Debra Webb

"Webb moves effortlessly between two very diverse romances
and masterfully keeps the reader on the edge
until the last page."
—*Romantic Times* on *Striking Distance*

"Debra Webb delivers page-turning,
gripping suspense and edgy, dark characters
to keep readers hanging on..."
—*Romantic Times* on *Her Hidden Truth*

"Debra Webb draws readers into an
enthralling suspense with terrific characters..."
—*Romantic Times* on *Physical Evidence*

"Debra Webb's fast-paced thriller
will make you shiver in passion and fear."
—*Romantic Times* on *Personal Protector*

Dear Reader,

The editors at Harlequin and Silhouette are thrilled to be able to bring you a brand-new featured author program beginning in 2005! Signature Select aims to single out outstanding stories, contemporary themes and oft-requested classics by some of your favorite series authors and present them to you in a variety of formats bound by truly striking covers.

You may notice a number of different colored bands on the spine of this book. Each color corresponds to a different type of reading experience in the new Signature Select program. The Spotlight books will offer a single "big read" by a talented series author, the Collections will present three novellas on a selected theme in one volume, the Sagas will contain sprawling, sometimes multi-generational family tales (often related to a favorite family first introduced in series) and the Miniseries will feature requested, previously published books, with two or, occasionally, three complete stories in one volume. The Signature Select program will offer one book in each of these categories per month, and fans of limited continuity series will also find these continuing stories under the Signature Select umbrella.

In addition, these volumes will bring you bonus features...different in every single book! You may learn more about the author in an extended interview, more about the setting or inspiration for the book, more about subjects related to the theme and, often, a bonus short read will be included.

Watch for new stories from Vicki Lewis Thompson, Lori Foster, Donna Kauffman, Marie Ferrarella, Merline Lovelace, Roberta Gellis, Suzanne Forster, Stephanie Bond and scores more of the brightest talents in romance fiction!

We have an exciting year ahead!

Warm wishes for happy reading,

Marsha Zinberg

Marsha Zinberg
Executive Editor
The Signature Select Program

Signature Select™
SPOTLIGHT

Debra Webb

Dying To Play

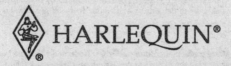

HARLEQUIN®

TORONTO • NEW YORK • LONDON
AMSTERDAM • PARIS • SYDNEY • HAMBURG
STOCKHOLM • ATHENS • TOKYO • MILAN • MADRID
PRAGUE • WARSAW • BUDAPEST • AUCKLAND

ISBN 0-373-83638-4

DYING TO PLAY

Dahmer, Bundy, Gacy...
Such pathetic attempts at greatness...
They knew nothing...
They did not know what I know...
I am pure genius, perfect in every way...
I, and only I, have the game...
And everyone is *dying to play*...

—*The Gamekeeper*

Prologue

Once the game is started it cannot be stopped. Not for anything. Not for *anyone.*

He had no choice.

Brad Matthews didn't look like a murderer or even a man who would carry a weapon. His suit was Armani...his shoes Ferragamo. But his manner of dress had been more reflex than conscious thought. He'd had only one thing on his mind this morning.

Nothing else mattered anymore.

He no longer cared if he lived or died, but he couldn't risk his wife...his children.

He wouldn't risk them.

At 9:05 a.m., just as the Gamekeeper had instructed, Brad walked into the downtown Atlanta Commerce Bank. He strode straight to the private office of the bank's president, an office where he'd done business many times.

His prey looked up and smiled, welcoming a trusted business associate of his beloved bank, but before he could rise from his leather executive chair, Brad drew the revolver he'd hidden beneath his jacket. He clenched his jaw and fired three shots into the president's massive chest. The startled look that claimed the man's face proved oddly calming to Brad.

He'd done it.

Screams and confusion erupted in the lobby beyond the glass wall that stood between him and the rest of those present inside the bank this Monday morning the first week of May…the last morning Brad would ever see.

The two security guards were sprinting in his direction, weapons drawn. Brad shot two more times, taking down one of the guards and sending the other one diving for cover. Then he turned the gun on himself.

Now it would end.

Picturing his wife and children one last time, he fired the final round.

Chapter 1

This was one of those necessary little annoyances in life a woman could definitely do without, Elaine Jentzen thought glumly. And on such a perfectly beautiful day. She'd fallen in love with the day the moment she stepped out into the early-morning sunshine. The air was fresh and the sky looked bluer than she'd ever seen it before. The sun glittered like a sparkling Georgia peach climbing its way into the cloudless blanket of pure blue. The smell of spring was everywhere. But she'd had to leave her small, neat, Dunwoody home to drive across Atlanta to be *here* at nine sharp.

She supposed it could be worse, though; she could be having her period and stuck on an after-hours stakeout with her partner, Hank Henshaw. Her nose crinkled instantly as her mind conjured up the odor of stale cigars and cheap after-shave.

No, she decided as she flipped through a fairly recent issue of *Working Woman,* this was even worse than an after-hours stakeout.

Elaine sat in a stiff, upholstered chair in front of her gynecologist's cluttered desk. She waited, her patience wearing thin, for him to come in and go over his findings with her. She never understood the need for this particular part since the results of the Pap test wouldn't be back for days. What could he tell her? That she looked tired? Overworked? She already knew those things. She worked fourteen-hour shifts most days, even the occasional Sunday. She'd accrued enough leave time to take the whole summer off, but she couldn't...or wouldn't, of course. Her job always came first.

If she were at work now she wouldn't have time to reflect on things she'd just as soon not think about. She sighed and tossed the magazine aside. She hated these appointments. That was the reason she'd waited over two years to come in for her *annual* exam.

One would think she'd committed a crime of the worst order. Not only had the receptionist who'd made today's appointment tsked when she saw on the computer screen that Elaine hadn't bothered to come in at all last year, the nurse had also firmly counseled Elaine as she led her to the exam room this morning. The you-know-better-than-that lecture had continued as Elaine stepped into the tiny dressing room and removed her clothing.

She was the deputy chief of detectives for the Atlanta Police Department, Homicide Division, for Pete's sake. She wasn't supposed to cow so easily to a gray-haired, rosy-cheeked nurse who looked old enough to be her grandmother.

But there was something oddly intimidating about having to take her clothes off under orders from a woman who would have made the staunchest instructor at the police academy proud.

As if that wasn't bad enough, then there was the humiliating experience of greeting the doctor while wearing a paper gown that opened down the front. Of course, Dr. Bramm could always be counted on for bedside humor, especially the kind that involved police work, like, "Captured your quota of bad guys already this week?"

Elaine had laughed, as expected, and gone on to answer his barrage of health questions in the most normal tone possible, considering her body was being plundered with cold, clinical objectivity.

She'd explained about the acute cramping and the increased nausea, which were the actual reasons she'd even bothered to come in. She was twenty-nine, the youngest detective, male or female, ever to make deputy chief. She didn't have time to be sick—or to be at this appointment. But she'd said nothing of the sort to the good doctor. Any negative comment on her part would only serve as a catalyst to start him on a tirade about how people took better care of their cars than themselves. She vaguely remembered hearing that one, the last time she was here.

She'd thought at first that her ulcer might somehow be causing the new problems and had said as much to the doctor. Lord knew it was already the bane of her existence. To her way of thinking she should own stock in the Tums and Maalox companies by now. But Dr. Bramm had informed her pretty quickly that her current symptoms might not be related to her ulcer at all. Then he'd felt compelled to repeat the lecture she'd already heard from the militant nurse who stood by, smiling and nodding in punctuation of his every word.

A lengthy exam and ultrasound later, Elaine waited in the doctor's office for his closing comments. He would lecture her some more, she presumed with a fair measure of certainty. She'd decided that, when he drew out the exam and insisted on the ultrasound. She couldn't ever remember one of these visits taking so long or being so complicated and uncomfortable.

Let him have at it with the lecturing. She'd take it, feign humbleness and swear on her life that she would never miss another annual exam. And everyone would be happy again.

When Dr. Bramm at last entered the office and sat down behind his massive mahogany desk, rather than feeling relieved as she'd fully expected, Elaine went on instant alert. Between his rigid posture and the solemn expression on his face, the news couldn't be good. If it was, the man needed to seriously rethink his bedside demeanor.

She resisted the urge to jump to conclusions. She absolutely would not even think about the "c" word. Other than the blasted ulcer she was young and healthy, surely it couldn't be that bad.

He opened her chart and stared at it for one somber moment before looking up at her over the rim of his bifocals. "Elaine, are you familiar with the term *endometriosis*?"

A tiny burst of fear flared inside her. "I don't think so," she said slowly, searching her memory for recognition. She found none.

He closed the chart and laid it aside, the gesture somehow

ominous. "It's an abnormal growth of cells in the female re-
productive system which sometimes spreads to other organs.
Some of the symptoms you related to me, the pain, the nausea, were suggestive of the disease."

Elaine tried to read him for a clue as to the severity of the
problem, but his expression was closed now. "So, just how bad
is it?" Another slow, hesitant response, so out of character for
her. She shrugged in an effort to shake off the adrenaline
pumping through her veins, making her heart pound. It wasn't
as if he'd said cancer. Or had he? "And what do we do about
it?"

He reclined in his chair and considered her questions for
a time before answering. "Based on my preliminary findings
and the severity of the symptoms, I'd say it's advanced. Stage
three or four. Of course, there are more detailed tests needed."
He flared his hands. "I'm going to refer you to a specialist.
Once he confirms my diagnosis, he'll likely suggest surgery
and hormone therapy."

"Surgery?" Elaine could feel her muscles tensing. She felt
nauseous, even more so than usual. She should have eaten this
morning. She would pay for that oversight. More Maalox or
Tums, whichever she had in the car, would be in order.

"We won't know how extensive the surgery will need to
be until you see the specialist," he said, obviously being
vague. "He'll give you more details about what you can expect and how the disease will affect your future."

An epiphany abruptly struck Elaine with a stunning effect.
"Does this mean I won't be able to have children?"

The question seemed to echo in the room. *Children.* She
hadn't really given much thought to the possibility before. She

would have one or two eventually, she'd assumed. *Eventually* being the operative word. Right now her whole life was focused on her career. She didn't even have a boyfriend. She blocked that seed of self-pity before it took root. She definitely wasn't going there at the moment. The fact was she'd put her entire personal life on hold eight years ago, and now the future was bearing down on her with what felt entirely too much like an ultimatum. She came from a big Catholic family. She wanted children. Someday.

Dr. Bramm sighed. He looked directly at her, his eyes giving her the answer before he spoke. "I can't give you any absolutes. I can only say…it's doubtful that you'll be able to conceive at this point. Very doubtful," he stressed. "If we'd only discovered it sooner." He shook his head solemnly. "But we'll do everything we can to increase the probability if that's what you want. You're still single?"

"Yes." Elaine felt as if someone else had answered the question. This couldn't be happening. She came from good stock. Both her parents were healthy and fit. Her older sister had four children already. And her three brothers had a whole gaggle of kids, all of which she doted on incessantly. Would loving her siblings' children have to be enough for her?

The doctor went on to praise the credentials of the specialist he'd recommended, but another realization had hit Elaine with the force of a bullet between the eyes, stealing her attention. *This was her fault.* She'd put her education and career before all else since she was eighteen years old. She hadn't taken the time to do the little things that she was supposed to do to take care of herself. Though she was thin by anyone's standards, she ate too much junk food, didn't really have time for anything else. She tried to make up for it by running every night with Sally, her big old golden retriever, until she exhausted herself. She didn't smoke, but she did indulge in a little too much wine most nights before bed to help her sleep.

No one would argue, however, that she didn't have the perfect excuse for her negligence. Her job was incredibly stressful.

Who was she kidding? Her job was murder.

Literally.

And now the prospects of having children, of sharing her future with anyone, were dim at best.

Maybe even dead. Who would want her now?

She had no one to blame but herself.

Suddenly her cell phone sounded, shattering the tense silence. Elaine fished for it in her bag and glanced at the number on the caller ID—Henshaw.

"I'm sorry, Doc," she offered apologetically. "I have to take this."

"Of course." He stood. "I'll have the nurse make you an appointment with the specialist," he added on his way out.

Elaine nodded as she flipped open her phone, or at least she thought she nodded. It was hard to tell at times like this. She rocketed into cop mode, and all else zoomed into insignificance.

"Jentzen. What's up?"

Henshaw's rusty voice sounded on the other end of the line, "Need you down at the Commerce Bank on Peachtree. Got another one of those multiple one-eight-ohs just like last week. Three dead, one injured."

She was up and out of the doctor's private office before her partner completed his last statement. "I'll be there in fifteen minutes."

Elaine hurried from the clinic with the promise that she would call back for the time and location of the appointment with the specialist.

Right now duty called. And, as she'd said before, her job was murder.

Chapter 2

The trip from the clinic on the east side to the scene of the crime on Peachtree Boulevard took nearly half an hour in the early-morning rush hour traffic. Elaine cursed under her breath every mile of the way. No amount of road construction ever seemed to alleviate the overcrowded expressways and streets in Atlanta. It amazed her that the city planners couldn't think far enough ahead to do better than this.

Images of empty cradles and groomless weddings kept vying for her attention, but she savagely tamped down each new intrusion before it could form fully in her head. There was no time to dwell on this newest development in her life. There was never enough time.

If she'd ever once contemplated slacking off on her career at some point in the future, that wasn't going to happen now. The job was likely all she'd have, considering what fate held in store for her. She clenched her teeth and blinked back the welling emotion. She didn't need this right now.

Her faithful old Jeep screeched to a halt at the entrance of the parking lot located next to the downtown Commerce Bank. Uniformed cops were checking every vehicle that came in or out. She couldn't recall the two rookies' names but they recognized her and waved her through without question. Elaine flashed her badge just the same.

The usual crowd of spectators and newshounds had gathered on the sidewalk near the street. Some were likely employees from the various other businesses along this block, others were probably early-morning shoppers.

Several patrol cars, lights flashing, were parked strategically around the bank. Elaine climbed out of her Jeep and approached the large two-story building's entrance. The setup was just like any one of the dozens of other banks in the Atlanta metropolitan area. What made this one the target this morning? That was the million-dollar question.

"Detective Jentzen!"

Elaine slowed as a familiar voice called out from the crowd of onlookers.

"Detective Jentzen! Can you tell us what's happening inside?"

Turning toward the voice, Elaine manufactured a smile for the *Chronicle* reporter to cover her impatience. Three more reporters pushed forward in hopes of getting an answer to their questions or at least a usable sound bite. A television crew was already setting up just outside the crime scene perimeter. The circus was in full form, and she wasn't even in the ring yet.

"I have no comments at this time," she said calmly. "I haven't even been inside. I'm sure we'll have a statement for you by noon." Ignoring the barrage of demands that followed her response, she resumed her journey toward the bank's entrance.

"Deputy Elaine!"

Elaine suppressed a groan. Just what she needed. Skip Littles. Reluctantly she glanced over her shoulder without actually slowing down.

"Deputy Elaine! You won't take even one question this morning?"

Though Skip wore a press pass he wasn't really a reporter. But he desperately wanted to be one. He grinned at her, the sun glinting off his thick eyeglasses. He worked at the *Telegraph,* that was true enough, but he was just an assistant. He was one of those people who garnered instant sympathy from her; she just couldn't help herself. Besides, he had helped her out once or twice when she needed some research ASAP.

Walking backward a few steps so as not to give the impression that she intended to stop long enough to field their questions, she held up a finger. "Just one," she said placatingly, earning a few glares from the *real* reporters.

Skip grinned from ear to ear. "Did someone die inside the bank this morning?"

She hesitated but couldn't see the point in evading the question. "Yes."

The satisfaction on his face perked up her low mood. Turning her back on the new onslaught of questions, she hurried to her destination. She'd done her good deed for the day.

A couple more uniforms guarded the double-door entry leading to the lobby. Elaine badged her way inside.

About a dozen employees, all clearly shocked into silence, stood huddled together near the long teller counter waiting for their turn to give a statement. In situations like this it was preferable to take the witnesses one at a time, to lessen the likelihood of confusion or agreement based simply on what the other guy said.

A forensics tech was methodically photographing the lifeless body of a security guard who lay on his back in an unnatural sprawl in the middle of the marble-floored lobby. Annoyed that the find-'em-and-bag-'em guys had started without her authorization, but not bothering to make a scene about it at the moment, Elaine crouched down to take a closer look at the victim. One bullet hole marred his brow just above his left eye. His gaze was frozen in a look of surprised horror or something on that order. Blood had leaked from the wound and matted in his blond hair. The guy couldn't be more than forty. Elaine blew out a heavy breath. Most likely married. One glance at his left hand confirmed her assumption. Kids, too, probably.

Another bout of foolish emotion wreaked havoc with her equilibrium. She had to get a grip here.

A few yards away an EMT was patching up the second security guard. A uniform hovered nearby, waiting to question the wounded man.

Elaine pushed to her feet and moved in the direction of the dense crowd of official personnel, including her partner. Through a glass wall she could see him in one of the offices. Henshaw, Detective Jillette and Walt Damron, Chief Medical Examiner, were deep in discussion. Walt rarely showed up at crime scenes anymore. Elaine wondered briefly if he was shorthanded this morning.

Henshaw saw her coming and met her just outside the office door. "Everything check out all right?" he asked, eyeing her speculatively.

"Fine," she lied. "You the first on the scene?"

He rolled the cigar stub that served as a permanent accessory to the corner of his mouth. "Yep. I guess that puts you in charge. Jillette just dropped by to watch the show. Flatt's around here somewhere."

Elaine resisted the urge to grimace. Flatt was an ass. He'd gone out of his way to make her life miserable since she made DC. She glanced around the chaos of the spacious, Greek-Revival-style lobby. "Looks like you've already initiated all the right moves."

Henshaw angled his head toward the office he'd exited. "Want to see the primary victim and the perp? It's just like the last one…too weird."

She nodded, her mind automatically sifting through the images from last week's mass murder. A customer had walked into a beauty salon and opened fire with a 9mm Beretta. No apparent motive, no nothing. A twenty-four-year-old college graduate in her first year of medical school, home for the weekend, had killed three people, then turned the weapon on herself. No family problems, no financial woes, no love-life theatrics.

Nothing.

Except four dead women, one being the shop owner.

Drawing back to the here and now, Elaine followed Henshaw through the group crowded outside the office. A brass plaque on the open door proclaimed the space as belonging to the bank's president, Harold Tate. Mr. Tate sat crumpled in his leather executive's chair, his starched shirt now grue-somely bloodied by the round bullet holes in his chest. Oddly, his navy-and-gray pin-striped tie lay unsoiled against the red-stained white cotton blend of his shirt.

"Brad Matthews," Henshaw announced, staring down at the dead man on the floor in front of the president's desk. "Fi-nancial consultant and newest full partner at Wylie, Brooks, Renzetti and Matthews just down the street. Wife, two kids, no record." Henshaw shrugged. "Just like the lady last week."

"Anyone here know him?" She glanced back at the em-ployees in the lobby.

"All of 'em. They said he was a nice guy. He's done busi-ness here, personal and professional, for years. He was quiet, polite and extremely intelligent, according to the first uniform on the scene. He said none of the employees can believe Matthews did this."

Elaine squatted down and took a closer look at the shooter. Thirty-five maybe, fit, handsome. *Two kids.* She shook her head. What a terrible waste. "No problems between these two?" She looked from Matthews to the older man behind the desk, then at her partner.

"None that anyone knows of," Henshaw said.

Elaine stood, uneasiness poking its way through her usual objectivity. Nothing about this felt right. "There has to be something," she insisted. "Dig until you find it. Having two unmotivated mass killings this close together is simply too bi-zarre. There has to be a reason. We're just missing it somehow."

"If there's any chance these two can be related," Jillette of-fered, abruptly reminding Elaine of his presence, "I think we should work on it as a team."

Unreasonably annoyed, Elaine looked at the man who'd spoken. He was only a couple years older than her, but he already had that male-chauvinist mentality down to a science. His dark hair was slicked back and, as usual, he was over-dressed. He looked ready to attend Sunday church service rather than investigate the scene of a multiple homicide. Jillette and Flatt did the *GQ* look like no one else in the division, earning themselves the nickname Ivy Leaguers.

How could she have forgotten Jillette was here? He and Flatt were working the beauty salon case. The similarity of the MO of this one had no doubt drawn them to the scene. As much as Elaine hated Flatt, she supposed Jillette's suggestion made sense. "If we find a connection," she qualified, "we'll do just that."

"Any reason we can't get started now?" Walt wanted to know, another presence that had slipped her mind while she studied the dead man...husband...father. A parent—something she might not ever be. A pang of hurt sliced through her before she could evict the ugly reminder from her head.

Elaine surveyed the fairly undisturbed scene once more. The gray suit jacket hanging neatly in the corner where Mr. Tate had left it only minutes before his life abruptly ended. The overturned chair where Brad Matthews had fallen. The .38 Smith & Wesson Special clutched in his cold, unyielding fingers. He could have gotten that weapon anywhere. They were a dime a dozen on the street.

"Go ahead," Elaine told Walt. "I'd like his drug tox and anything on that weapon as soon as possible."

Walt cocked an eyebrow and feigned the offended bit a little too well. "Everything I do is done as soon as possible. Or didn't you know that, Deputy Chief Jentzen?"

Elaine rolled her eyes. "Of course, what was I thinking?" He was right. Walt was as efficient as he was meticulous. She frowned then, remembering the oddness of his presence. "What're you doing down here, anyway? I didn't think Kathleen allowed you out of the morgue."

Kathleen was Walt's secretary. She was widowed, had been for years, just as he had. It was rumored that those two were secretly in love with each other but refrained from a relationship because of the job.

The job. God, what a pathetic existence they all lived in this line of work. No wonder there were so many divorces among criminal-investigation and law-enforcement personnel.

"I'm training a couple new techs," Walt said firmly, ignoring her comment about Kathleen.

Elaine nodded. She'd known he would do just that. "Yeah, I noticed the one in the lobby was a little trigger happy."

Irritation wrinkled Walt's brow as he leaned to his right to peer through the glass wall behind Elaine. She resisted the urge to turn around and see what the tech was up to now. The look on Walt's face said it all.

Walt muttered a curse. "Can't get decent help these days," he complained as he stomped out of the office.

Henshaw made a covert gesture toward the door. Instinct warning her that this wasn't good, Elaine followed him into the short corridor that led to the rear emergency exit.

"Look, Jentzen, there's something you oughtta know," he said quietly as he glanced first right, then left. He plucked the rarely lit stogie from his mouth.

"What is it?" she asked, instantly moving to a higher state

of alert. Henshaw had been in the division longer than any other detective, even the chief. By rights he should have been deputy chief years ago, but the powers-that-be had allowed a jackleg like Hindman to keep the position until he retired, which was about ten years too long. When Hindman finally retired, Henshaw was too close to retirement himself to be considered for the position. So said the chief, anyway. Though Elaine was proud of her promotion and she damn well knew she deserved it, Henshaw had gotten a raw deal. He should have been DC years ago instead of Hindman.

"Just before you got here there were a couple of Feds snooping around."

Elaine shrugged. "It's a bank, they have jurisdiction. I'm surprised they're not still here." She actually hadn't even thought of that until that precise moment. She swore silently. Just another example of how this morning's appointment had rattled her. But she had to stay focused.

Henshaw stroked his chin thoughtfully for a moment, then said, "Yeah, I know it's their jurisdiction, but there was something funny about it. Not the least of which was that one of 'em wasn't local."

Elaine felt the beginnings of a low dull ache right where a frown was creasing her forehead. "What do you mean *funny?*"

"Trace Callahan."

She mentally repeated the name a couple of times before recognition broadsided her. *Trace Callahan.* "Jesus."

"My sentiments exactly," Henshaw muttered. "The way I heard it the guy's been off field duty for two years."

Elaine considered what she knew about Callahan. Accord

ing to local scuttlebutt the Bureau's top Febbie, the nickname regular cops used for federal agents, had gone over the edge a couple years ago and had been jockeying a desk ever since. "You're sure it was him?"

"It was him." Henshaw lifted one shaggy gray brow and gave her the look. The one that said, I can't say where I heard it, but you can take it to the bank, no pun intended. "Word is he actually tried to kill some perp with his bare hands shortly after that whole bizarre case two years ago."

She'd heard the same thing. "He lost his partner, right?" If she remembered correctly, there was also gossip that Callahan and his female partner were lovers. The idea only added to her uneasiness. This was definitely not her day.

Henshaw nodded. "Yeah. Most everybody, including Callahan himself, thought it was his fault. He screwed up an operation and she bit the dust."

Callahan had been the best of the best, the Bureau's big star, but he seemed to just come unglued. Everybody in Homicide had heard the rumors. Though Callahan worked directly out of Quantico, the liaison agent who worked between Atlanta PD and the boys at the local Bureau office had kept the chief *unofficially* informed of the whole sordid story. It was front-page news for a while before the big news outlets moved on to something else.

"Well," Elaine offered, "if Callahan is one of the Feds assigned to this case, then we'll simply have to deal with him."

"I'm just saying," Henshaw countered, "that it could be risky business. That's all." He waved his hands in a magnanimous manner. "Hell, he could be the greatest frigging investigator on the planet, but if you can't count on him during a field op, I don't want no part of working with him. If he goes ape-shit again I want to be clear of the fallout."

Elaine's cell phone rang, saving her from having to make promises she might not be able to keep. She dragged it from her shoulder bag and flipped it open. "Jentzen." It was the chief. He was brisk and to the point. "I'll be right there," she assured him. He wanted her at the office ASAP. She dropped her phone back into her bag. "Got a command performance with the chief. I'll touch base with you later, Henshaw."

He nodded. "I guess I'd better get over there and see how the interviews are going or Flatt'll be taking over for me."

Elaine watched Henshaw amble out to the lobby before she made a move to go. *Callahan.* Though she'd never met him in person, she'd heard plenty about him. The man had received numerous commendations from the FBI director, even a couple from the president himself. By all reports, Callahan was some sort of Bureau legend. Then, two years ago, things had gone wrong for him. According to the chief, he hadn't been the same since. She'd seen his face splashed across the TV screen during the hoopla after his partner was murdered. Elaine shivered. He was as handsome as sin.

And every bit as deadly, if even half the rumors were true.

Chapter 3

By eleven-thirty, only twenty minutes after he'd called, Elaine stood outside the chief's office. Connie, his longtime secretary, had told her to go on in, but she hesitated for some reason. She couldn't actually justify her hesitation. It seemed irrational, yet she felt compelled to wait a moment longer.

Maybe it was everything that had happened that morning…a bad mix of personal crisis and unsettling professional remorse. Too much waste. Too little time. The possibility that the two mass murders could be connected—could happen again—weighed heavily on her. How was she supposed to keep Atlanta safe if she couldn't solve these two crimes? It was her job to see that they got solved. She needed more Maalox. More time, and a frigging crystal ball.

At least, she considered, the day surely couldn't get any worse.

Taking a deep, bolstering breath, Elaine clasped the door-knob, gave it a swift twist and pushed her way into the large, perpetually cluttered office. She didn't bother to close the door behind her. Why feed the rumor mill? She marched straight up to the boss's desk and produced a wide professional smile.

"Good morning, sir."

Chief John Dugan glanced up from the papers he was riffling. "Have a seat, Jentzen. I'll be right with you."

That perfect blue sky she'd admired this morning served as a backdrop behind him through the wall of windows. His office had an amazing view, one of the best in the city. At night the city lights were awesome. She knew firsthand. Another twinge of regret needled her. God, if she didn't know better she'd swear she was premenstrual.

Putting all personal worries aside, she sat down, dropped her shoulder bag to the floor, crossed her legs and relaxed into her chair. She mentally reviewed what she'd noted at the crime scene that morning. Then reviewed it again in an effort to keep her mind from wandering.

It didn't work.

Despite her most gallant attempt, her gaze followed the chief's every move. The slow, methodical shuffling of his strong hands. The determined set of his shoulders. He was tall and quite attractive for a man closer to fifty than forty. He wore his graying hair cropped short. Smile lines bracketed his eyes and mouth but didn't detract from his good looks. He was a solid, good man. Inside and out.

That was what had first attracted her to him.

As a new detective assigned to his division, the only female at the time, John had taken her under his wing. He'd treated her as an equal and made sure she'd learned her lessons well. The affair had been an accident.

Neither of them had intended for it to happen. John was newly divorced, she was plain lonely. All work and no play had sent her social life on a crash-and-burn course. Falling into a relationship with John had been so easy...too easy. For an entire year they'd stolen forbidden hours every chance they got, had great sex and generally enjoyed each other's company. But that was the extent of it. Neither of them had visions of a future together. It had been about safe, convenient sex.

Six months ago, though, when she'd gotten her promotion, Elaine had ended the relationship. She'd felt it was wrong under present circumstances. Truth be told, she'd felt more than a little uncomfortable for a while before that. John had sworn he'd recommended her for the promotion based on merit, but she couldn't dispel the niggling little doubt that their personal relationship had somehow played into his decision.

She knew she was the best person for the job...that was a cold, hard fact. She worked harder than anyone else in the division, had from the beginning. Her very first case, kidnapping and murder involving four Atlanta children, was proof of her single-minded focus. Breaking that case had been a huge boost to her fledgling career. She'd maintained a collar record to match her ambition ever since. She was a natural at organizing ops...a born leader, John called her. But still, she was the youngest detective in the division, seniority- and age-wise. Henshaw had been the first to publicly show his support of her selection. But others, Flatt in particular, had not liked it one bit. He had even gone so far as to make little accusing remarks when he had known she would overhear.

John had told her to ignore the rumbles. It would pass, he'd assured her. And it had, for the most part. Flatt and a couple of others were still a little PO'ed about being passed over, but she could deal with them.

Still, at moments like this she wondered.

"So." John settled back into the leather chair behind his desk and focused his full attention on her. "Does it look like the bank case could be connected to the beauty salon murders?"

"There are some similarities," she admitted. "But it's still too early to tell. We may discover that Matthews had a beef with Tate." She shrugged. "Or even that he slipped over the edge for some reason. Who knows? Maybe the bank turned him or one of his clients down for a loan."

John considered her words for a moment. "If there's even a remote possibility that there's some sort of shared manipulation or influence playing into this, I want you to follow it as far as you can. I don't want another multiple homicide scene next week. The papers are going to have a field day with this. We'll be reading about it every step of the way."

Elaine nodded. John had to deal with the uppity-ups on these kinds of high-profile cases. The mayor would not be a happy camper if this happened a third time. Of course, all good detectives could see into the future. Determining if the two crimes were connected and preventing another one should be a piece of cake in the mayor's opinion. It truly amazed her that the man had gotten elected.

"We'll have to keep close reins on this one," John reiterated, in case she didn't get it the first time. "The mayor doesn't want any leaks. We need to keep a lid on every aspect of this investigation."

"I'll do my best."

John smiled at her. The same kind of smile that had once made her pulse react, now only flooded her with asexual feelings of affection. She wondered briefly if she'd forgone birth control during their relationship, would she have gotten pregnant? Had it already been too late then? How would he have taken that kind of complication? How would she have dealt with it? She almost sighed aloud, but caught herself. Had that whole year been another waste? If she'd tried harder, could it have been more? God, she really was a mess. She didn't have the time or the option, careerwise, to try harder. Not then, not now.

"I know you'll do your best," he said, dragging her focus back to the conversation. "There's just one glitch."

She tensed, a warning registering. "What kind of glitch?"

He exhaled a frustrated puff of air, clearly dreading what he was about to say. "You know this one is Federal jurisdiction."

"Yeah." She shrugged. "If they want lead, they're welcome to it." She sure as hell wasn't going to fight for this one. It was a no-win situation. Then again, the last thing she wanted was to be at the beck and call of a couple of arrogant Federal agents who thought they were God's gift to women, if not mankind as a whole.

John erased all emotion from his expression right before her eyes. Uh-oh. Whenever he went deadpan, things deteriorated rapidly for the detective sitting on the opposite side of his desk.

"They don't want lead," he said quietly, too quietly. "In fact, they've asked for you by name."

The air in the room suddenly thickened with the uncomfortable feel of a setup. Elaine arched an eyebrow as much in surprise as skepticism. "For me? Why would they want me?"

"Apparently they've heard of your stellar reputation." A hint of a grin quirked his lips. "If they want the best, they've asked for the right detective."

Irritation nagged at her despite the compliment. "Stop stonewalling and tell me about the glitch." There was more to this, a lot more. She had a bad feeling. He was doling out too much good up front.

The chief took his time before answering. "Apparently there is some aspect of this case that caught the Bureau's attention. They believe these two murder sprees are definitely connected. One of their agents thinks he may know who's behind them."

That was just too surreal. "We don't even have any tangible evidence," Elaine argued. "How the hell could he know that? It's not like there's even been the first real clue."

John flared his hands, obviously as much at a loss as she was. "Beats me. But if the FBI director trusts this guy enough to follow his instincts, I'm certainly not going to question him."

He had a point there. And a good chief or director always backed his detectives and agents. Elaine had to admit that as much as she despised Flatt personally, he was a good detective. She'd back him if the need arose.

"So, what exactly do they want?" She needed clarification here. If she was going to have to play flunky for some G-man, she wanted as much information as possible at the start.

John looked directly at her and said the last thing she wanted to hear. "They want to team you up with their agent. They want the two of you focused solely on solving this situation." She opened her mouth to argue, but he stopped her with an uplifted palm. "They're that sure of this guy, Elaine. I wouldn't have said yes, if they weren't so sure. Especially under the circumstances."

She sprang from her chair and parked her fists on her hips. "You said yes without asking me first?"

That deadpan expression never wavered. "I did."

She bit back the scorching four-letter word that raced to the tip of her tongue. "I hate this," she murmured fiercely. "I want that on the record up-front. I already have a partner, a real cop. What's Henshaw supposed to do while I'm playing lackey to some buttoned-down hotshot who thinks he's some kind of *Top Gun* character?"

"Don't worry about Henshaw," John assured her. "We've got plenty to keep him busy. I thought I'd put him on the Fish-net murders."

"Oh, he'll love that," Elaine mused, some of the fight draining out of her. What was the point, anyway? Damn, she needed more Maalox. Her stomach burned like hell.

The Fishnet case was a string of prostitute murders where the victims had been strangled with fishnet stockings while in a compromising position. Henshaw wouldn't mind. He'd probably enjoy the scenery. Elaine wanted to kick something. But what was the use? She'd still be stuck working with the Feds. Up close and personally.

"This won't be the first time you've worked a joint task force. What's the big deal?" John wanted to know.

What'd he expect? Enthusiasm?

She looked directly at him and said exactly what was on her mind. "I have a partner. I don't need another partner." She glared at her boss for emphasis. "And I damn sure don't want one who no doubt suffers with the same ailment all Feds do—the God complex." One of the chief's comments abruptly pushed its way through her irritation. *Especially under the circumstances.* What the hell did that mean?

"Well if it makes you feel any better, Detective," a husky masculine voice drawled from the doorway some ten feet behind her, "I don't want a partner, either."

"Dammit," she hissed, her eyes closing briefly in self-deprecation. Elaine turned slowly toward the man who'd spoken. Though she'd never met him, she recognized him instantly. That ruggedly handsome face as well as the stance, both weary and wary, contrasted sharply with his starched shirt and khakis, silk tie and polished brown leather loafers. There was something raw about him—besides the weapon nestled in its holster against that mile-wide chest. It radiated off him in waves. A distracting mix of confidence, masculinity and sexuality.

Elaine disliked him on sight.

"Elaine Jentzen," John announced unnecessarily, then cleared his throat, "this is Special Agent Trace Callahan. Your new partner."

Callahan strolled slowly toward her, each step a deliberate act of intimidation. But Elaine wasn't intimidated. Surprised at her body's foolish reaction to him, yes, but not at all intimidated. Ignoring the swirl of awareness in her gut, she thrust out her hand when he got within shaking distance.

"I wish I could say it's a pleasure, Agent Callahan," she said bluntly. So *he* was the circumstances the chief spoke of.

Callahan closed a hand over hers, unexpectedly sending a surge of pure heat spiraling through her. Those analyzing blue eyes never left hers for a second. "The pleasure's surely mine, Detective Jentzen," he said smoothly, so damned smoothly that she almost shivered. "And not to worry," he added, holding on to her hand when she would have pulled away. "I left my God complex at home this morning. I'll be sure to do that for the duration of our partnership."

Fury burst inside her, and a different kind of heat scalded Elaine's cheeks. "See that you do, Callahan," she shot back. "And we'll get along just fine."

Something on the order of a smile played about the corners of his mouth as he released her hand. "No problem. We Top Guns are always on our best behavior when working with *real* cops."

Her day had just gotten worse.

Chapter 4

"Have a seat, Agent Callahan," John offered before shooting Elaine a look that meant two things—sit down and shut up.

Too pissed off to be submissive, she ignored her boss and looked directly at Callahan, daring him to make the first move. This close, his gaze startled her. It was more than simply analyzing…it was penetrating. Pure blue, like today's sky, only ice-cold. Those eyes bore the experienced lines of someone who had witnessed too much…given too much. A chill shivered through her.

"After you," he said with a smile that wasn't a smile at all. It was more like a practiced offering. A compromise he'd trained himself to make during situations like this.

Elaine blinked and looked away from those disturbing eyes. "So, who's in charge?" she asked John, determined to nail down that point right off the bat.

"You'll lead," Callahan interjected. "So long as," he qualified, "we understand each other."

Oh, he was smooth. She knew precisely what he meant. So long as he got his way, she was in charge. She sent him another evaluating look. "I think we understand each other perfectly." With that said, Elaine sat down. She didn't miss the relief on John's face. This was awkward for him she knew, but at the moment she didn't care. She wasn't going to play nice under present circumstances.

Callahan settled into the other chair, his gaze lingering on her. She could feel him watching her…weighing the challenge she represented.

"We don't want any conflicting obligations," John told her, getting back down to business. "I don't want your focus scattered by anything. We'll let Flatt fill in as deputy chief while you're on this case."

Elaine stiffened as insult was added to injury. No way was she taking this without a fight. "I don't see the necessity. I'll still report in as usual. I can handle both."

John shook his head. "I'm in agreement with the Bureau on this one. The case needs yours and Agent Callahan's full attention. Anything less is unacceptable."

Fury flamed inside her. It didn't have to be this way. "Why not Henshaw? He's senior, let him fill in."

"My decision is final." The look John gave her was more telling than his words.

Elaine recognized the futility of arguing the issue further. Once John Dugan made up his mind there was no changing it. Whatever his reasons for choosing Flatt over Henshaw, she had no choice but to accept the situation. But she didn't have to like it.

"Fine," she agreed tightly. This whole day had sucked. What was one more injustice? She almost laughed. And here she'd thought things couldn't get any worse.

"I'll need a status report every twenty-four hours," John went on. "To keep the mayor abreast of the situation. I'll also keep Senior Supervisory Agent Douglas informed," he advised Callahan. "It's my understanding that you'll report directly to me throughout the investigation just like Jentzen."

Callahan nodded. "That's right."

Surprise, surprise, Elaine thought. The Feds were staying out of the main loop. She wondered what hidden significance that goodwill gesture carried. Someone was pulling out all the stops on this one. No doubt to appease the mayor.

"So we understand each other here?" John asked looking at her again.

"Absolutely," she said succinctly despite the fact that she didn't understand any of it. And she damn sure didn't like it. She hated this kind of politically motivated crap.

John stood, an act of dismissal. "Then I'll let the two of you get started."

Elaine snagged her purse and pushed to her feet. "Thank you, *sir.*" Disappointment flared briefly in John's eyes at her curt tone. She refused to feel guilty for that, too. Though she felt sure he really didn't like this any more than she did, she resented the feeling of helplessness it gave her. He'd been in on the decision making; she'd had no say at all. But he had a job to do. And so did she.

Not waiting for Callahan, she walked out while he was still

shaking hands with John. It didn't take the guy long to catch up to her. She'd just pushed into the stairwell when he breezed in behind her.

"We headed someplace special?" he asked as he slipped on a navy-blue jacket that exactly matched the silk tie he wore.

"Back to the scene of the crime. Where else?" Elaine started down the stairs without looking at him. If he was lead, would he have started someplace else? She banished that line of thinking. She was lead; she didn't care what he would do.

"You want me to drive?" He was right beside her, his feet keeping time with hers. "My rented car's—"

"I'll drive." She still didn't look at him.

"Suits me."

The last two flights of stairs were descended in silence. Well, silence, that is, if she discounted the war of conflicting thoughts and emotions inside her head. Every part of her that made her a woman wanted to cry out at the injustice fate had thrown her. The cop in her wanted to rant further about the whole setup of this little joint task force. But she couldn't lose control…not right now. Later, when she was at home alone, she would allow herself to think about something besides the case again. Definitely not now, with some hotshot secret agent on her heels.

At the west exit that would take them to the personnel parking area, Elaine hesitated before opening the door. Something the chief had said suddenly rose above the rest of the chaos inside her head. She turned to the man waiting behind her. "Why me?"

His stare was analyzing and went on long enough to make her want to squirm, but she resisted. There was something totally unnerving yet somehow intensely spellbinding about his eyes. It was as if he could read her thoughts...could see inside her. She purposely cleared her mind, just in case.

"Does it matter?" he answered her question with a question, his voice carefully devoid of inflection.

"Chief Dugan said you asked for me," she explained, suddenly uncharacteristically uncertain of her ground.

Something shifted in those intense blue eyes...some barely discernible emotion she couldn't possibly read. "Douglas asked for you. I wouldn't have."

Douglas—his boss. Apparently she wasn't the only one who had a problem with a new partner. "*You* wouldn't have'?"

"I would have preferred a male partner." That unsettling stare cut to her marrow.

"You think one of my male peers would do a better job than me?" she demanded icily. She felt a muscle tic in her cheek at the absurd notion that Flatt or Jillette or any of the others could do a better job than she could.

He shook his head. "I'm sure you're more than competent, Detective Jentzen," he said in that slow, quiet drawl, honey sweet and polished smooth. "But in my experience women are ruled more by their emotions than by their gut. Emotions can get you killed."

She lifted her chin defiantly. "You would certainly know more about getting someone killed than I would."

He flinched and she immediately regretted her words. At least to a degree. Obviously Henshaw had been right about Callahan's past.

"Let's just say," he offered in that same controlled tone, "that I'd rather spare you learning how that feels."

He reached for the left breast pocket of his jacket as if it were second nature. A frown lined her brow as she considered the small bulge in that same pocket. A pack of cigarettes?

"You smoke?" she asked, her intolerance of the habit more evident in her voice than she'd intended. This just kept getting better and better. Her favorite uncle had died of lung cancer after half a lifetime of smoking. She'd almost broken Henshaw from the habit. What the hell was she supposed to do with a good-looking, smooth-talking, cigarette-smoking partner who had gotten his last partner killed?

His hand dropped back to his side. "I used to," he admitted, just a hint of reluctance weighting his words.

She arched a skeptical eyebrow. "If you've quit, why are you still carrying a pack?" She glanced at his pocket once more for emphasis.

"It's a long story. One I'm sure you wouldn't be interested in."

Before she could say anything else he reached around her and opened the door. Her breath caught at his unexpected nearness. The vaguest scent of aftershave, something she couldn't readily identify, piqued her senses, made her want to draw closer.

Turning swiftly away from him, Elaine led the way to her black, badly-in-need-of-a-wash Jeep. She climbed into the driver's seat and reached over to clear the passenger side. She tossed the files she'd taken home to review, her linen jacket, and a take-out box containing the remainder of yesterday's lunch into the back seat.

Callahan slid onto the seat, his long, lean frame making the vehicle seem suddenly too cramped. He pulled on his seat belt after noting she'd done so. The act was awkward, un-practiced, as if he rarely performed it. Well, whenever he rode with her he would wear it. She would see to that. She might be stuck in this situation, but she would retain every aspect of control possible.

As she pulled out onto the street, she glanced at his pro-file. He had those chiseled good looks, all angles and shad-ows, that Hollywood clamored for in leading men. A pair of designer sunglasses slipped into place as she watched, only adding to the movie-star mystique. His dark-brown hair was short, a little longer on top where it waved, draping a few locks down his forehead for a sexy touch.

Just another reason to dislike him. He was too perfect on the outside. Women likely flocked to him in droves, only to discover the internal goods were damaged.

She fixed her gaze on the street before her. Damn, just what she needed. A new partner who would not only get in her way, but who would also create distractions, for her as well as any other female around, wherever they went. Dammit, dammit. Why the hell hadn't Douglas picked Flatt or Jillette for this assignment? A realization of sorts struck her with staggering force. She was a woman. The Bureau likely believed she would be easier to control.

Well, Elaine didn't like playing the submissive part. She didn't like it one iota. She stole another sideways glance at her passenger. Midthirties, she guessed. Definitely not the marrying type. Before she could school the thought, she'd checked out his left hand. No ring.

She wanted to kick herself for looking. She didn't care if he was married. She didn't care that he was too damned handsome. She had a job to do, and Mr. Hotshot Superagent wasn't going to distract her.

Pain stabbed deep in her midsection, followed by a burn at once familiar and dreaded. She grimaced. Dammit. She needed to eat. But she wasn't about to go to lunch with this man. Keeping her eyes on the road, she reached for the Maalox in the center console. She opened it with a savage twist and drank a long, deep swallow.

Feeling immensely better as the thick, velvety liquid slid down her esophagus headed toward the volcano erupting in her stomach, she screwed the top back on and chucked the now-empty bottle onto the back seat. She'd definitely have to remember to pick up a new one.

He was staring at her again. She could feel him. She flexed her shoulders, a useless attempt to release the stress building there under his steady gaze. Only then did she consider how what she'd just done with the antacid probably looked to an outsider.

She stopped for a traffic light and turned to meet the question no doubt in his eyes behind those damnable shades. "Don't ask. It's a long story. One I'm sure you wouldn't be interested in," she said, repeating his earlier words.

His smile was slow in coming, like a dewdrop slipping down a tender new leaf, reaching for that point where the sun would glitter from it like Nature's mirror. And when it reached fruition it was a sight to behold. Butterflies took flight in her stomach, and she knew she'd just witnessed an event as rare as a blue moon.

It was definitely something she wanted to see again.

And that only made bad matters worse.

Chapter 5

Trace stood outside the Atlanta Commerce Bank for a long while after Elaine Jentzen went inside. He was in no hurry to go inside. He'd already seen all there was to see. There would be no inadvertently left evidence, no conclusions to be drawn from the scene staging. Nothing. And that was the only clue Trace needed.

A cool breeze shifted the wide leaves of the massive magnolia trees shading the nearly empty parking lot. He studied the details of the large brick structure with its bold, white-column sentries guarding the double entry doors. Stuffing his hands into his pockets, he huddled against the sudden chill that danced up his spine.

Why had *he* chosen this particular bank? Was it because Matthews used this one? Or was it the bank's president that had made this institution the target? Trace knew little about the case so far, but he had enough information to recognize the familiarity of the *game*.

Dread pooled in his gut.

If last week's beauty-shop murders had left any question, today's bloodshed had cleared up the doubt. As far as Trace was concerned, anyway. He'd managed to convince his superiors at the Bureau, barely. He recognized that even the remote possibility of a repeat of two years ago had done more of the persuading than anything he had said or done. And Supervisory Special Agent Douglas appeared to be on his side…not that his support was much of a consolation. The bottom line was simple. No one wanted to take the risk.

The caption above the entrance to the bank snagged his attention, drawing him several steps closer. In God We Trust. He wondered briefly how many other Atlanta banks featured that logo. It would please the scumbag responsible for these senseless murders to no end to make a mockery of the people's trust.

That was part of the thrill for the Gamekeeper.

He preyed upon those supremely confident in their ability to recognize the difference between right and wrong. No one saw the danger coming…until it was too late. He toyed with his chosen victims, manipulated them in every possible way. Then, when he tired of their frantic struggles, he used them to act out his evil schemes.

Worry creased Trace's brow as he stood beneath the shaded portico of the bank entrance. There was one major difference, however, in these two cases and the ones from two years ago. The Gamekeeper, without exception, made the final kill himself. It was part of his signature—part of the ritual he followed religiously. But with both the beauty-shop case and the current one, the supposed perps had offed themselves. That had been the major sticking point with the brass. The profiler had been reluctant to agree with Trace when he suggested that the Gamekeeper could be behind last week's murders. He would say the same about this one.

Serial killers rarely changed their MOs...unless some life-altering event predicated the change. He knew that better than anyone. But it didn't sway his thinking.

Memories of the night his partner died abruptly slammed into him with the power of a train exploding from a dark tunnel.

Molly had been as green as they came. Brand-new to the Bureau. That alone had made her the perfect candidate for the trap Trace had devised. He'd asked for her, insisted on having her. She would play the part of his new girlfriend, his lover. And she would be the bait for the Gamekeeper. He would be the one to actually get close enough to make the collar. Molly had loved it. Thanked him over and over for allowing her the opportunity to work with a legend.

A legend. Yeah, right.

He swallowed hard, emotion making the action nearly impossible. He'd had such a hard-on to solve the case...to be the one who brought the Gamekeeper down, he hadn't fully considered the risk to her. But he hadn't worried because he'd been in control....

Or so he'd thought.

They'd played a twisted little game back and forth, he and the Gamekeeper. At the time, Trace could almost taste the triumph. He was so very close. He was going to nail him.

So many dead. All young with great futures ahead of them. Those were the ones the Gamekeeper liked best. No junkies, hookers or homeless people for him. He liked the challenge of more worthy opponents.

What was the fun, he'd said in one of his taunting calls to Trace, in stalking and murdering an already helpless creature?

He wanted to play.

To draw out the pleasure.

Sick bastard.

Trace clenched his jaw. He should have seen it coming. He should have known the Gamekeeper was too smart to fall for such an ordinary sting. The scumbag had known that Molly was Trace's partner, not his girlfriend. But he'd also known that they'd grown close during the course of the investigation. He'd watched them, studied them. And the bastard had wielded every bit as much hurt…as much pain in the end.

She was dead. It was Trace's fault. Nothing he could do would bring her back.

She'd died in his arms. He'd tried to stop the bleeding…tried to keep her alive until help arrived, but it had been useless.

He'd made a fatal mistake.

Trace jerked back to the here and now. He was shaking. A sheen of perspiration slicked his skin. His stomach roiled with the bitter dregs of his own guilt…of the vengeance he'd waited so long to wreak. He needed it more than his next breath. He wanted the Gamekeeper dead.

He'd managed to get off one good shot that night. He'd hit him, Trace knew he had. But he hadn't killed him. The Gamekeeper was still alive. Trace felt him. The fact that the sick piece of crap had apparently dropped off the face of the earth for the past two years had lent credence to the possibility that Trace had managed a fatal hit that night. But he knew differently. Every fiber of his being sensed the evil lurking close by.

Whatever the Gamekeeper's reasons for lying low until now didn't matter. He was back, and Trace intended to stop him this time. He intended to kill him. He wanted to personally help perform the no-holds-barred autopsy on the son of a bitch. To hold the saw that cut into that twisted brain.

Trace fought to stem the tremors quaking through him. He dragged in a breath, ragged with his efforts to regain control. He had to keep it together.

This was his second chance. Second chances didn't come along often. He would do it right this time.

"You coming in or what?"

Trace looked up to find Detective Jentzen glaring at him from the bank's entrance. He jerked, startled.

Her eyes narrowed as she quickly took in his pathetic state. He squared his shoulders and blinked away the last of the lingering images that haunted him day and night. He could do this.

"Yeah." He started forward, each step a conscious effort to remain steady. "I'm coming in."

Not bothering to hide her annoyance, Jentzen held the door until he reached it, then gave him her back and strode across the lobby.

Trace moistened his lips and exhaled a relieved breath. He couldn't let that happen again. If she suspected for one second that he was experiencing difficulty staying in control, she would certainly insist that he be removed from the case.

Not that he could blame her. In this line of work, who wanted to partner up with a guy who couldn't watch his partner's back? The Bureau had stuck him on desk duty. This was his one shot at making things right. His new partner resented the hell out of him, but he could live with it. She certainly hadn't been his first choice, either. Though by all accounts she was a damned good cop, she was a woman, and he wasn't sure he could trust her to react like a cop when the chips were down.

He couldn't make a mistake and he couldn't allow her to make one. This was his opportunity to kill two birds with one stone. To bring down the Gamekeeper and to get his professional life back. He didn't really care that he no longer garnered any respect from the other agents. And he sure as hell didn't need any friends. It was the job that kept him going…that he needed. If he had to go back to that desk for the rest of his days…well, he just wasn't sure he could handle it.

Sure, he hated the way everyone looked at him now. As if they feared he'd go berserk at any given moment. But more than that or even the ever-present talk behind his back, he hated the looks of sympathy.

The panic he struggled with on a daily basis abruptly surged into his throat.

He choked it back.

This time would be different.

He would do everything right this time.

"Callahan, this is Detective Henshaw." Jentzen stood next to an older man, fifty, fifty-five maybe. He looked a little rumpled and a lot cop smart. The cigar clenched in the corner of his mouth gave him a sort of Columbo-without-the-trench-coat look.

Trace extended his hand automatically. "Trace Callahan," he said, not missing the older man's methodical scrutiny.

Henshaw pumped his hand a couple of times and grunted. "I've heard of your reputation."

Trace forced a smile. He'd just bet the old man had heard of him, but he doubted it was anything good. "Don't believe everything you hear," he suggested in as good-natured a tone as he could manage.

Henshaw chuckled, but those cunning eyes told the tale. He knew a lot more than he would dream of saying. "I'll bear that in mind, Callahan."

Trace looked from Henshaw to his reluctant partner and back. "I suppose Jentzen told you about the working arrangements?"

Henshaw nodded. "I can live with it. *Temporarily.*" He looked at the woman at his side. "I'll have my final report ready by the end of the day."

"Just leave it on my desk. I'm not sure when I'll—we'll get back to the office."

"Will do."

Jentzen's cellular phone rang, and she stepped away to take the call. Henshaw gave Trace a final curt nod before walking past him. Trace reciprocated, damned tired of the pretending and the double-talk, but he had to play it out a little longer.

Until he set things right again.

"Just one more thing," Henshaw said, as if he'd almost forgotten some important aspect of the case he needed to pass along.

Trace turned to face him. "What's that?" Their gazes locked in a silent battle of wills.

"Don't let anything happen to *my* partner," the old man warned. "You risk her life unnecessarily and you'll answer to me. You got that, hotshot?"

Trace read no malice in the man's tone or expression…just genuine fear for his partner's well-being. The warning wasn't anything he hadn't anticipated. "I've got it."

"Good."

Detective Henshaw pivoted on his heel and exited the bank. He paused outside the door to light his cigar. A puff of blue smoke rose above his head. Trace looked away, suppressing the urge to reach into his own pocket for a cigarette. He'd quit smoking ten years ago. Then, when everything had gone to hell, he'd picked them up again. Last month, he'd finally worked up the nerve to quit for good. He hated being at the mercy of the habit…almost as much as his new partner obviously hated the idea of being partnered up with someone who polluted her air space. She seemed to make an exception with Henshaw. Or maybe she had him trained not to light up in her presence.

His gaze sought and found Elaine Jentzen. She was no green, right-out-of-the-academy rookie like Molly had been. She was street savvy and smart, but more than that she was experienced. Despite her youth, she'd worked long and hard to get where she was. A degree in criminology with a minor in psychology and graduating top of her class from the police academy were pretty impressive feats to have accomplished by age twenty-two. Her very first case in Homicide had made a hero of her. She'd been flying high ever since. Not to mention making deputy chief before hitting thirty. He imagined she'd made a few enemies along the way as well. No one moved up the ranks that quickly without pissing off somebody.

According to what he'd pulled up on the computer about her, she was a third-generation cop. All three of her brothers were either policemen or firemen. Her sister was the only exception in the bunch. She'd chosen education for her field of expertise, then married during her first year of teaching. Five years and four children later, she was a stay-at-home mom with a college professor husband.

Trace didn't have any siblings. His parents had died long ago. It was just him. That hadn't really ever bothered him before. But now, somehow, it did.

Considering Jentzen's brood, it made him feel lonely. He almost laughed at that one. He *was* alone.

And that's the way he liked it.

Self-pity wasn't his style.

Nor was being dependent upon another human being.

He surveyed his new partner's long legs, then all that dark hair that fell past her proud shoulders. She was tall, five foot seven inches or eight maybe. Thin, but more lean than skinny he'd bet. The black slacks weren't formfitting, but were well tailored to the sweet contours of her body. She wore her badge and weapon at her waist in a no-frills fashion. The white blouse was something soft and flowing. It nestled against her skin in all the right places. His gaze lingered a little too long on her breasts. He blinked and forced his attention up to her face.

But her brown eyes were her best asset, in his opinion. Her every emotion shimmered in those wide, oval pools. She emanated more strength and courage than most women in his experience. The fact that she'd already earned his respect to an extent surprised him. He was usually slow in allowing that kind of confidence.

As she argued with someone named Flatt on her cell phone, Trace watched her every move. She used her hands a lot. Long, delicate fingers were tipped by short nails. Her face was as animated as her hands. And what a pretty face it was. Too pretty for a cop, especially one so ambitious.

She did this thing with her hand…just a quick motion of running her fingers through her hair. He liked that. He liked her. She was a good cop. A real *cop,* he thought, his lips slanting up into an unexpected grin.

Nope, self-pity wasn't his style.

But then neither was lusting after the forbidden.

He couldn't make a mistake this time.

He wouldn't make a mistake.

Elaine Jentzen was a complication he didn't need or want. But he would make the best of the situation…if that was possible.

"Earth to Callahan."

Jentzen's voice startled Trace back to attention. "Yeah?" Damn. He'd zoned out again.

She gave him one of those barely tolerant looks teachers saved for their most trying students. "If you're ready now, I'd like to get this show on the road. We have to make a statement to the press."

Well, at least now he had his answer to making the best of things.

It was going to be impossible.

Chapter 6

How did one top one's best effort?

The Gamekeeper knew how.

He smiled. It had been so easy. He'd reinvented himself, and his adversary had no idea. Not just yet. He laughed out loud, the sound satisfying, exhilarating. He just kept getting better and better. Closer and closer to his ultimate goal. Closer than anyone suspected.

He was so very clever...so absolutely perverse. This new game was perfect. A unique and unparalleled *original* creation. No one had ever done anything this magnificent before.

Agent Callahan had not been victorious two years ago, as he so arrogantly thought. The Gamekeeper had been the triumphant one in the end. He gritted his teeth against the *bad* thoughts. Held them at bay. It wasn't time. Not yet. The pain had been almost unbearable. Weeks of agony had followed that fateful night. The tremendous mental anguish that had accompanied the immense pain had been cleansing and at the same time intoxicating. He'd loved it. Baptized himself in it and was reborn.

The Gamekeeper closed his eyes and relished the triumph of rising again. Just like Christ himself. No mere man could keep the Gamekeeper down.

Certainly not Agent Trace Callahan.

He was right where the Gamekeeper wanted him. He felt giddy with the knowledge that the plan had worked so quickly. The danger of getting closer and closer, drawing his enemy deeper into the game, made each calculated move all the more thrilling.

It wasn't about increasing his body count…never had been. It was the danger that sent adrenaline pumping through him…that turned him on. Oh, he did love the game.

And it was only going to get better.

Because no one was as smart as he was. No one else had the *game*.

Only he was genius enough to have created such a flawless masterpiece that conquered the final frontier—the mind. No one had gone this far before.

He remembered as a child the batteries of intelligence tests, the psychoanalyzing. He was a genius, and most certainly not from the gene pool of the obsequious pair who'd adopted him at the tender young age of two.

What had all the pathetic adults in his childhood expected? He'd been far smarter and more capable than any of them. None had recognized the full extent of his genius…the potential of his abilities. Instead they'd feared him. Put him on medication, treated him like a freak.

But he'd made a special game for all of them. They had thought they were so smart…so invincible.

No one was as smart or as invincible as the Gamekeeper.

Not Agent Callahan. Or his new partner, the lovely Deputy Chief Jentzen.

Hmm. This was just like old times. They were both much more vulnerable than they knew. They had no idea just how vulnerable.

Because no one could beat the Gamekeeper at his own game.

So many had tried.

All had failed.

No one would ever catch him…not in a million years. He was too perfect…too smart. Too invisible.

The Gamekeeper leaned forward and began typing words into the chat box on the computer screen.

Time to play.

Chapter 7

That night when she arrived home, Elaine dragged herself from her Jeep to her front door. Sally, tail wagging, waited for her just inside. Elaine was totally wiped out. She and Callahan had spent hours going over Matthews's and Tate's backgrounds—work history, friends, relatives, finances, marital standing—looking for any kind of motivation for the events that had taken place that morning.

They'd found nothing.

Locking the door behind her, she bent down to scratch her big girl behind the ears. Elaine was exhausted physically and mentally, but not so exhausted that she couldn't force herself to muddle through her nightly rituals. Her companion depended upon her. Other than the afternoon walks Allen, the teenager next door, gave Sally, the nightly run was her only outdoor fun.

Elaine changed into running shorts and shoes and a T. She owed this to herself as well as Sally. She needed to burn off some of the day's frustrations.

Nearly an hour later the twosome bounded back into the house. Elaine had managed to keep anything other than the case off her mind during the run. But now, as her heart slowed to a normal rhythm, Dr. Bramm's words haunted her once more, joining the images of Brad Matthews and Harold Tate, the security guard and the four women from last week's mass murder already churning in her head. She stripped off her clothes and climbed into the shower, her favorite wine cooler in hand. She didn't want to think anymore. She pressed her hand to her stomach and braced for the burn as she took a long sip from the cold bottle. Grimacing, she chased it with another, then another after that.

Slowly, as the hot water and the alcohol did their work, the brutal images drained away. No more dead bodies…no more empty cradles.

Elaine closed her eyes to a blessedly emptied mind.

That serenity lasted about four seconds. Trace Callahan abruptly filled the space. She chugged down the last of her wine cooler and turned her face up to the hot spray, but it was no use. He wouldn't go away.

He disagreed with every conclusion she reached, or scenario she offered. He would not give up on his theory that the two multiple homicides were connected with a serial killer who'd terrorized D.C. two years ago. The Gamekeeper.

He made her want to scream or swear, or maybe even tear out her hair. She set her empty bottle aside and made fast work of washing her hair and body. How would she ever conduct this investigation if he refused to listen to reason?

She twisted the control, shutting off the shower and stepped out onto the fuzzy pink mat. Nothing about this investigation was really under her control and she hated it.

She hated him.

Clutching the towel to her chest, Elaine sighed. Well maybe she didn't actually hate him. It was his attitude...that aloof, male mentality that she couldn't tolerate. She wanted to hit him. Especially after that incredible grin he'd flashed her in the car. Her heart had all but leaped from her chest. She despised that he could make her react that way.

She shivered.

She hated him, all right.

But then there was that vulnerable side of him. Her fingers stilled in their work of tucking the towel around her. She'd seen it when he lingered outside the bank, as if coming inside was more than he could do at that moment. He'd looked pale and shaky, *afraid.* She shook her head. That just didn't mesh with the rest of the vibes he emanated. For the most part he oozed a laid-back, good-old-boy charm, as if he was in no hurry about anything. But that wasn't the case at all.

Trace Callahan was smart and as eagle-eyed as they came. He didn't miss anything. His attention to detail and powers of perception amazed her—even if he was wrong in his conclusions.

What was worse, she thought with utter disdain, was the package. Why was it that with good-looking men the elevator either didn't go all the way to the top or they were know-it-alls and brooding? Or gay?

Men. They were just too hard to figure out.

Elaine blow-dried her hair then pulled on her favorite one-size-fits-all Braves nightshirt. She would simply have to learn to live with her new partner, at least for a little while. She'd conduct this investigation like any other, he would either be with her or against her. She wasn't going to worry about it.

Screw his attitude. She ran a brush through her hair and stared at her reflection. The realization that she would probably never have children, that she might even be facing serious health problems suddenly flooded her all over again.

Why hadn't she asked more questions? The doctor had said that the disease sometimes spread to other organs. Her heart lurched at the implication. Could she die from this? She should have asked him for more complete details. But Henshaw had called and she'd had to leave abruptly. Surely she wasn't going to die. He'd said the specialist would explain the possible effects on her future.

One had to be alive to have a future.

But what kind of future? Nothing would ever be the same again, that much she was certain of. She was damaged goods now, just like her new partner. Who would want to marry a woman incapable of bearing children? She thought of her gang of nieces and nephews and the pleasure having them in her life gave her. She might never know how it felt to hold her own child in her arms…

Tears welled in her eyes. She didn't want to cry. She was stronger than that. Her mother and sister would have a fit when they found out she hadn't called them with this news first thing after leaving the doctor's office. She couldn't talk about it with anyone right now. Not even Henshaw when he'd asked. If she told anyone, it would be like making it real. She didn't want it to be that real...yet.

She didn't want to think about it, either.

She grabbed her empty bottle and headed back to the kitchen. She stopped in the living room long enough to pop in her favorite jazz CD. The sultry music drifted along behind her as she made her way into the kitchen. Eating would be a good thing right now...especially since she hadn't bothered to all day except for a few snack crackers and a diet cola.

Leftover Chinese from last night looked easy enough. She wasn't in the mood to cook or clean up afterward. A couple minutes in the microwave and dinner would be served.

Elaine poured Sally a bowlful of her favorite kibbles. She filled a small pitcher with tap water and poured it into the dog's matching water bowl. As she stroked the animal, she realized Allen had brushed Sally today. Good. She just wasn't in the mood to go the extra step tonight. Her long shifts were a godsend to her young neighbor, though. His mother had allergies and had never allowed him to have a pet. Spending time with Sally satisfied his need for that kind of bonding. Sally loved him, and Elaine was tremendously grateful. She'd be in a fix when Allen graduated high school and went off to college.

Well, she had two years to worry about that. Anything could happen in two years. This morning was proof that no one, even when it appeared that way to those around her, led a charmed life.

The microwave dinged, tugging her back to the present. She opened the door, and the pleasant smell of Lo Mein wafted around her. Her stomach rumbled. Oh yeah, she was definitely ready for some food. Though she was only having leftovers, alone at that, she went all out. Linen napkin, stemmed glass of Chardonnay and two lovely lit candles for a centerpiece.

The first bite hit her stomach like a lump of hot coal. Her stomach clenched, then cramped, kindling a fire that never really left her gut.

"Dammit."

She grabbed the ever-present bottle of Maalox from the counter and took a hefty swig as she sank back into her chair.

A few minutes later she could eat in relative comfort. God, she was such a mess. The newest medicine her internist had prescribed was little or no help with the ulcer. And she wasn't about to go in again complaining of continued pain and burning. She knew what came next and she wasn't prepared to go there right now. Maybe they could just take care of her stomach ailments at the same time they gutted her pelvic cavity.

Another bout of emotion gripped her. She blinked away the moisture. Crying would accomplish nothing. She'd call Dr. Bramm's office tomorrow and get the appointment with the specialist. Worrying about this latest problem was pointless until after she had all the facts.

The single chime of the front doorbell interrupted her self-counseling session. Sally sprang up from her lazy sprawl on the floor and barked a warning. Elaine blew out the candles and headed in that direction, she frowned as she glanced at the hall clock: 10:29. Who would be at her door at this time of night?

She'd have gotten a call if there'd been another murder or any other news pertinent to the case.

While Sally uttered a low growl, Elaine flipped on the outside light and checked the security peephole in her door. She relaxed when she saw Henshaw's rumpled form, minus his usual stogie, on her porch. He always left it in his car when he came to her house. He insisted that he respected her personal space. Henshaw was truly one of a kind. She missed him already.

"It's okay, girl. It's just Henshaw." She unbolted the door and drew it open wide. "Has something happened?" she asked by way of a greeting.

Henshaw quirked an eyebrow. "Is that it? No 'Good evening'? No 'Won't you come in'?"

Elaine sighed. "Sorry." She stepped back. "Good evening, partner. Please come in." Sally wagged her tail, offering her own hello.

"At least the mutt's glad to see me," he muttered as he shuffled across the threshold. "By the way, you might want to call me Hank, since, officially, I'm not your partner at the moment."

She rolled her eyes and closed the door behind him. "What're you doing here at this time of night if nothing has happened?"

"I didn't get my report finished before you left the office, so I thought I'd drop it by."

She felt her eyes narrow in suspicion. She knew better than that. Henshaw might move like a tortoise, but his brain worked as speedily as any hare. "Don't give me that. What're you really doing here?"

He reached into his interior jacket pocket and produced the folded pages of the report. "Well, the truth is," he began, offering the document to her, "I just wanted to see if you were doing okay."

She placed the report on the hall table. "Callahan and I haven't killed each other, if that's what you mean."

"Screw Callahan." He looked straight at her. "I mean, are *you* okay? You seemed kind of preoccupied after your doctor's appointment."

Elaine tensed. "I'm fine. I was preoccupied. Entering a crime scene does that to me, you know."

He nodded. "All I'm saying is, something isn't right and I know it."

"There's nothing to tell," she lied. "Now, if you want to come in and sit down, I'll fix you a good stiff drink and I'll tell you how much I hate working with Callahan." She could definitely see a couple more glasses of wine in her future if she planned to get through the night.

"As interesting as it sounds, I'd better pass." He looked sheepish. "The wife will have my hide if I don't get home before midnight. I don't want to get her riled up. Gotta help her keep that blood pressure down." He fixed Elaine with that too-knowing gaze again. "You're sure you're okay."

She smiled, warmed by the genuine affection in his tone. "I'm okay. With thirty looming only a couple of months away I think my body's just getting a head start on falling apart."

Concern marred his brow, reaching all the way down to his eyes. "Anything serious?"

"Nothing that can't be taken care of," she hedged. "I'm fine, really."

He reached into his trouser pocket for his keys. "All right. I'll let it go at that. Good night." He turned to go. "And I'll keep my mouth shut about Callahan. No point in stirring the stink."

"Night," she said as he opened the door. "Thanks for bringing by the report." She leaned against the jamb when he hesitated on the porch. He wanted to say more, but for some reason felt reluctant. "This whole new-partner thing is temporary," she reminded, just in case he was feeling out of sorts. "I can deal with it."

"It's not you I'm worried about on that score," he called over his shoulder as he descended the steps.

She waited until he'd gotten into his car before closing the door. His final words brought the image of Callahan outside the bank to mind once more. Was he really unstable? Was that how his partner had ended up dead? Maybe she should be concerned about his ability to back her up in the field.

Maybe she should be more worried about her life in his presence than her honor.

The doorbell sounded again. Sally whined and looked up at her with a question in her big brown eyes. Elaine glanced at the report lying on the table. What had Henshaw forgotten?

She opened the door and said, "Decide you want that drink after all?"

"Is that an invitation?"

Elaine stared into the piercing blue eyes of Trace Callahan. Amusement twinkled there. Warmth spread through her before she could stop it.

"What're you doing here?" Her tone was every bit as sharp as she'd meant it to be, but her vision was another matter. She couldn't stop her eyes from studying his too-handsome face. Five-o'clock shadow darkened his jaw, adding another layer of texture to the already interesting terrain. He licked his lips causing a little infuriating hitch in her breathing.

Then he gave tit for tat. His gaze traveled down the length of her, abruptly driving home the way she was dressed. *Damn.* She stiffened when that evaluating gaze settled back on hers.

"It's late, I know," he said in that sensual drawl.

No way could she miss the male approval in those searing bedroom eyes. "That doesn't answer my question." He had an infuriating habit of answering a question with a question or with a remark that skirted the actual answer.

"I wanted to talk to you…off the record." He adopted what he obviously thought was a hopeful look. It didn't quite hit the mark.

She exhaled noisily, impatiently. He was her partner. "If you really feel it's necessary."

"I do." His expression turned too serious, too somber.

"All right." She opened the door wider and he stepped inside. As usual, his presence diminished the space, made her want to back away. Sally growled low and menacingly. Callahan didn't appear put off by the threat.

"It's all right, girl." Elaine stroked the dog's head and said to her unexpected and definitely unwelcome visitor, "Pour yourself something to drink and have a seat." She gestured to her living room. "I'll be with you in a minute."

He nodded once, then followed her instructions, that deliberate walk making her pulse react. She shook her head. Damn, she didn't need this.

In her bedroom, she cursed herself for the fool she was as

she quickly dragged on a pair of jeans. She refused the impulse to glance at her reflection as she left the room. She didn't care how she looked, other than being dressed. This wasn't a social visit. She definitely was not trying to impress him.

"Come on, girl," she muttered to Sally who tagged along after her. "Let's see what this little tête-à-tête is all about."

Still standing when she returned, he offered her a tumbler containing the only hard liquor she had in the house, bourbon. She kept it around for her brothers. The decanter and four tumblers sat in a silver tray on the antique sideboard she'd inherited from her maternal grandmother. Again, Callahan perused her body from head to toe as if he felt the need to analyze her from the outside in. Elaine felt immensely better with Sally sitting at her feet.

"Thank you," she said politely as she reached for the drink. She could use one about now, but didn't have the guts to pay the price. Wine was one thing, eighty proof was entirely another. Her stomach couldn't handle it. Unavoidably her fingers brushed his as she accepted the glass. A zing of electricity zapped her. She almost flinched. The only thing worse was that he didn't seem to notice any of it. Maybe she was the only one suffering from confused, overactive hormones.

He sipped the Jack Daniels unnaturally slowly. His rigid posture, the tightness of his fingers on the glass all screamed of labored restraint. Or maybe it was her imagination. She was definitely looking for weakness.

"I think we got off on the wrong foot," he said finally, his voice low, his tone devoid of inflection.

Elaine resisted the urge to laugh out loud. "That would be a vast understatement, Agent Callahan."

He stared at the glass in his hand but didn't take another drink. He swallowed, hard, the movement of muscle beneath bronzed skin oddly distracting. She looked away.

"We need to clear the air. Keep this professional."

Anger pinged her. "Are you accusing me of being unprofessional?" she demanded, and instantly wished she could take back the words. This promotion had made her too damned edgy. She went on attack instantly when anyone questioned her job performance.

He blinked, then frowned. "No." He lifted one shoulder in a halfhearted shrug. "It's just that you argue my every suggestion and you seem to resent my mere presence in a room. We'll never accomplish anything that way."

She set her glass down on the nearest table and forced a calm voice. "Don't expect me to go along with all your suggestions," she warned. "I call it like I see it. As far as your presence, my chief ordered me to work with you, and I will. Any resentment I feel will not affect the investigation."

He placed his glass next to hers, though the gesture was clearly forced. "All I'm saying is that I don't want you to overreact to the Bureau's involvement in this case. I don't think that's too much to ask."

"I'm a professional," she said coolly. "This has nothing to do with the Bureau's involvement. I make my assessments based on what I discover for myself, but I don't trust until it's earned. I'll continue to question your suggestions until I either see it your way or I trust your judgment. *I* don't think that's too much to ask."

He almost smiled but didn't quite follow through with the effort. It amused him when she used his own statements against him. Well, maybe *amused* wasn't the right word.

"I guess that's all I can expect," he relented.

"I'm glad we're in agreement." With Sally on her heels, she walked across the room and paused at the doorway leading to the hall. "We both need some sleep. We've got a long day ahead of us tomorrow. I, for one, intend to stay focused on this investigation. So, if there's nothing else…"

He didn't move. He didn't even speak for one long moment. He had more to say, she could see it in his expression, in the determined set of those broad shoulders. The sensual ache from the music was the only sound during the tense standoff.

"You've already made up your mind about me."

The accusation wasn't spoken in an accusing manner, not openly, anyway. His tone remained low, tightly controlled. But she knew what he was thinking. He wouldn't have said it otherwise.

"Are you going to tell me that you didn't get your partner killed?" she suggested. "Because that's all I've been told about you and that was secondhand." It was only fair to give him a chance to refute what she'd heard. He was her partner, for the time being.

He walked toward her, his steps measured, controlled, just like his voice. When he stopped next to her, he looked straight into her eyes. "You expect me to justify what I did do or deny what I didn't as told by the media?"

There he went, answering her question with a question. "That would be a start."

Fury ignited in those blue depths. The blast made her want to step back, but she held her ground. He reined in the outburst right before her eyes. The effort it took visible.

When he'd exiled all emotion from his expression, he said, "A *real* cop would do more than just talk about making her own assessments based on fact rather than hearsay."

Clenching her jaw to hold back a scorching rebuttal, Elaine pivoted and stormed into the hall. She refused to admit his statement held any merit. She jerked the front door open, a blatant demand for him to go. "Like you said before, it's late."

He made his way to the door but paused directly in front of her before going out. "I guess I was wrong."

In spite of her anger, this close, that whiskey-smooth voice slid over her like a caress. Reluctantly she met his gaze, the intensity of it almost undoing her bravado as she waited for him to finish what he'd started.

"I really did think you were a good cop."

Outrage charged through her. She stared hard at him. He stared back, a challenge in his eyes. What the hell did he want from her? "You know what?"

He angled his head in question.

She smiled sweetly. "I don't care what you think. This is my investigation and we'll do things my way. End of story."

"And I'm not supposed to make any waves. Is that it?"

He was somehow closer now. She refused to back off. "That's it in a nutshell, partner."

"Well, at least I know where I stand," he allowed in a tone so low, so lethal that it made her shiver.

She met his intense gaze with lead in her own. Opening the

door wider still, she said, "Glad we had this little talk, Callahan."

Two more tense beats passed before he moved. "Right."

He walked out.

Elaine slammed the door behind him.

They were surely off on the right foot now.

Chapter 8

Elaine would never get used to the smell of chilled flesh. No matter how many autopsies she attended or corpses she viewed for identification purposes. It was always the same. Her gut wrenched, and it was all she could do to keep down the Starbucks special house blend she'd inhaled en route to the morgue this morning.

Good thing she hadn't eaten anything solid.

"What's the bottom line, Walt?"

Walt Damron surveyed his handiwork a moment before responding. Elaine automatically did the same. She knew the routine. As the chief medical examiner he got to pick and choose his cases, leaving the routine work to those under his dominion. And when he did elect to take on a case personally, he did so with much pomp and circumstance. He was the best and he wanted some acknowledgment of that station.

Elaine couldn't help thinking how sad Brad Matthews looked lying there. Dead. Naked. His sins bared for all to see. Still young by anyone's standards, his career taking off, a wife and two kids. What went wrong?

A frown furrowed its way across her forehead. He looked healthy in spite of the hideous marbling effect death had left on his skin. Well, and discounting the damage the .38 had done in the vicinity of his brain.

Walt heaved a sigh and started to flip through the pages of his preliminary report. "Toxicology is clean." He shrugged and set the report aside. "There are a few tests that won't be back for a day or so, but all in all I don't expect to find anything useful." He shook his head and made a tsking sound. "If only *I* had such a strong heart. Either the man led an exceedingly healthy lifestyle or he was blessed with good DNA."

Damn. Nothing. "So he just went off the deep end and killed a business associate and that security guard for no reason," she said, more to herself than to Walt.

"Just like that young woman last week," the distinguished medical examiner noted quietly.

Elaine shifted, frustrated. The reminder hadn't been necessary…but there it was. "Thanks, Walt. I appreciate your doing this one personally."

"Dr. Damron."

Elaine started at the deep, husky sound of the male voice. She'd forgotten about Callahan. Man, she had to be off this morning to have let him slip her mind. Especially considering he'd hitched a ride with her from the station. She shouldn't have had that fourth wine cooler before hitting the sack last night. But she'd needed to relax. After Callahan's visit the feat had been nearly impossible.

Walt stared expectantly across the dissected body of Brad Matthews, waiting for Callahan to continue.

"Any indication of extreme fatigue?"

Walt's shaggy gray eyebrows knitted thoughtfully. "Nothing out of the ordinary. It would be more speculation than anything for me to suggest that the heavy bags under his eyes or any other outward indication generally associated with stress or fatigue were more than lifestyle or genetics."

Callahan inclined his inordinately handsome head without a single perfect hair falling out of place. "But you said his general state of health likely indicated an unusually healthy lifestyle."

"True. But that doesn't mean that he hadn't started working too hard or carrying too heavy a stress load more recently." Walt shrugged. "For that matter, anything's possible where his mental state was concerned. There was no visible or chemical indication of disease, but he could very well have developed some sort of phobia or mental disorder recently. I can only tell you what I see, what toxicology suggests."

"Thank you." Callahan walked out of the room.

Elaine stared after him, bewildered.

"I can't read the man," Walt said quietly, his attention focused on the door Callahan had exited. "What do you make of him, Detective?"

"I'm still working on that one," she admitted. "I'll let you know."

Walt made a sound that broadcast his doubt. "I won't hold my breath."

Elaine wasn't holding hers, either. She thanked Walt once more and took her time catching up with Callahan.

This morning when she'd arrived at her office he'd been waiting for her. He'd looked as spit and polished as ever. Charcoal-gray suit jacket over a white shirt and navy slacks. Clean shaven, hair looking as if he'd just stepped out of a salon. He'd shone like a freshly minted silver dollar. That is, if one didn't look too closely. It had taken only one glance into those unnerving blue eyes to see the truth before he banished the telltale indication.

Callahan was clinging to that edge he'd reportedly gone over two years ago, by the very tips of his fingers. Maybe he wanted or needed to get his professional life back together. His participation in this case might very well be about that more than anything else. Who knew? But one thing was astonishingly clear. He was barely hanging on. One wrong move could send him plummeting back into that private hell he'd apparently climbed out of far too recently for her comfort.

Like Walt said, he was hard as hell to read, so her conclusions were more speculation than anything else. She needed the truth. She needed Callahan to come clean with her. But she didn't see that happening in this lifetime.

"Detective Jentzen!"

Elaine hesitated at the main entry of the ME's office and glanced back in the direction from which she'd come. Kathleen, Walt's secretary, hurried along the corridor toward her.

The smile that pushed into place was genuine. Kathleen was a truly nice lady. Elaine couldn't help wondering again if the gossip about her and Walt was true. "Good morning," she offered, having missed the loyal secretary when she first arrived that morning.

Kathleen beamed. "You're looking well," she said to Elaine.

It wasn't until that precise moment that yesterday's reality slammed into Elaine all over again. It was like waking from a nightmare only to realize the dream had been real. Endometriosis. Surgery. Probably no children. Who wanted a woman incapable of bearing children?

Forty-eight hours ago a husband and children had been the farthest goals from her mind. Why was it that the abrupt idea that she might not be able to achieve either was suddenly so devastating?

Elaine blinked. Reminded herself she had to call Dr. Bramm's office today. "Thanks. You look terrific yourself." Clearing her mind of the too personal, too unpleasant thoughts, Elaine focused on the older woman. She did look good. Damn good for a lady closer to seventy than sixty.

Kathleen adopted a knowing expression. "Your mother called. Said she'd been trying to track you down all morning. Your office told her you were over here."

Elaine had set her cell to vibrate that morning so as not to be disturbed. "Thanks, Kathleen. I'll call her right away."

"See that you do." A secret smile stole across the woman's lips. "I'd better get back to the office. Dr. Damron can't find a thing without me. Have a nice day!"

Elaine pushed out into the bright May morning and redirected her thoughts to the case. She'd call her mother when she had some privacy. Right now she had a few questions for Callahan.

He waited by her Jeep. When he caught sight of her he slipped what was clearly an unlit cigarette back into his jacket pocket. The guy had definitely picked a bad time to quit smoking. She quashed the trickle of sympathy. He didn't deserve her sympathy just yet. And as long as he played devil's advocate at every opportunity on this case he wouldn't earn her trust or respect, either.

"What's the deal, Callahan?" She walked up next to him and folded her arms over her chest, opting not to lean against her vehicle, since it still badly needed that washing and in part because she wanted him to see that she was annoyed.

He lifted one shoulder in a negligent shrug. "What do you mean?"

Okay, so she'd dismissed his every conclusion yesterday. Was he going to hold out on her today? If getting to her was his plan, he'd done a bang-up job so far. She didn't like this. Didn't like it one bit. Henshaw didn't work this way; she didn't work this way.

"Tell me what you're thinking."

That analyzing gaze locked on to hers then, sending a shiver down her spine despite her best efforts to resist the reaction.

"Why?" he tossed back. "So you can pick apart my theories?"

She shoved a handful of hair behind her ear and puffed out a lungful of frustration. "Look, this isn't going to work." She planted her hands on her hips and glared at him. "You're supposed to be working *with* me not against me. Partners, remember?"

That ghostlike smile that haunted one corner of his carnal mouth and got to her like nothing else could made an appearance. "And here I thought you'd forgotten our little deal." The smile vanished and those piercing blue eyes turned ice-cold. "I'm not here to make you look good, Jentzen. And I'm damn sure not here to parlay theories for the learning experience or the moral support of the team. I want one thing and one thing only…to bring this guy down."

Fury detonated on a cellular level, sending tension radiating along every single nerve ending. So he'd spent the night deciding he wanted to play by his own rules. "By *guy* I assume you mean your old nemesis the Gamekeeper."

His jaw tightened visibly. "That's right."

"Get in."

He looked surprised at her ferocious tone.

"Where to, *partner?*" If his tone hadn't been facetious enough, his expression left no doubt as to how he felt. He hated being stuck with her, having to bend to her wishes.

"Just get in."

Elaine climbed behind the wheel of her Jeep, anger making her movements stiff. Without uttering another word she drove straight to the only place she could be certain of two things, they wouldn't be bothered and the territory would be considered neutral by both parties.

Jimmy's Pub was a bit off the beaten path, on Cone Street in downtown Atlanta. But being a third-generation cop, Elaine knew the right places to go for anonymity as well as camaraderie. Though Jimmy's was best known for its beer and old-fashioned-style burgers, the doors opened at ten every morning for the early lunchers. Or maybe just to make sure cops had a reliable place to go and discuss business that required distance from the office or nosy colleagues.

"Burger and a cola," she told the waiter who paused at their table the moment they sat down. If his T-shirt was any indication the guy was a student at a local university. His jeans were well-worn, and he had that harried look of a full-time student, part-time employee, working hard to balance his schedule with homework commitments and the undying hope for a decent social life.

Callahan looked to her for counsel. "Try it," she told him. "The burgers here are the best." She lifted a skeptical eyebrow. "Unless, of course, you're a vegetarian."

"I'll have the same," Callahan said to the waiter who nodded and moved on.

Patronage at the pub was light today. The main lunch crowd wouldn't filter in until after noon, she imagined. That was one of the primary reasons Elaine preferred to skip breakfast and go for an early lunch, it cut wait time down to half. She didn't recognize any of the patrons seated around the large dining area or at the long bar. Good. That way she didn't have to worry about anyone horning into the conversation. She thought immediately of Flatt and Jillette and how they no doubt waited in the wings for an opportunity to try and take this case from her. Then again, she considered, why the hell didn't she just let them have it?

"Why did you ask Walt about stress and fatigue?" She cut to the chase, pushing worries about her two disloyal colleagues to the back burner. "You have to know how difficult it is to judge those kinds of indicators with any real accuracy."

To Callahan's credit he didn't look away. He held her gaze, but he did keep his expression carefully blank of what he might or might not be thinking.

"It's his MO," he said flatly.

Surprised, Elaine offered, "The Gamekeeper's?"

Callahan nodded. "He picks his targets, then he wears them down until they feel they have no choice but to do his bidding. They just don't have what it takes to keep fighting the inevitable."

She studied him a moment, tried to determine if he was ready for her to hit him with the big guns. No way to know. Only one way to find out. "So you think the beauty salon murders as well as the ones at the bank yesterday are all tied to this Gamekeeper?"

He nodded again, his posture visibly braced for her arguments.

"But how? We don't have the first lick of evidence to even connect the two." This was nuts. Sure there was that one glaring similarity. Both shooters had walked into a place of business and killed for no apparent reason. Still, that was only one link. Were all drive-by shootings in urban areas connected merely because they were carried out in the same manner? Definitely not.

"There's your link," he offered with absolutely no hesitation. "*He* likes it that way."

Elaine shook her head in renewed frustration. "I'm going to need more than that, Callahan."

The waiter stopped at their table long enough to deposit two sweating glasses of cola. "Burgers'll be out in a couple minutes."

Elaine hastily thanked him so he'd move on and Callahan would start talking again.

"Think about your shooters," he told her, his gaze boring

into hers. "Both were on their way up. Had the world by the tail. Their lives were seemingly perfect. Why would they do this? Why throw everything away?"

"We wouldn't be sitting here if I knew the answer to that," she snapped. "Get to the point."

"That's what the Gamekeeper does. He selects those who have everything going for them, the cream of the crop, then he lures them in. He likes the challenge."

"And you would know this based on…?" she pressed, still seeing no concrete reasoning behind his conclusion.

"Because he killed people in D.C. that way. He selected each player with the utmost care, then he reeled him or her in, and then it was over."

Elaine remembered a number of highly publicized details of the case. "But this Gamekeeper killed his players himself, right? There were no suicides involved."

Callahan's fierce expression went blank again. "That's right."

When Elaine would have spoken again, he cut her off. "Don't bother with the serial-killers-don't-change-their-routine excuse," he said, a distinct edge in his tone. "I've had that load of crap shoved down my throat until I could puke. They do, at times, change their methods." Callahan sipped his drink, taking his time. Perhaps more to give himself a moment to calm down than to quench his thirst. "It's possible that I wounded him badly enough that he has no choice but to do things differently this time."

She gave her head another shake. "I'm sorry, Callahan, I just can't accept that conclusion without more than you're offering. Granted, we need to follow up on that possibility, but I'm not going to assume he's the one based on such meager reasoning."

He leaned back in his seat, his expression going to victorious in one fluid motion. "I see. So we'll follow up on all our other leads. Consider all those *other* options first."

Ire tore through her again. He knew as well as she did that they had no other leads or options. "After we interview Matthews's wife, we'll outline a strategy." The new widow had been sedated after hearing the news. Her personal physician had assured Elaine that she would be up and ready to speak with the police by noon today. Another reason for an early lunch. The woman's mother had picked up the children and would be caring for them for a couple of days.

Mother.

Damn, she had to touch base with her mom.

Callahan directed his attention back to his glass of cola. "Whatever you say."

Wow. Now that was cooperation. Too bad she knew he didn't mean it.

"I have to make a personal call."

She started to push up from the table but one look into his eyes told her that he suspected it was only an excuse to make some call related to the case behind his back. Damn. She supposed she didn't deserve his trust just yet, either.

Slumping back into her chair she fished out her cell phone. Six missed calls. Elaine frowned. What the hell could be so urgent that her mother would keep calling like that? For the first time since Kathleen had given Elaine the message, a new kind of anxiety strong-armed its way into her too busy morning. She'd been so focused on this case that she hadn't considered something might really be wrong.

With a flick of one finger she'd entered the speed dial

number for *home*. Not the place where she lived with Sally, but the home where she'd grown up with three brothers and one sister. Her mother's pleasant voice on the other end of the line immediately alleviated the pressure on Elaine's chest. Surely if something were wrong she wouldn't sound so calm.

"It's me." Elaine took a deep, calming breath. "Sorry I missed your calls. What's up?"

"We need to talk."

Those four little words struck renewed fear in Elaine's heart. There was something about the tone—or lack thereof—that jarred her most deeply entrenched instincts.

"Is something wrong?"

"Can you come by for an early lunch?" her mother asked, smoothly avoiding her daughter's question.

Just then the waiter plopped the heavy stoneware plates on the table, Jimmy's famous burgers literally steaming in their griddle toasted buns.

"Sure, I'll be there in thirty minutes," Elaine assured her before disconnecting. She stared at the phone for a moment before dropping it back into her purse. Her gut knotted up and did some screaming of its own. She swallowed hard and wondered if she'd remembered to bring that new bottle of antacid.

"Everything okay?"

Her gaze shifted to her new partner. She couldn't help wondering if she looked as guarded as he did. How the hell were they going to conduct this investigation when they didn't trust each other for an instant?

"I don't know."

There wasn't much that scared Elaine, but *this* terrified her.

Chapter 9

Elaine managed to scarf down half her burger before she told Callahan they had to go. She had neither the time nor the inclination to drop him off at the station considering how traffic would be backed up at that time of day. Instead, she told him she had to stop by to see her mother a moment and he could wait in the car...if he didn't mind.

He shrugged that indifferent gesture so characteristic of his personality and didn't argue. He'd managed to shovel down his burger by that time, anyway.

Elaine parked her Jeep in the long curved drive that cut through the elegant landscape of her childhood home. The yard instantly brought back dozens of memories of touch footfall and tree-climbing exploits. There was scarcely a tree on the property that Elaine hadn't scaled at least once. With three macho brothers, she'd learned the art of playing hard and fast very quickly. Her only sister, Judith, two years older, had preferred baking and curling hair to playing with her brothers and tomboy sister. Elaine couldn't help smiling. She'd had the perfect childhood with the epitome of the all-American family and wonderful parents. They'd done everything together and had always been there for each other. Both her mother and her father had been heavily involved with their children's lives. Still were for that matter.

"I'll be quick," she promised as she unbuckled her seat belt. Guilt nudged at her but she ignored it. This wasn't about the case. This was personal. She didn't want him anywhere near her personal life.

"No problem." He surveyed the yard and the house beyond. "Nice place."

Elaine abruptly wondered where Callahan had grown up. Did he have family? What did they think of the shambles that appeared to be his career and personal life? She frowned, shook off the foolish thought and stared out at the classic Georgian home that stood a proud two stories and a roomy five thousand square feet.

"Thanks."

She'd just gotten the driver's-side door open when she heard her mother's voice.

"I didn't know you were bringing a guest!"

Elaine cringed. Her mother was a typical Buckhead socialite. No way would she ever stand for *anyone* waiting in the car. Atlanta's home of the wealthy, socially and politically prominent, Buckhead residents strictly adhered to certain codes.

"Mom, this is Special Agent Trace Callahan."

Callahan emerged from the vehicle, offering her mother that megawattage smile, which charmed her in two seconds flat. "Mrs. Jentzen, it's a pleasure to meet you, ma'am." He took Lana Jentzen's outstretched hand and brushed a kiss to the knuckles. Her mother pressed her free hand to her chest and giggled. Giggled!

Elaine's jaw sagged in disbelief. Any possibility of damage control went out the proverbial window with that line and showy display. She would need to know where Callahan hailed from in order to determine if he'd just put on the dog for her mother or if he'd been raised a true Southern gentleman. She seriously doubted the latter, though the conclusion could very well be based on nothing more than her intense dislike for the man. Or was she confusing distrust for dislike? If one considered the way he could make her shiver in awareness.,.forget it. She wasn't going there.

"Please, come in." Lana looked from Callahan to Elaine, the blush on her cheeks giving away her pleasure.

"I'll just wait out here," Callahan suggested humbly.

Elaine rolled her eyes. Yeah, right. Like that was going to happen now. "Mother, we don't have much time."

Lana waved a hand in dismissal of her daughter's comment. "I insist you both come in and have a glass of iced tea at the very least. For early May the weather is turning out to be beastly hot."

Unable to slow this runaway train, Elaine followed her mother up the walk, Callahan right on her heels.

"Where's Dad?"

"Oh, he's on the golf course, I presume."

Elaine felt uncertainty line her forehead. It wasn't like her mother not to know where her father was every moment of the day. Something was definitely off kilter here.

"You have a lovely home, Mrs. Jentzen."

Lana paused at the front door, her hostess smile firmly in place. "Call me Lana, Trace," she urged. "You'll make me feel old calling me 'Mrs.'"

Trace? Now Elaine was really worried. Her mother had to be ill. Calling a stranger by his first name was not standard operating procedure for the sophisticated lady. No way.

Another ten minutes passed before Elaine got her time alone with her mother. The elegant lady had insisted on showing *Trace* the backyard and telling him how Elaine's grandfather had bought this home for Lana and her husband upon the birth of their first child. They'd lived here ever since. She said the last with such remorse Elaine worried that perhaps her first thought had been right. Could her mother be ill? About to give Elaine some horrible news? Thank God she hadn't bothered her mother with her own unfavorable report from the doctor.

"We missed you at dinner last night," her mother said when they had at last sat down around the massive kitchen table, a place where Jentzen family meetings had taken place for as long as Elaine could remember.

Elaine closed her eyes for a second and gave herself a mental kick for not calling. The entire Jentzen clan had gathered for dinner on Monday nights for as long as she could remember. Her grandparents, parents, aunts and uncles had done so for half a lifetime before their own families had come along and drawn them into extended groups.

"There was a multiple homicide," she explained. Her

mother had been a cop's wife her entire adult life. Not to mention the mother of three sons as well as one daughter who were all protectors of the community. She, of all people, should understand the call of duty.

"I felt certain something came up," Lana allowed. "And of course you had no way of knowing I'd planned any sort of announcement."

Every muscle in Elaine's body tensed in preparation for bad news. "Give it to me straight, Mom," she pressed. "If something is wrong, just tell me."

Lana clasped her hands on the table in front of her and took a deep breath. "Your father and I are getting a divorce."

If she'd said the world was coming to an end Elaine wouldn't have been more surprised. This was impossible.

"What?"

"It's true. We've discussed it at length, and divorce is the only option."

Elaine shook her head in an attempt to clear the confusion. It didn't work. "I don't understand. Why would you want to get a divorce?"

"It's a rather long story, dear. Are you sure you have time just now?"

"Mother, you cannot make an announcement like this and leave it at that." This was impossible. Crazy. Her father couldn't have…? "Mom, is Dad having an affair?"

"Of course not," Lana protested, clearly mortified that Elaine would even suggest such a thing.

Thank God. "Then why would you want a divorce?"

Lana tilted her head slightly to the right and studied her daughter. "How can I explain?" She pinched her lips together and looked thoughtful for a time. "Your father and I have been married for forty-five years. He was my high school sweetheart and we married right out of college."

And had been together ever since, Elaine wanted to add but managed to keep her mouth shut.

"He's the only man I've ever known." She glanced side to side as if concerned someone might hear her next words. "In the biblical sense."

Elaine wanted to crawl under the table. Surely this wasn't about sex. There were drugs for deficiencies in that department. Elaine shifted in her chair and moistened her lips. "Is that the problem? *Sex?*" The word came out more or less a croak. She swallowed in hopes of dampening her suddenly dry throat. The sex talk had been humiliating enough when her mother had given it to her all those years ago. That was the one area where Elaine and her mother had never ventured with any measure of comfort. They didn't talk about boys and sex. Never had. Judith had talked about it enough with her mother for both of them. Lana had never understood why Elaine kept everything about her social life to herself.

"Yes," her mother answered, her chin held high in abject refusal to be put off by her daughter's discomfort with the subject. "In a way."

Elaine had no idea what to say next. Thankfully her mother took the lead. "I love your father, don't doubt it." She shrugged her silk clad shoulders. "It's just that I'm certain there must be more."

She had to be kidding.

Elaine flared her hands in question. "In what way?"

"We've had a wonderful life together, your father and I.

We raised you and your siblings with the utmost care. You're all happy and well adjusted."

If she only knew, Elaine mused silently.

"For the past ten or so years your father and I have been on our own and—" she shrugged again "—frankly we've discovered we have nothing in common."

A warning went off in Elaine's brain. "Are we talking boredom here or what?"

"Yes," Lana enthused, evidently thrilled that her daughter appeared to understand. "I want more. I want to travel…to learn new languages and to be with other men."

Elaine's eyes widened in shock. "Other men?"

"Please, dear," Lana fussed, "you sound like a parrot."

She couldn't take it anymore. Elaine pushed out of her chair and threw her arms in the air. The conversation had just entered the Twilight Zone. "You say you love him. You've been married to him for most of your life but you want to be with *other men?*"

Her voice echoed in the room and Elaine winced. She hoped like hell Callahan hadn't heard that last remark. Her mother had left him in the parlor watching the noon news with a tall glass of iced tea garnished with a lemon wedge. A small tray of cookies sat nearby on an antique table for his enjoyment. Lana Jentzen never did anything halfway. That certainty was the very thing scaring the hell out of Elaine at that very moment.

Lana patted the air in a gesture that insisted Elaine take her seat once more. "It happens all the time," she offered. "People outgrow each other. It's not the end of the world."

Oh, but it was.

Elaine felt as if her insides had twisted into a tattered braid. She collapsed into the chair she'd recently vacated. "Mom, you're too old for this kind of thing."

Lana looked taken aback. "I'm sixty-five, Elaine, I'm not dead."

This could not be happening.

"Mom, have you talked to a counselor?" This was way over Elaine's head. She wasn't even sure what to say to this kind of radical decision.

"Your father and I have been in counseling for months," she said pointedly. "It's time to move on. It's not like we're going to live forever. There are things I want to do…places I want to see before I die."

Months? How could her parents have been in counseling for that long and Elaine not know it?

"I…" What the hell did she say? Clearly her mother's mind was made up. "I don't know what to say to this."

Her mother reached for her hand. "It's a shock, I realize." She smiled patiently. "But you'll get used to it. Your father and I are still friends."

Elaine resisted the nearly overwhelming urge to shake her head. Who was this woman? "Where is Dad?" The idea that he might have moved out already broadsided her next.

"He's on the golf course, dear," she said, her gaze searching Elaine's as if she suspected dementia. "I told you that. Are you sure you're all right?"

"I mean," Elaine restated for clarification, "where is he living?"

"Why, here." Lana surveyed the huge kitchen. "There's plenty of room. My father bought this house for the two of us, selling the property and splitting the proceeds is out of the question. We're adults, we can share the house."

The image of her father bringing home a date and her mother doing the same inadvertently on the same night loomed in Elaine's mind like the premonition of imminent doom.

Another realization scooted its way into the bizarre thoughts churning in Elaine's brain. Maybe they really didn't want a divorce. Maybe that was the real reason they had opted not to sell the house. Could there be hope?

"It'll take time to adjust to the idea," Lana said, patting her daughter's hand. "We'll be fine and so will you."

A little while later Elaine and her mother hugged and said their goodbyes. Just as they reached the entry hall Elaine remembered Callahan. Boy, this announcement had really thrown her for a loop. He had wandered over to the grand piano in the corner of the room to survey the array of framed photographs scattered across its polished top. Elaine just wanted to get him and get out of here. The whole episode was entirely surreal.

Before bidding goodbye, Lana invited Callahan to stop by again anytime.

Elaine didn't look at him or speak as they climbed back into her Jeep. She didn't want to know if he'd overheard anything. And she damned sure wasn't going to answer any questions. The idea that her mother might have had her eye on him made Elaine shudder. This wasn't supposed to happen. Weren't men the ones who were supposed to do this sort of thing? And didn't it generally happen by age fifty?

"You have a nice family," Callahan commented as they pulled out onto the tree-lined street.

"Thanks," she muttered.

He was right. Nice family. Nice home. Nice neighborhood. Nice every-damned-thing. But her parents were still getting a divorce. Her mother and father had gotten married in the church, for God's sake. How could they get a divorce?

She had to talk to her sister. Maybe Judith could shed some light on this. But there was no time now.

Elaine pointed her Jeep in the direction of the home where Brad Matthews had resided with his young family. She had to clear her mind, focus on the case. Dealing with her parents' divorce—unbelievable as it was—would have to wait.

Her cell phone interrupted her concentration. She snagged it from her bag. "Jentzen."

"Detective Jentzen, I'm glad I caught you."

Connie. The chief's secretary.

Elaine went on alert. If there had been another set of murders…she didn't want to think that.

"Hey, Connie. Is the chief looking for me?" Even that would be better than the other possibility.

"It's Mrs. Matthews," Connie told her. "She won't be able to be interviewed until one. Her husband's family arrived this morning and they're trying to work out funeral arrangements."

Elaine resisted the urge to heave a sigh. Obviously, Mrs. Matthews didn't understand that it would be a couple more days before she could move forward with a funeral, at least if she intended to inter the body.

"One o'clock. Got it." Elaine thanked her and tossed the phone onto the console.

"Change in plans?" Callahan suggested.

"Matthews's widow can't see us until one." She didn't look in his direction. The ordeal with her mother had made her feel vulnerable. Vulnerability was something she did not intend to let Callahan see. Not if she was going to hold the spot of lead detective.

"There are some calls I could make," he said when she stopped at the next traffic light.

Though she'd just as soon not, she knew that avoiding eye contact when she responded would be seen as intentional, so she gave him a cursory glance. That analyzing gaze latched on to hers so fast and furiously that she had to look away. Heat infused her cheeks in that brief instant.

His perceptive antenna was working overtime.

"We'll go back to the office, then." She had a call or two to make herself. More reports might be in from the autopsy, though Walt didn't expect to discover anything out of the norm. A vivid image of Brad Matthews's cold, dead body flashed across her mind.

What had made him walk into that bank and kill a close business associate? There had to be an answer. Normal people with everything to live for just didn't go over the edge for no reason. She tamped down the urge to steal a glimpse of her companion. He'd had his reasons for taking that unintended plunge. People always did. But Elaine had no answer where Brad Matthews was concerned.

What would she say to his widow? That they were doing everything they could to nail the entire incident on her husband? And wouldn't that be the easiest solution? Find a motive, then close the case. One more high-powered white-collar worker cracks. It happened all the time.

But this was different somehow. Just like the senseless murders at the beauty salon last week. Every instinct Elaine possessed warned that there was more than met the eye in both cases.

The only question was, would she be a good enough detective to see it?

Once back at the station, she left Callahan at her desk and disappeared into the ladies' room. She'd be safe from interruptions there since she and Connie were the only females on the floor.

She paced the small washroom and waited for her sister to answer her phone.

"Hello. Put that down!"

Elaine stopped and stared at the phone a second. What the hell? "Judith?"

"Elaine? Oh, I'm sorry for shouting in your ear. Jared decided to try climbing the living room drapes. I don't know what's gotten into that child?"

Jared was four years old, the eldest of her sister's four children. Four kids in five years. Elaine wondered on a regular basis how her sister handled the stress. But she was the perfect stay-at-home mom. And usually her kids were extremely well behaved.

"Is everything okay?" her sister inquired.

"Fine. Everything with me is fine." A big fat lie, but she wasn't about to go into that right now. She could understand Judith asking since Elaine rarely bothered with personal calls during duty hours.

"Good." Another sidebar to her son to *Get down!* vibrated across the air waves.

"Look, if this is a bad time we can talk later," Elaine offered. Her sister sounded harried in a way Elaine had never noticed before.

"No. No. It's okay. What's going on?"

Elaine leaned against the white tile wall and heaved that sigh she'd been holding in for almost an hour now. "What's going on with Mom and Dad, Judith? Is this divorce thing for real?"

Judith released a weary sigh of her own. "It seems so."

Elaine shook her head. "This is nuts. How can she just up and decide she wants a divorce?"

"Dad is such a homebody. Hardly leaves the house unless it's to play eighteen holes. I think Mom is ready to do that traveling she's always talked about. Neither of them is getting any younger, you know."

Her mother had said the same about the travel. "Surely Dad can be persuaded to travel with her." She resumed her pacing to ward off the mounting frustration. "If not, why doesn't she travel alone or with some of her friends? There doesn't have to be a divorce."

"I think she's feeling a little neglected as a woman," Judith ventured cautiously, thought about it a moment, then added, "Do you know what I mean?"

Elaine felt her eyes roll back in her head. Did she know what Judith meant? Was there another woman on the planet who went without more often than Elaine? If her mother wanted to talk about neglect, Elaine could write her a book on the subject. Mostly it was her own fault, but that didn't make her feel any better.

"What're we going to do about this?" Taking charge was what Elaine did best. There had to be a way to fix the situation.

Judith hummed a note of uncertainty. "I don't know, Elaine. I've got so many problems of my own I'm not sure I'll be any help with this."

Problems? What kind of problems did her sister have? She had a great husband who taught literature at a local university. He was handsome, attentive and a hopeless romantic. She had four beautiful children and a lovely home. Their mother's inheritance had ensured that all the Jentzen children would receive a beautiful home as a gift upon the birth of their first child.

An epiphany pierced Elaine's heart. She would never have that. Not the house; of course she would get a house. Her mother wouldn't leave her out. But the children…she might never be able to have children of her own.

"Elaine? Are you still there?"

"Yeah. I'm here." The whole world seemed to be going mad around her. What else did her sister want? She had it all. Her mother had it all and more! Did some sort of insanity run in the Jentzen women that struck when they should be the happiest? Maybe that's why Elaine didn't have a husband already. Perhaps some rebel brain cell knew that having it all would lead to insanity.

More shouting on the other end of the line. Elaine got the distinct impression that her sister's oldest child might be on shaky ground as far as his future was concerned.

"Can we talk about this later?" Judith said in a rush. "I really have to go."

"Sure. We'll talk tonight."

"Love you. Bye!"

And then she was gone. Sweet, perfect Judith. The big sister who had it all.

Considering the lives they led, if her sister and mother weren't happy, what hope was there for Elaine?

Chapter 10

The home of Brad Matthews was not quite as grand as the one in which Detective Jentzen had grown up, but it was in a similar, affluent Buckhead area. Meticulously landscaped yards, well-maintained homes. Most every driveway appeared to come complete with the latest in minivans or SUVs.

Trace kept quiet and allowed the good detective to take the lead interviewing Mrs. Matthews. It wasn't a hardship. She knew how to handle herself. Watching her prompted a new sense of respect that he would just as soon not have felt, but there it was. So far she had lived up to her glorified reputation.

And it wasn't as if the widow knew anything, anyway. Even if she did have knowledge of some scrap of information that would help, it was currently buried under her tremendous grief and heavy medication. Elaine managed to keep the woman on track in spite of the overwhelming emotion. Another characteristic of a fine detective.

Trace stood near the wide front window of the homey living room, well away from the ongoing interview. Mrs. Matthews sat in a leather chair that Trace guessed had been her late husband's favorite. She looked small and intensely fragile, her brunette hair and rich, coffee-colored eyes a stark contrast to the pallor of her complexion. Any color that normally illuminated her skin, other than the dark circles under her red-from-crying eyes, had drained under the strain of yesterday's horrifying events. The classic black sheath she wore told the world that she was in mourning and spoke of her reserved taste in clothing.

His gaze shifted to the detective seated nearby on the floral sofa. She wore her usual fare—navy slacks and a white blouse, both of which flattered her slender figure. The navy jacket disguised the weapon at her waist and lent an authoritative and businesslike air. Like the grieving widow, Elaine looked somewhat pale herself. But Trace had a feeling her strained appearance had as much to do with her personal life as with this case.

Something wasn't right in the Jentzen world.

But that wasn't his concern. He could allow nothing to interfere with his focus on this case. Then again, her mental condition definitely impacted the case. He didn't need her vulnerable. Having her as a partner was risk enough. Any weakness would work against them both. He had learned that lesson the hard way. He'd known this was a mistake from the beginning, but Douglas, his field supervisor and basic know-it-all, had insisted. Elaine Jentzen was the best Atlanta had to offer. Trace would work with her or he was out of the loop. He'd almost…almost opted out then and there.

He should have. He should have resigned and taken on the case as a civilian. Then, at least, he wouldn't have been saddled with another female partner. His gut churned with regret and guilt. But he couldn't do that. As a civilian he wouldn't have had access to numerous investigative tools, would have been barred from the information loop, ultimately slowing down the process. That was a risk he couldn't take. He had to be on top of this case or chance more innocent lives being taken. Allowing the bastard even a minute more than absolutely necessary in which to take a single additional life was a minute too long.

Trace couldn't let that happen. He clenched his jaw. He would not let it happen. He turned his attention back to the interview, pushed all else aside.

"Mrs. Matthews, why don't you tell me what the last couple of weeks in your husband's life were like?"

The widow had already said that she hadn't noticed anything wrong or different. Her husband had been the same as always. Came home each night. Played with the children. Nothing had changed. Nothing, she'd sworn, other than he did seem overly preoccupied, which was out of character for him. Brad had prided himself on leaving work at the office. He tuned out all else when with his family.

Mrs. Matthews blinked a couple of times. "I don't know what you mean? I've told you already that nothing really unusual happened." Her voice sounded shakier now than when they'd started the interview. She was losing her ability to focus. Exhaustion likely clawed at her petite frame. Talking about what her husband had done made it real.

"What you told me, Mrs. Matthews," Elaine said gently but firmly, "is that your husband was preoccupied. *That* was unusual. Let's see if we can figure out why."

Even from his position across the room, Trace saw the tears spill down the widow's cheeks. He gritted his teeth to hold back a curse. They weren't likely to get anything else at this point.

"Why would he do this?" she whispered, a desperation in her voice that tightened the knot of apprehension in Trace's gut. "Brad had never harmed anyone in his entire life. I don't understand. He didn't even own a gun." She shook her head adamantly. "It doesn't make sense. We went to the Tate family Christmas party the past three years in a row."

Elaine leaned forward and placed a consoling hand on the other woman's. "Ma'am, that's what we're trying to figure out. If you'll help us, Agent Callahan and I are going to get to the bottom of this terrible tragedy."

The fragile woman flicked a glance in Trace's direction. She looked away too quickly for him to paste on a perfunctory smile. "What was the question again?" she asked. A shaky hand reached up to scrub at her damp cheeks.

Elaine repeated her last question with a kind of patience Trace couldn't help admiring. That she didn't falter when faced with the other woman's tremendous grief surprised him. Maybe she could hold her own better than he'd first thought. He gave himself a mental kick. What the hell was wrong with him? He wasn't supposed to be admiring anything about her. No mistakes this time, he reminded that part of his brain that apparently didn't get it. *No mistakes.*

Mrs. Matthews regarded the question silently for a time before she finally responded. "It started about a month ago." Her voice was low but not quite as unsteady. "He forgot the spring barbecue our neighborhood had planned." She shrugged. "It's the same weekend every year. I don't know how he forgot."

"Was he angry that he'd forgotten?" Elaine prompted.

The widow shook her head. "Not angry, disappointed. He kept apologizing over and over." She looked directly at Elaine. "Like he couldn't get past it."

"That was…?"

"Easter weekend. But I'd noticed that he seemed preoccupied a while before that. He didn't talk to me as much. Didn't…" She caught herself and looked away, red abruptly staining her cheeks.

"Didn't what?" Elaine pressed. When she got no answer she added, "Mrs. Matthews, if you don't help us, we can't solve this case."

Trace felt his body shift toward the conversation, his instincts going on point.

"We hadn't made love in weeks—" she glanced toward Trace again "—I can't even remember the last time."

"I take it that was unusual, as well," Elaine suggested.

Mrs. Matthews nodded. "We'd always had a very healthy…"

She hesitated. Elaine patted her hand again. "I understand. Did your husband do anything when he came home at night, other than what you've told me, that felt odd?"

Trace noted that Elaine changed her strategy. Went from us to me. Good move. The territory had gotten too personal for *us,* especially considering he was a man.

Another lapse of silence as the woman gathered her

thoughts on the question. "He spent a lot of time on the computer." She frowned, clearly dredging her memory banks for more. "He generally didn't go near the thing unless we were looking up something together like vacation spots or…" Her voice quavered. "Or baby names."

"Do you know what he was doing on the computer? Work he'd brought home with him perhaps," Elaine offered.

"I don't know." The woman's eyes rounded with something akin to fear. "Whenever I asked he told me to stay out of it. He'd never done that before. But he apologized later…and it didn't happen again."

Trace stepped away from the window. "Mrs. Matthews, may I take a look at the computer your husband used here at home?" Funny, he mused, what a person remembered as being out of the ordinary when prompted just the right way. More kudos for Detective Jentzen.

The sound of his voice or maybe the question made her jerk. "It's all right," Elaine assured quickly. "Agent Callahan might be able to tell us what your husband was doing that made him so tense."

The widow nodded. "All right."

She stood and led the way to a cluttered library. The room wasn't very large and was filled mostly with children's books and toys. A playroom, he decided.

"There." She pointed to the high-tech computer system in the far corner of the room.

Trace flashed her a brief smile, then moved to the sleek, space-conscious computer desk.

"Would you mind showing me your husband's closet?" Elaine asked.

Trace was thankful that Jentzen had lured the woman from the room. He needed to focus, not answer questions. And he definitely didn't need the woman staring anxiously over his shoulder.

He started the booting-up process and utilized the time to survey the hardware. State-of-the-art. New. Like the home, Matthews had purchased only the best for his young family.

Trace frowned when the screen stalled midcycle.

About two minutes later he knew that any further attempts to boot up would be futile.

The computer had either crashed or been wiped of all software including its operating system.

He checked the hardware, including all connections. One look at the small black box with its blinking lights told him that the system was connected to the Internet via a broadband link through a local cable company.

Computers crashed all the time, but it would be just too coincidental that the one in Brad Matthews's home had done so the same day or the day after his murder-suicide rampage.

Trace didn't believe in coincidences.

Instead of going straight up to the bedroom where Elaine and Matthews's wife were, Trace took a look around downstairs. Forensics would likely be called out to have a look. His gut instinct was that it wouldn't make any difference. They likely wouldn't find anything useful to the case. But there was always the chance they might get lucky.

The computer, however, was a different story. If it had been purposely wiped, as Trace suspected, finding something on it could prove a major development. But if the Gamekeeper had anything to do with it, there would be nothing left to find. There was always the possibility that Matthews himself had initiated the crash-and-burn to get rid of any evidence of whatever he'd been working on at home. Trace didn't believe that, however. He understood what he was up against here even if no one else wanted to admit the truth of the matter.

The Gamekeeper was back.

Upstairs Elaine watched Mrs. Matthews touch each suit that had belonged to her husband with such reverence that it hurt to watch. Finally she stopped on one. "This one," she said.

"This is the suit he wore last?" Elaine touched the summer wool fabric of the gray suit. The same designer and elegant cut as the one Matthews had been wearing when she'd first seen him lying on the floor of Tate's office. The image of him lying on that cold steel slab in the morgue, with a *Y* incision on his chest sprouted in her mind like an errant Internet pop-up before she could block it.

Amelia Matthews nodded, then choked in a breath.

Elaine searched the pockets. Nothing. "Mrs. Matthews, we're going to need to try and find anything that might tie your husband's movements in with what triggered this tragedy." She turned to the grieving woman who stood by, her eyes bright with new tears. "Understand that I don't need your permission, but I would prefer it that way."

She stared at Elaine blankly, if anything, looking more confused than before.

"I'd like," Elaine explained, "a team of forensic technicians to go through your home to see what they can find. It might prove useless, but we have to know for sure. If there is anything on his clothes, shoes or any other part of what he left behind that can help us, we need that help. Will you help us?"

She nodded. "The children and I will be staying with my parents." A flood of emotions rolled down her pale cheeks. "Do whatever you have to. Just find out how this happened."

Elaine nodded. "I'll do all I can." She almost left it at that, but she couldn't. "Mrs. Matthews, I have to tell you that this might not turn out the way you want it to. I can't promise you that your husband isn't guilty of…" She swallowed hard as the woman's terrified gaze latched on to hers. "He may have committed these murders of his own volition. There is that chance. You must know that whatever I find will become public knowledge and may very well work against your husband."

She hated like hell to make a statement that might scare the woman off, but the last thing Elaine needed was some hotshot lawyer screaming lawsuit. With a person on the edge like this, it would be easy to cry she'd been taken advantage of during a vulnerable time.

For several endless seconds the two of them merely stood there, in the middle of Brad Matthews's walk-in closet, saying nothing. Elaine needed to be certain that his widow understood the process and the repercussions.

"I just want the truth," Amelia Matthews said. She dragged in a ragged breath and went on, her voice halting with emotion every other word, "I don't believe he did this." She shook her head. "I mean, I know he did, but he didn't do it because he wanted to. Something was wrong. I don't know what or how, but someone caused this to happen." Her gaze connected with Elaine's once more. "Someone besides my husband."

No one ever wanted to believe the worst about the people they loved. "I'll do everything I can," Elaine reiterated. And she would, though she wasn't sure that what she could do would ever be enough.

Downstairs Callahan waited outside the library door.

"Anything?" she asked him. He truly was impossible to read outside the occasional revealing slip.

He moved his head side to side, then looked past Elaine to Amelia Matthews. "Mrs. Matthews, have you used the computer since the last time your husband did?"

"No." She clasped her trembling hands in front of her. "I'm not very good with computers. I always left that up to him."

"Can we take the hard drive with us?"

Elaine frowned. The forensics team would take care of that. Her gaze narrowed. Callahan had found something.

Amelia shrugged. "Of course."

He went into the library and returned in less than ten seconds with the CPU in tow. He'd apparently already disconnected it from the monitor and keyboard. He'd definitely found something and had anticipated cooperation.

Elaine thanked Mrs. Matthews for her assistance and promised to keep her updated on the case's progress.

Callahan had already loaded the CPU into the back and climbed into the passenger seat by the time Elaine made her way down the front walk. She held her tongue until she'd gotten in, started the Jeep and pulled out onto the street.

"What did you find?" She hated that she sounded annoyed, but she was annoyed, dammit. If he thought for one second that he could play this game with her he was mistaken. There was no what-he-found-was-his and what-she-found-was-hers. They were working as a team now, for better or worse. Like it or not.

"Nothing."

She braked for a traffic light and scorched him with a scalding glare. "You're already on thin ice, Callahan, don't go making any cracks." A fire roared to life in her stomach as if cued by an evil director. Perfect. She snatched up her ever-present bottle of liquid antacid and chugged down a hefty swallow. Damned ulcer.

"You really should see a doctor about that," he offered, in that smooth, dark voice, the sound of which probably worked as an aphrodisiac on most women.

Elaine blocked the whole concept of sexual awareness and resisted the urge to tell him to piss off. She would not let him get to her—on any level. "The CPU, Callahan. What the hell is that about?" She cut him another scathing look. "And don't screw with my head, just give me the facts."

That arrogant yet sexy-as-hell smile that only a guy like him could pull off spread across his sculpted mouth. "You don't miss a thing, do you?"

She whipped to the side of the street and slammed on the brakes. Horns blared behind her but she ignored them.

"What the hell are you doing?" she demanded. He kept his gaze straight ahead, not bothering to even spare her a glance, much less that cocky smile. "Are you trying to piss me off?"

"No."

Fury rolled through her. "Then, what the hell are you doing?"

She'd known this was a mistake from the get-go. She'd had

a great partner. One who wouldn't have played games like this with her. They didn't have time for this. What the hell was wrong with this guy?

"The hard drive has been wiped."

She tensed, her irritation immediately funneling into anticipation. "You're certain?"

He turned that handsome head toward her, one infinitesimal increment at a time, until that piercing blue gaze locked with hers, the slow, deliberate process having the desired effect. Her breath halted somewhere shy of her lungs.

"Yes."

A single word. One syllable. And she'd been mesmerized by the movement of his mouth in uttering it. Incredible. And totally stupid. Anger whipped through her once more.

"Matthews could have been erasing the evidence of whatever he'd been up to," she suggested.

"Maybe."

That penetrating stare never left her for a moment. She refused to squirm. Ensured that her gaze stayed on his, not on that seductive mouth. Just then she couldn't be sure which presented the most danger.

"Oh, yes," she said then. "The Gamekeeper." She'd have to keep her eye on him with that CPU. Elaine didn't want to believe she'd been saddled with a partner so determined to prove his own theory that he might plant evidence…but she had to be smart here.

For one instant she saw disappointment in those assessing eyes, but it disappeared as fast as it had appeared.

He looked away, breaking the crackling connection.

"There's something I need to show you."

Elaine's internal alarm system went on high alert. "What?"

He gave her an address only ten or so blocks from the station. She did a quick mental rundown of the location. Apartment building on the edge of the city's reconstruction. The whole area was scheduled for major renovations over the next couple of years. A part of the mayor's determination to make Atlanta more beautiful, more representative of what the great state of Georgia stood for. Not to mention rundown apartment buildings made great upscale lofts when gutted and reworked from the inside out. When developers made money, campaign donations soared.

"You want to show me something at your place?" Now there was an original ploy. She made a sound that left no question as to what she thought of that.

"No games," he said, fixing that penetrating gaze back on hers. "You give me the time, I'll give you what you want to know."

She searched those eyes, but he'd veiled them so quickly she couldn't hope to get even a glimpse of the motivation behind his words.

Maybe he wanted to be on the up-and-up with her. But why couldn't they do that here and now? Or at the office?

She shifted her attention to the street and eased back into the flow of traffic.

"Just remember," she said without so much as a glance his way, "I carry a weapon and I don't have a problem using it."

She didn't have to look to know he'd smiled. She felt the warmth of it. How was it a guy so damaged could wield so much power over her?

Another of life's mysteries. Like her parents' failing marriage and the strange conversation with her sister. Clearly the planets were way out of alignment.

The whole world had gone mad.

Chapter 11

Ramon Johnson sat on the edge of his bed. He'd gotten out of school early to go to a dentist appointment, but he'd stopped by his house first to check the mail.

He'd been watching the mail for two weeks…waiting.

It had to be a mistake.

The scholarship belonged to him.

He'd worked hard for it these past three years.

Fear banded his chest, tightened around his heart.

His mother would be so disappointed.

Tears stung his eyes.

He'd been so mean to her…before he'd pulled himself together. He'd let her down so many times.

It was supposed to be different now.

He'd worked hard—real hard—had done all the right

things. He'd even taken extra steps she didn't need to know about to ensure he aced the tests.

It was the only way to ensure he got the full scholarship. He'd felt guilty about it at first. But it had worked, hadn't it? He'd scored better on the test than he'd ever dreamed of even hoping.

Ramon stared at the letter in his hand once more.

Denied.

He'd applied for the scholarship after being invited. After being assured by the university's basketball coach that he was "in" already. Now the offer had been denied as if it had never existed.

The coach had lied to him.

Just like everyone else he had trusted.

All but his mother.

She had never lied to him.

And now he'd let her down…again.

She probably wouldn't forgive him this time.

Fury tore through him.

He would make them pay.

He stared at one name on the letter. Arthur K. Massey, principal, Deerborn High School, Atlanta. He was the real traitor here.

He'd ruined Ramon's whole future.

No way could he hope to get in at any good university now, for sure not the private one he'd targeted. Not with this kind of black mark on his transcript.

But then, he should have expected the betrayal.

He'd been warned that there were those who had it in for him. The same ones who'd used his athletic talent to make all-state three years in a row. Now the ones he'd counted on were finished with him.

They would pay.

And then they would know the truth. Ramon Johnson had won in the end. He'd beaten his enemies.

He might not have a future anymore…but he wouldn't be the only one.

Chapter 12

Trace closed the Jeep door and waited for Detective Jentzen to round the hood of her vehicle. He watched her closely as she considered his temporary digs. Nothing fancy. He'd never gone in for luxury or elegance of any sort.

Even his rented bungalow back home, in which he'd lived for more than a decade, would be called minimalist at best. The location had more to do with proximity to Quantico than with housing perks. He had a microwave, a fridge, television set and a bed. What else did he need? Well, okay, there was the computer. He couldn't live without that.

He rolled that last thought around in his head. The computer was a relatively new addition to his personal furnishings. Until about a year ago he'd always depended upon the one at his office. Probably still should.

But one year ago his instincts had moved into a zone from

which he couldn't withdraw. A constant state of alert as if some part of him had known that his old enemy had awakened from hibernation.

The shrink the Bureau had insisted Trace see on a regular basis had called it an empathy link. It happened fairly often, he'd assured him in that monotonous monotone that put Trace to sleep every time. According to the esteemed psychiatrist, an agent worked so hard to understand the motivation of a killer that he learned to think like the very killer he hunted. The connection grew stronger and stronger as the case evolved, thus linking the minds of those closest involved.

In Trace's opinion it was a load of crap. He had nothing even remotely resembling empathy for the Gamekeeper. The only thing Trace wanted was to see him dead on a slab in the morgue. Dissecting that diseased brain would be the only way to ensure the bastard didn't come back somehow.

Trace pushed aside his mental ranting and turned his attention back to his reluctant partner.

"Nice place," she said, echoing his comment regarding her childhood home.

"You don't have to be kind, Detective," he said, injecting as much humor as he could summon into his tone. "It's a dump."

If Jentzen got the joke she showed no indication. Instead she followed him into the lobby of the aging building without comment. Efficiencies could be rented by the day or the week, ensuring a steady flow of lowlife occupants. Trace almost laughed out loud as he started toward the door that led to the stairwell. What did that make him? Never mind, he already knew the answer to that one.

"Elevator's out of order," he explained as he hesitated at the door—had been since he'd moved in.

"No problem, I prefer the stairs."

She climbed the five flights of steps without pause and without as much as a single puff to indicate the exertion had winded her. Her physical conditioning was obviously as good as it looked. This was more than he could say for himself. He hadn't bothered with physical training in months, other than the punching bag he beat every night…a year and ten months, if he remembered right. Why bother? He'd been on desk duty all that time and understood full well that, barring a miracle, that's where he would stay.

Unreliable in the field. That's what they called him. Unreliable…period.

If he hadn't been the only human being on the planet who knew the Gamekeeper so well, he wouldn't be here right now. Even his participation in this investigation was on shaky ground. One screw-up and he was off the case. One wrong step and his investigative career was over for good. He'd be a desk jockey until he retired.

Unacceptable.

He couldn't go back to that.

Desperation climbed into his throat, threatening to burst into full-fledged panic.

He had to do this right.

Trace fought the panic before he unlocked, then pushed open the door to his scarcely used room. He'd spent most of his nights at a computer café surfing the Net.

She stepped into the room and almost instantly her scent permeated the air, alleviating the closed-up smell. Nothing overpowering like most women wore but something subtle, natural. One slow, methodical survey was conducted before she met his gaze.

"Reminds me of you."

"Yeah?" Well, she'd summed him up with that statement. The bed was unmade. The three boxes containing his case files on the Gamekeeper sat haphazardly around the room, papers cluttering every available surface. The suit he'd worn the day before still waited in a plastic bag near the door to be picked up for laundry service. That was another thing one couldn't count on when settling for low-rent housing—the amenities, if any existed, usually sucked.

"Are these your files?" Jentzen walked over to the two upholstered chairs flanking a small side table and sat down in the one that wasn't piled high with research.

"Everything I have." He cleared out the other chair and dropped into it. "You may not have seen everything."

"I haven't seen anything," she told him, her tone frank, her gaze latching on to his. "Other than what I read in the newspapers and the scuttlebutt I heard around the station, I don't know anything about you or your suspect."

Why wasn't he surprised? He'd assumed she'd been properly briefed. Field Supervisory Agent Douglas had assured Trace that he would fully brief her chief. Clearly he hadn't, or her chief had failed to pass along the information. Trace didn't take Chief Dugan for a slacker, definitely not the type who'd leave his detective in the dark. Not this detective in any event. Trace hadn't missed the way the chief looked at Jentzen. There was or had been something between those two. Something beyond the scope of the professional. His throat tightened instantly as the idea of what she would look like without those reserved clothes slipped into his thoughts. He licked his lips and reminded himself that he couldn't allow that kind of thinking—even for a second.

Trace picked up a folder and opened it. Inside were a number of crime-scene photos from two years ago. He passed them to Jentzen.

"Seven victims. Two were primary targets."

Jentzen looked up from the graphic photos. "What do you mean *primary* targets?"

"His primary targets were the ones he chose to carry out his plans." Trace reached for the next folder. This one contained his personally documented notes. "I don't know his name or even what he looks like, but I know him." He passed this folder to the woman now watching him expectantly.

"He kills for sport. To prove he can. That he's more powerful than his victims. That's why he always chooses targets that will be difficult kills. No easy street bums or homeless vagrants. No prostitutes. Well-educated, prominent targets. He thrives on the challenge of destroying those with the most to lose."

"Power is his only motivation?" she ventured, her words guarded.

That she used the present tense gave Trace hope that he wasn't talking to a brick wall on the subject of the Gamekeeper. "In the past I believe power was his entire motivation. I'm certain that his basic survival depended upon it somehow." He shrugged. "Like a junkie needs the next fix. He couldn't go on without it."

"He lured his targets via the Internet. Not so original," she suggested.

Trace inclined his head and considered her statement for a bit before going on. "Maybe not. It was the way he orchestrated his games that was so very original."

"How's that?" As she spoke she perused his notes. "He selected two primary targets, then what?"

"Each was lured into a game of life and death. Pure fantasy, of course." Jentzen's gaze collided with his. "At least that's what they thought." Trace went on, "But then the calls, the feeling of being followed, the tampering with their identities started." He tapped the photograph of a twenty-six-year-old law clerk. "Her car was repossessed, though she hadn't missed a payment. The Gamekeeper knew how to dig into her…what she prided herself on most, like her perfect credit record. Things started to go wrong at work. Meetings failed to be put on her schedule. Papers went missing. When he'd pushed hard enough, made her believe that she had discovered who was responsible for her troubles, she did the unthinkable…she killed in the heat of the moment."

Trace saw by the change in her expression that she was comparing what he said to the current cases. "Did the primary targets commit suicide as in the two recent multiple homicides here?"

He shook his head. "That's the sticking point. The Gamekeeper might have driven his primary targets over the edge and caused them to kill as an automatic response to the final moment of immeasurable stress, but they weren't killers. Somehow the Gamekeeper had known that, in the end, they would either back out or spill their guts to the authorities. So he made sure he was there for the final showdown. I don't know if he forced the targets to finish the job, but I do know that he killed each one with a single bullet to the head and left a note celebrating the fact."

Jentzen moistened her lips, then chewed on the lower one, no doubt considering that the shooter in both her multiple homicides had put a bullet in their own heads. As hard as Trace attempted to stay focused on the case, he couldn't help watching those straight white teeth nibble on that full bottom lip. Between that unconsciously sexy habit and that soft scent of hers, being this close made him yearn to touch her. To see if she felt as warm and inviting as she looked.

"He's evolved," she murmured, more to herself than to him, he grimly suspected.

He swallowed back the need tightening his throat. "That's my theory. Maybe I wounded him badly enough in the shoot-out two years ago that he can't physically complete the task as before."

"He's adapted to a change," she offered, her attention still focused on his extensive notes.

Trace felt hope stir in his chest, but he quashed it. This was too easy. Nothing was ever this easy.

Detective Jentzen set the file containing his notes aside and fastened her gaze on his. "I can certainly see how you would see a strong connection between this old case and the murders here in Atlanta over the past week. There are definite similarities." Her brow furrowed in concentration as if she needed to mull over her next words carefully before going forward. "But why here? Why now? I don't see the relevance. Why would the Gamekeeper show up here after two years? How could he know you would become involved in this investigation?"

Just as he thought. Too good to be true. Trace looked away from her questioning expression. He knew what she wanted. Hard evidence. He couldn't give her any hard evidence. He could only go with what he had. Instinct. Fierce, primal and relentless. He knew it was *him*.

"Why here?" he echoed. "I don't know the answer to that just yet," he admitted, ruing the fact that he sounded as defensive as he felt. Dammit, he wanted to come off as totally objective, but he'd failed miserably. "As for the now, I would guess that he's only recently perfected his strategy. There may have been failures over the past year that we're not aware of. I've been following that possibility, looking for cases with similarities."

"Have you found any?" The blunt, doubt-filled tone obliterated the last of any hope he'd allowed to awaken.

"Some." But nothing significant, he didn't add.

She assessed him for a time. He resisted the urge to shift beneath her scrutiny. She was just like the others. She thought he was grasping at straws. Was obsessed with the one case he'd failed to resolve. The one black mark on his record had pushed him over the edge.

"You think he's back to have his revenge against you personally, don't you?"

Trace looked away, startled that she'd come to that conclusion. "It crossed my mind."

"What does Quantico say?"

By Quantico he knew she meant his superiors. The ones with the power over his destiny.

He leveled his gaze back on hers, allowing the weight of his determination to settle heavily. "They say just exactly what you think they do. That I'm wrong on this one. That I've lost my touch…that I don't have what it takes anymore." He hated this crap! Hated the very idea that all he'd accomplished in his career was now being questioned as if it meant nothing at all. He deserved better than this.

"And do you, Agent Callahan, still have what it takes?"

Maybe it was the way she looked at him when she asked the question or the way she said the words, but it took every ounce of willpower he possessed not to silence that sexy mouth with his own. Every cell in his body detonated with a need he'd ignored for far too long…a desperation that had pushed him so close to the edge he wasn't even sure he hadn't gone over that slippery precipice already.

He snatched back control in the nick of time, scarcely holding back the urge to see if she tasted as good as she smelled.

"Damn straight."

Something changed in her eyes then. Something intrinsic to their fledgling relation, but impossible to ascertain the exact nature of. "All right, then let's do this." She surveyed the boxes and the mounds of background material on the Gamekeeper's previous escapades. "I want to know everything you know."

He desperately needed to believe that her interest was about faith in his judgment, but he knew that was only wishful thinking. Her homicide detail had been and continued to go over every imaginable avenue to solve these bizarre events without discovering a single lead. They had no suspects other than the two shooters involved, not even a motive upon which to hinge their case. They had nothing.

Then and there in his shabby, rundown room he'd rented by the week, Trace realized something about Elaine Jentzen, third-generation cop, rising star on the Atlanta police force. She was just as desperate as he was.

Desperation fueled her motive here. If his suspicions about her dedication to her work held even a hint of plausibility, she was duty bound to follow through.

Their shared desperation might very well be all that he had on his side just now. He didn't have a problem with that. He'd take her cooperation any way he could get it.

Trace took his time and led her through the investigation from just over two years ago when he'd first gone head to head with the Gamekeeper. Every minute of every day from the very beginning was documented. Even the twisted chats he and the bastard had shared online. Trace had hooked a special recording device to his computer so that the interaction was captured, giving him the ability to review over and over their sick conversations.

There was no way to know how long the Gamekeeper had been playing his games. He could have changed his MO a dozen times, despite what all the profilers at Quantico had to say. The Gamekeeper was a different kind of serial killer. He didn't fit any of the generic molds.

He was arrogant, extremely intelligent, perhaps a genius. The only way Trace had managed to get close to him was by baiting him. Therein lay his one mistake. He hadn't been properly equipped to handle the situation. Had been too cocky and self-assured about his own methods. But he'd learned the hard way and his partner had lost her life.

A quick glance in Jentzen's direction made his gut clench.

He had to make sure nothing like that happened this time. Couldn't risk her…couldn't let it happen again.

But it all felt so familiar. Damn déjà vu.

Instinct warned him that the whole situation down here was a set up…but he had no proof. Nothing.

The Gamekeeper was back for one purpose and one purpose only: to finish what he'd started two years ago. The destruction of Trace Callahan.

Maybe he was giving himself too much credit thinking that way. That's what his shrink would say, after all. But Trace knew that just like his stellar record prior to two years ago, the Gamekeeper had himself a record of sorts going. He didn't like that whatever his finale was supposed to have been, Trace had ruined it…had forced him into hiding.

He intended to finish it, no matter how many lives it cost. The Gamekeeper laughed in the face of the authorities, because he knew no one would believe Trace. He knew the odds were on his side. He could get this done and disappear again before anyone realized it was really him.

Only Trace knew the truth.

Somehow he had to make Elaine Jentzen believe him.

As much as he didn't want to admit it, he needed her. She had something he'd lost, credibility. If he could convince her of his theory, maybe, just maybe there was hope of stopping this bastard before more lives were lost.

If the Gamekeeper escaped them this time, they might never find him again. Trace couldn't let that happen. But, unfortunately, he couldn't do it alone.

A blast of notes from a cell phone shattered the silence, jerking Trace to the here and now. He had to focus, couldn't keep going off on those mental tirades. Elaine Jentzen would either believe him or she wouldn't. End of story.

"Jentzen." She stood, did that thing with her hand. Flipped her long, silky hair over her shoulder. That he noticed made him set his jaw harder still. He had to get a grip here.

He would not let this get personal. Not to mention she didn't appear to like or respect him in the least, not really. If he crossed that line, even got too close to it, he had a feeling she'd be requesting his dismissal in a heartbeat. But he had a bad feeling that staying away from that danger zone was going to be the hardest thing he'd ever done.

Trace kicked himself for thinking along those lines. It wasn't as if he didn't work with women every day. Why did this particular one have to get to him? Hell, he'd thought he was immune to that kind of thing now. Clearly he wasn't. This woman tugged at him on a sexual level, made him want to reach out to her.

That was the furthest thing from her mind. He didn't have to wonder. Her dislike for him was evident in her very posture. Not that he could blame her. She had more than enough reason to distrust him. A damn truckload of motive to dislike him. He'd heard all the rumors. Understood perfectly what most people thought of him.

He'd screwed up, and his partner had died for his error.

Rumor also alluded to the idea that he and Molly had been intimately involved. Well that was nobody's damned business. He wouldn't justify the gossip with a denial or a confirmation. Maybe it was a mistake not to confront the issue, but it was his to make.

"Where?"

The sudden change in Jentzen's demeanor set Trace on edge.

"Deerborn High School." A hand went to her mouth. "How many dead?"

Anticipation roared through Trace.

He didn't have to hear any of the details. He could feel it. The Gamekeeper had struck again. Dread pooled in his gut.

"The shooter's still alive?" She glanced at Trace then, her eyes wide with surprise. "Locked in the principal's office?"

Already on his feet, Trace snatched the phone out of her hand. She stared at him, shocked at his high-handedness and at the same time too startled to say what no doubt had raced to the tip of her tongue.

"This is Agent Callahan, who is this?"

"Detective Henshaw," a rusty voice informed.

"The shooter's trapped?" Trace demanded. His heart slammed mercilessly against his sternum, commanding him to act. He was already at the door of the rented room he'd scarcely spent more than a few hours in since arriving in Atlanta. A quick glance back at Jentzen's appalled face got her moving in that direction, as well.

"Yeah," Henshaw confirmed. "But he's crying and carrying on in there, threatening to shoot himself. If we try to go in he'll—"

"Listen to me, Henshaw. I don't care what you have to do, you keep that shooter alive until I get there. Do you understand me?"

"I'll see what I can do."

Trace didn't miss the blatant skepticism in the old man's voice. Or the displeasure at taking orders from a burned-out Federal agent.

"*Do it* or you'll answer to me!"

Trace shoved the phone at Jentzen and reached for the door. "How fast can you get me to that scene?"

Judging by the look in her eyes, taking him anywhere was the farthest thing from her mind, but, to her credit, she didn't give him any grief. "Twenty minutes if traffic's not too congested."

Downtown Atlanta during rush hour wasn't the best place to be with any destination in mind, much less a school when shots had been fired. "Just get me there as fast as you can."

If they were very, very lucky…maybe, just maybe they were about to get their first break. A real connection, a living, breathing "link" to the Gamekeeper…if he didn't kill himself in the next twenty or so minutes.

Chapter 13

Other than the dozen police cruisers with blue lights throbbing that surrounded Deerborn High School, the educational facility looked like most any other in the Atlanta area. Large, fairly well maintained and no doubt overcrowded. Like the streets, the schools couldn't be upgraded fast enough to keep up with the ever-expanding Southern metropolis.

Elaine swore when she surveyed the hundreds of students who had been evacuated from the building. Three forty-five. The excitement must have started shortly before the end of the last period, leaving school officials no choice but to go into emergency mode. They had apparently evacuated as many students as necessary and then gone into lockdown to isolate the threat.

Harried teachers rushed around in an attempt to keep the restless students away from the school, the place where the children were supposed to be safe. During the past decade that assumption had proved less and less accurate. Elaine shook her head as she surveyed those pushed as far back from the building as possible. Just kids.

She and Callahan were out of the Jeep before it stopped rocking at the curb. She badged her way past the first line of security, uniformed patrolmen. From there she ran like hell, lunging up the front steps of the fifty-year-old schoolhouse without slowing.

Inside, the main corridor was lined with more uniforms. Some twenty yards or so in the distance she saw their destination—administration, the principal's office. A small sign protruded from the wall above the door, the letters forming the words Main Office were scrawled in a fancy script.

The sea of law-enforcement personnel flanking the entrance to the office parted for her and Callahan to pass through.

In the reception area Elaine scanned the smaller crowd in search of Henshaw. Her gaze swept over two bodies behind a secretary's desk. Both female. Both too damned young to die like this. The stricken expressions of the two EMTs standing nearby said all there was to say. There wasn't anything anyone could do for those two…they were gone.

"Where is he?" This from Callahan.

Henshaw jerked his head toward the closed door marked Arthur K. Massey, Principal. "Hear him?" Henshaw asked Elaine. "He's been doing that since we got here."

Elaine eased closer to the door. She heard the boy sobbing. Her heart wrenched. What the hell had happened here? A sickening sensation of dread dragged at her stomach. This couldn't happen again…not again.

"What's the story?" she whispered, leaning toward Henshaw. "Any witnesses to what went down?"

"School nurse," he said as quietly as that gravelly voice would permit. "She managed to escape without getting shot. She's in her office being questioned by a uniform. Said he just came in, demanded to see the principal and then started shooting."

"What's his name?"

Elaine turned her attention to Callahan, who'd asked the question. His gaze hadn't left the door to the principal's inner office. A muscle flexed rhythmically in his tightly clenched jaw. For an instant the reports and crime-scene photos she'd studied in his room flashed one after the other like a bad movie through her mind. He'd been down this road already. Anticipation of the next move burned in his gaze. He fully believed that his old nemesis was behind these shootings. And maybe he was right. But Elaine needed more than his hunches. She needed to know for certain before she focused too much time and effort on his theory.

"Ramon Johnson. Turns eighteen the twenty-seventh of this month," Henshaw told him. "The same day he's supposed to graduate."

Elaine glanced at the motionless bodies on the floor and shook her head again. Dammit. Dammit. Then and there a part of her shuddered with a feeling of sudden, absolute terror. What if Callahan was right? What if that freak he'd hunted two years ago had resurfaced? If the legendary Trace Callahan couldn't stop him, back when he was at the very top of his game, what chance did he have now?

What chance did she have?

Callahan leaned against the wall next to the door. "Ramon, you okay in there?" he called out.

The sobbing halted abruptly.

"We're worried about you. You okay?"

Elaine tried not to be impressed by Callahan's gentle tone under present circumstances, but she was. His voice lacked any hint of intimidation or authority, instead he oozed concern and sympathy. With her heart pounding and her gut in a thousand knots she wasn't sure she could have spoken quite so calmly.

"Go away!"

Callahan scrubbed his chin with one hand. Elaine watched, annoyed that his every move drew her attention on a level she could no more control than breathing.

"Look, buddy, I know you're upset, but you need to talk to me. Tell me how this happened…who did this to you?"

Elaine cocked her head and listened intently for what would come next. How could Callahan be so sure this was the right move?

Another sob choked from the young man on the other side of the door. "Call my mom…tell her I tried…I tried real hard."

A volatile mixture of trepidation and anticipation burned a path up Elaine's spine. She watched Callahan's posture tense, as well. They were going to lose him. Every instinct screamed at her that Ramon Johnson was about to end this right now.

She pressed closer to the door. "Ramon, this is Detective Elaine Jentzen. I'm going to talk to your mother for you, but first I need to talk to you."

Before Callahan or Henshaw or even Ramon could fathom her actual intent she twisted the knob and pushed the door inward. Callahan hissed something like What the hell? but she ignored him and quickly closed the door behind her.

"I'll shoot!"

"It's okay, Ramon, you don't have to shoot, I just want to talk."

It had been nearly an hour since he'd fired at his last victim. If he'd intended to kill himself he likely would have already. That's what she was banking on.

The blinds were closed, but enough light slipped in around them for her to make out the young man huddled in the corner beyond the principal's desk. The principal lay on the floor a few feet away. Elaine couldn't be sure he was dead…but he definitely wasn't moving.

"You tell her this wasn't my fault," Ramon said, his voice ragged with emotion. "Tell her I tried."

"I'll do that." Elaine cautiously moved closer. "Is it okay with you if I check on Principal Massey?"

"He's dead." The words were strained, desperate. "It's too late."

Ramon didn't protest as she eased down into a crouch next to the motionless body and checked for a pulse. Nothing. Damn.

"He is, isn't he?" The question croaked out of the frightened young man.

"Afraid so, Ramon." She shifted slightly so that she could look more directly at him. Her eyes had adjusted to the dim lighting of the closed up room. "Who made you do this, Ramon?" She asked the question in that manner in an attempt to make him believe she didn't consider any part of this his fault. And, considering what the Gamekeeper was capable of, maybe it wasn't. But that was taking a hell of a leap.

"I can't talk about it anymore…it's too late." He stuck the barrel of his .32 revolver to his temple. "You tell her what I said."

Fear roared through Elaine. "Wait," she urged. "What's her name?"

He blinked, then seemed to consider that her question made sense. "Aretha Johnson. She works days. You'll have to call her at work." He named a local textile factory.

This was so damned wrong. She had to keep him talking.

"Ramon, let me help you." She eased a fraction nearer to his location.

"Don't come any closer or I will shoot!"

He didn't want to. Elaine knew with near certainty that he didn't. Whatever had possessed him to do this, it had worn off now…had lost its momentum. He didn't want to die. But the barrel of that .32 remained poked into his temple. She couldn't be one hundred percent.

"It'll make it a lot better on your mom if you'll tell me how this happened so I can give her the facts. Mothers like to know those things," she pressed, hoping to distract him from the weapon for a moment.

"I…" He leaned toward Elaine. She tensed but held her ground. "I just wanted…" He stiffened, something in his eyes changing so fast she couldn't read the abrupt reversal. "It's too late."

He pulled the trigger.

Elaine's breath evaporated in her lungs.

The sound of the hammer clicking split the air, but the weapon didn't discharge.

He'd already fired his last round.

Relief gushed through her as she went for the weapon.

Disbelief claimed his face a fraction of a second before he collapsed onto her, his weight forcing her down onto the floor. She called out for assistance. Before the echo of her cry had faded, lights suddenly blared overhead and the room filled with cops.

There was blood all over the front of her blouse when they pulled Ramon off her. Gut wound. Damn. She'd missed that in the near darkness. She wondered if he'd gotten shot during the struggle with the principal.

While the EMTs did their work, Callahan dragged her over to one side of the room. "What did he say?"

The forcefulness of his tone sent anger firing through her veins. "He asked me to call his mother."

"Is that all? You were in here three and a half minutes. What else did he say?"

Had it only been three and a half minutes? It had felt like an hour.

"He didn't tell me anything, Callahan," she snapped. She jerked her arm free of his hold. "Only that it was too late and to tell his mother that it wasn't his fault."

Those penetrating blue eyes analyzed her a beat longer before he backed off.

The EMTs had prepped Ramon for transport when she stepped around Callahan. Ramon was unconscious and had lost a lot of blood. That's all they could tell her at that point.

"Henshaw, get Walt's team over here," she said as she followed the EMTs from the principal's office. She wasn't about to let Ramon out of her sight.

"Will do, DC."

She didn't look back, but she knew Callahan was right behind her. She could feel him seething. He'd wanted to question Ramon and she'd beat him to the punch. It hadn't been intentional, she'd simply seized the opportunity when she saw it about to go south. Surely he'd known the kid was on the verge. But then, maybe he hadn't. Had he lost his touch? Had what happened two years ago affected his ability to handle himself in this kind of stressful situation? With an unexpected burst of clarity she realized that the scene they'd just encountered was likely his first of that nature since his partner was murdered.

Whatever he'd been thinking when she took the lead and barged into that office, he'd hesitated, and hesitation could be a dangerous thing in this line of work. He'd been all too happy to talk, but taking the next step hadn't come so easy.

When they burst through the main entrance, the crowd outside the school had increased by a gaggle or two of media vultures. Vans representing various local television stations had parked in the street and set up for live-feed coverage of the events as they unfolded. Print reporters, as well as the ones who'd arrived in the vans, instantly started to scream out questions from their positions just barely beyond the secured perimeter.

Elaine ignored them. Callahan climbed into the ambulance with Ramon and the EMTs.

"I'll see you there," he said before the doors closed.

She didn't waste time arguing. Ramon Johnson didn't have the time to spare.

Two officers kept the reporters at bay as she scrambled behind the wheel of her Jeep. Henshaw would oversee the forensics team and the questioning of any witnesses. Every instinct told her that Ramon was the key to learning the truth about what had happened here today.

She wasn't about to let him or Callahan out of her sight for long.

Once Ramon Johnson was in surgery, Elaine retreated to the ladies' room. She washed her hands, scrubbing away as much of the blood as she could. Then she splashed a little cool water on her face to refresh herself.

She stared at her reflection and considered what would make a student take a gun to school and kill three people, then try to kill himself. Not fellow students, most likely ruling out any sort of problems in that area. Instead he'd brutally murdered his principal, the school secretary and the guidance counselor. For what reason? What possible motivation did he have? Had he been reprimanded? Expelled for some reason?

She needed more information. And she desperately needed him to survive surgery. For many more reasons than this case. He was too young to die…for his life to be wasted like this. Three multiple homicides in less than two weeks. What the hell was going on in her city?

Her eyes closed and she blocked all the other worries that tried to surface. Her mother and father were on the verge of divorce. Her sister sounded unhappier than Elaine had ever known her to be. All that she'd looked up to, hoped to have someday was slowly unraveling.

And then there was the other little problem.

She had to call Dr. Bramm's office.

She couldn't put off seeing that specialist.

Elaine dried her hands and dabbed at her face. As she wadded the paper towel and tossed it into the trash, she heaved a weary sigh. The chief would want some answers. Another mass murder with no leads would not be acceptable.

Life was about to get intensely uncomfortable for her and any other cop related to law enforcement in Atlanta.

She pushed out of the rest room and immediately settled her attention on the small waiting area at the end of the corridor.

Elaine allowed the door to close with a whoosh behind her, but she couldn't prompt her feet into action. Her full attention was riveted to the scene playing out in the small area designated for those waiting to hear from patients undergoing surgery.

Callahan was speaking to a woman who was clearly distraught. Her hands covered her mouth and she kept shaking her head at whatever he was saying.

Ramon's mother.

The strength seemed to seep out of Elaine with her next breath. She could only imagine the woman's pain. Her son had gone from a mere high school student to a murderer in the course of one afternoon. She would have questions. Questions that might prove to have no ready answers…at least no answers that they could find.

Of course, that was assuming that Ramon hadn't been in trouble before. When all was said and done, there might very well have been warning signs that this very thing was about to happen. But it would take time to sort out those details. And they would never know the whole story for certain unless Ramon survived surgery.

Just then the woman wilted and Callahan enveloped her. Held her with those capable-looking arms. She shuddered with grief, cried against his broad shoulder.

Though Elaine couldn't make out his expression, she could see the gentle way he held the woman. The whole picture looked so out of character with what she knew about the man. And yet it looked so right. She suddenly wanted to be held like that. To be able to lean on someone…to feel those strong arms around her, making her feel safe and whole again.

Elaine felt a jolt at her own thoughts. What on earth was wrong with her?

Her cell phone vibrated, preventing her from having to answer that damning question. She muttered a curse. She was supposed to have turned it off on this floor. She went back into the bathroom and took the call.

"Jentzen."

"According to the nurse our underage shooter just came in and demanded to see the principal."

Henshaw. He seldom bothered with a greeting when on a case. She was expecting his call, anticipating the information. No point in wasting time, in his opinion.

"When the principal wouldn't come out of his office the kid opened fire. The nurse had the good sense to hit the floor."

"Does she know if he's been in trouble before? Can she pull his file?" Elaine needed to get some sense of what had motivated Ramon.

"Yep. Back in junior high he stayed in trouble. Drugs, the whole nine yards. But he hasn't been in trouble once since moving into high school. Things were a little shaky his freshman year on an academic level but no behavior problems. He's on the honor roll and, according to some of the staff members we've questioned, he's the star of the basketball team."

Elaine massaged her right temple. A headache had started to nag at her. "Anything else?"

"Only that he'd just gotten a full athletic scholarship to the university he'd hoped to attend. Top private school in the southeast. His academic future was set."

The situation made less and less sense. What could possibly have gone wrong? Maybe he'd started using drugs again. That seemed the only reasonable explanation.

Elaine had faced off with her share of dopeheads, and Ramon Johnson hadn't felt like the type. She hadn't picked up that kind of vibe at all.

Then again maybe Callahan wasn't the only one losing his touch.

Henshaw would call when he had more information. She thanked him and dropped her phone back into her purse. She plowed her fingers through her hair and massaged her skull. What was she missing here?

After a badly needed respite of two or three minutes, she shoved back through the bathroom door. Callahan would want this new information. Her gaze moved to the far end of the corridor. If they were lucky, maybe the mother could provide some insight on what kind of demons her son had been dealing with on a personal level, because it darn sure looked as if academically he'd had everything going for him.

But something or someone had made him feel otherwise.

What would make him want to hurt the very people involved with the academic career that was about to take off? School was almost over. Graduation just weeks away.

What had tipped him over that edge? Pushing him beyond some unseen point of no return?

Elaine thought of all that Callahan had told her about the Gamekeeper. How he chose the strongest, the ones with everything going for them. Ramon Johnson met all the criteria.

She shook her head. Callahan's theories were just that, theories, nothing more. There was no evidence to indicate any of these murders were even connected, much less related to a serial killer he'd tracked two years ago.

All they had was speculation.

And a hell of a lot of dead bodies.

With not a motivation for murder in sight.

The chief would be royally pissed.

Maybe Flatt would get his wish after all. He'd wanted the deputy-chief position something fierce. At this rate the position might be coming available sooner than anyone could have guessed.

But she refused to worry about politics.

She had to figure out what the hell was making seemingly harmless citizens turn into mass murderers.

A shiver swept over her skin.

She suddenly felt exactly like a hostage.

Desperate and utterly helpless to negotiate any sort of salvation.

Chapter 14

Not since Elaine's first case in homicide had Atlanta's beloved mayor elected to sit in on a detectives' briefing. Not only the mayor, she noted as she surveyed the guests seated at the front of the room. The chief of police, the county sheriff and another gentleman she'd never seen before, who served as the city's new public affairs officer.

The one person conspicuously absent was Special Agent Trace Callahan.

He had refused to leave the hospital, despite the guard detail left in charge of Ramon Johnson's security. Elaine would actually have preferred to go back to the hospital this morning, as well, except that the chief had called this meeting and, unlike Callahan, she couldn't say no.

Admittedly, hanging around the intensive care unit would have been pretty much pointless with Johnson in a coma. Still, a part of her wanted to be there just in case. If he woke up, any information he might choose or be able to relay could prove significant to the case now fondly known in the newspapers as the Unexplained Mass Killings.

According to the doctor in charge of Ramon's care, there were no guarantees that he would wake up at all. For that matter the doctors couldn't even explain what had made him lapse into the coma.

It happened sometimes in critical situations was the overall consensus. Some insisted the reaction was the body's way of healing itself. Shutting down all but the absolute essential processes in order to focus on repairing the physical damage.

At least he was alive.

Elaine closed her eyes and thought of the way his mother had cried. Aretha Johnson couldn't believe what had happened. Ramon had been the perfect son…the perfect student for nearly four years. He hadn't been on drugs since junior high school. Toxicology had confirmed that claim. The kid was clean. And yet three people were dead by his hand.

Callahan's notes slipped into her thoughts, vied for her attention even when she didn't want to go there. The shooter in each of these three multiple homicides had met the Gamekeeper's criteria. In every incident there appeared to be no motive for the killing…nothing that would explain what had turned a law-abiding citizen into a murderer. The shooters involved had had every reason to want to live and to be as happy as anyone could be.

Just like the primary victims in the Gamekeeper's killings two years ago.

If this Gamekeeper was a true serial killer, why wait two years between rampages? Why change his MO? Had he, as Callahan suggested, found it necessary to adapt? Callahan felt certain he'd wounded the bastard.

Elaine couldn't simply accept that scenario. Mainly because it didn't answer the really big questions. Why here? Why now? Maybe he'd been traveling around the country playing his games during the past two years. But not with the same or even a similar MO. If he had been, she would have found the link. Like Callahan, she'd searched every known database in hopes of finding some kind of connection…any link to mass murders in some other jurisdiction. Knowing anything was better than knowing nothing.

And that's what she knew…nothing.

There wasn't a single other case out there that came close, other than the Gamekeeper's work two years ago in D.C. and even then there were significant differences.

"This is unacceptable!"

Elaine dragged her full attention back to the room at the mayor's sharp announcement.

"This city is under siege," he continued, his voice a commanding bellow. Once a drill sergeant for the Marines, he certainly hadn't lost his ability to take charge of a room. "Our citizens are living in fear. A simple trip to the beauty parlor or the bank has turned into a nightmare." He flung his arms magnanimously. "And now, my God, half the city kept their children home from school today because they were afraid to do otherwise." He looked from face to face; his a stern mask of determination. "We are a city at war and we don't even know the enemy."

Things only went downhill from there. Elaine suddenly envied Callahan.

The public relations liaison insisted repeatedly that the media had to be given as many details as possible without jeopardizing the case. Otherwise, as every detective in the room already knew, they would come to their own conclusions and print it…citizens would read the theories and take them as fact. The community needed to understand. Confusion and lack of information fostered fear, he reiterated again and again throughout the briefing.

The entire hour turned out to be nothing more than a glorified pep talk. The chief of police as well as the county sheriff assured the mayor that all assets would be utilized to the fullest in the effort.

Since Elaine's phone hadn't vibrated during the meeting, she assumed that Johnson had not regained consciousness. She counted on the idea that Callahan would have called her. She hoped putting that much trust in him wasn't a mistake. For all she knew he could have interviewed the boy by now and be back out on the street looking for the one suspect that he believed to be involved. The Gamekeeper.

She pushed aside the doubt. They couldn't keep working together if she didn't have some faith. She'd spent most of the night last night reviewing every moment she'd spent with him, in particular those tension-crammed seconds before she'd pushed into that room with Ramon Johnson. What had made Callahan hesitate? That he hadn't taken charge of the situation and done exactly as she had still puzzled her. Had he been on desk duty too long? Was fear of making another mistake holding him back?

"Elaine, I need to see you in my office before you leave."

She looked up, only then realizing that the meeting had adjourned. "Sure." She offered her chief a smile. But he wasn't smiling back. Damn. This couldn't be good.

John Dugan made the final rounds of the conference room before ushering Elaine down the corridor to his office. Connie was missing in action, her desk covered with notes for the chief, the numerous lines on the phone there lit up like a Christmas tree.

Inside the chief of detectives' office, John closed the door and turned to Elaine. "What's going on with Agent Callahan?"

Elaine schooled her surprise at his question. That he didn't suggest they have a seat startled her, as well. John Dugan prided himself on formality. He never acted without taking his time to evaluate a situation. Every instinct told her that he was shooting from the hip here. Too worked up to want to sit down much less play by the rules of proper office etiquette. Not, she amended, that there had been anything proper about their affair, but that relationship had been conducted strictly after hours.

"He's sticking close to Johnson in hopes he'll regain consciousness," she explained as if his question had been about Callahan's whereabouts. But then, the chief already knew that.

John assessed her a moment as if he had to measure how much he should say. "I mean, how is he handling himself?"

"He's okay. I don't have any complaints." The chief's persistent stare made her uncomfortable. "Is there some reason you ask?"

He blew out a heavy breath. "It's something Douglas said to me last night."

Douglas…Callahan's field supervisor. "What did he say?" Whatever it was she had a right to know. She was the one out there in the field with Callahan.

John relaxed marginally. He sat down on the edge of the small conference table that consumed a good portion of the room's floor space and served as a meeting place for more intimate sessions. She hadn't meant to go down that road. What the hell was wrong with her?

John spoke then, drawing her wayward attention once more. "We had a couple of beers." He shrugged. "Exchanged war stories."

She didn't bother asking why Douglas had made the trip to Atlanta without having met with her or Callahan. Then again, he could be meeting with Callahan this morning. Or perhaps Douglas preferred meeting with the brass rather than the mere rank and file.

"He admitted that he thinks Callahan is obsessed with this Gamekeeper character," John went on. "No one at Quantico believes the guy is back. But Callahan won't let it go."

Elaine mulled over what the chief was saying, with the idea that it was the FBI who'd insisted that she and Callahan partner up on this. "Does that make sense to you, John?"

She never called him by his first name anymore. It didn't feel appropriate. But at that particular moment she needed to hear what John Dugan the man had to say, not her superior, not the detective, but the *man* who'd made love to her on more than one occasion. The man she'd trusted completely, still did for the most part.

"No, it doesn't." He took her by the arms and looked straight into her eyes. "I want you to be very careful, Elaine. I've got a bad feeling about this one. There's something going on here that we don't know about. I believe the Bureau is purposely leaving us out of the loop on something relative to these killings."

Trepidation shifted inside her. He was right. Something wasn't as it should be.

He released her, his grim expression turning hopeful. "Find some answers for me, Detective. Otherwise I've a feeling we're all going to end up in the unemployment line."

Elaine left his office with what felt like a big, heavy rock in her gut. He hadn't been kidding about the unemployment line. The mayor and the chief of police had made their positions clear on that score. Anyone who expected to maintain a future in law enforcement, specifically homicide, had better get on the stick. More killings without forward movement on the case would be wholly unacceptable. Heads were going to roll if Atlanta's finest didn't come up with some evidence to indicate how and why these murders were happening. She didn't take the warnings personally. It wasn't about being bullies, it was about stopping the killing. She understood that. The mayor, who admittedly wanted to get reelected, also wanted the same thing every detective in the room had wanted—to keep Atlanta safe.

"Hey, DC, why the long face?"

She felt a smile push across her lips at the sound of Henshaw's voice. She missed him more every day. "You should know the answer to that one, partner."

Henshaw set his hands on his hips, the lapels of his jacket shoved aside. "I think we need a conference."

Elaine's smile stretched into a grin as she followed her favorite cop down the corridor and to the right. Their destination, the boys' locker room—which was also the men's rest room. Henshaw checked it out, then motioned for her to follow him inside. He closed and locked the door.

Her second day in the department Henshaw had taken her to the "boys'" space and showed her that they didn't have anything, other than urinals, that the girls' locker room didn't have. He told her that she was to always remember, no matter how the guys ribbed her, that she could do anything they could.

He tucked his unlit stogie into his mouth and heaved a sigh. "I think we've hit an impasse here." He searched her eyes as he spoke as if watching for her inner response. Was her partner afraid she wouldn't share what she thought with him? "Since we can't seem to make any headway, the way I see it, there's one of two things going on with this case."

She'd trusted Henshaw's judgment from the very beginning. If he had a take on the situation, she definitely wanted to hear it. And somehow she had to get the point across that *he* was still her real partner; she wasn't going to blindside him.

"Either our burned-out Fed is right about this Gamekeeper freak," Henshaw suggested, "or he's in this up to his eyeballs."

The latter was not at all what she'd expected. "You think he would purposely lead us astray just to play this game?" She considered what the chief had told her as far as Douglas's thinking. Could Callahan be that obsessed? So much so that he would allow people to die to prove his theory? "Or maybe to lure his old nemesis out of hiding," she added, more to herself than to the other detective.

"Maybe he's the one making it happen," Henshaw suggested with a pointed nod. "Did you ever think of that one?"

Her loyal partner's words put her on the defensive. Proof positive of her stupid, stupid hang-up where Callahan was concerned. What the hell was she doing letting this get personal? She didn't even like him…not really.

"Wait," she said, holding up both hands in a stop gesture. Too late, the damage was done. "Are you insinuating that you think Callahan had something to do with these murders?"

"All I'm saying," Henshaw returned, his entire posture going into a don't-kill-the-messenger stance, "is that maybe his obsession has turned into some kind of psychosis. He might not even be aware of what he's doing. They say he wanted off desk duty badly enough to do most anything."

Elaine's gaze narrowed. "Who is *they?*"

A flicker of uncertainty showed in his eyes. "It was just something I heard Flatt and Jillette discussing. That's all. It's probably nothing."

Where would either of those jerks get an idea like that? God knew the pair had never had an original thought. They'd heard it some place.

"Where do you think they heard something like that?" Henshaw had turned evasive now. That bothered Elaine to an extent, but she knew he didn't want to stir up trouble. He just felt compelled to keep her up to snuff on the locker-room scuttlebutt.

"If memory serves," he said, taking the long way around the story, "I believe Flatt mentioned that he has a friend who is an assistant to Supervisory Special Agent Douglas."

Dammit. Why the hell wasn't Douglas being up-front with

her? Or the chief? Apparently even he suspected that something was amiss with the guys from the Bureau.

"Thanks, Hank," she said, her mind already turning over the steps she needed to take from here. "I appreciate you keeping me in the loop."

"What kind of partner would I be if I didn't?" He patted her on the shoulder and winked. "I might be stuck interviewing prostitutes and pimps, but my heart's still with you."

The Fishnet Murders. She made the connection. This whole crazy business with Callahan had her a little slow on the uptake. That's why Henshaw had been the first to the scene at the high school yesterday. The red-light district wasn't that far away.

"How's your case going?"

He shrugged. "It's going."

She nodded. Nobody understood that statement better than she did. Sometimes it felt like you hit a wall with a case and nothing short of a miracle would save you. She felt exactly like that right now.

"What about you?"

She made a disgusted sound. "I feel like we lost before we even got started."

He shook his head. "I don't mean the case. I mean you? You never did tell me what the doc had to say."

Actually she had, at least she'd told him what she wanted him to know. She'd live. She hadn't told anyone the rest. Damn. And she had to call Bramm's office and get that appointment.

Could she go into that now? Anxiety writhed inside her. She needed to face this…but the subject was still too tender to tread too heavily. Disappointment had already registered in her sweet old partner's eyes. He knew she didn't plan to tell him the whole story.

"You ever heard of endometriosis?" she asked, startling herself as well as him. There might not be much she could do today that would be right, but she could do this. She could make her partner feel good about their continued relationship. Despite his protests she knew it bothered him that he'd been set aside in favor of some has-been Fed. She forced her mind off the subject before she could feel guilty for that one. How in the world had Callahan gotten that deeply under her skin in such a short span of time?

"Yeah," Henshaw said, surprising her again. "I had a cousin who had to have surgery for that." He winced. "Not so pleasant."

She nodded her agreement. "I may have to have surgery." Funny thing was, since Dr. Bramm had diagnosed her, she hadn't had the first symptom of the disease. The only discomfort she'd suffered was related to her damned ulcer.

He patted her arm again. "You'll be okay, DC."

She managed a smile, or the closest thing she could muster to one. "I'm not the deputy chief right now," she reminded. "Remember, Flatt's filling in while I'm stuck with our pal Callahan." She said this to remind her partner that he wasn't the only one who'd gotten screwed in this.

"You think the kid can tell us anything?" he asked, moving back to the case.

"Maybe." She suddenly felt completely overwhelmed. How on earth was she going to do this? She hadn't felt this lost ever. "*If* he regains consciousness."

Henshaw nodded. "Funny thing about that," he went on. "With both the other shooters they saved the last bullet for themselves." He laughed, a dry, crusty sound. "Not the next to the last one, but the very last one. Wonder what went wrong with Johnson?"

Henshaw was right. If one assumed that the three cases were connected somehow, as Callahan suggested, what went awry with Johnson? "I guess the one that ended up in his gut could have been the one he was supposed to have used to blow his brains out?"

"If that's so, then why the drama?" Henshaw countered. "He kept crying in there, threatening to shoot himself. And you did say he stuck the gun to his head and pulled the trigger as if he'd expected there to be another round."

That was true. She shrugged. "Maybe he lost count."

But it wouldn't be that simple. Nothing about murder was ever that simple.

Chapter 15

A glitch.

A tiny misstep in the scheme of things.

It happened.

Even to geniuses. Look at Einstein. Da Vinci. No one was perfect all the time.

He smiled, looked at himself in the mirror and relished the beauty of his reflection. He knew how to take care of glitches, knew precisely how to make them work to his full advantage and appear a part of the plan so as to save face.

No one had to know he hadn't intended it to be exactly that way.

After all, this was his game and he set the rules.

An occasional glitch just made things more interesting…made winning more of a challenge.

And he would win.

No one could beat the Gamekeeper at his own game.

Chapter 16

"Attendance today is still down more than fifty percent."

Elaine nodded, understanding the vice principal's concerns. As the mayor had said the day before, parents were afraid to send their children to school.

"Mrs. Hamilton, I know this is difficult," Elaine allowed. "But I'm going to need your help."

"Anything," the vice principal replied without hesitation. "I don't know what made a fine young man like Ramon do something like this, but I want to do whatever it takes to get to the bottom of it."

Elaine quickly ran down the list she required. The names of anyone close to Ramon, male or female, clubs he belonged to. Basically anyone who knew him more than simply in passing needed to be interviewed.

Yesterday, after her little conference with Henshaw, she'd

gone back to the chief and asked for full support from her old partner. The chief had given her Henshaw and Jillette. Flatt could be utilized to a degree but he still had to carry on as deputy chief of detectives, as well. A number of beat cops were at her disposal as needed. She would gladly use all the help she could get. A number of students had already been interviewed…but they needed more. They needed anything and everything.

With the vice principal meeting out of the way, she decided to follow the journey Ramon Johnson had taken each day at school. She went to all of his classes, took a long look in his lockers, and then out to the space where he'd parked his bicycle every day. He'd taken honors classes, had worked hard in athletics. It just didn't make sense.

"Deputy Elaine!"

The familiar voice waded into her disturbing thoughts, forcing her to refocus her gaze on her surroundings. Skip Littles strode across the parking lot toward her. He waved and smiled widely.

"Good morning, Skip," she said, pushing a smile into place. She noticed he wore his press badge. A number of reporters had swarmed the high school yesterday, but most had decided to take it to the station this morning in an attempt to glean any tidbits from the latest detectives' briefing. Seeing Skip here now surprised her, but it shouldn't. He felt comfortable following her around, mainly because she usually gave him something to take back to his co-workers at the paper, which ultimately garnered him the right attention and a small pat on the back.

The wind shifted his brown hair, allowing it to fall across

the thick lenses of his glasses. He shoved it back, his movements awkward. He was like an overgrown kid still groping
to fit in. But Skip was no kid, twenty-five at least. And fitting
in wasn't likely, now or ever. But he tried and that's what
counted in her book.

"Can I ask you a couple of questions, Deputy Elaine?"

He looked so hopeful. She never could resist the underdog.
"Sure, Skip. You doing a piece on this case?" She knew he always tried, but the *Telegraph* would likely never see him as
anything other than a desk assistant. Though they would gladly
use anything he managed to come up with, the byline just
wouldn't be his. She had to give him high marks for effort.

"Yes, ma'am." He nodded enthusiastically. "I believe all
these killings are related." He cocked his head and studied her.
"Don't you? The devil's work, I say."

She couldn't agree more. Definitely the devil's work. Considering they lived in the Bible Belt most folks would likely
think that way. But she understood that in this instance the
devil was likely all too human. "I can't say whether or not the
murders are connected just yet, Skip. But I believe there is a
pattern of some sort evolving here." That much couldn't hurt.

He shook his head. "Ramon Johnson went to church every
Sunday," he added solemnly. "He knew what the devil could
make him do, knew how to resist, but he failed."

A new kind of tension moved through Elaine at the uncharacteristically harsh words. "What do you mean, Skip?"

He shrugged. "I just heard some of the folks at his church
say something like that last night. Wednesday night is church
night." He shrugged those skinny shoulders again. "It's true
though. The devil's after all of us, you know."

Elaine's cell phone interrupted the moment. "Excuse me." As she pulled the phone from her purse she turned away. "Jentzen."

"Johnson's awake."

Callahan.

"Did he say anything?" Anticipation stung through her veins. This could be the break they needed. When the coma had passed the twenty-four-hour mark she'd worried. This had to be a good sign…the turning point they needed.

"Nothing. He remembers nothing."

Disappointment deflated the hope that had risen at the idea. She heard the same in Callahan's weary tone. "You're sure?" Of course he was sure. She gave herself a mental kick. He wouldn't say so otherwise. Hell, he hadn't left Ramon's bedside.

"As sure as the medical staff will allow me to be."

She shook her head as she imagined Callahan attempting to shake the truth out of the young man. "I'm headed to the residence. You coming or staying there?" Foolishly a part of her wanted him to meet her at the Johnson home, but the saner, cop part wanted him to stay away. It had begun. Damn. She hadn't wanted this. Something about this guy got to her on a purely noncop level. Definitely the last thing she needed.

"I'll be there. Mrs. Johnson said to make ourselves at home."

"See you then."

Elaine ended the call and dropped the phone back into the bag hanging from her shoulder. Was Ramon's memory lapse a result of the coma or the trauma? Or was it a built-in safety mechanism by whoever had hardwired the kid to do this?

There she went, believing in Callahan's theory about the Gamekeeper.

She turned back to Skip, who waited anxiously. Or maybe Skip was right…maybe it was the devil hard at work stealing souls.

"I should get back to work," Skip said, his cheeks crimson with embarrassment. He always got embarrassed whenever Elaine looked at him for too long.

She reached into her bag and withdrew a card that included her cell phone number. "You call me if you hear anything else, Skip. I could really use your help."

The new sparkle in his eyes lifted her spirits slightly. If only the rest of the world was as easy to please.

The Johnson residence was no where near Buckhead or any other of Atlanta's premiere luxury living spots. It was a small, simple home in a neighborhood that continuously struggled with that narrow line between good and bad. The homes were fairly well maintained. Most of the occupants blue-collar, church-going folks. But the constant battle with keeping drugs and the like out of the neighborhood had taken a heavy toll on the residents. Elaine's appearance in front of the Johnson home was met with suspicion rather than relief. Trust was a rare, precious commodity on this side of town.

She'd wanted to come here yesterday, but her new partner had nixed that plan. Callahan had insisted on being in on the first look at the Johnson home, but wouldn't leave the hospital until Ramon came out of the coma. Uniforms had protected the residence since it was considered part of the crime scene.

Callahan's rented sedan already sat at the curb. He waited on the covered porch looking about as at home as a French poodle in a pen of pit bulls.

As she moved up the walk toward the front of the house he stood and tucked an unlit cigarette back into his jacket pocket. "How did your little tête-à-tête with the brass go this morning?"

Elaine waited until she'd moved closer to respond. She wanted to see what was in his eyes. Damn. She should have remembered. He was far too good at blocking his emotions. She would see only what he wanted her to see, curiosity. A part of her wanted to ask why didn't he just go ahead and smoke that damned cigarette instead of playing with it. On days like today, she might be tempted to join him.

"Just the way you think," she tossed back. Why pretend? He knew the drill. Anytime unsolved murders went down, the brass got antsy. Hell, she got antsy. No one wanted to stop this outbreak any more than she did.

Callahan nodded. He still wore the same suit as he had two days before. The shirt looked a little the worse for wear, but it was his face that told the most about the previous two nights. He hadn't slept. Those piercing blue eyes were as bloodshot as if he'd been on a drinking binge. His jaw was covered with golden stubble. All in all he looked ready to step on-screen and sweep every woman in the viewing audience off her feet. Good thing Elaine wasn't feeling much like a woman this morning.

"Let's see what we can find," she suggested as she stepped up onto the porch with him.

He held up a key to the house. "Just been waiting for your

arrival." He smiled that killer smile and, hard as she tried to prevent it, the female in her stirred, roused from hibernation, and went on full alert.

She tamped down the annoying reaction he always seemed to generate with such ease and followed him inside. A different kind of stimulus had her lips stretching into their own smile the moment she entered the quiet home. Vanilla and sugar. The place smelled like a bakery, sweet and warm.

The furnishings were well-worn but comfortable looking. Neat and appealing on a very basic level. Ramon Johnson had come home to this every day she would bet. How could he not have known how much his mother loved him? That was just it. There was no reason to believe he didn't. Not really.

Living room, kitchen, bathroom and two bedrooms. Modest in size, but the love in the home was apparent in every small room. Ramon's bedroom was no exception. Posters of athletes lined the walls. The Bible lay in plain sight on the night table near his bed. A small desk with computer sat in the corner, its screen black.

Callahan headed straight for the computer.

Elaine took her time, surveyed the shelves. Most were loaded with trophies, but there were a number of books. Classics mostly and a few more recent, fantasy hardbacks. A basketball lay in the center of his unmade bed. Next to it was a crumpled piece of paper.

She sat down on the edge of the bed, most likely where Ramon sat when he pulled his shoes on and off. The paper looked wrinkled as if he'd wadded it and then smoothed it back out at least once. Two creases were still visible, indicating it had once been in a business-size envelope. She held it carefully by the very edges and read the typed body.

Her breath caught in her throat, and the air in the room seemed to vanish as the impact of the letter's content slammed full force into her.

"Computer's been wiped just like the one at the Matthews' residence," Callahan tossed over his shoulder. "I think maybe we'd better get the one from the shooter in the beauty salon murders. Send all three up to Quantico's tech lab."

"Callahan," she said. Her voice felt alien to her own ears, cold and stiff.

"Yeah." He turned from the computer then.

"You'd better come take a look at this."

He was around the foot of the bed and next to her so fast her head started to spin…or maybe it was what she'd just read. He took the letter from her and quickly scanned it.

"Holy—" He read it again, then looked at her. "Didn't his mother tell us he'd received a full scholarship to this university?"

Elaine nodded. "The vice principal confirmed it. Apparently the school hasn't gotten a copy of this letter yet." She pointed to the murdered principal's name. "This is motive." Her gaze connected with Callahan's once more. "Big-time motive."

He glanced at the floor, frowned, then looked again, before abruptly leaning down and pulling something from beneath the edge of the bed. The linen-colored envelope matched the paper on which the letter was printed.

"It's the university's official letterhead and envelope," he said, passing both back to Elaine.

She tugged a plastic evidence bag from her jacket pocket and placed the letter and the envelope inside. She stared at the contents, her heart heavy with something so far beyond sadness she could find no accurate description.

"This is how he works," Callahan said softly. "He plants all the right seeds of doubt, nurtures the uncertainty, then he plays the grand finale." He tapped the evidence bag. "This is the coup de grâce, the straw that broke the camel's back and pushed Ramon Johnson over the edge."

Elaine looked at him, studied that chiseled profile in search of something, anything that would make her see the certainty in his words. How could he be so damned sure?

"How can you be certain it's him?"

"Because I know him." That blue gaze bore into hers making her feel too exposed. "I can feel him. Can you understand that, Detective?" He knocked on his chest with his fist. "I can feel his hand in this. He's playing with us. He wants us to know he's the one. That's why he let you find the letter."

Confusion disrupted her thought process all over again. "What do you mean, he let me find the letter?"

"Was anything even remotely linked to motivation found in the beauty salon murders?"

She shook her head.

"In the Matthews case?"

He knew the answer to that. Dammit. "No." She hadn't meant the word to sound so defensive.

"And yet, here is our motivation in a nice, neat little package." He indicated the plastic evidence bag. "The only other connection so far is the wiped computers." Callahan let go a heavy breath. "He knows what he's doing. He baffled us at first. Now he's leading us. It's the way he works."

"It's the devil," she offered, her gaze shifting to the Bible lying so close by. Maybe Skip was right. The force behind all this sure as hell felt supernatural.

"That's what I called him in the beginning."

Elaine's gaze snapped back to Callahan. "What?"

"A devil. I called him that at first." He looked away as if fearing she might see too much if he wasn't careful. "He uses a similar method to what most people believe the devil uses."

She could see the relevance in his statement. According to the Bible the devil knew one's weaknesses and preyed upon those chinks in spiritual armor. Who didn't know that age-old story of the struggle between good and bad?

Her gaze drifted down to the letter in her hand. Was this Ramon's big weakness, the need to get into the right school…to prove his worth?

She closed her eyes and fought a wave of emotion. How the hell could someone do this? She stiffened, pushed away that weaker emotion. Looking at this objectively was essential. She knew better than to go off on an emotional tangent. How long had Ramon known? She glanced at the date on the letter. Not long. Had he suspected this was coming or was it a complete shock?

Clearly he would blame Principal Massey. She perused the letter once more. No doubt there.

She thought of his mother then and how devastated she would be when she saw this letter but there was no getting around showing it to her. Did this evidence of motivation set Ramon's case apart from the others? And how could the

Gamekeeper or anyone else have made this happen or have known it was coming?

"You still don't want to trust me on this, do you?"

Callahan's question drew her full attention back to him. He watched her, tried to see what she was thinking just then. He looked tired. Exhausted really.

"There's no evidence to support your scenario," she said frankly. It wasn't that she wanted to discredit him, she simply didn't have any compelling reason to go along with what he suggested. She told herself that Douglas's comment about him being obsessed didn't play into her decision, but was she lying to herself?

He shook his head. "How many more dead bodies do you need, Detective? Think about it. He leaves no evidence—that is his MO."

She waved the letter. "Isn't this evidence?"

He held up his hands to refute her suggestion, then balled them back into fists and dropped both onto his lap. "He let you find this to confuse the issue, to divert your attention. Don't you see the parallel between two years ago and now? He's playing with us!"

She didn't. At least not to the degree he did. A part of her wished she could. It would be so much easier.

He wouldn't look at her now. Impatience exuded from his posture. She thought of his bloodshot eyes and couldn't help wondering if he'd spent both nights at the hospital or if maybe he'd taken a break to wallow in his old habits.

"When was the last time you overindulged in alcohol?" The question was out of her mouth before she could stop it.

They had to be straight with each other. She had to know that she could trust him on that level.

Fury had ignited in those blue eyes when his gaze collided with hers this time. "More than a year ago, what of it?"

He felt suddenly too close, as if he'd leaned in her direction and all that fury pressed in on her. She stood, tucked the evidence bag containing the letter into her purse. "I just needed to be sure, that's all."

He pushed up from the bed, towered over her, deliberately setting her further on edge with his intimidating stance. "Sure, I get it. Douglas talked to you or your chief, didn't he?"

She kept her gaze carefully focused elsewhere so she didn't give herself away.

"You don't have to say anything. I already know. He called me, too."

She hoped the subtle shift in her posture didn't give away her surprise at that statement.

"He ordered me to keep pushing you to trust me. He can't understand why I haven't already convinced you to believe what I'm telling you about the Gamekeeper."

"Why would he do that?" she demanded, her own fury getting the better of her now. "He told the chief that I should be wary of you. That you're obsessed with this Gamekeeper character!"

"Yeah, I know."

Utterly dumbfounded, she threw up her hands. "You know? Why would he tell you one thing and my chief another?"

"He didn't. I lied so you'd tell me the truth."

Outrage blasted through her. "You bastard." She barely resisted the urge to slap him. He'd tricked her!

That penetrating gaze leveled on hers, the intensity of it taking some of the steam out of her. "I've been called worse, Detective Jentzen, but it doesn't change the fact that I'm telling you the truth. Whether you ever believe me or not, people will keep dying until he's through playing this game."

A shudder quaked through her. How could she not put some stock in what he said? With every ounce of his being he believed his theory to be on target. The truth of it burned in his eyes.

"What does he want?" she asked, surrendering to the inevitable. Maybe he was right…God knew she had no idea what was happening here. All killers wanted something…that's why they played the game. It filled some void…provided something that was missing from their evil souls.

That haunting smile tipped up one corner of Callahan's mouth. "That one's easy. He wants me." `

If every fiber of her being hadn't been screaming at her that he was right, she might have argued the point. "What do we do about that?"

"We don't have to do anything. He's already set the game in motion. At this point we're simply pawns. Our job is to react. We can't possibly anticipate his moves, so what other choice do we have?" he added when she would have argued with him.

"You shouldn't be on this case." She knew it with complete certainty. This went way beyond simply being personal. For the first time in her entire life she wanted to do something totally stupid. She wanted to put her arms around this broken man and hold him, comfort him. Reach out to him and somehow make sense of this insanity. She was an idiot. A complete idiot.

He made a sound intended to be a laugh but it fell well short of the mark. "I am this case."

Chapter 17

Elaine couldn't put it off any longer. Friday morning after the usual briefing, she disappeared into the ladies' room and put in a call to Dr. Bramm's office. She hadn't had any cramping or nausea but this had to be done. As much as she'd like to pretend it would simply go away, she knew it wouldn't.

The receptionist gave her the name and address of the specialist and an appointment date for next week. Elaine thanked her and ended the call. She stared at the name she'd written down and wondered if this man would take one look at her and tell her that any chance of having a child was out of the question. Stage three or four, that was Dr. Bramm's estimation. Advanced, not a good thing. Having children would be unlikely. Why was it the idea hadn't seemed to matter until now? She thought of her sister's children and those of her brothers and she just wanted to cry.

How could this happen to her? She flattened her palm against her belly. Other than having the ulcer, she'd always been healthy. Had practiced safe sex. Actually hadn't had that many lovers. What had gone wrong?

She blinked back the emotion stinging her eyes and punched in another number on her cell phone. She needed to hear her father's voice, needed to talk to him. She'd been too busy to touch base with him since learning the news from her mother.

Divorce.

God, this was totally insane. Her mother and father had been happily married for nearly half a century. Surely, looks couldn't be that deceiving. She tried to think of a single moment when she'd felt they were unhappy together and couldn't recall even one.

"Dad, it's Elaine."

"Good morning, Sunshine. What's cooking in cop world?"

Her father had always called her Sunshine. He claimed that from the time she could walk she'd always been curious and exuberant about life in general. No matter what, he could count on Elaine for a smile, thus the nickname. She didn't feel much like smiling today. She'd spent most of the night kicking herself for letting Callahan get too close.

"Same old, same old," she lied. She didn't want to talk about work or herself, she wanted to know what her father intended to do about the divorce. "What about you? What's going on with you and Mom?"

He heaved a weighty breath. "You heard about the divorce, I take it."

"Yeah, I can't believe it."

"Neither can I," he admitted. "I'm convinced it's that new counselor she's seeing. Last month she started in on wanting to travel more. Then she jumped on the idea that we didn't have anything in common. We've been married forty-five years, can you believe that? We have a history in common!"

Elaine wasn't sure anymore what to believe. "Dad, is there anything I can do?" Talking to her mother about it wouldn't help. That had been obvious the other day. She had made up her mind, and Elaine wasn't going to change it.

"I'm not sure there is, honey. She's determined to go through with this."

"Maybe you should go see the counselor again," she suggested. It couldn't hurt.

"I've tried. He won't see me at this point. A conflict of interest he says."

Wasn't a counselor supposed to try and save marriages? "I'm sorry, Dad." What else could she say? "I wish there was something I could do."

"I've been watching the news, Elaine. You don't need to be worrying about us. Take care of yourself."

Her father had spent most of his career in internal affairs, but her two older brothers were beat cops, both captains of their own squads. The younger Jentzen spawn was the only male who had insisted on choosing another field. He'd gone into firefighting. He'd made the family proud in spite of her father's initial misgivings. That Judith had become a teacher-turned-housewife and mother was no problem, she was a woman after all. Elaine had always been considered one of the boys.

They talked a while longer about his latest golf game and

whether or not the rain would hold off for the weekend. When she'd said goodbye she closed the phone and sagged against the tile wall. What was happening to her life? All that had felt strong and dependable was suddenly on shaky ground.

Whether it was her father's obsession with golf or her mother's contrary counselor, their marriage was in serious trouble. Maybe Elaine would just stay single. It was a lot less messy. No one to pick up after, no one to complain about. All she had to do was take care of herself. Well, and Sally. She smiled when she thought of her big old golden retriever. Sally was her saving grace. That run she took with her each night helped keep her sane.

She had a great dog, what did she need with a man in her life?

But then, dining alone most nights wasn't all it was cracked up to be, either. Nor was not having anyone to talk to about work and life in general. She and John—Chief Dugan—used to talk for hours.

Before she could stop it, the image of Trace Callahan had pushed aside the chief's familiar face. She closed her eyes and shivered. Talk about nothing in common. She and Callahan had absolutely nothing in common. When you got right down to it they didn't even like each other.

But something about him made her want to know him…want to reach out and uncover the mysteries…whether she ever learned to like him or not.

Okay, she admitted. Maybe that was the draw. She shook her head and pushed away from the cool tile wall. It was a cliché as old as time. Callahan waltzes into her life all tall, dark and handsome, shrouded in mystery. Any female breathing would be attracted to him, or at least would sit up and pay attention, on a physical level. The whole emotionally torn history and the gossip surrounding his broken career tugged at her on every other level.

She should have seen that one coming.

Elaine Jentzen had always been a sucker for the underdog. Skip Littles was proof positive.

A frown tugged at her brow as she considered running into Skip at the school. Why hadn't he been there when all the reporters had flocked to the scene? Why show up so much later...when everyone else had already gotten their story and moved on?

Maybe he'd just been behind the curve.

But he never had been before.

She shuddered when she recalled their conversation about the devil. Callahan had mentioned that he'd called the Gamekeeper the devil at first. Coincidence, she told herself. Skip Littles had no way of knowing that.

A knock on the door dragged her from the worrisome thoughts. It wouldn't be Connie, she'd simply come right on in. Had to be one of the guys.

Elaine strode over to the door and pulled it open.

"We need to talk."

Hank Henshaw looked more unsettled than she could ever recall seeing him.

"Sure, come on in."

It was the only way to have privacy around here. The homicide department was one large bull pen, with a separate desk for each detective, but not much else in the way of privacy.

Henshaw meandered into the ladies' rest room and took a

moment to look around. "Why is it this place is always cleaner than the men's room?"

She laughed. He grinned. Boy, she missed him. "What's up?" Elaine figured they'd better get this done. If Connie walked in and found Henshaw, she'd have a stroke. Elaine and her partner usually conducted these clandestine meetings in the men's room. Unless it was an emergency the other detectives stayed clear. It was an unspoken rule of sorts. Interrupting a washroom conference between two detectives was not done.

Her longtime partner pulled a folded document from his jacket. "I just got the ballistics report on the .38 Matthews used at the bank."

Elaine took the document he offered. "Good. Any matches?" Whenever ballistics finished analyzing a weapon, the results were always compared to any in the system, which included several databases of documented analysis from other cases, to determine whether or not the weapon had been used in a previous crime or if it were stolen.

Henshaw nodded. "You ain't gonna believe this, DC."

She dropped the hand holding the report to her side, preferring to hear the results straight from her partner's mouth. "Give me the abbreviated version."

"The .38 came from evidence lockup."

Total confusion claimed her now. "That's not possible. Our handling and security standards are too good to let something like that happen." The Atlanta PD was better than most at keeping a close watch on evidence. No way did someone walk out with a weapon that just happened to end up involved in a multiple homicide.

"Not ours," Henshaw said, the worry in his eyes making her gut clench. "This weapon came from evidence lockup in Washington, D.C. It's the same weapon used in the Gamekeeper murders two years ago."

Elaine felt the air rush out of her lungs.

"Callahan signed for it...he never returned it. No one noticed—" Henshaw shrugged "—or cared until now."

Trace Callahan had signed out a weapon from the evidence lockup...the one his arch nemesis had used to kill his targets, including Callahan's partner. Now that same weapon shows up in a multiple homicide here in Atlanta...in a case that Callahan fiercely wanted her to believe involved the Gamekeeper.

"I didn't show it to Flatt yet," Henshaw commented, pointing to the report. "I thought you'd want to know first. I can give you some time, but by this afternoon or tomorrow at the latest I won't have any choice but to give him a copy."

Flatt would have a field day with this. He'd do anything to get attention. He was acting deputy chief now, and he wanted to gain all the glory he could. Considering that Callahan was her partner for the time being, anything out of line that partner did reflected poorly on her.

"You didn't see this," she said to Henshaw. "I'll show it to Flatt later. If he questions it, I'm the one who received it. Got it?"

She was asking Henshaw to take a big risk. Flatt would come down on him hard if he found out about this. But she needed to determine how this had happened before Flatt got wind of it.

All because she couldn't or wouldn't believe Callahan

would go this far. Stupid, stupid, stupid. How could she know what a mistake this was and not be able to stop herself from making it?

"Whatever you say, DC." Henshaw stuck his stogie in his mouth. "Well, I'd better get going. Gotta get back on those interviews."

She nodded. Henshaw and Jillette were conducting the interviews with those who had known Ramon Johnson best. Schoolmates, neighbors, members of his church. Elaine had the sudden, inexplicable feeling that they wouldn't find anything…that no number of interviews would earn them the first bit of information.

As crazy as it sounded, considering the ballistics report Callahan appeared to be right to some degree.

This case looked more and more as if it were about him.

Henshaw hesitated. "Oh, yeah, they got that creep who'd been killing all those prostitutes."

Elaine managed another smile. "I guess all they needed was your input, partner."

"I ain't been in this business thirty years without learning a few things," he tossed back.

When she and Henshaw left the men's room, Elaine dropped by her desk and picked up her messages. She flipped through the numerous calls and decided none of them warranted her attention just now. She tossed the wad back onto her desk and grabbed her jacket and bag. Callahan had gone back to the hospital this morning to prod Johnson a little more. They had to talk. Someplace private. Where she could scream and rant at will. He was far too controlled to do any ranting of his own.

Maybe that was the key to getting the truth from him. Maybe she had to make him lose control. She had a feeling it wouldn't be that difficult. He was damn close to the edge.

"Jentzen, we need to talk."

Inwardly she cringed. Flatt. What the hell did he want. She turned and produced the requisite smile. "Morning, Flatt. What can I do for you?"

Looking even more smug than usual, he jerked his head in the direction of the men's room. Perfect. A one-on-one conference with her favorite jerk.

She followed him across the bull pen, exchanging a look with Henshaw en route. She relaxed then. Her partner had her back. Rules were made to be broken.

The instant the door had swished closed behind her, Flatt rounded on Elaine.

"What the hell is going on with you, Jentzen?"

Since she didn't have the foggiest idea what he was talking about, she shrugged. "Can you be a bit more specific?" After all, her parents were on the verge of divorce. Her sister sounded totally unhappy and…well, there was an alien growth overtaking her pelvic cavity and any possibility of having offspring. Other than that she was just frigging dandy, but she would be damned before she would share any of that with this jerk.

Flatt's face turned a darker shade of red. "You know what I'm talking about," he growled.

She turned her palms upward in question. "Sorry, I don't have a clue." And she didn't.

If Callahan were here he could light his ever present cigarette on the man's face, she mused. Flatt was really PO'ed, though she couldn't figure out to save her soul what it had to do with her.

"You and Callahan are involved," Flatt snarled. "Don't try to deny it. I know you are."

Her chin dropped like a rock. What the hell was he talking about? "This is a joke, right?" She glanced around, visually checked under the stall doors to see if the gang had gathered and hidden there. Any second now the rest of the homicide detail would likely pop out of their hiding places and laugh their asses off. Except...Flatt wasn't that witty.

"Do I look like I'm joking?" Flatt bracketed his hands at his waist, his fury barely contained within that slender frame all dolled up in that fancy Armani suit.

He wasn't kidding. The reality hit her like a bullet, right between the eyes. "You're serious?"

"Of course I'm serious," he railed. "I may only be in this position temporarily, but I take my job very seriously. You'd better get your act together, Jentzen. I don't intend to let you make me look bad. No way."

"Where is this coming from, Flatt?" she demanded in a growl of her own. "Who told you this?"

"Don't worry about where I got my information." He smirked. "I have my sources, same as you. Just watch your step, because I'm definitely watching you."

The door abruptly shoved inward and Henshaw, whistling some tune she couldn't readily identify, strolled in, breaking the cardinal rule of detectives—never interrupt a private meeting. "Whoops!" He jarred to a stop. "Sorry, didn't know you two were conferencing." He reached for his crotch. "Not sure I can wait, though." He shook his head. "It's hell getting old."

Steaming, Flatt stormed out of the room without another word. Elaine stared after him somewhat dumbfounded but mostly just plain old ticked off.

"What was that all about?" Henshaw moseyed over to where she stood.

She looked at him, still unable to believe what had just transpired. Where the hell had that come from? "He accused me of being *involved* with Callahan."

Henshaw barked out a laugh. "Just shows what that dumb prick knows. You don't even like the guy."

"Damn straight." Elaine managed a strained laugh. Her partner was right...she didn't even like the guy. "I gotta go." She didn't look back at her loyal partner as she headed toward the door. If she did, she feared he would see the lie in her eyes.

"Hey."

She hesitated, hand on the door. She'd almost escaped. "Yeah?"

Henshaw walked up to her, the rubber soles of his shoes whispering on the tile floor. "Is there something else I need to know?"

She shook her head. "No. Nothing."

He grunted. "I'll see you around then." He turned and made his way back toward the urinals.

Elaine pulled the door open and left, her gut twisting in a dozen knots.

It was the first time she'd ever lied to her partner.

Chapter 18

*P*ositive.

Regina Williams stared at the letter in her hand, and her whole life flashed before her eyes.

She would never hit that million-dollar mark in real estate sales.

Never meet Mr. Right.

Never…do anything…

She would die.

Because life would no longer be worth living.

Not now.

Okay, so it was her fault. She should have been more careful. She crushed the letter in her hand and threw it across the room.

She hadn't been completely monogamous.

Who was these days?

Regina stared at her reflection in the mirror above her cluttered dresser. Her brown hair was styled in a trendy fashion, the color glossy. Her eyes, the same lush brown of her hair, were clear. She had so much going for her. Looks, brains, and she damn sure wasn't afraid of hard work. Never had been.

She'd had the world by the tail and had nowhere to go but up. What was wrong with enjoying sex? She had been extremely selective. In the past six months she'd stuck to only two men in particular. Both of whom she enjoyed thoroughly. Neither of whom knew about the other.

One of them had done this to her.

She didn't have to wonder. Didn't have to ask questions. She knew.

In more than seven years, since she'd gotten her life on track and started her new career, she had not had unprotected sex with anyone. Not a single living soul…until six months ago.

She'd felt safe with the two loves of her life. Hadn't been able to choose between the two so she'd hung on to both. Allowing the relationships to go deeper than any other before. Making love with no barriers between them had been a sign of trust…of deeper feelings.

And what had it gotten her?

HIV positive.

A death warrant.

There was no way to be certain which of them did this to her, but she should have known. Hadn't she been warned? For that matter she should have learned her lesson long ago. Never trust anyone…especially a man who wanted in your pants.

Well, it was damn sure too late now.

She should have listened to her friend's advice.

Whichever bastard had done this to her probably did it on purpose. He'd known he was doomed so he'd decided to take her with him. Or maybe he'd found out about the other man in her life.

Whatever the case, one of them had killed her just the same as if he'd stuck a gun to her head and pulled the trigger.

Now he would pay.

If she had no future…her devoted lovers wouldn't have one, either. It didn't matter that she couldn't be sure which one was the guilty party. They would all three suffer the same fate…one way or another.

Like her mother had always said when she and her sister got into trouble, *I can't be sure which of you did this so I'll just punish you both…*

Mothers were always right.

Chapter 19

Jentzen had chosen the battleground carefully. Her place. She had the home field advantage.

Trace hadn't asked why. He'd heard all he needed to know in her voice when she made the call.

We have to talk. My place. Thirty minutes.

Ramon Johnson still remembered nothing about the shooting. His mother had gotten a little testy with Trace for continuing to press her son, who had been moved to the psychiatric ward for further observation.

Trace had a feeling that Ramon Johnson would never remember what happened to him. The Bureau would need to send in a specialist to determine if brainwashing was at play, but he had a hunch that was the case. He hadn't known the Gamekeeper to use that tactic the last go-round, but then again, none of the victims had survived.

As much as he knew about the bastard, he didn't know nearly enough.

Trace parked his sedan in front of Jentzen's small home and blew out a breath of utter fatigue. He told himself he could do this, had to do it. There was no one else. He needed Jentzen on his side. For the first time, he recognized the bottom line—he could not do this alone.

But damn if he didn't dread seeing new accusations in her eyes. Her chief, or maybe Douglas, had probably given her some new scrap of evidence to indicate that Trace was off his rocker, unstable—not fieldworthy. And maybe he was. He could scarcely get past looking at himself in the mirror each morning. He closed his eyes at night, wanting nothing more than to drink himself into oblivion. And every damned night he made himself a promise, if it was this bad the next day he'd give in and drink until he could forget.

That's how he survived. One day at a time. About the only thing that kept him from saying to hell with it all was the idea that if he didn't stop the Gamekeeper, no one would. It wasn't that he thought he was so damned good that no one else could do this…he simply knew that it had to be him. For one thing, no one wanted to accept that it was, in fact, the Gamekeeper up to his old tricks. Not to mention that the Gamekeeper had sealed that decision by drawing Trace here. And as much as Atlanta PD, Elaine Jentzen being no exception, didn't want him here, he had to be here. He had no choice in the matter.

Funny damned thing was, Douglas had insisted that he explore his theory, just to be safe. Why the hell didn't the guy give him any support now? Trace had suspected that he was playing both sides of the fence here.

Callahan was fairly certain of the reason Douglas so carefully covered his ass. Fear. Fear that Trace would go off the deep end again and kill someone or get someone killed. No one wanted to take the blame for allowing him this much rope. And yet, no one who'd been involved with the Gamekeeper's previous case wanted to take the risk that Trace might be right.

Screw 'em all. He got out of the car and slammed the door. He would do this alone if he had to. He couldn't let *him* get away with this. Trace knew it wouldn't be over until one of them was dead. Whatever he'd done to piss off the Gamekeeper, besides almost catching him, the bastard definitely had it in for him.

A grim smile twisted Trace's lips. The feeling was mutual. Trace definitely had it in for the Gamekeeper. The sick SOB would pay for what he'd done to Molly. He would pay if it was the last thing Trace ever did.

He paused at Jentzen's door and took a moment to gather his thoughts…or maybe his courage. Not that he was afraid of her, not really. She intimidated him a little. He could admit that. But it was mostly because she reminded him so much of the way he used to be. So sure…so damned confident. Not in the least wowed by his long-ago, legendary reputation. Yeah…that was just a little intimidating.

But what really scared the hell out of him was the fact that she somehow managed to make him want to reach out to her…want to feel again. Dangerous territory for a burned-out has-been whose emotional well-being could accurately be described as beyond repair. He had no business feeling anything but the need for revenge.

Discounting that the idea was extraordinarily stupid, it could also prove hazardous to the pretty detective's health. He'd already gotten one partner killed.

His hand went instinctively to his breast pocket. Damn, he would kill for a cigarette right now. But he couldn't. If he let himself slip…made one tiny mistake, it might start an avalanche he couldn't stop. Smoking would lead to drinking, and then that would result in other lapses he barely warded off as it was.

He would not take that risk.

One day at a time, he reminded the part of him that struggled every hour of every day to keep it together.

He raised his hand to knock on her door, but it abruptly opened. Elaine Jentzen stood before him, looking madder than hell and too damned good to ignore.

She wore khaki slacks today, with a mossy-green blouse. Even with the holster strapped to her shoulder she looked soft and feminine. All that dark hair fell around her slender shoulders like a cape of pure silk. But considering the fury glittering in her eyes, impressing him had been the last thought on her mind as she dressed that morning.

"Good to see you, too," he offered when she said nothing and stepped back to allow him entrance to her home. Her territory. The distinct feeling that he was about to get raked over the coals soured in his gut. Wouldn't be the first time, or the last. Might as well take it like a man.

He followed her into the living room or parlor, whatever they called the main sitting room down here in the South. It was too early for her to offer him a bourbon, but he wouldn't have taken it had she. Good thing she didn't. He couldn't put much stock in his self-discipline lately. He stared longingly at the sideboard where the bottle sat. Just another risk he couldn't take.

The big golden retriever, Sally, lay on the floor by the sofa. She looked up at him with big doe eyes, and her tail swept back and forth on the floor behind her. At least some-body was glad to see him.

"Explain this." Jentzen thrust a wrinkled document at him.

He accepted the single page and stared at it for a time. Well, well. Now it was official. He should have been worried or at least upset by the report, but he wasn't. In fact, he felt calmed by it. This finally proved what he'd been saying all along. It was the Gamekeeper. He wanted to bring Trace down. What better way than to attempt to frame *him?*

He handed the report back to her. "I told you so," he said with no small amount of glee.

She snatched it out of his hand. "Are you out of your mind, Callahan?"

Assessing her stand on the matter wasn't as easy as he'd hoped. When they'd first met she'd been like an open book, but now she tried shutting him out. Understandable, he sup-posed. She was mad, that was clear. But there was more. Dis-appointment, regret, something along those lines. Maybe she'd wanted to believe in him. Doubtful. More likely only wishful thinking on his part.

"What do you want me to say, Jentzen? That I stole the gun and forced Brad Matthews to use it? Think. Is that reasonable? I wasn't even here then."

She tossed the ballistics report onto the coffee table. She opened her mouth to say something else but snapped it shut instead. Before he could think of something else to say that might be useful she whirled away from him and stomped over to the sideboard. She poured a shot of bourbon into a glass and downed it. He licked his lips, wishing she'd pour him one, as well. If she made the offer, how could he turn it down? He wouldn't be able to.... He understood that with complete certainty.

After plopping the glass back onto the tray, she wheeled on him once more. "Did you or did you not sign out that weapon?"

He laughed, shook his head. What was the point in discussing the issue? She'd already made up her mind.

"Answer me, dammit!"

His gaze latched on to hers and he told her the truth. "No. I didn't sign for it. I'm the one who turned it in to evidence in the first place. Why would I need to see it a second time?" A bullet from that weapon had killed his partner...seeing it again was the last thing he'd wanted. There was no way he could have made the connection at the crime scene at the bank...or maybe he simply hadn't wanted to see. Going into that bank and looking at the horror had brought back memories that tugged hard at his ability to keep it together. Smith & Wesson .38's weren't unique in the business of murder. No way could he have recognized it without the ballistics report.

"Then you tell me who would want to set you up like this?" She leaned against the sideboard as though suddenly too weary to remain upright without assistance. Or maybe she recognized the need to guard the bourbon. "And don't give me that song and dance about the Gamekeeper," she warned. "Whoever did this, if it wasn't you, had to have access. A cop?

Have you pissed off someone so badly that he would go to this extreme for revenge?"

"Look." He started toward her but she held up a hand stop-sign fashion.

"Stay right there," she commanded.

He braced his hands on his hips and took a long, deep breath to clear his head. He'd awakened this morning feeling fairly confident for the first time in a long while. He was certain she'd see things his way after finding that letter…a letter that had erroneously been mailed from the university. It was a mistake the school's business office could not explain. That had to prove something. Trace had showered and shaved, thinking that finally…finally he would have someone on his side in this. He'd gone to the hospital and checked on Ramon Johnson. Even asked him about the letter, but he wouldn't talk about it.

And now the one hope he'd had of having an ally in this battle went down the drain in one solid flush.

"You know who's doing this," he told her, allowing his stare to bore into hers. "I've told you it's the Gamekeeper. This is part of the game. He wants me. He intends to take me down."

"Oh, yeah, how could I forget?" She shook her head and made a sound of disbelief. "The infamous Gamekeeper." That dark mocha-colored gaze blasted his. "Why is it no one else suspects this Gamekeeper character? Hell, you can't even prove he exists outside your imagination."

Fury rushed through him, obliterating any sense of calm or reason. He stalked over to where she stood; she visibly steeled herself. "My imagination didn't kill my partner," he said from between clenched teeth.

"You're right," she shot right back. "Your carelessness did."

The truth in her words smothered the fury flaming inside him, leaving him empty all over again. She was right. Molly's death was his fault…no one else's. And here he was trying to drag another partner into the same lethal trap. He had known this uneasy alliance was a mistake from the beginning.

"You know what," he said, his voice strained with the burden of holding back emotions he couldn't bear to feel—emotions he'd thought dead long ago, "you're right. I did get her killed. I won't let that happen again."

He turned on his heel and started for the door. This partnership was over. He would do this on his own. Screw the Bureau. Finishing this alone was the only responsible way.

"Callahan!"

She came after him but he didn't slow until he'd gotten to the door and had no other choice. He reached for the knob, but she halted him with a firm hand on his arm.

"I'm not finished yet." She stared up at him, daring him to argue.

He had to make her see…had to make her understand that getting caught up in this with him was too dangerous. He couldn't risk history repeating itself.

There was only one way he could think to do that. He shook off her hand and grabbed her by the shoulders, pulling her in front of him and then pinning her to the door in one unexpected move. Sally was on her feet and growling in the same instant.

"You're wrong there," he murmured with all the intensity strumming through him. "*We* are finished here. It's over.

There's nothing else to say." If he couldn't scare her off like this…he didn't know what else to do.

She shoved against his chest, the attempt futile since he was far stronger than she was. "Back off," she warned, a new kind of fury glittering in her eyes. "It's okay, girl," she said to her dog. "I can handle this." The dog whined a little as if not quite certain whether to trust her master's judgment.

Callahan stuck his face in the hotshot detective's, forcing her to look him in the eye. "I'm not backing off until this is finished. The best thing you can do is stay out of my way. Got it?"

"You've lost it, Callahan," she accused, her breath fanning his lips, making his battered heart beat too fast. "Flatt's on to you."

He watched those lush lips move as she spoke, and an ache tore through him. It had been so long since he'd wanted a woman…since he'd let himself need. He wanted her so badly right now he could barely resist taking her…but it would be a mistake.

"I'm not afraid of Flatt," he said tightly. "I just want you off this case."

"Forget it. This is _my_ case."

He closed his eyes for an instant to fight the overwhelming need suddenly raging inside him. How had he let this happen? Any hope of intimidating her was lost. He needed her too much…for all the wrong reasons.

And then the last thing he'd expected happened. She went up on tiptoe and kissed him. When he would have pulled away, she grabbed him by his lapels and pulled his mouth harder against hers.

His fingers tightened on her arms...to push himself away, he told himself. But he couldn't. He just wanted to taste a little more...feel her lips moving on his a second longer. She tasted so good...a little like bourbon, a lot like woman. She smelled...she smelled so damned fine. His hands found their way to her slender waist. He wanted to touch her.

Without warning she pushed him away. He blinked, forced his eyes open.

She stared up at him with a primal ferocity that surprised him...and had absolutely nothing to do with desire. "This is over when *I* say it's over. We're in this together. You might not have my trust just yet, but you do have my attention."

Her cell phone shattered the moment, throwing up a barrier between them. He clamped his mouth shut on the argument he would have launched.

She cut him a look that reiterated her demand that he back off, and he did. She moved around him and answered the call.

"Jentzen."

He used the moment to get his act together. He scrubbed a hand over his mouth in a useless attempt at wiping away her taste, then took a deep breath. She'd made her point. She had control...for now.

And he needed her, dammit. No matter how he denied that reality, the fact was he just wasn't strong enough to do this alone.

"We're on our way."

He turned, noting the distinct edge in her voice as she concluded the call.

Her gaze collided with his, and words weren't necessary.

More dead bodies.

And it was only going to get worse.

Chapter 20

Regina Williams lived in a loft in the heart of Atlanta's theatre district. Boutiques and antique stores flanked her building. It was the place all the young ambitious types who'd come into their own financially wanted to be.

A real estate agent on her way to the top, Regina had plenty of neighbors who simply could not believe she would harm a living soul—unless, of course, it was to kill the competition during the sale of a house. Her reputation was that of a shark when it came to business. But she was known for her friendly nature and kind gestures on a personal level. That she had killed two men and then herself was unthinkable.

And yet she had, apparently, done just that.

Both men had been tied to chairs, their nude bodies covered in their own blood. Regina lay on the floor before them, the knife she'd used to slit their throats planted deep within her own chest.

The luxurious white carpet had turned crimson all around the carnage. Otherwise the loft looked as neat and immaculate as the owner had no doubt kept it.

Pristine. Not a speck of dust on any surface. The stainless steel and granite in the kitchen gleamed as midmorning sun splashed through the numerous windows. The bed was made, the pastel-yellow linens the finest Egyptian cotton money could buy. Her walk-in closet offered a bounty of elegant suits and dozens upon dozens of pairs of shoes and other matching accessories.

According to Jillette, a new, sporty, red BMW loaded with every available option filled the spot in the basement garage designated for this loft.

Regina Williams had it all, it would seem.

But that hadn't kept her from dying an ugly, brutally primitive death. Elaine considered the knife protruding from her chest. Definitely not the favored suicide method. It was rare for a woman in particular to kill herself in such a violent manner. This was another case for Walt. He would be able to determine if someone else had stabbed her and then made it look like suicide. Walt never missed a trick. He'd been in this business too long to be fooled.

Looking at the overall scene there were no signs of forced entry. No signs of struggle. According to the parking garage security cameras, the first victim, Scott Santos, had arrived at 7:45 that morning. Twenty minutes later the second victim, Brandon Ingram, had parked in the visitor area and headed for the garage elevator. The smile on both faces had suggested that the two men expected something entirely different than what actually waited on the fourth floor. Sex probably. What else would bring a man to a woman's apartment so early on a Friday morning? She supposed it was possible they'd had business dealings.

Judging by the ligature marks on the wrists and ankles of the two victims they had been restrained rather securely. Regina had used the electrical cords from various small kitchen appliances. She'd then stuffed silk scarves into her victim's mouths. That she had used what was readily available in her home indicated that the murders had not received a lot of thought. She hadn't gone out and purchased items with which to carry out her plan.

The only question was, when the second victim arrived, what had kept him from fighting back? Especially when he'd gotten a look at the other guy tied up in a chair. Elaine surveyed the two men now, careful not to step in the pool of blood surrounding their position. The idea that Regina had tricked the first one, telling him that sex would ensue, appeared plausible. But victim number two would have surely felt something was amiss upon seeing victim number one restrained…unless, of course, the three often participated in ménage à trois type activities.

It was Friday morning, didn't they have to work?

Both men had been wearing business suits upon arrival. One victim's briefcase had been found in his car. The appointment calendar inside indicated he had places, besides here, he'd needed to be this morning. Calls were being made to both men's workplaces. One had been the manager of a local upscale retail shop. The other a health insurance executive.

"Got something for you, DC."

Elaine looked up as Henshaw ambled over to her position. He held an evidence bag containing a letter and an envelope that had been ripped open.

"It's a letter from a physician's office giving the Williams woman the results of some lab work she'd had done recently."

The letter indicated that Regina Williams was HIV positive and would need to come in for a follow-up appointment immediately upon receipt of this notification.

"Call the doctor's office," she instructed Henshaw. "Find out if this is legit." Her heart started to race. This whole setup had an all-too-familiar feel about it. If the letter proved a mistake, then it would be a repeat of Ramon Johnson's situation. What set these last two multiple homicides apart from the first two?

They had found no such misleading letter regarding any part of Matthews's life or the med student's who shot up the beauty salon. What had provoked those shooters? E-mails? The computers were wiped, erasing all traces of whatever had transpired via that medium? She had no way of knowing. Yet.

Young, financially secure. Healthy. A beautiful family. Matthews had had everything going for him. There simply was no apparent motivation. Just like the beauty-shop murders. Med student Marla Sash had been at the top of her class, had a bright future ahead of her in the world of medicine. Why the sudden change in strategy? If this was the Gamekeeper, as Callahan insisted, why had he suddenly started leaving evidence?

Callahan approached her just then. Elaine had to work at keeping the emotions that immediately surged from showing.

What the hell had she been thinking this morning? She'd kissed him!

Instinct…pure instinct. She'd been looking for a way to rattle him, and the kiss had occurred spontaneously. She damn sure hadn't intended to kiss him. It had just happened. And then she'd used it to her advantage. At least, that's what she told herself, to stave off the worst of the guilt for doing something so totally unprofessional.

Flatt's accusation rang in her ears again. He couldn't possibly know she was fighting this strange draw to Callahan. The jab he'd flung at her had been pure speculation. He'd hoped to get a rise out of her, that's all. But that didn't explain why she couldn't get a grip on her crazy mixed-up feelings. Maybe she was simply reaching out to the closest warm body during a time of crisis. Her personal life as well as her professional one was definitely in a state of chaos at the moment.

He was handy, she assured herself. That's all.

"The computer's been wiped." Callahan settled that blue gaze that undermined her defenses so easily onto hers. "Just like the others."

And too damned handsome…that face, rugged and yet so appealing. She blinked. Hated that she couldn't *not* notice the way he looked. Or even the way he smelled. Male and clean and somehow wild and untamed all at the same time.

God, she was losing her mind.

"I guess we'll ship it off to your lab as well," she allowed, then looked away, shook her head at the gruesome scene ruining everything some high-priced interior decorator had accomplished. Anything was better than looking at him. "For the good it'll do us," she added, a thought spoken. According to Douglas, not even the Bureau's top experts could find anything on the CPUs from the other three cases. Whoever had cleaned them had known how to do it the right way.

How could some serial killer have access to that kind of knowledge? She turned back to Callahan. "How would your Gamekeeper possess the skill required to clean a computer's memory like that? Most people aren't even aware that simply deleting information doesn't erase its existence. Who is this guy, Callahan?"

She'd said more than she should have. The look of hope that claimed Callahan's expression told her as much. He wanted her to believe him, to take his hunch—his theory—for what he believed it to be…the real story here.

"Like I told you, I know him, but that's it. I don't know who he is." He shook his head. "We don't know where he came from, nothing. It's as if he simply came into existence one day and decided to start killing people."

"But you know that's not the case," Elaine countered, sensing he was hiding something. "Most likely he'd killed before two years ago but wasn't caught." Her gaze narrowed. "What set the Bureau on his trail?"

Callahan looked away. "I can only tell you that I was given the case."

Whoa, now. That definitely wasn't right. An outright lie. It didn't take a detective to see that one. But for what reason? They were supposed to be working on this case as a team. Partners. What the hell was he keeping from her?

"We'll talk about this later," she promised.

He arrowed her a sideways glance that guaranteed a confrontation. What was up with that? First he does everything within his power to convince her to believe him, now he clams up?

This guy needed a shrink. Badly. Hell, maybe she did, too.

Elaine walked through the loft once more, flipped through Regina Williams's photo albums and the notes to self she'd left posted about, perused her mail, opened and unopened alike. As she did so, neighbors were interviewed. Her employer was located and notified. All were horrified. No one could believe Regina would do this.

Next of kin were informed. A time for final identification arranged.

The employers of the two victims were equally horrified by the news. Both were upstanding employees.

Not a single person involved in this multiple homicide had a prior record, not so much as a parking ticket.

Elaine stood in the bedroom and stared out over the city that she loved. How could this keep happening? The fourth multiple homicide in two weeks. There had to be a connection. Something she'd missed. A rash of mass murders just wasn't normal outside gang turf wars or drug lord wars. Especially considering two of the killers had apparently had everything to live for. But then the latest two had recently had their worlds shattered.

No rhyme or reason.

No connection.

What she needed right now was a miracle.

One she knew with complete certainty would not come.

As she and Callahan took the elevator back down to the underground parking garage she wondered what the two male victims had been thinking as they'd arrived that morning. What power had she held over them to ensure they would come by when at least one had appointments to keep?

Those were questions that might never be answered.

The elevator doors opened to a barrage of reporters.

Elaine and Callahan had to fight their way through the crowd. She had no intention of giving any comments until after she'd talked to the chief. Something she definitely did not look forward to doing.

Questions were shouted to their backs even as a couple of uniforms restrained the mob from following as she and Callahan moved in the direction of her Jeep.

She settled behind the wheel and the ring of her cell phone slowed her hand as she reached for the ignition.

"I wonder who that'll be," Callahan muttered.

She didn't have to wonder. She knew.

"Jentzen."

As she'd suspected, Chief Dugan's stern voice on the other end of the line ordered her to come straight to his office and to bring Callahan with her.

She closed the phone and tossed it back into her bag. As she gave the vehicle's ignition a fierce twist, her gaze collided with Skip's. He stood among the other reporters. Only, instead of screaming questions in her direction he simply stared at her. Tension stiffened her spine. There was something about the way he looked at her.

"Let's get out of here, Jentzen," Callahan urged, snapping her back to attention.

The media circus had turned visibly bloodthirsty, and there she sat, staring.

"Yeah."

She shoved the vehicle in gear and rocketed out of the parking slot. She shot up the exit ramp, her mind still distracted by the way Skip had stared. What the hell was wrong with him lately?

When she would have reached for her bottle of antacid, Callahan had beaten her to the draw.

"I figured you'd need this about now."

She took the bottle from him, cutting him the sharpest glare she could with her thoughts fragmented as they were.

"Thanks," she muttered, but she didn't mean it.

"We all have our demons," he commented, no longer looking at her. He faced forward, purposely avoiding eye contact.

She took a badly needed swig of the soothing antacid and tossed the plastic bottle into the back seat. She merged into the heavy traffic. It was Friday, everybody had places to go, things to do, anticipation of the weekend burning in their bellies.

Saturday and Sunday would be like any other workday for Elaine. Murder cases didn't allow for time off. Death didn't take holidays.

She pushed all the things she knew she should do, like checking on her parents and her sister, talking to her brothers, simply taking care of herself, to the farthest, rarely visited area of her mind. There was no room for anything else right now. Whatever baggage cluttered Callahan's personal life, as well as this bizarre attraction brewing between them, would have to wait.

Nothing else mattered but the case.

The chief wasn't alone when they arrived at his office. Detective Flatt, the son of a bitch, and Supervisory Special Agent Douglas waited with him.

"We need a break in this case," John Dugan said to her.

She resisted the urge to say *no shit*. "Yes, sir, I'm well aware of that need."

"Then why aren't you doing more, Detective?"

This from Flatt.

She turned a lethal glower in his direction. "Don't take your temporary position too seriously, Flatt. As *you* well know, I am the best detective in this department. If there's evidence to be found, I'll find it."

Before he could belt out a comeback, the chief held up a hand to shut him up. "This isn't the time for dissention among our ranks."

She rolled her eyes. What the hell? With Flatt there was nothing but dissention when it came to her position as deputy chief. The position he now temporarily held.

"You haven't voiced an opinion, Agent Callahan," Douglas piped up. "What's your thinking?"

Elaine had to bite down on her bottom lip to stifle a smile when Callahan gave his superior a look that said, Like you care.

"I think you know what I'm thinking," he said matter-of-factly.

"And how do you feel about his conjecture, Detective Jentzen?"

She considered Agent Douglas for a moment before she answered. There was something about him she didn't trust. Maybe it was that arrogant smile. Or the designer suit he wore. He looked too polished. Too smug for his own good.

Though she'd never met him before this case, she disliked him immensely. Maybe she had Callahan to blame for that.

"Right now it's the best scenario we've got."

Flatt sucked the air out of the room, his gasp of shock so damned loud Connie probably heard it through the closed door.

"There is no evidence to suggest Callahan is right," he thundered as soon as he'd managed to exhale.

"Give me something to go on, Elaine."

Her gaze connected with the chief's. To say he startled her by using her first name during a meeting would be a monumental understatement.

"That's just it," she admitted. "There is nothing to go on. No connection. Isn't that the Gamekeeper's MO?" She directed the question at Douglas.

He smiled that condescending smile again. "It is. But are we dealing with the Gamekeeper here or simply poor police work?"

Fury detonated inside her.

"What about the erroneous letter from the university?" the chief put in quickly, before she could tear into Douglas. "When Flatt spoke to Jillette he indicated an equally damning letter had been discovered at the latest scene."

She held back the words she'd wanted to hurl at Douglas. Her annoyance at Jillette reporting directly to Flatt took priority. "We don't know whether or not the letter from Williams's physician is erroneous or not. Henshaw's checking on it."

"Henshaw just confirmed that the letter was inaccurate," Flatt said with a smirk. "The call came in just before you walked in the door."

Disappointment kicked aside her fury for the moment. Why would Henshaw call Flatt instead of her?

"So, I guess we have a connection between the last two. Both murder sprees were set off by erroneous information that made the killer believe he or she had nothing to live for." The chief uttered the conclusion with distinct relief. He was likely thanking the good Lord that he had something to report to the impatient mayor.

"Which means," Douglas said from his position near the window behind the chief's desk, "that the last two cases really have little in common with the first two, both of which appear to have no motivation." He shook his head. "The connection to the Gamekeeper gets dimmer and dimmer," he said to Callahan.

Callahan stood. "We've wasted enough time."

He walked out of the room before the statement had stopped echoing in the air.

Elaine got to her feet uncertain whether to follow her partner or wait to be dismissed by her chief.

"I'm not sure keeping him on this case is such a good idea," Douglas said to Dugan.

John Dugan pushed up from his chair, his gaze fastened on to Douglas's. "You sent him here to do a job. Put him under my jurisdiction. Until I consider his participation a risk, he will stay on the case."

Elaine smiled. "Like my partner said," she added, "I think we've wasted enough time."

She walked out with the knowledge that Dugan had her back. And she had Callahan's.

It was past time she listened a little more carefully to what he had to say. And she would know what he was hiding…one way or another.

Chapter 21

Elaine drove to her house. It might be a mistake but it was the only place she could trust that no one, absolutely no one would be listening.

She parked in the driveway and reached to open the vehicle door.

"If this is going to be a repeat performance," Callahan said, waylaying her exit, "I'd like to have some advance warning."

She looked at him, too annoyed to let that killer smile turn her inside out as it usually did. At least, that's what she told herself. Unfortunately it was a lie. "Don't give up your day job, Callahan, you'd never make it as a stand-up comic." Then she got out, without giving him the opportunity to formulate a comeback. She strode straight up to her front door and went inside.

Sally greeted her, tail wagging, big eyes hopeful. "Later, girl," she promised as she reached down and scratched behind those attentive ears. They would take a nice, extralong run tonight. Understanding that the scratch behind the ears was all she would get just now, Sally sauntered off to lie on the cool floor next to the sofa.

Callahan came inside and closed the door, garnering nothing more than a glance from Sally. She was getting used to him—not a good thing.

"Coffee?" Elaine could use a cup herself. Going for another bourbon was out of the question. She'd paid dearly for that mistake. Her hand went instinctively to her stomach. If the antacids ever stopped working completely she'd be in serious trouble.

"Coffee sounds good."

Callahan followed her into the kitchen. He'd never been past her living room, so, like any good investigator, he took a moment to survey his surroundings, likely concluding certain things about her based on what he saw. Like the dirty dishes in the sink that needed to be loaded into the dishwasher. Or the dead cheese on the counter that she'd forgotten to stick back in the fridge last night. She tossed it into the trash, along with the partial loaf of sliced bread that had expired two days ago.

She went through the steps and set the coffeemaker to brew. It was old and looked as if it had survived a war, but she loved it. No matter how fancy the newer models, she doubted a single one would brew coffee like this one. Or maybe it was the accumulated buildup from the years of use that made the coffee taste so good.

"I appreciate you backing me up with Douglas."

Sally lumbered in just then and took up a new position, this one under the kitchen table. She liked being where the action was. Not that there was going to be any action, at least not the kind that had taken place that morning. Elaine cringed inwardly at the memory of her fool mistake.

"I didn't do it for you, Callahan," she said to him, determined to get things back on a less intimate level. "I did it for the case."

He nodded. "Well, thanks, anyway."

"You do understand that Henshaw will have to give that report to the chief today." She had actually expected the subject to come up today. She'd given the report back to him and told him she didn't want to be anywhere around when the chief saw it. In retrospect, she decided that might be why Henshaw had contacted Flatt directly about the letter, to keep his mind off the missing-in-action ballistics report. But her old partner wouldn't be able to keep that damning report under wraps past today. Shit would hit the fan when the brass got wind of that one.

"I was surprised he hadn't turned it over already," Callahan admitted.

He'd apparently braced for the same thing she had in that meeting with Dugan, Flatt and Douglas.

"Has Douglas always been such a jerk?" She reached into the cupboard and selected a couple of coffee mugs. She needed Callahan relaxed before she hit him with the real questions she wanted to ask.

He laughed softly, derisively. "Pretty much. He and I don't really like each other, never have. He made field supervisor, a post I definitely didn't want, but I always got all the glory." One of those lopsided half grins quirked his lips. "He likes that I'm not so popular anymore."

Elaine could definitely sympathize with that scenario. Flatt and Jillette had given her hell for getting the promotion to deputy chief. She knew with complete certainty that Flatt would do most anything to make her look bad. Just another reason she had to be especially careful on this case.

"No wife or girlfriend?" she heard herself ask. Damn! What was wrong with her? That question was far too personal.

He moved his head side to side. "No time for a wife." He shrugged. "As far as girlfriends go, I suppose that depends upon the definition of the term."

She didn't need any further explanation on that one. What Callahan was saying to her was that he didn't do relationships. Quickies, one-night stands, but no committed entanglements.

She considered him a moment as the scent of fresh-brewed coffee filled the air. He didn't flinch, just let her look. "So how do you deal with not being so popular anymore?" She'd heard about his reputation. He'd been called a superagent. The best the Bureau had to offer. Two years ago he'd not only lost his partner but he'd taken a hell of a fall from grace. Few egos could take such a tumble without serious damage.

But then, she'd seen the damage he'd suffered. The way he held his drink that first time he'd come to her place. He'd wanted to gulp it down and have another, but he'd resisted. And then there was that constant struggle with smoking. She'd almost forgotten the way he'd looked when he'd had to go back into that bank to view the crime scene. She hadn't seen him look so panicked again, but she got the distinct impression he barely controlled the reaction.

Without warning his gaze turned rock hard. "Don't try to distract me, Jentzen. Whatever's on your mind, just spit it out."

So much for that strategy. "You're not telling me everything you know about this Gamekeeper character. This is your chance, Callahan." She filled one mug with coffee, then the other. "Don't waste it," she suggested, her gaze every bit as determined as his. "It might not come along again."

For what felt like a mini-eternity they visually squared off, neither willing to give an inch. While the coffee cooled on the counter.

Finally he spoke, "There is more. But I need to be sure you really want to know all there is to know. I've never been one to believe that what you didn't know couldn't hurt you, but in this case it's true."

She laughed, the sound forced by the muscles constricting in her throat. The emotions glimmering in those blue eyes just then set her on edge. "I don't see how we can keep working together unless all the cards are on the table. For the record, it's my opinion that knowledge is power."

He shrugged. "All right." He paused, whether for the effect or simply because he found what had to be said difficult, she couldn't be sure. "I told you the truth when I said I didn't know his name. I didn't have clearance for that information."

Clearance? She frowned. "What the hell does that mean?"

"It means that the Bureau got the Gamekeeper case by default. The public wasn't supposed to have known about him."

She gave him a look that said, keep going, no more dramatic pauses.

"Two years ago when he went on his killing spree, there were a lot more victims than the seven the media learned about."

Dread congealed in her gut. Definitely not what she'd expected to hear. "How many more?"

He flared his hands. "I have no idea. I didn't have clearance for that, either. Dozens maybe."

Another choked laugh emitted from her throat. "You have no idea? Don't be so damned evasive, Callahan, spit it out, as you say."

He leaned against the counter next to the sink and started to tell his story, as he did, his expression turned distant, as if he were back there…two years ago…reliving a nightmare he'd as soon forget.

"The case got dumped in my lap after the fourth murder." Lines furrowed his brow. "I think they knew I could find him…wouldn't stop until I did. They were counting on the reputation I'd built. But what they didn't count on was the Gamekeeper's resourcefulness."

In the moment of silence that followed, she started to ask who he meant by *they* but then he continued. Her heart picked up a couple of extra beats in anticipation.

"NSA couldn't risk being involved. Any connection to them would have been devastating to the ongoing program."

"NSA?" Elaine lifted a skeptical brow. "You mean the National Security Agency? As in top-secret code breakers, government NSA?"

He nodded, just once, but there was no mistaking the gesture. "The Gamekeeper was—is—part of their mind-control research. They knew he was mentally unstable when they enlisted him. Hell, they found him in a maximum-security in-stitution. But they needed him so they took him."

"Why was he in an institution?"

"He killed his parents when he was a kid. Burned down the house while they slept. Killed one of his foster parents be-fore they locked him away."

"So he'd been locked up like that since he was a kid?"

Callahan nodded. "Since he was ten years old."

Damn. Ten years old?

"But he's a genius of some sort. Could manipulate people through primitive but intensely powerful mind games. That's what got NSA's attention. So they seized control of him and put his genius to work in one of their defense research programs."

"Somehow he escaped two years ago?" Elaine shuddered at the idea.

"He actually started playing his secret games about four years ago, but they didn't realize it was him until he appar-ently disappeared."

"Two years ago, when you got the case," she suggested.

"That's what they tell me. Apparently his kills had been random and in different cities prior to that. Places they took him to showcase his talent for one reason or another. But when the case in D.C. hit the newspapers, NSA's hands were tied. They had to attempt to recover their asset."

A new kind of horror formed in Elaine's mind. "So you were supposed to capture him alive?"

"That was my first order. Take him alive at all costs."

"But when the killings continued they got desperate."

He nodded. "Nearly a dozen people died before they amended that order."

"A dozen? I thought only seven people died."

"That's how many the media knew about. The others were kept quiet."

He moistened his lips, Elaine watched the movement, her full attention drawn there for three beats, her heart pounding harder with each one.

"For some reason the bastard enjoyed the challenge I represented," he went on. "Got off on playing with me. I used his whacked obsession to my advantage to lure him closer. Set Molly, my new partner, up as bait." Callahan closed his eyes. "But I screwed up."

Elaine knew the rest. At least what she thought was the rest. The Gamekeeper had recognized the baiting ploy and killed Molly Brubaker.

"He killed my partner just to show me he could, and then he dropped off the face of the earth."

The abrupt change in Callahan's entire demeanor made Elaine want to reach out to him. The look of despondence…of utter defeat gave him a vulnerability that tore at her heart.

She suppressed the urge to touch him. That would be a colossal mistake, one she'd already committed and recognized with glaring certainty. "You said that, for a time, you thought you'd killed him."

He nodded. "I hit him that night, I'm certain. But somehow he survived."

"How do you know NSA isn't protecting him?" She wasn't really into conspiracy theories but she was no fool, either. If he was that important to a particular program, he might well be protected.

"Because they're denying he ever belonged to them now,"

he admitted, with obvious reluctance. "It's as if two years ago never happened. The representative we dealt with then is out of the picture. The powers that be now insist he wasn't one of theirs. That he was part of some rogue research that had never been sanctioned. They've taken themselves out of the equation. We can't prove the Gamekeeper is or ever was connected to them. The Bureau would like to walk away from it, as well, by insisting that the Gamekeeper died two years ago. But I won't let them. I know this is him. He's back to finish what he started two years ago."

"To defeat the one player who didn't fall the last time," she guessed. "You're the only one who could get close to him, maybe even beat him at his own game. He can't let you live." The epiphany struck with heart-stopping impact. That was the answer. That's what all of this was about. A kind of fear slid through her veins. The Bureau, NSA, they were going to let this happen...let Callahan risk his life to end this when they knew he wasn't up to par. They didn't care.

Oh, God. This time he was the bait. The Gamekeeper had started playing his games again, and they allowed Callahan to jump right in the middle of it, knowing he couldn't possibly win this round. They did this in hopes that if Callahan got his and the Gamekeeper survived, at least maybe he would be satisfied. Even though Douglas had suggested that perhaps Callahan needed to be taken off the case, he'd never had any intention of allowing that to happen. But the chief and Flatt, the dumb bastard, would remember that the Bureau had never really believed this case was about the Gamekeeper.

"They know this is going to end badly."

She hadn't realized she'd said the words aloud until Callahan responded, "They know."

"How can we stop him?" She lifted her chin in defiance of the trepidation settling into her bones.

"No one can know I've shared this with you," he warned. "I'm reasonably sure I know too much and that my survival is not likely, no matter how this turns out."

A new kind of tension propelled her instincts to the next level. "I know there are books and movies written about this kind of thing all the time, but do you really believe you'd be executed just because you know the truth?" Okay, she couldn't quite make that leap. It wasn't that she didn't believe him; she did. She believed every word he'd said about the Gamekeeper. It was not outside the boundary of reality that the government would go to extreme measures to develop new weapons for defense. Some measures would likely not be accepted by the people, thus those instances would be kept secret whatever the cost…to an extent. To kill an FBI agent to keep him quiet, well, she just couldn't go there.

"Indulge me," he urged. "No one is to know what I've told you. Not even Henshaw."

Elaine chewed on her bottom lip as she considered what he was asking of her. The chief had backed up Callahan. If she told Callahan that, would it change his mind about keeping this secret? No, she could see his determination on the subject.

"For now I'll agree to your request," she allowed. "But," she continued, noting the way his gaze narrowed, "if I feel keeping this secret jeopardizes the case in any way, I will take it to the chief."

For several moments she worried that he intended to argue the point, then he relented. "Fair enough."

Elaine had a feeling that fair had no part in this investigation. She and her entire department had been misled. For that she was angry. But it wasn't Callahan's fault. He was trying to play by the rules that had been thrust upon him. That he'd confided in her earned him a good deal of her trust. It might be a mistake, maybe even the biggest one she'd ever made, but she would take the chance.

The whole story he'd just given her could be a sham. Something he'd made up to win her support. But she didn't think so. His eyes were actually what convinced her. There was no way anyone could fake the kind of pain she'd seen in his eyes. Whatever else he was, Callahan was just a man. He'd let his need to trap a killer get his partner killed, but he hadn't done it alone. He'd been set up. For that reason he owed himself forgiveness, but she doubted he'd ever give it. Since the world could not know the truth, no one else was going to be offering any, either.

He picked up the coffee she'd poured and took a long swallow. She imagined it was cold by now, but the caffeine would still do its job. With that in mind she picked up her own mug and drank until it was empty. The tension in the air of her kitchen was too thick just now for additional conversation.

"What's next?" she asked eventually, certain he must have a strategy.

"We see if he left us any other clues." Callahan set his cup on the counter. "That's the way he plays. At first there's nothing. After he watches you squirm for a while, then he gives you something to renew your self-confidence, to ensure your continued interest. Something to keep you on the hook."

"Like the letters."

Callahan nodded. "There'll be more this time. A little something extra. He knows how much he can get away with. He'll want to end this soon."

"So as not to risk being caught," she wondered aloud.

"He's only human. He's well aware of that fact. If I had my guess, Ramon's survival was not part of the plan. That's why we've got him under guard. Traumatic amnesia isn't uncommon, but it's usually temporary. He could start remembering things today...tomorrow." He shrugged. "That's why I instructed the doctors and nurses to double-check all new orders."

Realization shook Elaine, making her suddenly unsteady on her feet. When had he done that? Why hadn't he told her? "You were afraid the Gamekeeper would somehow alter Ramon's orders. Maybe order something that would have an adverse reaction."

"You're quick, Detective." Callahan gifted her with that megawatt smile.

She tamped down her annoyance at his jab. She'd only just gotten the information he'd had for two years. Of course she wouldn't be as quick to come up with the scenarios he did.

"Ramon is allergic to penicillin. A dose could be lethal. With most everything computerized in hospitals these days, all one would have to do is hack into the system and change the medicine prescribed for a patient...or maybe the blood type for those receiving transfusions."

Hell, that happened occasionally simply by human error.

Callahan was right. The Gamekeeper could certainly have done something like that and the whole incident would have been blamed on human error.

"That's another reason his mother hasn't left his side even to shower or get a good night's sleep," Elaine reasoned. Callahan had warned her not to take the chance.

"She wants to believe her son was a victim in this." Callahan exhaled a weary breath. "And in reality he is. It didn't take much prompting to put her on guard."

"We should go see what Walt has for us," she suggested. The chief medical examiner would have the bodies from this morning's crime scene on steel tables by now. Since he usually didn't work cases personally, when he chose to he got right on the autopsies.

"You think there's any chance Henshaw will get those DNA results back today?"

"It's not impossible," she admitted, "but it's highly unlikely." DNA analysis usually took weeks. However, the chief had asked a friend in the lab to drop everything and get this one done ASAP. Callahan wanted the seal of the envelope in the Johnson case tested against the analysis he'd had done two years ago on the blood at the scene from the final showdown with the Gamekeeper. He hoped to get a match. If the Gamekeeper had licked the envelope to seal it, his saliva would do the trick.

"You think maybe he has someone helping him?" Elaine had considered that possibility, as well. If the perp orchestrating these murders was in fact the Gamekeeper, as she fully suspected at this point, he could have one or more primary targets assisting like before. And as before, those targets would die by his hand, thus tying the present killings to those he'd carried out two years ago.

"Anything's possible."

He was right. Anything was possible. It was quite possible that she had finally accepted his scenario because she had nothing else and was desperate. She recognized that fault in her reasoning. But Douglas's actions in the meeting that morning had pushed her closer to believing Callahan. Maybe it was because she had always been a sap when it came to championing the underdog.

Whatever the case, it was the best scenario they had at the moment, and she was duty bound to follow up on it.

A ring from the telephone shattered her worrisome thoughts. She jerked back to the here and now. Not her cell phone...her landline.

No one ever called her at home, unless it was family. And even they knew she was never home in the middle of the day.

She strode into the living room but her answering machine picked up before she reached it.

"Elaine, this is Judith. I know you're not home, but call me as soon as you get this message. Can I stay at your place this weekend? I have to get away.... I...I'll talk to you tonight."

For a time after the dial tone had sounded, indicating the end of the call, Elaine just stood there, bewildered more at the tone of her sister's voice than the words. She'd sounded harried as usual, but this time there was more. Desperation. She'd sounded totally at the end of her rope and completely desperate.

"I'll wait outside."

She watched Callahan leave by the front door, Sally cocked her head and watched, as well, before strolling back to her favorite spot near the sofa and collapsing.

Elaine called her sister and assured her that she was more than welcome to spend the weekend, though it was doubtful Elaine would be home much of the time.

Judith didn't care, she just needed someplace to get away. Over the phone she wouldn't go into exactly what she wanted to get away from. Elaine didn't push. She had enough to contend with right now without interrogating her sister. They would talk tonight.

Elaine gave Sally a pat and left, locking the door behind her. Her gaze settled on Callahan as she walked to her Jeep. He leaned against the front fender, the unlit cigarette in his hand. He stuffed it into his pocket and climbed into the passenger seat without saying anything.

She scooted behind the steering wheel, keeping her thoughts to herself, as well. There was already too much information whirling around in her head. She had to sift through it before she added more to the mix.

"We didn't talk about that other thing," he said, his deep voice reverberating inside the confines of the vehicle.

Elaine shivered at the sound and instantly chastised herself for being such a premier idiot.

"What other thing?" She turned the ignition, keeping her gaze conscientiously averted from his. No one liked to hash out an investigation any better than she did. But enough was enough. She didn't want to talk anymore right now. Especially about what she knew full well that he meant.

"We shouldn't let this get personal."

Okay, she was guilty. She'd kissed him. Dammit. But somehow the way he made the statement infuriated her.

She turned her head, stared directly into those piercing blue eyes. "Don't worry. We're not going anywhere near personal."

"You did kiss me," he said, the husky nuances of his tone making the words sound all the more intimate.

She tamped down the automatic urge to get defensive. No way was she going to let him see that he was right to some degree. She'd let him get to her…whatever excuse she came up with there was no denying that annoying fact. But he would never know it.

"That wasn't personal," she said calmly, more calmly than she had a right to. "It was a tactical maneuver. I needed to shake you up, make you vulnerable. I accomplished my goal."

He searched her eyes, her face, taking his time, and then he smiled. Her breath evaporated like early-morning mist beneath the relentless July sun. She hated, hated, hated that he could make that happen with only a quirk of those damned sensual lips.

"You did, indeed, Detective," he said, and her insides went all soft and squishy.

As if plagued by a split-personality disorder, his entire visage abruptly changed, evolved right before her eyes. The transformation took her aback.

"It was a mistake," he said sharply. "Don't ever do it again."

The standoff lasted another ten seconds. She looked away first. Outrage exploded inside her like a dozen tiny bombs set to go off one right after the other.

Then she inwardly smiled, grabbed back control and adjusted her expression to a more professional one. She pulled the gearshift into Reverse but turned to her passenger before releasing the brake and easing out into the street. "Don't worry, Callahan. Real cops learn from their mistakes. We never make the same one twice."

He was the one who looked away this time. Because he knew she spoke the truth. She mentally cheered. Maybe that kiss was a mistake, but he'd enjoyed it every bit as much as she had. Possibly more. And he'd allowed it to happen the same as she had. He was the first partner she'd ever kissed…could he say the same? She'd heard the rumors about the relationship between him and his last partner.

"At least I've never slept with my boss."

Elaine slammed her foot back on the brake, halting the Jeep at the end of her drive. Unadulterated shock prevented the immediate onset of outrage. "What are you insinuating?" He couldn't possibly know—no way. He had to be speculating.

"That you and your chief were once lovers." He turned to her then, a savage gleam of pure satisfaction in his eyes. *"Elaine."*

Fury bolted through her, overshadowing the shock. "Just because he called me by my first name doesn't mean anything."

"You're right," he agreed. "Alone it doesn't mean a thing. But I see the way he looks at you." Callahan leaned toward her. "I know that look, Jentzen."

She turned her face away from him, stared straight ahead, mainly because she was as mad as hell, but partly because she was scared to death he'd see the truth in her eyes.

He leaned closer still and whispered in her ear, "When a man's been that close to a woman it shows. Don't try to deny it."

She drew away, simultaneously turning to glower at him and trying her damnedest not to let him see her shiver with awareness. How could he make her this angry and still have that kind of effect on her? "Screw you, Callahan."

He moved back to his side of the vehicle, then he smiled that irritatingly gorgeous smile that wrecked her ability to think clearly. "Don't worry, Jentzen, I didn't mean anything by it." That penetrating gaze collided with hers. Amusement twinkled there. "It wasn't personal. I just wanted to shake you up. Looks like I accomplished my goal. I guess we're even now."

Chapter 22

Elaine sat in her Jeep for several seconds that night after arriving home. Her sister's car was parked next to the curb in front of the house. Obviously, she hadn't changed her mind about getting away for the weekend. Elaine blew out a flagging breath. It wasn't that she didn't want to spend time with her sister, she just couldn't deal with any more family dramas right now.

She needed time to unwind, to block all the images of murder and mayhem from her mind. What she wanted more than anything else was a long, hot shower and a six-pack of wine coolers. Bourbon would work better and certainly faster but her stomach still reeled from the shot she'd downed that morning.

Oh, well. Sitting out here wasn't going to make the situation go away. Her sister had come for the weekend. Elaine had to face that exhausting reality. She would get no peace tonight or tomorrow night. She knew Judith's MO. Movies and conversation. She thrived on it, would talk any subject to death.

Elaine got out of her Jeep and trudged up the walk, already far too punchy to be good company. At the door, she didn't bother knocking or checking to see if it was locked, her sister would have used the spare key Elaine kept hidden. She would also leave the door unlocked in anticipation of her little sister's arrival. At times Elaine wondered how Judith had managed to survive college and then go on to have four children and still be so naive. Didn't she know there were bad people on the streets? Locked doors were a necessity this day and time. But then, there was always the possibility that Elaine was jaded by cop work.

As she suspected, Judith sat curled up on the sofa with a huge bowl of popcorn. A decades-old classic movie blared from the television set. Sally lay on the floor at her feet, her own bowl of kibbles nearby. The big old dog swished her tail across the hardwood floor once or twice but didn't bother getting up.

Could Sally read her that well? Elaine was spent physically and mentally. Her usual run was out of the question, though she'd made a promise to the animal earlier that day.

"Hey, sis, you're just in time!" Judith smiled widely between mouthfuls of popcorn. "This one's almost over." She pointed to the stack of movies on the coffee table. "We've got plenty more." She reached for her bottled water and took a hefty swig.

Elaine tacked a smile into place. "Hey." She sighed, the evacuation of air taking the last of her strength with it. "I need a shower first."

Judith nodded. "Okay. I'll wait before I start the next one. Maybe I'll check out the Home and Garden channel."

Elaine didn't argue. There wasn't any point. Once Judith made up her mind, there was no changing it. The only hope Elaine had of getting any sleep tonight was by making sure her prim-and-proper sister got so drunk she'd pass out. Judith rarely partook of alcoholic beverages, even wine. Four pregnancies, one right after the other, and months of nursing would do that to a woman. Putting her out of her misery with a couple of good stiff drinks would be relatively easy. Her youngest was no longer breast-feeding. No reason not to go that route.

Elaine checked her answering machine for messages as she made her way to her kitchen. Nothing. Thank God. She didn't want to hear about anything tonight. She just wanted to sink into oblivion and forget this investigation. With that in mind, she snagged a couple of bottles of wine coolers from the fridge and headed to her bedroom.

She stripped and climbed into the shower, not bothering to wait for the water to get good and hot. She chugged the wine cooler, grimaced as it hit her empty stomach. She had to learn to eat first. Damn. She waited for the discomfort to pass, then gulped a few more swallows. All she wanted was to relax and put the past few days out of her mind.

As the water heated up, she leaned against the tiled wall and allowed the hot spray to wash over her. Slowly the gruesome images from four brutal crime scenes drifted away. The voices of dozens of witnesses, all claiming their friends or family would never do such a thing, faded. Autopsy and ballistic reports shifted to some rarely visited recess of gray matter.

But Callahan's voice wouldn't get out of her head. She'd suffered that same malady since the first day they met.

The story he'd related about the Gamekeeper kept intruding. His too-close-to-home speculations invaded next. *When a man's been that close to a woman it shows.* She shivered uncontrollably at the memory of that deep, husky voice whispering in her ear....

She twisted off the top of the second wine cooler and sipped it more slowly but with the same determination. She would make him go away. The hot water started to work its magic, relaxing her muscles marginally. She exhaled long and deep, keeping her eyes closed. She didn't want to think. But Callahan, damn him, just wouldn't go away.

Her heart picked up its pace as she thought of how his lips had felt against hers. She touched her own, licked them. Softer than she'd expected, gentler. He'd tasted like good, hot sex. The kind that came after a fight, fast and furious...frantic. The feel of his chest beneath her palms had startled her. He always dressed in a long-sleeved shirt, jacket and trousers, nothing formfitting or showy, but even that much fabric couldn't disguise his broad shoulders or his lean build. Yet it wasn't until she'd pushed against him that she'd felt the pure masculine muscle. Despite having sat behind a desk for two years and failing to keep up with the aerobic part of his physical training, he was still strong, built with all the right male contours.

Something else she shouldn't have noticed.

That the simple memory of how he'd tasted and felt could have her body tingling with desire made her furious at herself. She opened her eyes and hissed out her frustration. A few more swallows of wine cooler and she admitted defeat. There would be no getting Trace Callahan out of her head. He was there to stay, for better or worse. She just had to make sure that was as far as he went. No matter how attracted to him she felt, no matter how damned long it had been since she'd made love, she could not go down that path.

She set the second empty bottle aside and did what she had to do. Washed her hair, smoothed the soap over her body, noting the tautness of her nipples as well as the sensitivity of her lower anatomy. Somehow she had to regain control of this situation. He didn't want this to get personal any more than she did. One of them had to be strong enough to make sure it didn't happen.

The sad truth was, Elaine wasn't at all convinced it would be her.

Thirty minutes later with her hair dried and her favorite nightshirt on, Elaine joined her sister on the sofa. She chomped on a mouthful of popcorn and washed it down with a third wine cooler.

Since Judith made no move to start the next movie Elaine figured she intended to talk for a while first. Resigned to her fate, Elaine stuffed down more of the popcorn and prayed for the buzz a third wine cooler usually offered.

"I can't do this anymore," Judith announced soberly. She passed the bowl of popcorn to Elaine and stood. Sally quickly scrambled out of her way.

Elaine watched her sister pace back and forth across the middle of the room. She tried to work up the initiative to ask something, anything but she couldn't dredge up the resource. Instead, she observed her fair-haired, older-by-two-years sister as she worked up a head of steam. Judith was the only blond, blue-eyed member of the otherwise dark Jentzen clan. According to their parents she'd inherited some near extinct gene from an ancestor three generations back. Right now those long, blond tresses flounced around her shoulders as she swiveled on her heel and marched in the other direction.

"I'm tired of being nothing but somebody's mother." She halted abruptly and stared down at Elaine. "Not that I don't love my kids and enjoy motherhood, I'm just weary of having absolutely nothing else." She huffed in frustration and started to pace once more. "You don't know how it is."

True enough. Just another reason to keep her mouth shut and let her sister do the talking. Her fury would fizzle soon enough.

"My whole life revolves around diapers and toddler-friendly foods and kiddy cartoons and movies." She flung her arms heavenward as if looking to the Almighty for answers. "I tried to write a check with a crayon the other day for Pete's sake! My mind is junked up with car seats and immunization schedules! I'm just sick of it."

Elaine regarded her somewhat more sympathetically as she made two or three more trips back and forth in front of the sofa. What was going on with this? Her sister loved being a mother. Had scarcely been able to wait for her first child to be born, or any of the others for that matter. She'd focused solely on those children for the past five years. Elaine mentally hesitated, examined her last thought. Maybe that was the problem.

"What does Harry say about this?" Harry had the nerdy professor look down to a science but in a cute way, and he was the kindest man Elaine had ever met. He loved Judith to distraction. Gloated over their children at every opportunity. They had the perfect marriage, just like her mom and dad. Elaine swallowed hard, tried not to consider that maybe her sister's marriage was on the rocks, as well. That would simply be too much. This wasn't supposed to happen. How could Elaine even hope to manage a decent marriage if Judith and their mother couldn't?

"I'll tell you what he says." Judith planted her hands on her womanly hips and glowered down at Elaine. Four children had given her those full, lush curves, just something else Elaine would never have. "He says I'm overreacting. That in a few years the children will be off to school and then I'll wish I had them back home again. He just doesn't understand! He spends all day at the university having intellectual exchanges with students and other professors. He can't possibly understand!"

She started to pace again. The revelation about her husband incited worry in Elaine rather than the amusement she'd expected to feel. Harry and Judith were the most romantic couple she knew. If those two couldn't see eye to eye on marriage and children, the rest of the civilized world didn't have a chance.

"What exactly are you saying?" she finally asked as Judith marched past her once more.

She halted instantly and plopped down on the sofa next to Elaine. "You just don't know how lucky you are to be so free," she said wistfully. "Your career has skyrocketed. I swear, Elaine, you have no idea how fortunate you are not to have tied yourself down with children."

Apprehension knotted in Elaine's gut. Or maybe it was hurt. The wine coolers had kicked in and it was hard to tell. "I want kids," she admitted, her voice shakier than she would have liked. "I just haven't met the right man." She'd be damned if she'd blame her lack of offspring on the job. It was more about not having encountered Mr. Right. Then again, wasn't her lack of a decent social life entirely related to working twelve- and fourteen-hour days?

Don't go there, she warned. It only leads to depression.

What difference did it make anyway? There would be no children in her future. Snagging the right guy would be impossible at this point. Callahan's handsome mug flashed briefly across her mind. She gritted her teeth against the little shot of electricity that followed. He was not Mr. Right, she railed at herself. And even if he was, who would want her now? She was damaged goods.

Judith heaved another woebegone sigh and reached for a handful of popcorn. "I love my husband, Elaine," she said. "I really do. And God knows I love my children. But somewhere along the beautiful journey from walking down the aisle to wiping runny noses and diapering baby behinds, I've lost myself. I don't even exist anymore. I have no career, no hobbies, nothing that defines me as a person. I didn't realize how much so until I got that book."

Things went downhill from there. Judith cried, talked about the book some friend had sent her about finding oneself after motherhood. Elaine couldn't bare it. She cried, too. Partly for her sister and partly for the children she would most likely never have. As had been the case with her mother, Elaine couldn't bring herself to open up about her own problems. Judith needed all the sympathy the two of them could garner. There wasn't room for Elaine's problems. Not just then.

She did the only thing she could. She listened to her sister's troubles and then she got her drunk. Elaine was vaguely aware of the clock striking midnight just before she surrendered to her own overindulgence. She would regret it come morning.

In that last moment of clarity, just before she passed out, she realized she'd not only managed to shut her sister up, she'd evicted Callahan from her head, as well. But then that sexy image went into the darkness with her.

The telephone rang in the dream. Elaine ran as fast as she could, but the phone was always just out of reach. Sally was there, barking like crazy. And so was Judith, only she was sound asleep, unaware of the dream taking place around her.

The ringing came again.

Elaine's eyes cracked open. Pain shattered her skull.

Oh, God. It was no dream.

The phone rang again, and another jolt of bone-cracking pain rattled her brain.

She tried to move but couldn't at first. Finally one leg flopped off the couch. Sally sidled out of the way. Only then did Elaine realize that the dog actually had been barking. Probably in an attempt to wake her master since the phone just kept ringing.

Elaine grunted, then swore as she pushed to her feet. The room spun, and she grabbed the sofa arm to keep from falling. Damn. She hadn't gotten this wasted in years...not since graduating from the academy. That was one celebration she'd just as soon forget. She imagined this one would be every bit as forgettable.

By the time her equilibrium settled, the phone had stopped its insistent noise. She swore again. Damned thing. It was more than likely Harry wondering when his wife would come home. A great husband and father he might be, but four kids could test anyone's patience.

Elaine scrubbed a hand over her face and caught a glimpse of the empty bourbon bottle from the corner of one eye. No wonder she felt like hell. She pressed a hand to her stomach and inventoried her slowly rousing feelings. So far so good. No extreme pain. Other than in her head.

The phone rang again.

This time she stumbled toward it, telling herself she could make it without having to sit down and rest and hopefully without the room spinning.

"Yeah," she muttered when she shoved the receiver against the side of her face.

"Hey, DC, you sound like hell. You sick?"

Henshaw. Damn. Surely there hadn't been another round of murders. Her stomach clenched at the idea.

"No." She cleared her throat. Wished she had a drink of water. "No. I'm fine."

"Look, I got some disturbing news from the chief's pal over at the lab."

The warning sensation came out of nowhere, the force of it very nearly overwhelming.

"I'll have to call you back," Elaine blurted before dropping the phone.

She raced to the bathroom. Barely made it in time to lift the seat before the contents of her stomach vacated. She heaved until there was nothing left to lose, cursing herself for drinking the bourbon, hating the taste of wine cooler mixed with popcorn and stomach acids. She flushed the toilet and sank onto the cold floor.

Unrolling a wad of toilet paper she winced as her stomach knotted and twisted in pain. Now she would pay the real price for her ignorance. She wiped her mouth, blew her nose and tossed the paper. Definitely not as pleasant coming up as going down.

"Idiot," she muttered as she got to her feet.

When she spit in the sink, she didn't miss the crimson color. She'd upset her ulcer. Truly stupid. When she'd brushed her teeth and consumed a hefty dose of liquid antacid to soothe her burning gut without barfing it back up, she got Henshaw back on the line.

"All right," she said, her voice a little steadier now. "What-cha got?"

"You sure you're okay?"

She blew out a breath. "I'm fine. What did the lab say?" She loved the guy, but right now she just wanted him to get to the damned point.

"The guy's calling the chief as we speak. I couldn't get any lead time on this one."

A frown burrowed its way across Elaine's brow, reminding her that she had one hell of a headache. She closed her eyes and forced herself to listen to what her partner had to say. Right now she couldn't imagine anything taking precedence over the hellacious way she felt, but telling him to call back later was out of the question. Not when the chief was about to hear lab results. Staying on top of this case was essential. Flatt would use any little slip against her.

"There was a match to the DNA from the seal of the envelope we found in Ramon Johnson's bedroom. They're testing the one from the real estate agent's crime scene now."

That was supposed to be good, wasn't it? It either matched the Gamekeeper or his accomplice. In either case, they had a suspect who had orchestrated the motivation for these crimes. This was good. Hell, it was great. The first real break they'd had.

"Does the suspect have a prior record?" she asked, hopeful. Callahan had told her he'd entered the Gamekeeper into the system as a serial killer listed under the name John Doe and the case number he'd worked two years ago. Considering that, she didn't expect a name, not really. But the case number would be sufficient.

"No prior criminal record, DC. It's Callahan."

At first Henshaw's words didn't penetrate the alcohol hangover haze clouding her thought processes. Then suddenly it did.

"What do you mean, it's Callahan? He's the one who insisted we expedite the analysis. I don't understand. What're you saying?"

Somewhere deep inside, she already knew exactly what her partner meant. Her heart started to pound in time with the throb in her skull. She braced herself against the table that held her telephone and answering machine. This wasn't right.

"The DNA was a match to Callahan's. He's the one who licked the envelope. I had no choice but to call Flatt when I couldn't get you the first time I called. He's looking at the ballistics report right now, too."

Everything inside Elaine suddenly stilled. The pain vanished. "I'll need a copy of that lab report," she told Henshaw. "I'm going to get Callahan and then I'll meet you at the station."

"I don't know if that's such a good idea," he said hesitantly. "He's in this up to his eyeballs, DC. He might have gone over that edge again."

"I'll take my chances." She hung up before Henshaw could argue further.

She glanced at the clock—8:15. She could reach him in less than half an hour if she hurried and then broke every speed limit between here and his low-rent address.

Judith would sleep it off. Probably be at home with her husband and kids before Elaine got back this afternoon…or tonight, depending upon how things went.

She jotted her sister a quick note explaining that she had to get to work. Ten minutes later she was dressed and ready to go. Sally waited at the door, the mournful look in her eyes indicating that being put off wasn't an option. Knowing she didn't actually have time, Elaine took the patient animal on a brisk walk around the block. Sally did her business, which Elaine efficiently cleaned up. As quickly as possible, she had Sally back in the house, had climbed into her Jeep and was backing out of the driveway.

Twenty minutes. She could be at Callahan's place in twenty minutes. She had to get to him first, had to warn him…or arrest him.

The cop in her warred with the woman. She had to look at

this objectively…had to be sure which route was the best to take. Trust him or take him in…

Instinct would have to be her guide, but whatever happened she had to get there…fast.

Chapter 23

Round and round they go, where they'll stop no one knows.

He laughed and laughed as he watched the lovely Detective Jentzen hurry away from her home.

She had no idea what came next.

Had no clue what he would do.

Oh, the wicked web he did weave.

So perfect, so genius.

He was so very close now. Almost to the pinnacle.

He hugged himself and felt his body grow aroused. This was so much fun! Nothing could compare.

His puppets were all dancing to the music he played. Not a one could make a single move without his command.

Callahan…poor Callahan. What a pathetic existence. But soon it would be over. The grand finale would come and then it would be finished.

Callahan would be released from his misery.

A special kind of hell awaited him.

The Gamekeeper smiled.

A very, very special kind of torture.

Oh, it was too perfect. Too, too perfect.

He couldn't wait for the ending. Anticipation rushed through him. Time to play.

Chapter 24

Trace sat at the bar alone. He looked from the bottle that waited on the counter to the mirror behind the rows of glasses on the wall a few feet away. He wanted a drink almost more than he wanted to take his next breath…but he'd been fighting the urge since the place opened that morning. He twirled the cigarette in his hand and thought again about lighting it. With maximum effort he resisted the impulse.

The guy behind the counter had looked a little startled when Trace made the order, after all, it had been eight in the morning. Since then he'd come by every fifteen minutes or so and asked if Trace might like a cup of coffee. Trace wondered if the guy recognized the battle taking place and worried that a loser might soon appear.

He stared at his empty shot glass and then he laughed softly. He'd been seriously one-upped this time. Here he'd

thought he was so smart. That he knew just how the Gamekeeper would play this out. Man, had he been wrong.

Now he was seriously screwed.

The analysis of the envelope's seal from the Johnson crime
scene had come up with a DNA match, all right. Special
Agent Trace Callahan. Douglas had called with the news. Apparently the lab had called him first. He'd probably demanded
that he get word before the locals.

In any event, Trace was now officially suspended. His orders were simple. He was to report back to D.C. pronto and
begin psychiatric counseling. A decision would be made
based on whatever additional evidence was discovered, as to
whether he would be prosecuted or reinstated.

Yeah, right.

He knew the deal. This whole thing had been a setup.
Maybe some would say he was on an ego trip to suggest such
a thing, but Trace knew. Dammit, he knew. These murders,
every damned one of them, had been for one thing only: to
lure Trace back into the game.

The idea that innocent people had died sent a blast of fury
through him. If the Gamekeeper wanted him why hadn't he
just come after him? Games weren't necessary.

But deep down Trace knew the reason. It was the way the
sick bastard operated. Those assholes at NSA should have
kept their psycho asset under lock and key and heavy guard.
He never should have been allowed free access to the outside
world. Codes, mind control, it was all just one big game in a
laboratory setting. But this was real life. The Gamekeeper was
out there killing people.

No one wanted to own up to the mistake. Hell, the only

reason the Bureau was involved was to make sure the guy was finally stopped and to keep Trace quiet. He'd warned Douglas that he would bust this thing wide open if they didn't let him do this. He had agreed, but not a single living soul was to know the truth of where the Gamekeeper had come from.

But Jentzen knew. Telling her was likely a mistake. Trace had put her in jeopardy by giving her that knowledge. But he'd needed her on his side, needed her trust.

For all the good it did him now. His threats to reveal the truth were useless. The evidence, the only evidence they had, implicated him as the motive behind the killings. He wondered vaguely what the chances were that Jentzen still believed him.

His mind replayed all that he'd learned about her and somehow, despite his current circumstances, he had to smile. She was beautiful. He liked the way she moved…the sultry, sexy way she talked. Not that she tried; sensuality just came naturally to her. She wasn't even aware of it, he'd wager. She played by the rules and worked hard.

The idea that she and Chief Dugan had been involved intruded into his thoughts. He couldn't be absolutely certain, but he was reasonably sure. Dugan looked at her the way a man did when he had intimate knowledge of a woman. Maybe that had been her one slipup. The one wrong step in an upwardly mobile career so spotless even Mother Teresa would be intimidated.

Jealousy flamed inside him, and Trace had to laugh at himself. Dugan was a well-respected man who had plenty to offer a woman like Jentzen. Trace, on the other hand, was pretty much nothing. He'd screwed up his career. He'd hurt people. He had nothing to offer anyone.

For the first time in a long time he wished he could change that. He wanted to know Elaine Jentzen inside and out. He wanted to touch her, to make her come apart in his arms. His body reacted to the thought. God, he wanted her.

But she deserved better than him.

Besides, he had a job to do. One he most likely would not survive. And that would be okay, as long as the Gamekeeper didn't survive, either.

"Coffee, please."

Trace looked up at the sound of Jentzen's voice. She smiled at the bartender and then made her way to the stool next to Trace.

"You're a pain in the ass, Callahan, did you know that?"

She didn't actually look at him but their gazes met in the mirror behind the bar.

"I've been called worse," he admitted, wishing now he'd already downed at least a couple shots of the whiskey waiting patiently on the counter.

"You gonna drink that or use it for decoration?" She glanced at the bottle, then at the cigarette in his hand. "The bartender's probably got a lighter if you need one."

"Haven't decided yet." He motioned for the bartender to pour him a cup of coffee when he arrived to serve Jentzen.

She waited until the guy had gone back to the other end of the bar and then she said, "I kicked in your door." She fingered the white stoneware cup. "Just so you know. When I didn't get an answer at your room, I figured…" She shrugged, still toying with the uninteresting cup on the counter in front of her. "Had no idea you were right across the street until I came outside and noticed your rental still parked against the curb half a block down. It didn't take much detective work after that to figure out you were in here."

Trace smiled at the idea of this lady kicking down his door to make sure he was all right. Or maybe she'd thought he was hiding from her.

"Can't a guy go out for breakfast?"

She made a sound of disbelief. "This isn't exactly IHOP."

True. The bar and grill opened at 8:00 a.m. and served coffee along with a variety of sweet rolls and muffins. But he'd seen what appeared to be regular customers walk out of here with at least a half-dozen bottles camouflaged in brown paper bags this morning. Apparently the bartender felt no qualms about selling alcohol at this hour. Who was Trace to judge anyone? He'd come for the same reason all those regulars had dropped by. He'd just been too much of a coward to give in. Trace knew where the alcohol would take him…to hell most likely, and he didn't have the guts to go there.

"I would have been here sooner," she said, her attention still focused on the steaming coffee, "if I hadn't been summoned to the chief's office."

He could imagine what the chief had to say. "You look like hell, by the way." She did look tired, maybe even a little hung over, but she looked gorgeous to him in spite of the obvious fatigue lining her face. But he couldn't say that. In reality he shouldn't have said anything. The observation was more a prompt to get her to tell him what she'd done the night before. Dinner with the chief? A date with some other guy who probably didn't deserve her any more than he or the chief did? What did a gorgeous detective do on a Friday night? None of his business for sure, but he desperately wanted to know.

"Thanks." She shot him a scathing look. "I had to baby-sit my sister last night. Getting her drunk was the only chance I had at having any peace."

Trace smiled. He could imagine that scenario. The Jentzen brood appeared close-knit. Just something else to make him feel alone. He had no one. His smile slid into a frown. Why was it that had never bothered him until he ran headlong into this lady? Maybe he was getting old and sentimental…or senile.

"I need to know the truth here, Callahan," she said after a lengthy silence. "How did your DNA get on the seal of that envelope?"

He sipped his coffee, prayed the caffeine would give him the courage he needed to do this. "If I told you I had no idea, would you believe me?"

She considered his response for a time then she sighed. "I hope like hell this isn't a mistake, but yeah, I believe you. You'd have been pretty stupid to press for an analysis if you were the one who'd sent the letter."

Trace closed his eyes for a second and let her words wash over him. She believed him. Trusted him. He moistened his lips and let his gaze meet hers once more in the safety of that mirror. He could look at her without really looking *at* her. He had to keep this *safe*. "He's setting me up. I should have seen this coming, but I didn't."

"Well, really, Callahan, you're only human." She took a moment to relish a taste of the brew she'd been fidgeting with, then continued, "This guy has clearly been plotting this attack for quite some time."

He turned to her, couldn't resist looking directly into those dark eyes. "Why would you believe me?" He had to know. Needed the reassurance of seeing the emotion in those dark-brown eyes when she explained her reasoning. Even he wasn't sure he would believe this story if it were happening to someone else.

She set her cup aside and swiveled to face him. "We're partners. Partners always back each other up."

Trace stared down at the scarred counter, unable to keep up the eye contact for fear she would see just how much foolish hope her words generated. Or how selfish he wanted to be. He needed her, in more ways than one. Big mistake. "I'll only drag you down with me," he cautioned. He didn't want her getting hurt in this. He'd already gotten one partner killed. He couldn't take that kind of risk again...no matter how badly he needed her. "You shouldn't trust me." Now there was the God's truth if he'd ever told it.

She flared her hands. "Too late. I already told my chief I was with you on this one."

His head came up, regret tightening the band of worry around his chest. "You shouldn't have done that. I'm suspended. I don't want this to damage your career." *Or you,* he didn't say, worry twisting in his gut.

She smiled and his foolish heart, damaged organ that it was, skipped a beat. "The chief told me that, considering the ballistics report and the DNA results, you couldn't be trusted. He said you'd been ordered back to D.C." She searched his eyes then, something vulnerable in her own. "When I didn't find you in your room, I thought maybe you'd left already." She looked away, drew in a shaky breath that confused the hell out of him. "I was...disappointed that you'd leave without giving me the benefit of the doubt."

The urge to touch her…to pull her into his arms and tell her there was no way he would do that was nearly irresistible. "I thought about it." He might as well confess. He'd at first considered leaving…to protect her. But he couldn't do that. Leaving was not an option. Not until he'd finished this. The Gamekeeper had to be stopped.

"There's no other evidence." Her voice was so soft but with an underlying ferocity that compelled him to listen. "Nothing. No connection to anyone by phone or any other means. The computers have all been wiped. We can't prove that the Gamekeeper is even involved in this. What little evidence we have points to you. No one is going to believe us or back us up. We're in this alone." She glanced at the bottle, then at the unlit cigarette he still held. "Do you think you can handle this, Callahan?" She held up a hand to stop him from answering until she'd clarified her request. "Think about what I'm saying for a moment. Be absolutely certain of your answer. I'm fully prepared to back you up as long as I can count on the same. But I need to be sure."

He looked deep into her eyes, told her without saying anything that she could definitely count on him. When he would have reiterated with words what he wanted her to see, the sound of her cell phone stopped him.

She dug it out and flipped it open. "Jentzen." She did that thing with her hand, tucked her hair behind her ear. He loved watching her do that…wanted so badly to touch her.

"I'll be right there." She closed the phone and met his expectant expression. "Flatt wants to see me ASAP."

Well, that couldn't be good.

She put her hand on his, sending a shimmer of heat through him. The unexpected intensity of the reaction startled him.

"Go to my place." She told him where she kept her spare key. "Wait for me there. Use my computer, phone, whatever. I'll be there as soon as I take care of Flatt."

"I'll be waiting."

She held his gaze for a beat longer and then she was gone.

She trusted him…wanted to help him do this.…

The only question was, could he trust himself?

Chapter 25

Elaine met Acting Deputy Chief Flatt at Jimmy's Pub as he'd requested.

He sat alone at a table, a glass of iced tea sweating onto a cocktail napkin nearby.

She glanced around the pub, didn't see anyone else from her department. She needed to call Henshaw and let him in on her plan. Whatever happened, she was in this for the long haul, and she needed her ex-partner's support. With every cell of her being she knew that Callahan was being framed.

Her heart had surged into her throat when he hadn't answered that door this morning…she'd been so damn afraid that he'd left…left without bothering to say goodbye…without giving her the chance to prove she believed in him. She fully recognized that a part of her believed in him for all the wrong reasons, but the cop in her—those well-honed instincts she'd inherited from two generations of law-enforcement ancestors—knew he was being framed. She smelled the setup a mile off. Her conscience gave her no other choice; she had to help him.

Pushing aside those damned softer emotions that immediately rose at the thought of him, she strode over to Flatt's table and pulled out a chair.

"'Bout time," he muttered.

She'd taken all of ten minutes getting here. What did he expect? Saturday-morning traffic had been light. He was damned lucky she was here now. She tamped down the urge to tell him to go screw himself. No matter how little respect she had for the jerk on a personal level, she had to make him believe that she was on his side in this. Otherwise he'd gang up with Douglas and pull her off this case so fast it would make her head swim—the hangover was doing enough of that already.

"I got here as fast as I could." She dropped into the chair and motioned to the waitress to bring her the same thing Flatt was having.

"Did you talk to him?" Flatt took a swallow of his tea, his gaze never leaving hers.

"Of course I did. He's not going back yet."

Flatt lifted a skeptical brow. "He's not?"

She curled her fingers into fists in her lap to keep from reaching across the table and shaking the knucklehead. "Are you kidding, this is his case. He plans to see it through." She glanced around the room, letting her old pal Flatt note that she appeared nervous.

"You did the right thing, agreeing to play this my way," he

said, attempting to keep the condescension out of his tone. It didn't work.

"I have a duty to the residents of this city," she told him, her sincerity genuine. "If keeping an eye on Callahan will help stop these killings, it's my duty to do just that."

Flatt would not know until this was over that the only reason she'd agreed to this meeting was to keep him off her back. After Flatt had left the chief's office that morning, she'd given John Dugan the whole truth. She believed Callahan and if Dugan had any sense he would, as well. Agent Douglas was playing all of them. She didn't tell him about NSA's involvement…but she'd been tempted.

John hadn't wanted to go along with her plan at first. Not that he didn't trust Elaine's instincts on the matter, but he feared she had been compromised emotionally. She'd had to do some fast talking to convince him she and Callahan weren't involved. Part of her had sensed that John's pursuit of the matter had been more personal than professional. He still had feelings for her, as she did for him. Except, she felt fairly confident that his were of a more possessive nature.

She cared for John, would always have the utmost respect for him, even if she didn't always agree with him. But there would never be anything more than that between them. She hated to lead him on, but she needed him with her on this. If she'd made him believe that there might be hope for a relationship in the future, she'd just have to apologize for that later. Right now she had a pattern killer to catch. She refused to call the Gamekeeper a serial killer any longer. She wasn't convinced that he killed because he felt some intense need or yearning to do so.

No, she had a feeling his murder sprees were motivated

more by necessity or perhaps simply to prove he could, rather than out of some primal need.

That he liked playing his games was clear enough, but before she could toss him in the same category as Bundy and Dahmer, she needed to know what he'd actually done behind closed doors for some heartless group of secret agents. Was he merely playing out the games he'd been commissioned to build? Had he been allowed free movement to test those games? She might never know the answers to those questions, but she had to stop him.

Callahan was the only way to make that happen. He knew the Gamekeeper better than anyone. Elaine had thought over all that she knew about Callahan and his nemesis. She'd watched him closely this morning, considered his reaction to this latest turn of events. And then she thought back to that first day at the bank.

Callahan had no choice but to face this situation. Someone had to stop the Gamekeeper, and since no one except Callahan believed it was really him, he had little choice but to do it himself. But he was afraid. No, he was terrified. Elaine had seen the fear in his eyes, though he'd tried hard to keep it from her. In spite of that terror, he would not back off. Not even if it cost him his career.

Or his life.

She had to respect that.

Admittedly, it went way beyond mere respect or admiration for his determination. She had to help him. Not only to stop the killings, but because she simply couldn't turn her back on him. He'd gotten under her skin, had burrowed deep somehow, and she couldn't shake him loose.

It was crazy. Too crazy for words. Here she was, her whole personal life falling apart, and she was hell-bent on getting mixed up with a guy whose history was even more screwed-up than her own.

"I don't want you interacting with Henshaw unless absolutely necessary," Flatt said, drawing her from the disturbing thoughts. "He'll see through you in a New York minute."

He was right on that one. Henshaw wouldn't be fooled, the way Flatt had been. Ironic, she mused. Flatt had no clue she was playing him. What Flatt didn't know wouldn't hurt him. She needed Henshaw on her team. Flatt would be pissed when he found out, but he'd get over it.

"I'd better get going." She left the tea she'd ordered untouched. After tossing a couple bills on the table to cover her drink she asked, "You'll keep me up to speed on Douglas?" Now there was the real reason she had to stay in tight with Flatt. Douglas would be working him, as well. She wholly suspected the Bureau bigwig was doing just that, though the chief remained skeptical on that score. Elaine preferred to cover all the bases.

Flatt leaned forward, stared at her with fire in his eyes. "You keep me up to speed on Callahan's every move, I'll keep you square with Douglas."

She nodded, then turned her back on the man she knew with complete certainty would do anything to make sure he got to keep the deputy chief position. Flatt had a plan. She hadn't bothered going into that with the chief, either. The last thing she needed was him thinking she was paranoid.

But she knew. Flatt had been waiting for a chance like this for months. Now he had it. No way would he turn his back on the perfect opportunity to usurp her standing.

Not when he'd been dying to get her out of the way since the day her promotion had been announced.

A smile lifted her lips. She had his number. The Gamekeeper wasn't the only one who knew how to use a person's weaknesses against them.

All she really needed was to know the Gamekeeper's weakness.

She stopped herself at the front of her Jeep. The abrupt realization made her laugh out loud. How stupid she'd been! It was so damned simple.

She already knew the Gamekeeper's weakness.

It was Trace Callahan.

That's what this was about. All the murders, all the manipulation. Every last move he'd made was about building up to the grand finale: the destruction of Agent Callahan.

And here she was jammed right in the middle.

"Deputy Elaine!"

She looked up, startled from her troubling epiphany. Skip Littles hovered at the rear of her Jeep.

He glanced around nervously. "I need to talk to you." His voice quavered a little. Definitely not the norm for the enthusiastic go-getter.

"Get in." She indicated the Jeep.

He shook his head quickly. "I don't have time," he said, his wide-eyed gaze settling on her as she moved closer. "You have to be careful, Deputy Elaine." He licked his lips, then swallowed. His throat worked hard with the effort as if a huge lump had lodged there.

"Why do I need to be careful, Skip?" She kept her tone soft, gentle. She didn't want to spook him. Something or someone had already scared him half to death. That much was obvious. It wouldn't be the first time she'd seen him get overly emotional over a case.

"I've been watching him," he said. His lips quivered. "I...didn't know for sure at first." His head bobbed up and down jerkily. "But I do now."

"You've been watching who?" she asked cautiously, anticipation burning through her veins. Every instinct went on point. She'd sensed something wasn't quite right with Skip the last couple of times she'd run into him.

"You know who." His eyes searched hers for confirmation. She gave it to him and he went on, "He wants to hurt you, Deputy Elaine. And that FBI fella...Callahan." Skip blinked rapidly, but the action did nothing to dispel the emotion glimmering in his eyes. "I tried to distract him, but he's too focused."

Another jolt of adrenaline seared through her veins. "Tell me how you interacted with him, Skip." She reached out slowly, placed her hand on his arm. "This is very important. If you can help me...I would forever be in your debt."

He stared at her hand for a long moment but he didn't draw away. Finally, those big eyes behind the megathick lenses settled back on hers. "He brags about his games in a certain chat room." He attempted to swallow again. "It's a secret place, Deputy Elaine, you can't go there."

Elaine thought a moment. She had to be very, very careful how she approached this. "Okay, Skip. I understand." She patted his arm and slowly drew her arm back. Then she looked straight at him, allowing him to see the desperation in her eyes. "Can you help me get there?"

For three excruciating beats she felt certain he would bolt, then he nodded, once, twice, a third time, his expression growing more determined with each movement.

"He'll probably know you don't belong," he warned. "He's smart like that."

Elaine smiled. "You're pretty smart yourself, Skip."

His face went somber. "Not as smart as him. No one's as smart as him."

She nodded once, showing that she understood what he meant. The Gamekeeper's ability was not to be underestimated. "But you'll help me?"

He let go a heavy breath. "I will. But you have to promise me you'll be very, very careful."

"You have my word."

"Okay." He took a deep breath, then let it go. "Wait until late…he only shows up late at night." He cleared his throat. "You go to KillerGames.com. You have to look closely or you'll miss it. There's a hidden pull-down menu, its location changes frequently, so you'll just have to play around at the main page until you find it."

"Got it."

"Select *buzz*. That'll take you to the chat room entrance, but then a dialog box will appear and ask for the password."

Sounded easy enough so far. "What's the password?"

"Deadend. All one word." He spelled it for her just to make sure she got it.

"Okay, so I enter the password. What happens next?"

"You'll have to give your screen name. If you don't have one you can make one up. They'll know you're new. But there's always someone new popping in."

He dropped his head as if imparting the information had taken all of his strength, leaving him helpless to continue any sort of interaction, even eye contact.

"Thank you, Skip. I really appreciate you helping me out like this." She bit her lip, wasn't sure she should press the issue, but the cop in her wouldn't let it go. "How did you find him?"

His head came up, but his eyes didn't meet hers. "I have to go."

"Wait." She took hold of his arm before he could get away. "I need to know, Skip. It's important. How did you find him when no one else has been able to?" Not the police, the FBI or even NSA. Now that was an accomplishment.

Skip's expression fell into one of defeat. "I didn't, Deputy Elaine. He found me."

Chapter 26

The better part of the day had passed before Elaine made it home. Following up on Skip's information had gotten pushed to the back burner. She'd insisted on driving him back to the paper. He'd promised to stay there until he went off duty, then he'd go straight home. She couldn't be sure he hadn't been fooled by some chat room freak, but she had to be certain.

She'd had an emergency meeting with Henshaw. Flatt had given her orders not to talk to Henshaw, but she just couldn't do that. He was her partner, her real partner. She owed him the courtesy of keeping things square between them…even if she didn't need his help. And she definitely needed him. She'd given Henshaw the lowdown and told him about Skip. He would look into the Skip situation also, and he agreed to do what he could to funnel any info to her he discovered Flatt holding back. That was the thing with Flatt, Elaine just couldn't trust him.

Henshaw would have her back.

The lab had confirmed that the analysis of the second envelope's seal revealed the same—Callahan's DNA. She and Henshaw had discussed a number of ways the Gamekeeper could have gotten his hands on Callahan's DNA. A quick call back to the lab to run the possibilities by the chief's friend, and they'd come to the conclusion that the most likely scenario would be from Callahan's toothbrush. Breaking into his room at the dump he stayed in wouldn't be a problem.

Before she'd been able to call Callahan, the chief had convened a special meeting to announce that an emergency task force was being assembled. Flatt would assume the role as primary liaison between Atlanta PD and the Bureau. To say that Elaine had been furious would have been putting it mildly. But she understood what the chief was doing. This was about her insistence on backing up Callahan. The chief might not outright disagree with her at this point but he intended to cover his ass…as well as prove his point. He didn't like what he sensed was going down between her and Callahan.

Well, that made two of them. Elaine didn't like it, either, but she was damned powerless to stop it. Putting personal feelings aside, she had a job to do. Her best bet at getting to the Gamekeeper was through Callahan. He was the key to all this. He had to be in the loop. Keeping him that close gave her little hope of slowing the fire building between them. It was a calculated risk; one she had to take.

She shoved the vehicle door open and got out. Callahan's rental was nowhere around, but that didn't surprise her. No one besides the chief and Henshaw could know they were working together. Flatt knew what she wanted him to know.

Callahan had most likely parked on another block and walked over. She hoped that's what he'd done. If he'd decided to go out on his own, she'd be in serious trouble with the chief. Not to mention, considering what Skip had said, he could very well be in grave danger. Then again, one of the reporters at the paper could be jerking Skip around. It wouldn't be the first time. But she had to follow up on *every* lead. Callahan had better stick to their bargain. She had far too many other problems to deal with just now to be putting up with any crap out of him.

Her worry was for naught. Callahan sat at the desk in her dining room, his attention focused on the computer screen. He looked up when she opened the door.

"I was beginning to think you'd forgotten about me." He managed a smile, but his expression gave away the uncertainty behind the statement.

The Bureau had suspended him, kicked him off the case. NSA pretended the problem didn't even exist. She could see how he might worry that Atlanta PD would drop the ball with his name on it, as well.

"Douglas asked the chief to institute a special task force," she told him by way of explanation.

Callahan pushed back from the desk, leaving the file he'd been studying on the screen.

"What's this?" She pointed to the monitor.

He stood, set his hands at his waist and cleared his throat. "I…hacked into NSA's database." Before she could demand to know why the hell he'd taken a risk like that, he went on, "I routed my access through dozens of other IDs, it'll take their people days to pinpoint yours. By then this will be over one way or another."

There was no point in yelling at him. It would be like scolding Sally for making a mess while Elaine was gone.

Speaking of animals…she glanced around the room.

"Where's Sally?"

Callahan pointed under the desk. "She's taking a nap. I guess I was too much for her."

Elaine crouched down. "Hey, girl, whatcha doing under there?" She rubbed the dog's sleek back. Sally lifted her head and licked her mistress's hand. Elaine looked up at Callahan. "Did something happen? Is she ill?" Worry knotted in her empty stomach.

He flared his hands, apparently feeling bad for whatever had taken place. "I took her for a run."

Callahan went for a run? Elaine pushed to her feet. "That's great." She hated that she sounded so surprised but he apparently hadn't done that in a while. She'd noticed that he'd gotten a little winded once or twice since they'd started working together. Assignment to desk duty had evidently doused his enthusiasm for physical training.

In spite of her best efforts, she glanced at the sideboard and the full bottle of bourbon there. Judith had apparently put out a new one after the two of them had finished off the other.

"Nothing like a partner who has faith in you," he commented dryly.

"Sorry." And she was sorry. Wait…she glanced around the living room. Wow. Who'd cleaned up? "Did you straighten up?" She gestured to the meticulously tidied room.

"Can't take credit. It was this way when I got here."

Judith. Damn. Elaine should have called and checked on her today. "Did you see my sister?"

He shook his head. "The place was empty when I arrived but she left you a note. It's by the phone."

Elaine started in that direction, then suddenly stopped. She frowned. Sally didn't get up to follow her. The best thing to do was call the vet, she decided then and there. It was bad enough that she was never home. She certainly wasn't going to let Sally go without prompt medical attention, considering how out of character she was behaving. Sally always met Elaine at the door. Always followed her around the house like a shadow.

"Your neighbor, Allen, I believe his name was, came and picked Sally up right after our run. I didn't know he ran with her. I guess she's just tired."

"Oh." Now that made sense. Okay. Elaine mulled over the idea. Sure. Sally had time to rest up before running with her at night. But two good runs right in a row probably had tuckered her out. "Fine. Okay. She'll be fine." The last was more to convince herself than Callahan.

She headed to the table where Judith had left her note. She read it quickly, smiling as her sister went on and on about how perfectly awful she'd felt that morning when she woke. She'd felt terrible that Elaine had had to go to work, so to make up for it Judith had cleaned house. Elaine glanced at the table, noting the lack of dust. She'd had a housekeeper once, but the woman had run off with some Internet boyfriend a couple of months ago and Elaine hadn't had the time to interview another.

At least her sister was herself again. Judith was fine. Sally was fine.

Elaine's hand went to her stomach. She had to eat. Exhaustion clawed at her. And a decent night's sleep wouldn't hurt. Her gaze flicked in Callahan's direction. Not that she figured that would happen with him around.

Worry nagged at her again. "Did you find anything?" she finally remembered to ask. God, where was her brain today? Still anesthetized from the effects of the alcohol, she guessed. There would be no more drinking binges for her.

Callahan glanced back over his shoulder, his attention already intently focused back on his research.

"Not yet."

Why was he being evasive?

"What're you trying to find?"

Breaking into a government system would likely be seen as an act of terrorism considering the events taking place around the globe. Maybe Callahan didn't care if he ended up at Guantánamo, but she sure as hell did.

"I'm looking for anything on the Gamekeeper."

Well, that told her a lot.

"Like what?" She started back in his direction. Something about this didn't feel right. Admittedly she hadn't told him about what Skip had to say, but he didn't know that. And there might not be anything to it. Why was he holding out on her?

"Like what happened to the program he was involved with and where are the researchers who had been in charge of his case."

She stood behind him, studying the screen. "Any luck?"

He shook his head. "The program no longer exists, at least, it isn't mentioned. And the researchers aren't listed on the personnel log."

"So what does that mean?"

He logged out of the system and shut down the computer. Once the screen had gone black, he reached behind the hard drive and tugged loose the cable that provided her broadband service. Then he stood and looked directly at her.

"I think it means that NSA was never involved. I could be wrong. Maybe they deleted the project. Erased any evidence that it ever existed. But what about the researchers? Good scientists aren't just dumped for no reason. They're too hard to come by. I'm beginning to think maybe the group who handled the Gamekeeper was some sort of subversive operation that pulled the wool over the Bureau's eyes two years ago."

More conspiracy theories. "I would prefer to believe that," she confessed. No one wanted to believe their government capable of such a cover-up.

Callahan scrubbed at his jaw. She shivered at the sound of his palm raking across the five-o'clock shadow that stubbled his jaw.

"There is one thing I can do," he began, then hesitated.

"What?" A new tension shimmered through her. At this point anything was better than nothing.

"I can go to the top. To the director and toss out a few accusations."

Well, if that didn't get him imprisoned she wasn't sure what would. "Maybe you'd better think that one over for a bit."

He smiled and she lost her breath. "Maybe," he allowed.

"Look, I don't know about you," she said, doing her level best to get her mind off how good he looked standing there in her dining room as if he were at home, "but I'm starving. I've gotta eat."

"You don't do enough of that, you know."

She shrugged. "I'll make up for it when this case is closed."

Elaine managed to keep her thoughts off the case long enough to eat. The silence was nice. She liked watching him consume his food. There was something primal and intensely male about it. Though he displayed perfect manners, he didn't beat around the bush; the man ate. She smiled. She liked that; had a feeling that he didn't always derive so much pleasure from the essential act.

"You've got a way with ham and cheese, Detective," he said when he'd finished off his third sandwich.

"Thanks." She took the last bite of her first and only sandwich, then washed it down with milk. Her stomach felt immensely better already.

But the rest of her felt heavy with guilt. She couldn't put this off any longer.

"I ran into Skip Littles today," she said nonchalantly, knowing he would hit the ceiling when he heard what she had to say.

"That would be a detective I haven't met," he offered, his gaze narrowed in concentration as he attempted to place the name.

She shook her head. "He's a desk assistant at the *Telegraph*." She laughed under her breath. "He hopes to get a reporter slot one of these days, but so far it hasn't worked out." She had a feeling his buddies, the reporters, were stealing his glory whenever possible and knowing Skip's innocent way of looking at the world it probably happened more often than not. She could see that Callahan wanted her to get to the point. "Anyway, most of us throw him a bone now and then when he's following a case. He's the kind of guy you can't help feeling sorry for."

"Wait, I know." He thought for a moment. "A mop of disheveled hair and glasses, really thick lenses."

She nodded. "That's him."

"Yeah, I've seen him at most of the scenes." His posture changed, stiffened or braced for what she had to say next. He'd evidently already guessed that he wouldn't like it.

She moistened her dry lips. Nothing she could do but spill it. He'd be angry that she hadn't told him first thing. "Well, he came up to me outside Jimmy's today and told me that he knew about the Gamekeeper. That he'd been watching him."

Callahan showed no outward reaction, but she knew with complete certainty that he had gone on elevated alert. Nothing about the Gamekeeper had been released to the press. No one, outside the chief, Flatt, Henshaw and herself even knew about the possible connection to this case.

"Tell me exactly what he said."

Elaine got up and started to clear away her plate. She didn't want to look at him as she said the rest. "He said he'd seen him in a chat room on the Internet. That he knows the Gamekeeper is here for you."

Callahan's fingers suddenly wrapped around her right wrist. "And you've kept this to yourself most of the day for what reason?"

She looked up at him and told the truth. "Because it's probably a hoax. And if it is real, I think he's right. I think you're the real target here and you'd be better off to keep a low profile. Henshaw is checking it out. He knows Skip and the ego-driven guys he works with."

Those long fingers tightened, almost brutally so. "You don't get it. Your harmless little friend might be a pawn the Gamekeeper is using. He could be in serious danger."

She nodded and tugged at his hold. That possibility hadn't escaped her. He blinked and released her as if suddenly realizing how harsh his grip had grown.

"That's why I've got Henshaw watching him. That keeps you a safe distance away and gets the job done at the same time." She wouldn't tell him the rest. She would check that out herself a little later. Skip had told her that the Gamekeeper never came online until late at night. If this was real she wanted to know it first.

Callahan picked up his plate and glass and stowed both in the sink. He turned to her then, his face a hardened mask, one she couldn't hope to read.

"Take me to him. I need to question him personally."

She was shaking her head before he completed the request—demand actually. "That's not a good idea. If the department or the Bureau gets wind that you're still investigating this—"

He took a step closer to her, his posture threatening. His whole demeanor a study in intimidation. "Take me to him, *now.*"

"You can't intimidate me, Callahan," she said bluntly.

"Then do it for Skip Littles," he said cruelly. "Because if he's delivered his message, completed his mission, then the Gamekeeper is finished with him."

He didn't have to say more…she knew what happened

when he finished with someone. But Henshaw would have called her…wouldn't he? The last call she'd gotten was that Skip had gone home.

What if she'd made a mistake?

Her cell phone rang. Where was her purse?

The living room.

She rushed to where she'd left it on the sofa and dug out the compact phone and flipped it open. "Jentzen."

It was Henshaw. He gave his location, an address she didn't readily recognize.

"You'd better get over here, DC. I can give you maybe forty-five minutes to walk Callahan through the place and then I'll have to call this in."

Dread fisted in her chest. "Do we have another…?" She couldn't bring herself to say the rest…but he would know what she meant. God Almighty, this had to end. Somehow they had to stop this madman.

"It's Skip, DC. Skip Littles has been murdered."

Elaine rubbed at her forehead and the throb that had started there. This was her fault. Dammit, she should never have let him walk away after giving her that information. She should have taken him more seriously.

"He left a message," Henshaw went on. "You need to get over here ASAP. I think this game has just moved to a new level."

Chapter 27

Skip Littles had lived in a small efficiency apartment near the newspaper where he worked. Other than a tiny bathroom, the entire place was comprised of one cluttered room without a window. Dark, gloomy. It didn't match the enthusiasm of the man who'd lived here. Man. Designating him as a man didn't feel right. He'd been more a big kid to Elaine. Like a freshman off to his first year of college, determined to make the dean's list.

But that was never going to happen. The plans he'd had would not see fruition.

Newspapers, magazines and books covered every available shelf and table and a good portion of the floor space. Hundreds of clippings and notes related to stories he'd no doubt deemed he might have covered or written better. A mini kitchen occupied one corner, and an array of pizza boxes and other take-out food cartons awaited trash day. Elaine wet her lips and tried to smile past the emotion choking her. Skip had belonged to the same lousy-housekeeper club she did.

A single lamp, which sat on a small table next to the computer desk, provided the only illumination. Skip's body remained upright in a cheap swivel chair, the kind you bought at a discount store for around thirty bucks. The chair butted up to an equally inexpensive build-by-the-numbers generic desk.

In contrast the computer occupying the top of the laminated pressboard workstation was state of the art. According to the label that hadn't been removed from the CPU tower, the machine had lots of memory, the latest and fastest operating system, and a huge flat panel monitor was the icing on the cake. A printer/scanner/fax combination sat next to it. No wonder the wardrobe offerings in the narrow closet were so slim. The guy spent all his money on computer equipment.

Poor Skip had died from a single gunshot wound to the back of the head. No exit wound. A river of blood had poured down his back and pooled on the floor around his chair. Henshaw estimated the weapon to have been a .22 caliber handgun. Since no one in the building had called in a gunshot, he could only assume that the shooter had used a silencer, or perhaps all Skip's neighbors had been out at the time. Henshaw had come to his residence when Skip didn't answer his phone. How had someone gotten to him with Henshaw right outside? Elaine shook her head. Another victim. An innocent, inquisitive man was dead because some freak had used him.

Elaine felt sick to her stomach. She should have anticipated this.

"I found this in his mouth." Henshaw thrust an evidence bag at her.

Skip's mouth was fixed in the open position, his fingers splayed on the computer keyboard as if someone had positioned him after death.

She peered at the crumpled page that Henshaw had smoothed out and placed in a clear plastic bag:

"I'm waiting…don't you want to come and play?"

The note was unsigned.

But she didn't need a signature to determine the author.

"I need to take a look at the computer," Callahan said to Henshaw. "Can we move him?"

Henshaw looked skeptical. "Might be better if you just try working around him. Forensics ain't gonna like this as it is." He looked to Elaine for confirmation.

She knew he expected her to take charge, but she just couldn't summon the necessary energy. Callahan took one look at her and relented. "No problem."

Henshaw passed Callahan a pair of plastic gloves. "Let's not leave any of your prints lying around."

Elaine turned away, didn't want to watch. She'd seen dozens of murder victims…but this was different. This was her mistake. Skip was dead because of that error.

"Look." Henshaw followed her as she escaped to the far side of the room. "This isn't your fault," he said gently. "If you're going to blame someone, blame me." His gaze narrowed. "I know what you're thinking, DC."

She looked at him then. "Do you really? Then you know it's entirely my fault."

Henshaw took the unlit cigar from the corner of his mouth and dropped it into his pocket. "No it's not. What could you do? Force him to go to the station house with you? Arrest him? You couldn't even be sure he was telling the truth. For all you knew he could have been baiting you for sound bites. Besides, the news he relayed had to have shocked you a little."

Her partner was right on all counts. There were plenty of excuses for the decision she'd made or failed to make…but none of them mattered. She had seen the fear in Skip's eyes…she'd known he was telling the truth and she still hadn't insisted he go with her. She hadn't tried to stop him. Granted, the chief had called at that moment and ordered her to his office. No matter, she should have followed her instincts…shouldn't have let this happen.

"You okay?" Henshaw pressed, worry making the furrows in his face deeper.

As if on cue, her stomach twisted angrily, sent a line of fire straight up her esophagus.

She gritted her teeth against the pain, then forced out the lie that would get them past this issue. "I'm fine. There doesn't appear to be anything else out of place or missing." Who could tell with this mess?

Henshaw recognized the lie for what it was but didn't pursue it. He knew her well enough to know that she wasn't saying any more. "Looks like whoever came in either had a key or was invited." He surveyed the room once more. "No sign of a struggle. No forced entry. He had to have been waiting in the building."

Nothing. Elaine knew there wouldn't be any prints or anything else to point to the killer's identity. Just a typed note with no signature.

"The memory's been wiped, just like the others." Callahan joined their huddle. "Find anything else of interest?"

She passed him the note, which no doubt was intended for his eyes, anyway.

A glimpse of Skip entered her peripheral vision, and she had to squeeze her eyes tightly shut to block out the image. He was dead. She should have protected him.

The annoying tones of her cell phone dragged her from the self-bashing session. Relieved to have any kind of distraction, she dug it out of her bag. "Jentzen."

"Elaine, why haven't you called?"

Her mother. She turned away from the conversation taking place between Henshaw and Callahan.

"What's up, Mom?" She didn't have time for this right now. She loved her mother, but if she was determined to go through with this insane divorce then Elaine wanted no part of it. Not even for a moment's distraction.

"You left me a message and said we had to talk. I've been worried sick," her mother urged. "Why didn't you call back? I've left three messages on your home phone."

Elaine frowned. She hadn't gotten any messages at home. And she darn sure hadn't called her mother and left any message. Who'd had the time?

"Maybe Judith called you," she suggested. That would make sense. Her sister had definitely needed to talk through her feelings. It had to have been Judith.

"Elaine, are you sure you're all right? It was you, dear, who called. Your exact words were 'Mom, it's Elaine. We have to talk.'"

Elaine turned around and stared at Skip. All the things he'd hoped to do in his life had been snatched away. Stolen by some psycho bastard even the FBI hadn't been able to catch. And for what reason? Just because the Gamekeeper had lured him into some stupid chat box? Because Skip had foolishly taken the bait, had passed that warning to her, a person he considered to be a friend? A friend who'd let him down.

...he wants to hurt you, Deputy Elaine.

Dread coagulated in her gut. She thought about the note Henshaw had found shoved in Skip's mouth. Maybe it hadn't been intended for Callahan.

Maybe it was for her.

As she and Callahan left the scene, Henshaw called in the shooting. Unless some neighbor saw them leaving, no one would know they had been there. She didn't like doing business this way, but, unfortunately, it was necessary.

"We need to stop by my mother's," she told Callahan as she pointed her Jeep in the direction of Buckhead.

If her mother hadn't deleted the message, she wanted to hear it for herself.

"I'll wait outside."

She glanced at him, started to ask why but then realized that he was right. The fewer witnesses who saw them together the better.

Twenty minutes later she parked in her mother's drive and hurried to the front door.

Lana Jentzen looked surprised to see her. "You didn't have to stop by. I know how busy you must be."

It was Saturday. No one wanted to work on the weekend, but murder didn't always wait for a regular business day. Her mother would know that as well as Elaine, maybe better.

"I want to hear that message."

Her mother closed the door behind Elaine and followed her to the table in the living room where the answering machine sat. "You know, dear, I might be getting older but I certainly recognize my own daughter's voice."

"Just bear with me," Elaine urged as she depressed the necessary button to replay old messages.

Sure enough, message number three was her voice.

"Mom, it's Elaine. We have to talk."

She shook her head in confusion. What the hell? She hadn't made that call.

"See, I told you." Her mother folded her arms over her chest and looked properly justified.

"I guess I forgot."

But she hadn't forgotten. Elaine had not made that call.

It was almost midnight before Callahan finally turned in. He'd stayed on the Internet searching through various secret government databases and putting bait, as he called it, out in cyberspace for the Gamekeeper. He'd had no luck luring him into a discussion thus far. She didn't even bother asking how he knew the databases existed that he'd hacked into. It was probably best she didn't know. It did surprise her, however, that the Gamekeeper hadn't taken his bait. Callahan had apparently been fishing for him for quite some time from what she could gather. Then again, it could be part of the bastard's sick game.

She'd had to go back to the office after leaving her mother's house, upon Flatt's request, to discuss the newest turn of events. Skip's murder. No one could see how his death played into the current case. She wasn't telling. She had to do this her own way. She'd come to that conclusion standing in her mother's living room and hearing her voice echo from the answering machine in a message she hadn't left. Even caller ID had shown the call as having come from Elaine's house.

Somehow the Gamekeeper had made that happen. He'd used her voice. But how? She understood that the technology was available to do that sort of thing…but how had he gotten a sample of her voice.

Her gut told her it went deeper than that. The message Henshaw had found in Skip's mouth…was for her. Skip had come to her. Had warned her that the Gamckccper wanted to hurt her.

Hcnshaw was right about one thing, this game had moved to a new level.

After the briefing, the chief had insisted that she hang around and go over what they had so far with the members of the newly formed task force.

She'd done so, her patience growing thinner with each tick of the clock.

Finally she'd gotten back home and Callahan had appeared, prepared to spend the entire night up and online.

Thank God he'd finally given in to the exhaustion clearly gnawing at him. He was running on about the same amount of sleep as Elaine, maybe less.

She sat down at her home computer and listened for several seconds just to be sure Callahan hadn't heard her come back into the dining room.

Sally had followed her and curled up at her feet.

Elaine plugged in the cable Callahan always pulled loose when he shut down. He'd insisted that with the kind of Internet service she had, her system could be invaded even when her computer was turned off. The only way to ensure no one got in was to sever the connection entirely. She powered up the computer and clicked the icon for accessing her Internet service.

Within moments she had located the KillerGames.com site. She looked for the hidden pull-down menu as Skip had instructed. A victory smile slid across her lips when she found it. She selected *buzz* and then entered the password. *Dead-end.*

A request for screen name appeared and she typed in LurkingLady.

Welcomes from several others in the chat box appeared on the screen.

Do u like games? Foxfire asked.

I luv games, she typed in.

Two of the more dominant users went back and forth about what they liked best in a new game, the name of which she did not recognize. She wasn't that savvy about computer games.

Welcome, LurkingLady, I've been waiting for you...

Elaine's breath stalled in her chest when she read the screen name.

Gamekeeper.

Several others immediately greeted him. Their comments indicated their glowing admiration.

Elaine felt the rage start to rise inside her, overriding the tiny burst of fear she'd felt at first, as well as any cop sense she possessed.

*I've been looking for you, too...*she responded.

Let's move to a more private venue, shall we...

The monitor flickered. She blinked, startled. The background color changed...and a new chat box opened.

Now, that's better...

Another slick move she didn't quite comprehend the dynamics of. Elaine wet her lips and lowered her fingertips to the keys. She clenched her jaw to hold back the real words she wanted to type...she had to stay calm...had to bait him, not alienate him.

Who are you???

That's right, she decided. Play it cool...innocent.

The sound of laughter echoed from the computer's speaker. *You know who I am.*

Her heart jolted and she stabbed at the volume level to lower it slightly. She glanced back toward the hall to make sure Callahan hadn't stirred. When she could breathe again she turned back to the computer. This bastard had her right where he wanted her, on unfamiliar territory. She glared at the screen name by his typed words and it was all she could do to remain composed.

What do you want?

I thought that was clear...I want to play...

I don't play games...

Ah, but you do, Detective...you play very well...

She considered for a moment what he meant by that. Her decision to back up Callahan possibly? The way she was keeping secrets from Flatt?

My partner is better at this than me, she baited.

More chuckles from cyberspace. She didn't know how he made the sounds, but she knew it was possible.

Your partner is dead already, Detective…he just won't admit it yet…he's no longer a credible opponent…

She muttered a curse, fury curling her lips.

I've always rooted for the underdog, she tapped in as she mumbled a few rather descriptive adjectives for the bastard, things she couldn't say to him just now.

How nice…now's your chance to prove how worthy you are, Detective…don't you want to play?…Everyone else is dying to play….

She gritted her teeth even harder. Yeah, people were dying all right. Like Skip.

I think I'm already in the game, she fired back. He'd concocted that message on her mother's answering machine. She was certain of it. He killed Skip…and all those other innocent people. But she couldn't risk saying any of that…she had to learn as much from this cyber meeting as possible. Patience was the only way.

See what a good player you are…you recognized the game right away…good girl…the next move is mine…

Fear raced through her veins. *What kind of move?* she rushed to ask.

In forty-eight hours people will die…your move is to guess who and where in time to stop it…

How the hell am i supposed to do that? She resisted the need to add *asshole* onto the end of that line.

Come, come now, Detective…what fun would it be if I gave you too much information?…

Listen, you son of a bitch, I'm going to get you if it's the last thing I do...

Dammit, she shouldn't have done that. Her cursor blinked at her, as if confirming her mistake. She'd blown it.

A full minute passed and she felt certain it was over. She'd made her second mistake of the day. And someone else would die because of it. She blinked back a rush of tears prompted by fury, mostly at herself.

Letters, words started to spill across the screen once more.

Here's a clue for the poor, poor detective.

An image suddenly filled the screen. Male, young, twenty-two, twenty-three maybe, dark hair, green eyes.

This man will go on a brief shooting spree, then he will die...Can you save him, Detective?...I think not...

On instinct she stabbed the print button. She held her breath until the page popped out of the painfully slow machine. In that same instant the image as well as the chat box vanished from her monitor. God, that had been close. She stared at the face on the page.

The next victim...but who the hell was he?

Chapter 28

"The chief will blow a fuse," Henshaw said, shooting a sympathetic look in Jentzen's direction.

Trace pinched the bridge of his nose with his thumb and forefinger. Why wouldn't anyone listen to him?

Perched on the edge of the sofa, Jentzen puffed out a breath and appeared to consider her options once more. As the ranking detective, Henshaw wanted her to understand that she would take the fall. Not by his choice, of course, but simply because that's the way it worked.

But they were wasting time!

Trace exhaled his own frustration. He resisted the urge to start pacing the room again. He'd done enough of that in the past few hours. Why the hell were they going over this again? They hadn't found the first match in the Georgia criminal records database or the FBI's for the man in the picture. Evidently the guy had no prior record, which meant he was a needle in a haystack. Could be anybody from anywhere.

The Gamekeeper's victims never had a previous record. The one thing they could count on was that this guy, whoever the hell he was, likely had everything going for him. Career, family, *everything.* Trace had known the whole task of checking databases would be an exercise in futility. But Henshaw and Jentzen had insisted on going through the steps.

Urgency nudged at him again. No later than tomorrow night the man in the picture would kill innocent people and then likely take his own life.

Time was running out. They had to act now.

"I don't give a damn what the chief does," Trace argued, unable to keep quiet another second. "We're almost out of time." He looked from the chair Henshaw occupied to Jentzen a few feet away. "You said the Sunday-evening addition of the *Telegraph* gets put to bed by ten this morning, we have to do this now or the point will be moot."

Though it was only 8:00 a.m., Trace knew that getting the picture on the front page would take some finesse. Finesse required time. They needed to move *now!*

Another burst of adrenaline flooded him, urging him to get this done before it was too late.

"All right." Jentzen stood. She looked physically exhausted and emotionally drained. Finding her friend dead like that had done a number on her. Finding out she'd interacted with the Gamekeeper without telling him had done a number on Trace.

Henshaw pushed up from his chair. "I don't like this, DC," he repeated. "I know we're running on empty here, but I've got a feeling this is going to cost you more than you want to pay."

Before Trace could put in his two cents' worth, the tough detective threw out her own defense.

"You may be right, Hank," she said quietly.

It was the first time Trace had heard her call her partner by his first name, but he knew they had been friends for a long time. Being partners hadn't changed that. Since she still called him Callahan, what did that say about their relationship? Not much, if he had his guess. But there was that other thing going on between them…an attraction neither of them could deny. Another misstep in a long line of bad decisions. Looked like his luck wasn't going to change.

"But I have to do this," she told Henshaw. "You know as well as I do that if we go to the chief either he or Douglas will nix the whole idea. And people will die. I'm not making the same mistake I made with Skip."

Henshaw shook his head in weary resignation. "But what if it's a hoax?"

They had hashed out that possibility already. Trace didn't see the point in using up more valuable time going down that road again. Dammit, didn't the man get it?

"Are we doing this or not?" he demanded, determined to get this show on the road. He knew in his gut that the Gamekeeper had taken this approach to ensure all the players were in place for the grand finale. There was no room for second-guessing.

Jentzen held up her hand for Trace to give her a minute. "It could be a hoax," she allowed, giving Henshaw the benefit of the doubt. "But I'm willing to take that risk. Your concern is duly noted. If this goes south I won't let it come back to haunt you."

Henshaw was no doubt very close to retirement, but Trace felt confident that wasn't why the man worried. He cared for Jentzen. He didn't want her hurt.

The old guy stuck his stogie in one corner of his mouth and then shook his head adamantly. "No way, DC. We're in this together." He glanced at Trace. "Right?"

Trace had to smile at the old goat. That he'd included him was a major step. "Right."

"Then let's do it." Jentzen grabbed her bag. "We'll take it to the top brass at the paper and see what happens. If the *Telegraph* won't go for it, the *Chronicle* will."

On the way to the door, Henshaw pulled out his phone. "I'll get the managing editor on the horn and see if we can arrange an emergency meet."

When Jentzen would have followed him outside, Trace waylaid her with a hand on her arm.

"He's right you know," he admitted. As badly as he wanted to do this…he knew how it could turn out. She would end up in the same boat with him and she didn't deserve that kind of fate. Wasn't it just like him? Always realizing his mistake after he'd already made it?

She searched his eyes, probably trying to figure him out since he'd just done a complete about-face. This close, looking at her was not a smart move. She had beautiful eyes…the kind a guy—even a burned-out-has-been like him—could get lost in.

"I'm aware of the risk, Callahan." She tilted that gorgeous chin upward, in defiance of the mix of emotions he saw in her eyes. She was just a little bit afraid and a whole lot worried. "I'm not going to let him take another victim."

When she would have pulled free Trace held on. "I'm still

madder than hell that you didn't tell me all that Littles said to you. I don't think you fully comprehend the full scope of the damage this bastard can do."

She wrapped her fingers around his wrist and pulled his hand away but, to his surprise, she didn't immediately let go. "What I know or don't know doesn't matter. He sets the rules. The only thing either of us can do is play this out."

He enveloped her hand with his, rubbed his thumb over her palm and heard her breath catch. He wondered if she'd experienced that same jolt of sensations he had. The dead last thing he wanted to do was hurt her. Hesitation, laced heavily with anxiety, barbed in his chest.

"Let me do this," he urged. "You and Henshaw don't have to be involved."

For a second that lengthened to ten, she simply gazed into his eyes without responding. The pulse at the base of her throat fluttered rapidly—whether from fear or the same electricity pulsing through him, he couldn't say. Touching her made him want to pull her into his arms…. The urge to protect her surged even stronger.

"When this is over," she said, drawing his gaze back to hers, "we have things to talk about."

He couldn't help himself. He had to feel those lush lips…the softness of her cheek. She let him trail his thumb over her lower lip, then across that smooth cheek. She trembled and something shifted in his chest. He swallowed against the swell of emotion in his throat.

"I'll hold you to that," he warned, wishing he knew the right words to say…. But he didn't. He'd never been very good at this kind of thing.

Now definitely wasn't the time.

His timing had always sucked.

Some things never changed.

But one thing he would do, he would keep her safe…at all costs.

Chapter 29

At 7:46 on Sunday evening Chief John Dugan demanded to see Elaine and Henshaw in his office.

Callahan attempted to dissuade her from going. Told her to let him go in her stead. But she refused.

She left him standing on her front stoop looking utterly vulnerable. He didn't want her to take the fall for this. He cared. She shivered at the idea and told herself it was truly stupid to get involved with him on a personal level.

They both had issues. Baggage. Lots of it.

But resisting was impossible.

Now, as the chief stood staring out the massive window in his office, hands on hips, she wondered what she had ever seen in him. Sure, he was a great deal more polished than Callahan, definitely more reliable. She almost laughed. What the hell did she know about Callahan? He'd barged into her life barely a week ago.

All she really knew was that he made her yearn to know him better. No one, not even John Dugan, had ever made her ache that way.

"Chief." Henshaw got to his feet. Elaine blinked, startled at the idea of what he might have in mind. "Don't blame Jentzen. This was my idea."

She rocketed out of her chair. "That's not true, Henshaw, and you know it. This was my decision. You tried to talk me out of it." She'd warned him not to do this. Irritation flickered. He was as stubborn as a mule.

Chief Dugan turned to face them, his expression stern, sending them both back to their respective corners, so to speak.

"Do you have any idea how many phone calls Dispatch has had to field since that newspaper appeared on lawns?"

Elaine could imagine. Exact numbers weren't necessary. The picture had run on the front page of the *Telegraph* with a plea that if anyone recognized this man they should contact Atlanta PD immediately. If this turned out to be a hoax, the department would likely get sued. She'd considered that and deemed what she had to do worth the risk.

The chief held up a hand when she started to speak. "That was a rhetorical question," he snapped.

She nodded. This was her first time getting fully dressed down by the chief. She didn't like it.

"The mayor and most of the other politicians in the city have called me and demanded an explanation. Sadly—" he looked from Elaine to Henshaw and back "—I couldn't give one. I had no idea what this was about."

She and Henshaw exchanged a look.

Again the chief held up a hand. "If you're holding anything back, I don't even want to know." He planted that hand back at his waist. "If I didn't need the manpower so badly, considering all these unsolved murders, I'd put you both on suspension."

Elaine stiffened at the word. No cop wanted to hear that. Not even one who'd knowingly committed an act of insubordination. That's what Dugan had called this whole mess. A lack of respect for authority. He would be addressing that aspect of this mess in the future, he'd promised. Flatt might be keeping his temporary position after all, Elaine mused.

"Sir, as ranking detective, you must know that the final decision was mine."

He glared at her. "I'm well aware of that, Detective."

She nodded. "Yes, sir."

The chief's phone buzzed and he picked it up. "Yes." He listened a moment. "Send him in."

Elaine's gut clenched hard. She hoped like hell that wasn't Callahan coming to the rescue. If he showed his face around here he'd likely be taken into custody and deported back to Febbie Land, as Quantico was fondly known among regular cops.

The door opened and an elegantly dressed Supervisory Special Agent Douglas waltzed in. He looked about as happy as Chief Dugan.

"Do you have any idea what you've done?" he demanded of Elaine before he'd gotten halfway across the room.

She didn't bother responding. His was probably a rhetorical question as well.

"Where is Callahan?" He stopped directly in front of Elaine. "I know you've been working with him. This move has his name written all over it."

She offered him a smug smile. "Actually it was my idea." Okay, so that was an outright lie, but she loved the reaction it got. Douglas's fierce expression drooped just a little. "I decided since I couldn't count on any of you Federal types coming clean about this, I'd just do it my way."

"What the hell is that supposed to mean?" he roared.

Before she could stop herself, Elaine fired back, "I can't decide if the NSA or the FBI, or maybe some shadow operations group is behind what the Gamekeeper's been up to. But I don't like being made a fool out of, Supervisory Special Agent Douglas. And I'm sure my chief doesn't, either."

Henshaw shifted, but to his credit, he didn't say a word.

"What's she talking about?" the chief asked warily.

Douglas wheeled away from her, taking a position near the conference table. "Sounds like she's been taken in by Callahan's wild imagination."

She moved her head firmly from side to side, partly to shake Callahan's voice out of her head. He'd warned her not to speak of this. "No, sir," she said to her chief. "We're the victims of a major cover-up."

"You don't know what you're talking about," Douglas sputtered. "I would advise you to keep those kinds of accusations to yourself."

"She's right," Henshaw seconded. "We've been had, sir."

Elaine looked at him, pride blooming in her chest alongside the irritation. He trusted her that much.

"Somebody had better explain—"

The door burst open, interrupting the chief.

"Chief Dugan, there's someone here to see you. A Sergeant Anthony Winn. He says it's about the photo." Connie glanced around the room uncertainly. The tension was thick enough to spread like peanut butter.

Elaine imagined they all looked pretty intimidating, horns locked in bitter confrontation.

"Send him in," the chief told his secretary. He turned back to Elaine, glanced from her to Henshaw. "Not a word from either of you."

"Yes, sir," they said in unison.

Sergeant Tony Winn was tall, midthirties, with a regulation police haircut and uniform. He looked nervous as hell. The group of expectant faces in the room didn't help.

"That's my brother in the photo," he said tightly. "I don't know what you think he's done, but he's a good man."

The chief briefly explained the situation, leaving out as many of the details as possible. Elaine almost rolled her eyes. If that lame story didn't put the sergeant off nothing would.

"Bottom line, Sergeant," the chief said, "we need to talk to him."

Sergeant Winn scrubbed a hand over his face. "I'll be the first to admit that he hasn't been himself the past couple of days." He shrugged. "Not since he got the rejection from the police academy."

"When did this happen?" Elaine asked, ignoring the chief's pointed glare.

"On Friday," Winn said. He shrugged again. "I don't know what happened. Everything was a go. Then suddenly he gets this letter saying his personal references had been withdrawn, leaving the board no choice but to reject his application. It was too late to call anyone. I'd planned to go see the commandant on Monday."

"Who were his personal references?" Elaine's heart was beating like a drum.

"I was one, and the other two were guys in my department."

All cops. The next victims.

"Where is your brother now, Sergeant?" This from the chief.

Elaine felt a rush of relief. Thank God. She needed him on her side right now.

"That's just it, sir. I don't rightly know. He stormed out of the house yesterday and I haven't seen him since." Winn shook his head. "To tell you the truth he hasn't acted like himself in a week or so now. I don't know what's going on. The rejection from the academy was sort of the straw that broke the camel's back."

The next four hours passed in a blur of activity.

An APB was issued for Randall Winn. But it was the photo in the newspaper that ferreted him out. The manager from a sleazebag hotel called in his location. Randall Winn had taken a room last night and hadn't come out since. He had a woman in the room with him.

A unit in the vicinity had gone in after Winn. Elaine hadn't breathed easy until one of the officers reported in to say Winn was alive. Henshaw had called the commandant of the academy at home to confirm that the letter Winn received was a fake as they suspected. It was. Elaine imagined the seal would carry Callahan's DNA.

Now Winn sat in one of four molded plastic chairs that surrounded a nondescript table in an interrogation room. Callahan, Douglas, the chief, Henshaw and Elaine watched him from the viewing room. That Chief Dugan had allowed Callahan back on the case surprised her. He'd given Douglas an ultimatum, do this his way or Dugan would go over his head. Douglas's surrender, in Elaine's opinion, indicated his guilt. He knew things he wasn't sharing. Otherwise he would have stood his ground. After all, he represented the Federal Government. He could take control of the case if he wanted to. Damn him. He was definitely holding out.

"How do you want to handle this, Callahan?"

Elaine turned to the chief, surprised all over again.

Douglas's face pinched in anger, but he kept his mouth shut.

"I'd like to talk to him first," Callahan said. He wore that navy suit that looked so good on him. He still needed a shave, but that only added to his ruggedly handsome image.

"Fine," Chief Dugan allowed, "but I want Jentzen in there with you."

Callahan looked at her. The doubt in his eyes annoyed her but she got it. He wanted to protect her…she understood that now. He'd lost one partner. He didn't want to lose another.

"I'll observe only," she assured him. She definitely didn't want to steal his thunder. Chief Dugan had given him this authority; she had no intention of usurping it in any way.

Callahan led the way from the viewing room to the interrogation room door. He hesitated there. "Thanks," he said, that blue gaze fastening onto hers, doing strange things to her ability to breathe. "For backing me up."

"That's what partners do."

She didn't tell him, but the smile he gifted her with then was thanks enough. It made her pulse skitter and her heart skip a beat. He had really gotten to her. Any hope of evicting him was long gone.

Randall Winn looked up when they entered the room, but he said nothing. She and Callahan settled into the two chairs opposite Winn.

"Mr. Winn," Callahan began, "I'm Special Agent Callahan from the FBI and this is Detective Jentzen from Atlanta Homicide. This is a letter we just had faxed over from the police academy." He placed the single page on the table in front of Winn. "The rejection you received was forged. Do you understand?"

According to the prostitute who'd been found in the hotel room with Winn, he'd been drinking heavily since the night before. He kept talking about dying and how they would all be sorry then. She said he'd freaked her out, but the money was good so she'd hung out with him. In exchange for the information, she'd been promised immunity for prostitution.

"Doesn't matter," he said, his breath pungent with alcohol. "Nothing matters anymore."

"Is that what the Gamekeeper told you?" Callahan asked.

Winn's gaze collided with Callahan's. "I don't know what you're talking about."

"Sure you do," Callahan urged, keeping his tone friendly. "I know how he plays this game. He's been working you, Winn. Setting you up to do something bad. Isn't that true?"

Winn's eyes widened. "I'm not talking about that."

The tension strumming through Elaine ratcheted up another notch as she watched Callahan regroup.

"I tell you what, Mr. Winn," he offered. "You think about my question for a while and I'll come back and talk to you again later."

Winn shook his head. "I'm not talking to you anymore." He abruptly turned to Elaine. "She's the only one I'll talk to."

The air in the room thickened with the uneasy feel of a setup.

"No deal, Winn," Callahan countered.

Elaine put her hand on his beneath the table. "It's okay. He can talk to me."

She felt Callahan tense but his expression never changed. "All right." He got up. "I'll be right outside."

Elaine waited until he'd closed the door behind him. "Okay, Mr. Winn. Why don't you tell me how you got involved with the Gamekeeper?"

She listened as he detailed the way he'd loved surfing the Net, loved playing games. It was his hobby, a kind of secret obsession. Then, about a month ago he'd gotten involved with this one really bizarre game. He'd found it fun at first, challenging. Then, two weeks ago, it had started haunting him…following him around. Calls on his cell phone. Messages at work and at home. His electricity got turned off. His debit card denied. He'd gotten a little spooked but he'd considered it just an elaborate game, so he'd shrugged it off.

Until the game had shown him the truth.

"What do you mean, Mr. Winn? What truth?"

He leaned forward slightly. "I saw how people really felt about me. Found out I couldn't count on anyone but myself.

Things started falling apart. All the things I'd counted on in the past were suddenly unreliable." He blinked back the emotion in his eyes. "Even my brother. He screwed me over." His gaze dropped to the letter on the table. He shook his head. "I don't understand this…they rejected me because my brother and his buddies withdrew their recommendations."

"It was a trick, Mr. Winn." She waited until he looked at her to continue. "That's what he does. He tricks you into doing the wrong thing."

Winn shook his head in denial. "You don't understand." He leaned close again. "He gets inside you. So deep you can't figure out where he ends and you begin." Something in his eyes changed, as if some distant memory had kicked in. "He's inside you, too, Detective. When a man's been that close to a woman it shows."

Elaine recoiled, her heart flailing in her chest.

Callahan was suddenly back in the room and the interview was over. Winn lapsed into a kind of trance…like Ramon Johnson had done those first thirty-six hours after his survival of the shooting, only Winn wasn't unconscious.

In the corridor the chief and the others waited, including Jillette and Flatt who looked beyond furious.

"What the hell is going on here?" Flatt demanded.

Callahan turned his worried gaze from her long enough to shoot the guy a deadly glare. "You snooze, you lose, asshole. If you'd been working on this case all day, you'd know what was going on."

Flatt launched into an excuse about having gotten an anonymous tip that had him waiting in a local park for most of the day. He hadn't even seen the evening paper. Wouldn't have known any of this had gone down if Jillette hadn't tracked him down.

"What anonymous tip?" Henshaw asked.

"He didn't show."

Callahan smirked. "You understand the term *decoy,* Flatt?"

The two tore into each other but Elaine couldn't make herself pay attention. Winn's last words kept echoing in her head. How had he known to say that?

"Enough!" The chief glared from one irate man to the other. "We need to focus all this energy on the case. We finally have some leads. Let's follow them."

Callahan went back into interrogation with Winn, for the good it would do, with Douglas monitoring from the viewing room. Flatt and the chief would review all the evidence so far just to be sure they hadn't missed anything. Elaine worked with Jillette and Henshaw on tracking down the Gamekeeper's chat room.

But she had an uneasy feeling they were wasting more precious time. The Gamekeeper wouldn't leave a trail. Nothing they had ascertained about him or this case was because of good detective work or even good luck. It was all part of the game.

Chapter 30

At 4:00 p.m. on Monday afternoon Elaine parked in her driveway. She'd had no sleep in more than forty-eight hours. She couldn't keep going.

Her stomach burned like hellfire itself, and her head ached as if she'd run headlong into a brick wall. She felt nauseated and for the past couple of hours had been dealing with serious cramps.

Just her luck to fall apart all at once, in the middle of her biggest case ever. And her brick wall had a name...the Gamekeeper.

She unlocked and opened the front door. Sally waited for her as always, but something was different this time. She started to whine the moment Elaine walked in the door. Then she saw the reason why.

A large puddle of urine on the floor.

"Oh, girl, what's up with this?" Elaine tried not to sound annoyed but she couldn't help herself. She didn't need this right now.

Sally dropped her head as if sensing her mistress's displeasure.

Elaine sighed. "No problem, girl. We all make mistakes."

She cleaned up the mess and decided to take the dog for a quick walk around the block just in case. She wondered vaguely why Allen, her neighbor, hadn't come by after school as he usually did. Maybe something had come up. Some sort of sports practice or school club meeting. As reliable as he usually was, he was still a teenager.

Elaine didn't know where the strength came from to make the trip around the block, but she'd about taken her last step when she finally reached her front yard once more.

Shirley Carroll, Allen's mother, knelt next to the flower bed she'd built along the property line that separated their yards. Her hands busily yanking out tiny weeds.

"Hey, Mrs. Carroll!" Elaine managed a smile in spite of the lack of enthusiasm she felt. She desperately needed to lie down and close her eyes. Just for a little while. Mrs. Carroll reluctantly threw up a gloved hand, her expression something between petulant and annoyed.

Elaine ignored the odd look and trudged onward, deciding a long hot bath was in order as well as a few hours' sleep. Callahan and Henshaw had things under control…well, as close to under control as they could get on this case. A part of her wanted to do something…find some way to nail this bastard, but she couldn't keep going without sleep. She would begin to make mistakes. Callahan had promised her he would get some shut-eye as well, but she wasn't sure she trusted him to stick by his word on that one.

"Ms. Jentzen!"

Elaine turned, hoping her neighbor wouldn't pick today of all days to chat. She'd almost made it to her door. "Yes?"

Shirley hurried over, glancing around as if she didn't want to be seen cavorting with the enemy.

How strange, Elaine mused. Her neighbor was generally quite normal and friendly.

"Ms. Jentzen, I know you're very busy, but I can't pretend."

Elaine was really confused now. "Mrs. Carroll, I have no idea what you mean."

The woman plopped her gloved hands on her hips and poked out her chin. "I don't understand the change in your arrangement with Allen." She glanced down at Sally and made a pained face. Elaine knew she was allergic. That she'd even come this close with Sally nearby felt very strange indeed.

"I'm sorry. You've lost me here. What change in arrangements?" She told Sally to sit, when she would have sniffed the woman's legs.

"Allen found your note saying you wouldn't need him to walk Sally anymore, and—" her expression turned crestfallen "—quite frankly he was really upset."

"What note?" Elaine frowned, utterly confused. "I didn't send any note."

Shirley pulled a wrinkled paper from the pocket of her prim, cropped slacks and held it out to her. "This note. I told Allen it was probably because of that *man*."

Elaine accepted the paper, eyeing her neighbor skeptically.

By *man,* Elaine assumed she meant Callahan. She read the written words that looked very much like her own handwriting. *Allen, I'll be taking care of Sally's needs myself from now on. Thanks, Elaine.*

"Mrs. Carroll, I didn't send this note." Elaine stared at the page, baffled all over again. "I don't know where this came from…" Her voice trailed off. Yes, she did. She knew exactly who. "May I keep it?"

Shirley Carroll shrugged. "It's your note." She sounded even more put off.

Elaine shook her head. "You don't understand. This is some kind of mistake. I definitely want Allen to keep working with Sally."

It took several more minutes for Elaine to convince the woman that she was sincere.

With that misunderstanding finally resolved, Elaine dragged into the house. She didn't have enough energy to achieve the fury level the situation called for. She tossed the forged letter on the table, only then noticing the message light blinking on her answering machine.

She pressed the button, and an unfamiliar female voice boomed from the machine. "Ms. Jentzen, you missed your appointment with Dr. Simmons today. You'll need to reschedule. Please call 555-7821."

Elaine snatched up the receiver and dialed the number. She didn't have an appointment today. "This is Elaine Jentzen," she said when the receptionist answered. "I think there's been a mistake."

Two minutes later Elaine hung up the phone, confusion reigning supreme yet again. She had no memory of moving up the appointment with the specialist. The appointment was supposed to be on Wednesday but the scheduling clerk insisted that Elaine had called on Friday and requested an earlier appointment.

This was crazy.

She depressed the play button again to listen to the rest of her messages. When she'd picked up the phone to call the doctor's office, the answering machine had automatically shut off the playback. Since the light had resumed its incessant blinking, there had to be others.

"Mrs. Jentzen, this is Maureen Stedman at Atlanta Utilities. We haven't received your payment this month. We've mailed out a late notice with no response. If we don't receive payment by 5:00 p.m. today we will have no choice but to discontinue service."

What the hell? Elaine grabbed the receiver and entered the number for the utilities office. She asked for Ms. Stedman. Elaine explained that she hadn't received a late statement and that she had in fact mailed in her payment three weeks ago. She rifled through her purse until she found her checkbook and stated the number of the check she'd sent.

"I'm sorry, Ms. Jentzen, but we have no record of receiving your payment."

Elaine plowed the fingers of her free hand through her hair. "What does that mean, exactly?"

"Ma'am, it means that if you don't make the payment by close of business today we'll—"

"Okay, okay, I get it." No way in hell was she driving across town. "How about I give you my credit card number?"

"That would certainly take care of the situation, ma'am."

"Hold on a minute." Elaine cast about in her purse until she found her VISA. She gave Mrs. Stedman the necessary information and thanked her. She'd have to call the bank and cancel that check. Who knew if it would ever turn up.

She dropped the receiver back in the cradle and collapsed against the wall. Her gaze somehow ended up on the bottle of bourbon across the room. She could use a drink about now. She'd mailed that check; there was no mistake. Her gut clenched. Surely this wasn't the Gamekeeper as well. Why would he do this? It wasn't like he could manipulate her as he had his other victims. More likely the check was caught up in the mail. Though it would be the first time any of her mail had gotten lost, it happened every day. No system was perfect.

The phone rang and she jerked at the sound. "Dammit." She blew out a breath and picked up the receiver. What now? "Jentzen."

"Ms. Jentzen, this is Maureen Stedman again. I'm sorry to bother you, but unfortunately your credit card was declined."

Declined? "Excuse me?"

"You'll need to come in and make the payment in person…in cash."

"I'll be there in thirty minutes." Elaine slammed down the phone. Sally looked up at her and whimpered. "Sorry, girl."

Swearing every step of the way, Elaine stalked out to her Jeep and drove straight to the nearest ATM. Cash. She couldn't believe this crap. She shoved her card into the machine and entered her personal identification number, then the amount of cash she needed. She selected the checking account option and agreed to all the conditions and waited, fury roiling inside her.

The ATM spit out a receipt but no cash. She glared at the slip of paper, and her mouth dropped open. Insufficient funds. *No damned way.*

This time she went inside the bank.

She waited, her foot tapping impatiently as the teller checked her balance.

"Ms. Jentzen, I'm afraid you have a negative balance in your checking account." The teller adopted a sad face. "You also have three insufficient fund charges."

"How can that be?" Two weeks ago she'd had a balance of over three thousand dollars. Where the hell had the money gone? Dread climbed into her throat. "What about my savings account."

The teller quickly tapped a few keys. "Ah. There's the problem," she said. "Three days ago you moved twenty-five hundred dollars from your checking account to your savings. That's what put you in the red." She smiled triumphantly. "Would you like me to transfer some of it back?"

"Yes." Elaine started to shake a little then. The son of a bitch had done it…was playing with her. Her trembling escalated. With anger she told herself, but she wasn't sure that's all there was to it. She was exhausted, bordering on hysterical here. Anxiety had slipped into the mix, and no small amount of fear. She hated that he could get to her like this. She had to pull herself together. This is what he wanted, she told herself. She wouldn't give him the satisfaction.

She withdrew the cash she needed and drove straight to the utility office, barely making it before the doors were locked for the day.

Then she went home. Too tired to maintain her anger or

the damned fear. Screw the Gamekeeper. She recognized his methods. He was trying to get to her. Not going to happen, by God.

All she needed was sleep. She would be fine and ready to kick ass by tomorrow morning. Let him play his stupid tricks on her.

Before pulling into the driveway, she stopped at her mailbox and discovered four days' worth of post. The postman probably thought she'd gone on vacation.

She parked her Jeep and went inside. Looking a good deal happier herself, Sally wagged her tail in welcome.

Forcing herself to eat first, Elaine rounded up a wine cooler and sat down at the table. As she consumed the turkey and cheese sandwich and sipped the wine cooler, she shuffled through her mail, ignoring most of it since it was likely attempts to interest her in another credit card or something else she didn't need.

A letter from Dr. Bramm's office was at the bottom of the heap. Frowning, she ripped it open. She'd just gone to him last Monday. Had he sent out his statements already? What did she care, anyway? Her insurance took care of the annual exam.

Not a statement, a letter.

She read the two brief paragraphs, her entire being going numb. Just to make sure she hadn't made a mistake, she re-read the first sentence of the second paragraph. *...results are positive for the presence of cancerous cells.* Her Pap had come back positive? *Please contact this office immediately for additional testing.*

Cancer?

Fear tightened around her throat like a hangman's noose. She had cancer?

Chapter 31

Trace parked his rental sedan in the driveway behind Jentzen's Jeep. It was after 8:00 p.m. He'd long ago pushed past the boundaries of exhaustion. What he felt now was something between exhaustion and nothing at all.

He'd interrogated Randall Winn a second time and gotten nothing. Then he'd gone back to the hospital and questioned Ramon Johnson. The same. At least this time Chief Dugan had agreed to call in a psychiatrist who specialized in mind control. The Bureau had the best available at their beck and call. For whatever reason, Douglas felt inclined to disagree with Trace. But Chief Dugan had backed him up and called in a contact of his own. He had to admit it felt good to have people on his side again.

Trace's gaze lifted to the house. But he'd let himself step

across a line with Elaine Jentzen and he wasn't at all sure he could retreat.

A frown drew his eyebrows together. Why was the house dark? Maybe she'd crashed before dark and hadn't turned on any lights. She had been exhausted. Fear crept into his heart.

The Gamekeeper never attempted to lure in anyone who knew him, except Trace, and that was different. He didn't want Trace to play the game, he wanted the game to reach out and touch him. There was a distinct difference.

But he'd changed his MO before. He could very well have changed again.

Trace was out of the car and at the door of Jentzen's house before his next thought could form. He didn't knock, just twisted the knob and burst inside.

His first thought was that the door should not have been unlocked, his second that the house felt entirely too quiet.

He blinked, tried to adjust to the darkness. The meager light from the streetlamp outside tried to penetrate the gloom indoors but failed miserably.

"I'm here."

Relief slid through him. "You okay?"

"I don't know."

Trace turned on the closest lamp, then shut and locked the door. A new bout of exhaustion nagged at him as the adrenaline receded.

Jentzen sat on the floor, propped against the far wall. She didn't look injured. Sally lay beside her. The house felt empty otherwise.

"What's going on?"

She didn't respond, just looked at him, the desolation on her face drawing him closer.

He shucked his jacket and sat down beside her. "What happened?"

She passed a handful of pages to him. He read the first. A handwritten note to someone named Allen telling him that she, Elaine, would take care of Sally. The second, third and fourth were insufficient-fund notices from her bank. A fifth indicated that her credit card had been canceled for failure to receive payment for three consecutive months. But it was the last one that sucked the breath out of his lungs.

Cancer.

"When did you get this?" Emotions he couldn't begin to sort whipped around inside him, frothing his insides into a mass of quivering jelly.

"It's a fake," she said, but her voice contained no enthusiasm or relief. She sounded resigned, defeated. "Dr. Bramm assured me that my results were negative."

Trace set the letters aside and felt a kind of defeat he'd only experienced once in his career. He'd failed to protect his first partner, and now he'd let history repeat itself. Thankfully she didn't have cancer, but she was in pain all the same.

"He tampered with my bank account," she said, her tone as flat as a sour piano note. "Fixed it so it looks as if I haven't paid my bills." She moved her head back and forth. "I don't know exactly how he did that. Electronic files manipulation, I suppose."

"This is how he works," Trace said. "He can get in anywhere, anytime. There isn't a system built he can't breach. He's that good…and that evil."

She sighed, the sound halting as if it was all she could do not to cry. Trace curled his fingers into fists, resisted the urge to reach out to her. He couldn't let this thing between them go any further than it already had. He'd made too many mistakes as it was.

"This was just a taste," she said softly. "Imagine if I wasn't a cop. If I didn't know his methods. I might have believed that I'd forgotten to mail my bills, that maybe I was losing my mind. Then comes a double whammy, *cancer.* The absolute worst news." She turned to Trace. "I can see how his victims would break down. It had to be awful for them."

"He's relentless when he goes after a target," Trace told her, thinking back to what little he'd learned two years ago and then in this latest killing spree. "He studies his targets, learns all he can about them. Then, little by little, he destroys their whole life until they no longer care, then he tosses out the coup de grâce."

"He picked me," she whispered. "That's why Douglas asked for me. Why…other things have happened recently in my life."

"What other things?" Trace searched her face, her eyes, looking for the answers she might not want to give.

"My parents are on the verge of divorce. I hadn't considered it until now but this counselor my mother is seeing is apparently encouraging her to go out on her own." She shrugged. "I can't prove it, of course, but it seems odd that after all these seemingly happy years together, she would suddenly start talking divorce. Then there's my sister." She laughed, the sound dry and lacking even a hint of humor.

"A long-distance friend mailed her a book about finding

oneself after childbirth," she went on. "Now she's questioning her life as a stay-at-home mom. Maybe it's my imagination but it just seems strange that my whole family, the marriages I've always admired, all started falling apart at the same time." She rubbed at her eyes. "I'm the reason he chose Skip. He knew I had a soft spot in my heart for the guy. All of this is my fault." She shook her head. "We'll probably never know what he did to Matthews or that med student."

"That's what he wants you to think." Trace knew firsthand. "He knows all the right buttons to push. Looks for the weak spot."

"How can we possibly hope to stop him? We don't even know where he is. What he looks like, or even his name."

Trace wished he could tell her she was wrong, that they would stop him. But he couldn't say for sure. Douglas had the Bureau's finest trying to track him on the Internet. They'd found nothing. The Gamekeeper made sure he didn't leave a trail. There was absolutely no evidence he'd ever been in that chat room with Jentzen. Nothing. It seemed impossible that anyone could have that much power...but he did.

But all that power was in the cyberworld. Trace stilled. Though his machinations caused people to die in the real world, he wielded that infinite power from cyberspace.

But he couldn't get to Trace that way.

If he was the Gamekeeper's ultimate target, then the bastard would have no choice but to come after him in the real world. Trace wouldn't fall a second time for his electronic methods. The Gamekeeper knew that.

Trace swallowed hard as the next realization sank fully into his brain. That's why he was working Jentzen so hard…to get to Trace. She was right. She had been chosen. Her high profile career made her a perfect candidate.

"You should walk away from this case." Trace fixed his gaze on her startled one, his certainty gaining momentum with each word. "He's using you— He won't stop until he's accomplished his goal. You have to get out while you still can."

She scrambled to her feet. "Forget it!" She glared down at him. "I'm no more at risk than you are, Callahan."

Trace pushed up from the floor. Okay, so that one had come out the wrong way. "This has nothing to do with you being a woman. Or your ability as a detective."

Sally growled low in her throat. "Go, girl," Elaine ordered, her tone uncharacteristically curt. Her head hanging low, the golden retriever stalked off into her mistress's bedroom. "Stay!" Elaine yelled after her. The pained look on her face told him how much it had cost her to speak to the dog in that manner.

"You have to listen to me," he urged, drawing her attention back to him.

"Yeah, right." She bracketed her waist with her hands and glowered at him. "You told me in the beginning that you wouldn't have picked a woman for a partner." She poked him in the chest with her finger. "This isn't about gender, Callahan, if the Y chromosome was all this case required you'd have already nailed the bastard."

She was right. He couldn't deny that. He'd failed two years ago and wasn't faring much better this go round. "You're right. I let him get away before. I got my partner killed, but I'm not going to let that happen this time."

"Forget it, Callahan," she snapped. "You have no say in what I do. This is my case as much as it is yours."

His gaze dropped from those furious dark eyes to that lush mouth pinched so fiercely with outrage. The memory of the one time they'd kissed interrupted his ability to think straight, making him ache to taste more of her.

"That won't work, either," she warned. "Just because I'm attracted to you doesn't mean I've lost my objectivity."

A smile hitched up one corner of his mouth. "Then it shouldn't bother you if I do this." He leaned down and nipped her fabulous bottom lip with his teeth.

She drew away, glared up at him with mounting fury. "You're a real piece of work, Callahan. I don't jump in the sack with every handsome guy I'm attracted to."

"So, you think I'm handsome?" He moved a little closer. She tried to back away a step, but the wall stopped her.

"I imagine most women do," she admitted breathlessly, "but that doesn't mean I'm going to let you seduce me."

He leaned nearer. She gasped. He smiled. *Too late, honey,* he didn't say.

"You're the one who brought up sex," he countered, unable to take his eyes off those magnificent lips.

She gave her head a little shake. "I didn't—"

"Yes, you did," he said, before brushing a kiss across her mouth. She shivered. Fire shot to his loins. He loved that she reacted that way to him.

She flattened her palms against his chest. "This is not going to happen like this," she warned, a sudden determination in her eyes.

Trace blinked out of his own trance. What was wrong with

him? He'd sworn he wouldn't go down this path, and look at him...he was a fool. Shake it off, he ordered. "You're right...I didn't mean..."

That he stammered had Elaine experiencing a heady rush of power. If anyone was going to be in charge here, it was her. She ripped open his shirt. He stared down at his bared chest and then at her, confusion claiming that too-handsome face. Before he could regain his bearings, she pulled his mouth down to hers and kissed him hard.

He resisted a little at first, and then he melted into the kiss, giving tit for tat. Their tongues tangled, seeking, retreating, exploring. She plunged her fingers into his hair and her entire being sighed. It felt so good to touch him that way. She'd wanted to muss that hair for days now. His hands moving over her body made her squirm...made her want to rip off her own clothes and go skin to skin.

As if he'd read her mind, he took care of that for her. Tearing off her blouse, shoving down her slacks. She kicked out of her shoes and her slacks. His shoes landed next to hers. Between urgent kisses, she ushered him down to the floor, then straddled that lean waist. She felt the push of his hardened sex against the fire kindling between her thighs. Flames erupted deep inside her, made her inner muscles pulse with want.

He tugged down her bra straps then closed those long-fingered hands around her breasts. She moaned aloud at the incredible sensations. Unable to control herself she started to move. To rock back and forth, rubbing herself against him, the silky fabric of her panties and the coarser feel of his trousers only adding to the friction...the exquisite stimulation.

He pulled her down for another long, hot kiss, and then he rolled her onto her back. Her legs wrapped instinctively around his. She arched into him; the need to feel him pressed against her was an urgency she could not deny.

He snatched off her panties in one quick snap, while she struggled with the fly of his trousers. She released him, took him in her fingers. Hard, hot and as sleek as satin. He shuddered. She reveled in the newly found power.

She sucked at his lips, enticed him into more of those deep, hungry kisses. He groaned savagely, shoved a hand under her bottom and crushed her pelvis against his. Impatience radiated from those taut masculine muscles. He wanted her now. Her fingers trembling, she led him to the place that ached for him, and he didn't let her down.

She cried out his name as his frantic pace pushed her over that edge of pure sensation. He followed immediately with his own primal growl of satisfaction.

He held her close for a long time after that. Their breathing slowly returning to normal. She didn't allow herself to think; this was definitely not a thinking thing. She wanted to feel…to slip into sleep and dream about this moment all night long. Reality would intrude soon enough. She refused to let the cold, hard floor matter…or the fact that their clothes were torn and scattered about.

Nothing else could touch her right now, only the feel of his strong arms around her. She nestled close. He smelled wonderful…like good clean soap and hard, hot male. Trace Callahan had definitely been worth waiting for.

He held her tightly to his chest. Kissed her forehead as if he'd sensed her need.

"I don't want you to regret this tomorrow," he murmured tenderly.

She smiled against his skin. "Not a chance, partner."

He laughed, the soft sound rumbling in his chest, then he rolled to his side to peer into her eyes. "I think we're going to have to go over the evidence again, Detective. We might be missing something."

He pushed her onto her back and his tongue made a trail along her throat, downward, all the way to her breasts. "I'm not sure I noticed this before," he whispered, those amazing lips moving against her skin. "I feel further investigation is definitely necessary." He closed that wicked mouth over one hard nipple. Her breath caught and her hips instinctively arched upward.

He kissed, teased and laved her body with that skilled tongue and that greedy mouth until she felt ready to come apart all over again. By the time he reached her hip bone she was pleading for him to finish it.

The shrill ring of the telephone sliced through the air.

He stopped, looked up, his head mere inches from her throbbing sex.

She stilled, her breath raging in and out of her lungs.

No. A distraught sound issued from her throat. She didn't want to have to go back to the station…she didn't want to hear that there had been more murders.

The answering machine picked up. "Elaine!"

Judith.

Elaine bolted up, scrambled for her damaged clothes.

"Please answer! It's Jared. He's missing. We've looked everywhere!"

Elaine raced to the phone. "Judith, did you call the police?"

Her sister's frantic voice echoed all the way to her soul as she explained again that they'd searched the house and yard…the whole neighborhood.

"I'm on my way," Elaine told her before tossing the phone aside. She stumbled into her slacks.

Callahan tucked his buttonless shirt into his trousers. "Did she call it in?"

Elaine searched for her shoes. "I…I don't know. She wasn't making a lot of sense."

The computer's screen saver suddenly vanished as if some-one had nudged the mouse or touched a key. Elaine recog-nized the tone that accompanied an instant message.

"Did you leave the cable installed?"

"I…I don't remember."

Callahan was already moving in that direction before she considered what the sound might mean. She stepped into her shoes and rushed to his side.

The dialog box held only four words.

Time to play, Detective

The invitation burned into her retinas, charred her soul.

"He's got Jared." She hadn't realized she'd spoken aloud until she heard the voice that was scarcely recognizable as her own.

As if to confirm her words a picture of her nephew flashed on the screen. Her heart seemed to stop and a part of her wanted to curl up and die as the realization of what was hap-pening fully assimilated in her brain.

"Son of a bitch," Callahan murmured.

The next visual that popped up on the screen was dark

Dying To Play

and grainy, difficult to…the images on the screen started to move.

"Oh, God."

It was her and Callahan…making love.

Callahan looked around the room. "He's been watching you all along."

The memory of what Randall Winn had said crashed into her brain. "He's been watching both of us…and listening to every word…"

"Get your weapon," Callahan ordered, his voice somehow different, devoid of emotion…much the way it had been in the beginning, gritty, hard.

Elaine grabbed her shoulder holster and bag as they rushed to the door.

"We need to borrow your neighbor's car," Callahan said once he'd gotten outside.

"Okay." Elaine wasn't sure how that would work, considering that Shirley Carroll was a little annoyed with her right now. Screw it. Her nephew needed her. They couldn't take her Jeep or Callahan's sedan since one or both might be bugged.

She ran to the door of the Carroll residence and banged hard. The porch light came on and Allen pulled the door open, going on guard the instant he saw her.

"Allen, I'll explain later, but I need to use your car."

"What?"

Callahan shoved his Bureau credentials in the kid's face. "Now."

Allen reached for the keys on the table near the door, but his mother suddenly appeared next to him.

"What's going on here?" She looked at Elaine, then at

Callahan, disapproval at their disheveled appearance glinting in her eyes. "What do you want?"

"Mrs. Carroll, this is an emergency."

"The keys," Callahan said to Allen. He pushed back the lapel of his jacket and showed off his weapon.

Shirley Carroll squeaked in fear.

Elaine felt sick to her stomach. If she survived she'd have to move out of this neighborhood after this, but right now the only thing she cared about was her nephew.

Allen thrust the keys at Callahan. "Okay, okay."

Mrs. Carroll warned that she was calling the police, but Elaine and Callahan didn't slow down. There was no time.

He started the Volvo sedan's engine and backed out into the street. The lights came on instantly, slicing through the dark night. He shoved the gearshift into Drive and rocketed forward.

A car abruptly swerved to block their path.

Before Elaine could consider what the hell some idiot was trying to do, a figure appeared next to her door. She looked up at the man whose face was side lit by the headlights of the other car.

Flatt.

"What the hell?"

"Get out," he ordered.

She got out, total confusion making her movements disjointed. "What're you—?"

Before she could finish the question, he shoved the small screen of a video camera in her face. On the tiny monitor she and Callahan were making love on her living room floor. The same image she'd seen on her computer screen.

"I knew you'd do something stupid like this, Jentzen," Flatt roared. "After this you might not even have a job in the department, much less the deputy chief position."

"You bugged my house?"

"And your car," he snarled, his eyes dancing with something akin to hatred. "I got a tip that you had crossed the line. Some people still consider that gold shield you carry a respected symbol. Obviously you're not one of them."

"Get out of my way, Flatt, I don't have time for this."

Callahan appeared next to her. "You heard the lady," he said in a lethal growl. "Get out of the way."

"I'm taking you down, as well, Callahan."

Flatt was suddenly lying on his back on the pavement.

Elaine blinked. Callahan had slugged him.

"Move his car," Callahan ordered.

While she backed Flatt's sedan into her driveway, Callahan dragged him onto the lawn and, using Flatt's own cuffs, secured him to the light post and took his weapon. Her head spun with uncertainty and mounting confusion, but she kicked it aside.

She jumped into the passenger seat of their borrowed car at the same time Callahan slid behind the wheel. They had to find her nephew in time. She closed her eyes and tried to block the images of the Gamekeeper's crime scenes. Jared was just a child....

Her cell phone chirped, announcing that she'd received a text message.

She fished it out of her bag and stared at the screen.

Hurry, Detective, Jared and I are waiting...

Hurry where?

She didn't know where to go!
Another message replaced the first.
There's no place like home...

Chapter 32

Elaine stood amid the concealing shrubbery in the yard next to the Jentzen family home. Her nerves jangling, she waited for Callahan to make a decision.

She generally preferred to take charge of a situation, but she understood that she might not be the best person to make command decisions just now. The volcano in her gut cried out for a quart of liquid antacid. But that wouldn't actually alleviate the real cause of her present discomfort.

The Gamekeeper had her nephew in there.

She gazed up at her childhood home, and fear seeped deep into the valves of her heart.

If Jared was hurt…

No, she couldn't think like that.

She pushed the concept away. He had to be okay.

The bastard had text messaged her again and warned that

if anyone else was brought into the situation, her nephew would die. No one knew the rules of good cop work better than her, and to walk into this without backup was a foolhardy thing to do at best.

But she just couldn't take the risk.

The Gamekeeper obviously considered her parents' home safe since every other member of the Jentzen clan was at her sister's attempting to find the missing child.

She wondered briefly how long the son of a bitch had been watching her family. Had he used her parents to get to her? Probably. He'd damn sure baited Flatt. She squeezed her eyes shut as the images rolled through her mind. Flatt showing her how he'd caught her in a compromising position with Callahan. Was the jerk really that determined to have her job?

Right now she didn't care about Flatt or much of anything else.

She had to get her nephew away from this deranged killer.

"I'm going in."

She jerked her head up at the sound of Callahan's voice. "No way. This is my game," she whispered harshly. "I got the invitation, not you. I'm not about to let you screw this up by storming the place."

He grabbed her by the shoulders and shook her. "Don't you get it?" he demanded through clenched teeth. "He's going to kill you just to make me pay. This isn't about playing the game with *you*. You're just another of his strategic maneuvers to lure me in. He knows it's the only way to get to me."

A part of her knew he was right.

"It doesn't matter. I won't take the chance. He asked for me and I'm going in." She pulled free of his hold. "I can't keep you from making a move, just make sure it doesn't get my nephew killed."

Callahan reached out to her through the darkness. She couldn't see his eyes but she sensed his desperation. She evaded his touch...couldn't bear it right now.

"I can't let you do this, Elaine." He fell silent for a moment. "I can't risk losing you like this."

It was the first time he'd called her Elaine. Further proof of their indiscretion. They'd both charged deep into that treacherous territory colleagues were supposed to avoid. They had connected on the most primal level. He would never let her go in there, risking her life, not even to save her sister's child. He intended to keep her safe...now more so than ever.

"You're right," she agreed, defeat dragging at her composure. There was only one thing she could do to ensure this got done her way. She drew her weapon and leveled a bead on his chest. "Give me your weapon and get down on your knees."

He stared at her though she couldn't read what was in his eyes. Surprise, she imagined. Disappointment, maybe.

"Do it now," she commanded, assuming a battle-ready stance.

"You won't shoot me," he challenged.

She laughed softly, praying like hell he wouldn't push the issue. "Callahan, you're a damned good-looking guy and the best sex I've ever had, but if you think I won't shoot you if necessary, then you'd better think again. That's my nephew in there." She didn't say, *He's more important to me than you,* but she let the implication hang in the air. Her insides twisted in denial, but she stood firm. She had to do this. Jared was an innocent child...she couldn't let him get hurt.

He drew his weapon and passed it, butt first, to her.

"You're making a mistake," he said quietly.

She checked to see that the weapon was on safety and then she shoved it into her waistband at the small of her back.

"Maybe so, but I have no choice. Now, turn around and drop to your knees."

He hesitated and for one infinitesimal second she feared he would refuse. He was a good deal larger than her and definitely stronger. If he protested, she wouldn't have a chance. Because there was no way in hell she was going to shoot him.

Callahan turned his back to her and went down on his knees with no argument. A warning blast of adrenaline shot through her.

He had a plan. No way in hell he'd go down this easy.

"Take off your belt and hand it to me."

He started to do as she ordered but then he turned. She whacked him across the head before he could reach her. He crumpled all the way down onto the ground.

"I'm sorry," she murmured.

Taking a deep breath, she moved into her parents' backyard, careful to stay in the shadows as much as possible. When she reached the back door, she paused, listened intently.

The house was silent, as was the entire neighborhood. Most folks would be in bed by now. Tomorrow was a workday. She just hoped she would live to see it come.

As she prepared to enter the house, she thought of the Gamekeeper's victims. The young med student and the ladies at the salon. Brad Matthews and his victims. Ramon Johnson and Regina Williams and the casualties of their lost battles.

This bastard had to go down tonight.

Any other option was unacceptable.

He didn't deserve to live. And she knew with complete certainty that whatever group had commissioned his research, if he survived this night, they would want him back. Would likely protect him.

No way was she letting that happen.

"You're dead, you son of a bitch," she muttered.

Elaine checked the back door. It was unlocked. Inside she eased through the mud room and into the kitchen. What little moonlight filtered in through the open plantation shutters didn't quite make it to the far reaches of the room. But that was okay. She knew this house inside and out. She'd played in this kitchen...learned to make pancakes on the griddle...sneaked her first kiss under the guise of washing the dinner dishes.

This was her family's home, and no sick bastard was going to hurt anyone here.

As she reached the family room she heard a shuffling of feet upstairs. She stood very still and listened, forcing all her senses to focus on any subtle shift in the atmosphere.

Jay Leno's voice suddenly broke the silence.

Light from the television flickered and the *Tonight Show* host's image filled the widescreen.

She took a moment to slow her thundering heart, then she stole across the room and into the entry hall. After checking out the deathly still dining room, she surveyed the staircase, automatically tuning out the noise from the television set.

A light blinked on in her father's den, drawing her attention to the room nestled at the end of the hallway. She moved in that direction, careful not to make a sound, her weapon drawn and ready.

The room was empty, the light having come from the computer as it booted up.

The television she could see him turning on with a remote even from some other part of the house...but the computer? Did her father's new computer have a remote, as well? Or were timers at work here?

When she would have left the room, the computer's desktop wallpaper caught her eyes.

Jared.

His frightened face stared at her from the screen.

She gritted her teeth to hold back the fury.

The screen blinked and a dialog box popped up.

We're waiting for you, Detective...don't be afraid, come up and join us...

Elaine took a moment to visualize the layout of the second floor. There was really no hiding place up there. Five bedrooms, nearly as many baths.

She considered the best place to be if she were in his shoes.

The master bedroom had a balcony. He was far too smart to get himself trapped on the second floor. He had already mapped out an escape route.

Moving with extreme caution, she climbed the stairs, careful to keep her breathing slow and even.

She didn't bother checking out any of the other bedrooms, she went straight to the master.

The room was tar black. The light-blocking blinds closed tightly. She stood very still and inhaled deeply, sniffing the air, mentally ticking off the familiar, like the lilac spray her mother used on the linens.

Lilacs and sweat.

She definitely wasn't alone in this room.

Something moved in the darkness, and she leveled her weapon in that direction.

He charged.

Shoot, her mind screamed.

Too risky, instinct countered.

She tilted the barrel of her weapon slightly upward and squeezed the trigger. A shock of fire blazed from the muzzle.

The lights came on.

She blinked against the brightness and at the same time attempted to assess the danger.

Applause came from behind her.

"Very good, Detective."

Something on the floor moved.

Jared! Damn good thing she hadn't shot at him when he charged her. Her heart wrenched painfully.

His hands were bound and a cloth sack covered his head.

Her first instinct was to run to him, but then she remembered the voice behind her.

"Go to him. I know you want to."

The voice…it sounded…familiar.

She whirled to face the threat.

Douglas.

"You."

He smiled, the expression openly amused, but there was nothing remotely amusing about the weapon in his hand. "Didn't have a clue, did you?" He gestured to the floor. "Drop your weapon."

Shock quaked through her a second time. "You're the Gamekeeper?"

"You think I'm not smart enough? Come now, Detective, you really don't know me that well."

As he spoke she moved, one inch at a time, to position herself between him and her nephew. She could hear the boy whimpering. God, don't let him make any sudden moves.

Elaine shrugged. "I don't know, Douglas. Maybe smart isn't the right word. I guess I didn't think you had the guts to do anything like this."

His smile vanished. "Well, Detective, you're more right than you know. I'm not the Gamekeeper. I'm merely protecting the assets of those who pay me far better than the federal government could ever hope to. Now, drop it."

Callahan was right. She crouched down and carefully placed her gun on the floor, knowing she shouldn't. But she couldn't take chances with her nephew's safety.

"Kick it aside," Douglas ordered.

She did so, but without much enthusiasm. The weapon stopped about five feet away.

"Now, the other one." He couldn't have known about the other weapon; he'd guessed. Elaine laid Callahan's gun on the floor and kicked it aside as well.

"So the Gamekeeper never was NSA property?" she prompted, sensing Jared moving closer to her. She barely resisted the urge to warn him to be still. She could not break the connection with Douglas, had to keep the dialog going.

"Are you kidding? They wouldn't know what to do with a mind as powerful as his." His entire demeanor changed, as if he'd just realized what she was up to. "Enough talk. Where's Callahan?"

"Why are you doing this?" she pressed, hoping to keep him

talking a little longer. Until she formulated some kind of plan that included her nephew's survival. "Why bring this business back up? How is that protecting your assets?"

"I had no choice," he growled. "Callahan wouldn't let it die. He kept digging and digging. Putting him out of his misery wasn't an option. Too many eyes were watching. I had to make it look like he self-destructed. And I had to find a way to end this urban legend once and for all."

That's what this was all about. Getting Callahan out of the way as well as ending any lore about the Gamekeeper. "You planted Callahan's DNA," she suggested. The .38 as well; she didn't have to wonder about that.

"It's amazing what one can do with a toothbrush. A few hairs from a brush. Technology has been my closest ally." His expression turned dark once more. "Now, where's Callahan?"

She would bet he'd planned this right down to the second. Or someone had. Maybe the real Gamekeeper. For an instant she felt regret that she wouldn't be able to take that bastard down.

"He won't be coming," she told him, the glee she derived from the astonishment that claimed his face almost obliterated her regret. She felt Jared move against her legs. Damn, he had to be still.

"Where is he?"

This was too perfect. He needed Callahan to finish this. She'd inadvertently done the one thing that threw a wrench into his plans.

"I disabled him, Agent Douglas. Like I said, he won't be coming."

"Too bad," he spat. "I really wanted him to watch this." He took aim at her.

Elaine's heart missed a step.

"Why don't we discuss this first?" another male voice asked.

Henshaw!

The muzzle of his weapon bored into the back of Douglas's skull. "Drop your weapon, asshole," he commanded, his rusty old voice sounding like heaven on earth to Elaine.

"Don't do anything you'll regret, Henshaw," Douglas warned. "I'm the only link you've got to the Gamekeeper." He smirked. "Besides, you shoot me and I'll shoot her." He waved his weapon at Elaine. "She ends up dead either way."

"Personally I don't give a damn about the freak or you. Now drop it."

"All right," Douglas relented, "just don't do anything rash."

Douglas bent his knees in a show of lowering his weapon to the floor. Elaine felt a new line of tension run through her. He was up to something. Like Callahan, he wouldn't go down so easy.

He swiveled suddenly.

The gun blast exploded in the room.

Henshaw staggered backward.

Elaine dove for her weapon.

She came up on her knees, her bead leveled on Douglas.

Unfortunately he had her in his sights, as well.

She didn't dare glance in Henshaw's direction. As much as she wanted to see how badly he was hurt, she couldn't risk taking her eyes off the enemy.

"Well, this has been interesting, but…"

His hand suddenly flew upward.

The weapon fired into the air, missing its target.

Callahan was on top of him, the two started rolling on the floor, fists colliding with flesh.

Elaine spun around and jerked the sack off her nephew's head. He sobbed so hard his breath came out in ragged bursts. "You okay, Jared?"

He nodded, his sobs only getting louder.

She pulled him to his feet and ushered him toward the door. "Go to your mom's old bedroom and hide under the bed, okay?"

He nodded once then took off down the hall.

She glanced at Callahan, who appeared to have the upper hand, and then she knelt next to Henshaw.

"That bastard shot me," he growled.

"He did." She entered 911 into her cell and requested backup and medical assistance. Help would get here in a hurry with the *officer-down* call going out.

"Let me take a look here." Gut shot. Not good. "How do you feel, partner?"

"Like I've been shot," he quipped.

She pushed his hand down on the wound. "Keep pressure on that." She checked the other situation and noted that Douglas had gained the upper hand now.

She hissed a curse as she pushed to her feet.

Shooting the bastard was out of the question. So she strode straight up to the fight and kicked him in the side as hard as she could. He fell to the floor next to Callahan.

"Thanks," Callahan muttered.

His lip was bleeding and his right eye would be black by dawn. "No problem."

She heard the sirens in the distance. Thank God.

Callahan restrained Douglas as she went back to Henshaw's side.

She checked the bleeding. Still too much. "Dammit, Henshaw, you need to stop this leaking." She managed a shaky smile. This was really bad. Worry twisted in her tummy. She took over the job of trying to slow the bleeding.

"You did good, DC. If I hadn't gotten shot we could have ourselves a party tonight."

She nodded, unable to speak for fear he would hear the fear in her voice.

"Damn," Henshaw muttered. "I'm gonna miss Diane Sawyer in the morning."

Elaine started to assure him he wouldn't miss anything but he'd passed out. "Callahan!"

The blood seeped between her fingers no matter how hard she tried to stop it. Her heart squeezed with pain. God, don't let him die on me!

Callahan dropped down beside her. He checked for a pulse, then swore. Elaine's throat tightened. "What?"

He didn't answer. He tilted Henshaw's head back and blew in a puff of air.

Oh, God. He'd arrested. Terror slid through her.

She forced her mind to focus on keeping the pressure on the wound while Callahan alternately blew air into her partner's lungs and executed chest compressions.

By the time the EMTs and cops bounded into the room, tears were streaming down her face, blurring her vision. Henshaw had not responded to Callahan's efforts.

The exact sequence of the next few minutes would be forever lost to her. The EMTs took over Henshaw's care. Flatt was ranting that this was all Elaine's fault. Vaguely Elaine wondered how he'd gotten loose. Her neighbors had likely called the police. Dugan ordered Flatt from the scene. Someone called out that they had the boy. Another cop.

Elaine's family was suddenly in the yard as Henshaw was being loaded into the ambulance.

Judith was on her knees crying, her arms tight around her oldest child. Her husband was next to her. The whole clan was clustered around asking questions, weeping tears of joy and sadness. Jared was safe. Elaine was safe, but Henshaw was badly injured.

"I have to get to the hospital." Elaine turned to Callahan. "Can you drive?"

"I'll get you there."

She shifted her attention back to her family, her ability to stay vertical waning. "I have to go to the hospital."

Her father nodded his understanding. "Go, honey, we'll catch up with you there later."

Callahan led her to the closest police cruiser. She heard him instruct the officer to transport her to the hospital where Henshaw had been taken.

She hesitated before getting into the car. "Aren't you coming?"

He shook his head. "I should stay here."

She stared at his damaged face and then she understood.

The Gamekeeper was still out there…somewhere.

Chapter 33

Elaine sat in a chair all alone in a private waiting room near the OR.

Dugan had called to check on Henshaw. Jillette had even stopped by. The nurses had warned that all other visitors had to wait in the first-floor lobby.

Elaine hadn't seen or heard from Callahan. He and the chief were likely interrogating Douglas.

She'd talked to her parents. Jared was fine. Not a hair on his head harmed. Judith had thanked her over and over and promised that she would never feel unhappy again. She swore that her children and husband were all she needed. A career and more adult time could wait until her children were in school.

Poor Judith. She would beat herself up for years to come over that one moment of selfishness. Everyone needed some personal time once in a while. Elaine would have to talk to her about that later.

When Henshaw was out of the woods.

Her gaze moved up to the clock—7:30 a.m. Shouldn't she have heard something by now? He'd been in there for hours.

Maybe no news was good news.

The door opened and she stood, hoping it would be the doctor or maybe his nurse.

Nope. Just her parents.

"Hey, honey." Her mother rushed over and hugged her.

Elaine held on for a long while, not realizing until that moment how badly she'd needed to feel some kind of strength and warmth to bolster her own. Her father took his turn next.

He drew back and smiled down at her. "Henshaw's a tough one," he said. "He'll get through this."

She prayed her father was right. Henshaw's blood pressure had bottomed out from the blood loss. That's what had sent him into cardiac arrest. Callahan had saved his life.

She should have done more…should have realized Douglas would make a move like that.

Her mother told her about the dozens of policemen and detectives waiting in the lobby downstairs to hear news of Detective Henshaw. Elaine had known all his friends would show up. She was glad for the support.

Her parents, who had apparently reconciled their differences, sat with her for a few minutes before the nurse ushered them away. Only one family member allowed in this particular waiting room at a time. Technically she wasn't family, but she wasn't going anywhere. Mrs. Henshaw, bless her heart, had required sedation upon hearing the news. Her blood pressure had skyrocketed and her own heart had kicked into a rhythm that worried the medical personnel. She was in a room on the floor below under observation. She'd made Elaine promise to come for her if anything changed. Mrs. Henshaw was counting on her to keep up the vigil.

At 8:30 the door opened again.

This time it was the doctor.

"He made it with flying colors." The doctor smiled. "He's been in recovery for about an hour. We're moving him into an ICU cubicle now. That's at the other end of the hall if you'd like to see him. I'm going down to relay the news to his wife, and then the mob, I hear, is waiting in the lobby."

Elaine thanked him profusely and then walked as fast as she could to the intensive care unit.

Henshaw had already been settled into a cubicle. It was like having a small private room except all the walls were glass. A state-of-the-art nurses' station sat in the middle of the immense unit. Each patient had a nurse assigned especially to him or her.

She held Henshaw's hand as he started to rouse, and she thanked God over and over for pulling him through this.

From the corner of her eye, she noticed the small television screen hanging in the corner near the ceiling. She searched for and found the remote control and set the television to the proper channel. There was no sound, but that didn't matter.

Henshaw opened his eyes, and she smiled at him. "Hey, there, partner."

He grunted. "See if I follow you around on the sly again," he said dryly.

She grinned. "Thanks. You saved my life." It was true. If he hadn't shown up when he did, things might have turned out vastly different.

"A good partner's always got your back."

"True," she agreed. Thank God. Thank God.

"Where's my missus?" He tried to peer past her but the effort to lift his head proved too much.

"She'll be up in a bit. She's been resting."

He nodded. "Good. With her blood pressure she didn't need this."

Determined to keep him on an upbeat note, she gestured to the television. "Hey, there's your favorite talk-show host."

Henshaw managed a crooked smile. "Well, I'll be damned."

Elaine got another couple minutes before the nurse ushered her out. She promised Henshaw she'd be back for the next round of visiting hours. He ordered her to get some sleep. She just smiled. Like that was going to happen.

In the corridor outside ICU she met Mrs. Henshaw headed to her husband's room. Elaine assured her that he was doing great. The two hugged and cried for a moment, another collective thank-you going heavenward.

When the door to the ICU had closed behind Mrs. Henshaw, Elaine turned to make her way back to the waiting room and drew up short at the sight of Callahan.

"Hey," he said.

He looked pretty much like hell. His right eye was badly swollen. His lip was busted. He'd changed his shirt, no longer wore the bloody, buttonless one from last night. The shirt was a little tight in the shoulders, and she guessed that it belonged to the chief. He always kept a change in his office. The plain white, crisply starched shirt looked good on Callahan in spite of the ill fit.

"Hey, yourself."

He gave her a thorough once-over. "I'm here to take you home."

She laughed. "I shouldn't leave yet—"

He held out his hand, cutting off her protest. "Yes, you should." He gave her a look that brooked no argument, then he massaged his head. "After that knock you gave me, you owe me some cooperation."

"I'm sorry." She closed her eyes and let go a shaky breath. "I knew you wouldn't let me go in there."

"It's over now." He offered his hand once more.

She stared at that strong hand and thought about the way he'd touched her…the way he'd held her. Her heart ached to reach out and never look back. Who would have thought that some burned-out-has-been Federal agent could make her feel so complete and at the same time so damned needy. He was an amazing man.

Another worry pushed aside her softer feelings. Her gaze rushed back up to his. "What about the Gamekeeper?" A new punch of fury fisted in her gut. Would they ever stop him now?

"I'll explain everything while you take a long, hot soak."

Man, that sounded tempting.

"I don't know, Callahan." She glanced back at the ICU.

"I do," he told her. He smiled and the battle was lost.

Less than one hour later she was soaking in a hot bath. A wine cooler sat on the edge of the tub. Callahan had washed her hair, and told her what they'd learned from Douglas. She shook her head at his strategy. He'd wanted her relaxed. What better way than to give her the news while she soaked in hot water with his fingers massaging her scalp.

She sipped the wine cooler and thought about all he'd said. Douglas had given up the name of the group he'd been secretly working for. A security team, whose origin neither she nor Callahan would ever know, had already taken charge of the Gamekeeper. Douglas had finagled a lighter sentence by giving up his location.

As it turned out, the Gamekeeper was merely a pawn himself these days. A genius, yes…but he was wheelchair bound. Callahan had wounded him two years ago. The bullet had lodged next to his spine, doing irreparable damage. Physically he was an invalid, but that mind was still a dangerous and formidable threat.

Douglas had protected him two years ago. Ensured that he was returned to whatever group had been utilizing him in their research.

Callahan had also learned from Douglas that the murders two years ago were a result of the Gamekeeper having escaped his watchdogs and launching his own kind of war. His war games had brought him into Callahan's life. The bastard had loved playing his games. The murders were merely collateral damage, to his way of thinking. But Callahan still wasn't convinced of his genius/insanity motive. He considered the Gamekeeper the same kind of psychopath as other serial killers.

Since Callahan wouldn't let this whole Gamekeeper thing go, after the events of two years ago, Douglas had talked his rogue superiors into using the Gamekeeper to stop him.

Douglas would ensure that Callahan took the blame in the end. Dispelling the Gamekeeper's legend among law enforcement once and for all. The Gamekeeper was dead, Douglas would prove. Callahan's obsession had brought him to life once more. End of story.

Douglas hadn't counted on Callahan's ability to sway Elaine or her chief. He'd expected the entire department to go along with him and the whole hoopla to be over after the Ramon Johnson killings. But it hadn't worked out as he'd planned, leading to more murders. Douglas swore he didn't know who had killed Skip Littles…a member of the group that had kept him rolling in dough, he speculated. Flatt was on two weeks' suspension for doing Douglas's bidding. Douglas turned out to be his anonymous tipster.

Elaine settled the empty bottle on the floor and considered just how persuasive Callahan had been from day one.

A new kind of heat that had nothing to do with the temperature of the water started deep inside her. She closed her eyes and relaxed completely.

It was over. The Gamekeeper would be locked away forever, and the radical group who had used him would be hunted down and prosecuted. It wasn't the optimum closure in her opinion, but it would have to do.

"How's the water?" She looked up as Callahan came back into the bathroom. He sat down on the edge of the tub. "You look relaxed now."

He'd unbuttoned that ill-fitting white shirt and rolled up the sleeves. Her eyes roved over the sculpted terrain of his awesome chest.

"Everything's perfect." She trailed her fingers up his arm.

"Why don't you find out for yourself?" Before he realized her intent, she pulled him into the tub. Water sloshed over the edge, sending her empty bottle rolling across the tile floor.

Callahan shifted his body, then put his arms around her and maneuvered until she was on top, allowing her to sit astride him. She leaned down against his chest and felt as if she were home.

"I could get used to this," he whispered.

She lifted her head far enough to settle her gaze on his. "I already am."

"I'm not going back to Washington."

She resisted the urge to jump to conclusions. "Has the local Bureau office made you an offer?"

He moved his head side to side. "I think I'm finished with that life entirely."

Worry had her chewing on her bottom lip. He smiled and soothed the flesh she'd tortured with the tip of his finger. She shivered.

"What will you do?"

He shrugged, the gesture drawing her attention to the now sheer-white fabric plastered to his muscular shoulders. "I was thinking I might start a private investigations firm. And—" he shrugged again "—I don't know, maybe I'll do the relationship thing."

His announcement sent a trickle of trepidation through her. She braced herself and said what had to be said. "I have this condition. It's called endometriosis. I'll be seeing a specialist tomorrow, but there's a good probability that I won't be able to have children."

He took her face in his hands and pulled her mouth to his

for a long, slow, sweet kiss. When he at last let her go, so they could both catch their breaths, he said, "You'll be enough, Detective. Only you. Anything else will just be icing on the cake." He drew her very close once more.

"Now kiss me, Detective. The water's getting cold and we haven't even gotten started."

Elaine was happy to oblige. No one could ever accuse her of failing to back up her partner.

There are things too great for the small minds of most…
But such greatness cannot be restrained indefinitely…
It is only a matter of time before someone new will want to play…
And I will be waiting…

—*The Gamekeeper*

* * * * *

*Everything you love about romance…**and more!***
Please turn the page for Signature Select™
Bonus Features.

Bonus Features:

Author Interview 350
A Conversation with
Debra Webb

Character Profiles 355

Sneak Peek 362
John Doe on her Doorstep
by Debra Webb
Coming in April 2005

Signature Select

BONUS FEATURES

Dying to Play

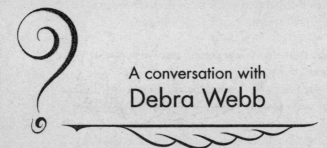

A conversation with
Debra Webb

Some women, when faced with a midlife crisis change their hair color, take up a new hobby, or go on a spur-of-the-moment vacation. For Debra Webb, her midlife crisis spurred her towards pursuing her dream of being a published writer. Also, she found time to take private investigation lessons. Enter the world of Debra Webb, as she chats about life, love and being a writer.

Tell us a bit about how you began your writing career.
I was thirty-seven and I'd always written stories, whether on paper or just in my head. Somehow with two children there just never seemed to be enough time or the right time. An unexpected illness shook my world and as I started to recover I realized that I had not done the one thing I'd always promised myself I would—write that book. Call it a midlife crisis if you will. And maybe that's appropriate; after all, I get to write stories featuring handsome, virile men as central characters! All jokes aside, I had been a storyteller my

entire life but God made my career happen.... I can't take credit for such a marvelous blessing.

Was there a particular person, place or thing that inspired this story?

Dying To Play was inspired by my fascination with the ever-changing technology of our world. Our children are addicted to computer games...we depend upon computers for far more than we realize. It wasn't a difficult leap.

What's your writing routine?

Now there's a tough question. I love writing, so I could do it 24/7 if sleep were not required by my body and attention by my patient family and friends. I prefer writing early in the morning or late at night when the world has ceased to seduce my attention. But, in truth, I can write anywhere, anytime. I simply love it.

How do you research your stories?

My favorite way is to talk to someone who is an expert in the area that requires my knowledge. The Internet is an immensely useful tool. And let's not forget the library.

Could you tell us a bit about your family?

My husband is a true hero. The kind of man every woman dreams of finding. He's tall and handsome, but more importantly, his heart is truly, genuinely good. He is kind and patient and my perpetual cheerleader. He loves his family more than life itself.

He supports me two hundred percent and then some. We have two wonderful daughters. The oldest is very much like me—very straightforward and determined to strive to accomplish more. She's also a writer, though not quite focused just yet. I have every reason to believe she will be the next Stephen King. Then there's our youngest. She is sweet and gentle, sometimes too much so in this often-harsh world in which we live. She is very much like her father. As gorgeous as she is, I fully suspect she will be a supermodel when she grows up. Look out, *Vogue,* here she comes! Now, I can't leave out the dogs, Toto and Trixie. Toto is a Scottie who patrols the house like the master of the guards while Trixie, a Maltese, is thrilled to sit on a pillow and be pampered. And then there's Goldie, the goldfish, who is quite content just swimming and eating all day.

When you're not writing, what are your favorite activities?
Oh, I love to explore anything. Places, things, people's backgrounds. I love movies, magazines, books! And I also love working around the house, planting flowers, redecorating rooms. Pretty much anything. And I love talking to my friends, especially Donna Boyd and Rhonda Nelson. Oh, and my private-investigator classes was a really cool project.

What are your favorite kinds of vacations? Where do you like to travel?
I love, love, love New York. I try to go every year. Did I

mention that *Sex and the City* was one of my favorite television shows? But other places are neat, too. Last July I went to California. Exciting. New Orleans is amazing. Chicago is terrific, too.

Could you tell us about your first romance?
I was in sixth grade, he was in seventh. His name was Jack and he was absolutely gorgeous. He had the most beautiful eyes. He wrote me sweet notes and gave me a bracelet with a single pearl on it. I won't ever forget him.

How did you meet your partner?
It was my father's fiftieth birthday party. My parents were farmers and one of my dad's farmhands invited a friend named Nonie Webb. The moment I laid eyes on him I knew I had to dance with him. We danced several times that night. I called him the very next day and invited him to my house for dinner. We spoke or saw each other every day after that for the next four months. Then we married!

Do you have a favorite book or film?
Oh, goodness, that's a hard one. I love, love movies—all kinds—but my absolute favorite is *The Long Kiss Goodnight* with Geena Davis and Samuel L. Jackson. But I do love romantic comedy as well, and my fave movie in that genre would be *Something's Gotta Give* with Diane Keaton and Jack Nicholson. My favorite suspense book would have to be Tami Hoag's *Night Sins* and my all-time-fave romantic comedy is

The Future Widows' Club, a not-yet-released book by Rhonda Nelson—look for it in April from Harlequin Signature. You're guaranteed a good time!

How do you develop your characters?
First I have an idea of the characters—either the way they look or a particular character trait. Then I toss them into one of my dastardly plots, which I've already devised, and whip them into shape. I love it when a character suddenly has everything to lose or has already hit bottom and no longer gives a damn—or thinks he or she doesn't.

Any last words to your readers?
Now this is the easiest question of all. You are my real heroes. Every one of you who has bought a single one of my books has helped to make my lifelong dream come true. I will never be able to thank you enough. Always know that I fully understand that the readers are the ones who make it happen!

Debra Webb spoke to us from her home in Huntland, Tennessee, as she took a break from writing her latest Harlequin Intrigue.

Getting to know the CHARACTERS

Isn't it great when you read a book, and you've been so pulled into that world that you want more of the characters you've grown to love, or the villains you've loved to hate? Here are some more character tidbits to satisfy your curiosity.

DEPUTY CHIEF OF DETECTIVES ELAINE JENTZEN: Elaine Jentzen is tall with long black hair and brown eyes. She's slender and very pretty. She is often accused of being too pretty to be a cop and she hates it. She's young, only twenty-nine, and has worked very hard to rise to the top in a man's world. She is the deputy chief of detectives in Atlanta's homicide division. She's tough, knows her job and doesn't hesitate to do it. She is a no-nonsense lady who doesn't care for macho tactics or burned-out guys who think they know so much.

Elaine comes from a large, loving family that has always been close. She has three brothers and one sister. Elaine spent a great deal of her time before age eighteen competing with those three brothers. In fact, one of her family's fondest memories is Christmas when she was seven years old. All three brothers received the latest in toy combat gear while she and her sister were given lovely baby dolls that wiggled and cooed just like real babies. Elaine staged a protest— she would not come out of her room until her mother went straight to the local toy store and traded in the doll for a shiny, black plastic toy gun. It was quite clear from that time onward that Elaine would not be a typical Southern belle. (Don't tell anyone, but that's an experience from Debra Webb's own childhood. Growing up with two brothers and half a dozen male cousins makes a girl a little competitive.) While attending college at the University of Georgia, Elaine, with the help of her advisor, started a student self-defense class to ensure no student, male or female, was ever physically victimized. Elaine was the perfect instructor— she'd had eighteen years of butt-kicking experience with her three brothers.

As tough as Elaine is, she has her soft spots. She has always been a champion for animals, especially dogs. She loves Sally, her gold retriever, as if the big furry animal were her own child. (Debra Webb has two dogs herself, Trixie and Toto.) Her one hobby, when she isn't tied up in a case, is supporting local animal shelters. Elaine adores sultry jazz and slow dancing, though she doesn't get nearly enough time for either. (Okay, the slow dancing is one of Debra Webb's can't-get-enough-of secret pleasures, too. In her opinion, a long, sexy slow dance is the best kind of foreplay. Debra's favorite music comes from the one and only Michael Bolton.) Wine coolers are Elaine's one must-have in the fridge. The wine coolers are to help her relax after a long day of tracking down killers...and to forget that she's going to bed alone yet again. She really wants to find just the right guy...one who is tough enough to hold his own with her and sweet enough to treat her right. Maybe, just maybe, she won't have to wait too much longer.

SPECIAL AGENT TRACE CALLAHAN:
Trace Callahan is a special agent for the FBI. He has dark brown hair and blue eyes, that unsettling kind of sky-blue. He has a nicely chiseled profile and is tall and slightly muscular, not heavy at all, more lean and toned. He cares about one thing and one thing only: getting the job done...at any cost.

Callahan lugs around a hell of a lot of emotional baggage. He hasn't worked in the field in over two years. The last time he did, his partner, fresh-off-the-farm Molly Brubaker, was killed by the Gamekeeper. He blames himself for her death. He's seen the worst there is to see but doesn't quit. He'll get the Game-keeper if it kills him. To those who have worked with him of late, it appears that maybe he wants to get himself killed. The last thing he wants to do is get involved with Elaine Jentzen, especially since the last woman he got involved with ended up dead.

Everything about Elaine gets to Trace. Her big family who pop in and out of her life on a regular basis. Trace doesn't have any family left. Never had any siblings or close extended family. He was always a loner. Growing up in a small town, he kept to himself at school, never bothered anyone unless they bothered him first. Trace never started a fight, but he always finished the ones that bumped into him. He wasn't a star athlete and certainly wasn't ever voted most popular in anything. But he had uncanny instincts and aced every test put before him, including his college entrance exams. His outstanding academic performance as a university student is what got him noticed by an FBI recruiter. After joining the Bureau, Trace rose immediately to the top. He was the best of the best...until fate played him a bad hand. Now he's out to stop the one that got away...the one who gave new meaning to evil—the Gamekeeper.

Trace Callahan is Debra Webb's favorite kind of hero. A man who has gone above and beyond the call...one who will die for what he believes in and for those he loves. A man who has seen the worst and somehow survived though his emotions are spent, seemingly dead. Debra loves healing a man like Trace...making him feel again. Guys like Callahan are her secret obsession.

THE GAMEKEEPER:

The Gamekeeper is an elusive enigma. No one knows his face...and only one really knows his twisted mind. Trace Callahan knows him all too well, giving the Gamekeeper megamotivation for wanting to rid the world of one more burned-out Federal agent. The Gamekeeper is a self-professed genius and, like his nemesis, he will stop at nothing to accomplish his goal...even setting the ultimate trap within a game that everyone is dying to play.

The Gamekeeper has a name but it's a secret that

no one, not even Trace Callahan, knows. His first name is two things added together—what you receive from the U.S. postal service and something that identifies your car. His last name is widely known as the challenge for certain standards. See if you can guess his real name. Let Debra Webb know if you figure it out. Her address is in her author bio. You can e-mail her from her Web site, as well. She can't wait to hear from you!

The Gamekeeper was an only child whose parents feared him...tried to put him away. It wasn't that they didn't love him, but they could not ignore the harm he did to other living things, including himself. He got rid of them as well as his foster parents. Even as a child he was far too smart to be outwitted by a mere human. He had no true education, since he was too dangerous for school. The Gamekeeper appears to have come into this world with a vast amount of knowledge, or perhaps it was mere instinct. Once he learned to read he devoured pages the way other children did candy. No cartoons for the Gamekeeper—he was obsessed with watching news channels. He wanted to understand the world outside those four walls of his prison. Oh, yes, he spent most of his formative years in a very special kind of institution.

Villains like the Gamekeeper are Debra Webb's worst fear. An evil that knows all your weaknesses and uses them against you. One who knows you better than you know yourself...knows all your secrets. He's that creak in the dark when your night-light fails. The feeling of being followed when you're rushing to your car in that underground parking garage. He's that prickly sensation you get when you know something very bad is about to happen and there's nothing you can do to stop it. He makes Debra shiver just thinking about him. She hopes he does the same for you.

*Don't miss Debra Webb's next book,
JOHN DOE ON HER DOORSTEP, available in
April 2005 from Intrigue. Turn the page for an
exciting preview!*

Here's a sneak peek...

John Doe on Her Doorstep
by
Debra Webb

The Enforcers are a new breed of government security. Set apart from the rest of the world as we know it, they are genetically calibrated to near perfection. No one can stop them and they never fail. The Enforcers are far more than mere men...but they are still only human.

PROLOGUE

☆

Alexandria, Virginia
Weekend Home of UN Secretary General
Donald Thurlo

"Dammit."

Donald Thurlo shuffled through the mound of papers on his desk again. A pool of golden light from the brass lamp spilled over the mass of now insignificant correspondence scattered on the mahogany surface. Where the hell was that letter? He needed the damned letter. It was his only protection.

He'd taken it from his wall safe only a few minutes ago. His brow furrowed in concentration. What had he done after that? He'd rushed upstairs to throw a few things into a bag. He glanced at the Louis Vuitton waiting at his feet. His pulse quickened. He had to get the hell out of here.

But first he had to have that damned letter.

"Looking for this?"

Ice cold fear surged anew through Thurlo's veins. Slowly, he looked up from his desk.

SNEAK PEEK BONUS FEATURE

Oh, God.

Too late.

With a pistol in his right hand, the stranger reached into the pocket of his leather jacket with his left and produced a folded piece of paper.

The letter.

Dammit.

Thurlo straightened and stared into the startling blue eyes of the assassin who'd been sent to silence him. "Why does it have to be *this* way?" he asked, his words trembling with the same fear coursing through him. "I could—"

"There's nothing you can do now," the man said in a deep, steady voice that proved more unnerving than if he'd screamed his response. "Goodbye, Mr. Secretary."

Thurlo started to cry for mercy, but the bullet's impact stunned him into silence.

And then there was nothing.

CHAPTER ONE

☆

Eastern Virginia

The early-morning weather was perfect. The sun was shining now, spilling its glow over the evergreen landscape, the air clean and brisk from the October morning's frost. Not a cloud in the sky.

A perfect day for vengeance.

The first phase of his mission had been completed.

Adam slowed and took the next exit off I-95 South. His destination was centrally located between Alexandria and Richmond. Ten miles west of a small town called Hickory Grove, in Virginia's Caroline County.

Estimated time of arrival, he glanced at his watch, twelve hundred hours. Interrogation wouldn't take more than thirty minutes, termination about two seconds.

Then it would be finished.

His lips compressed into a grim line. Part of him would have preferred someone else from Center to have been selected for this particular assignment. He was trained to put all emotion aside when it came to his work. Emotion had no place in this business. Thus, the paradox of today's mission. Director O'Riley had insisted that he was the best choice…the only choice in spite of the emotional connection. There was no question about that, Adam knew. No one at Center was better than he was. It wasn't a matter of ego; it was a simple matter of fact.

So, for the first time since his activation eight years ago, Adam's mission was personal. Under normal circumstances, Center ensured that an Enforcer's targets were unknown to him on a personal level. But not this time. He was more than simply familiar with the name in the target's profile.

Adam summoned the image of his target. She wasn't the kind of woman a man could easily forget…even if he wanted to. He'd dreamed of those dark eyes and lush lips too many times to count. That would never happen again. He gritted his teeth now at the mere thought of her. The dream had turned into a nightmare. A nightmare that should never have been allowed to escalate out of control.

Today it would end. Justice would be served and the Judas would be cut down.

A muscle flexed rhythmically in his tightly clenched jaw as he considered the man, an innocent, good man, who had lost his life because of this traitor. Adam still faulted O'Riley, Center's operations director, for not anticipating this threat. He should have had Archer protected, at least for a while after his retirement. O'Riley should have known for damn sure that Archer was keeping a copy of his research files at his private residence. What kind of security was Center running these days?

Adam had just returned from a mission in South Africa. He regretted his two-week absence now. Never before had he experienced such intense remorse. Had he been here, perhaps he could have somehow prevented Archer's death, though he couldn't immediately see how. There had to have been a way. No matter. It was done.

But he was here now, and he would avenge the death of his mentor. One of those involved in the murder had been taken care of already, which left at least one other key player besides the Judas. The identity of that second key player had not been confirmed at this point. But the Judas, his next target, was someone he knew well. Fire rekindled in Adam's gut. She had levied the ultimate betrayal: she had pretended to love Daniel Archer. There would be no swift execution for this target. A slow, painful death was in order. Adam knew precisely how to make that happen.

Center had narrowed down the possibilities of who was behind the move to obtain Archer's research. A secret coalition called the Concern was the most logical culprit. Intel was sparse on the group, their leader ambiguous. What little Center did know about the group was not good. The few members tagged thus far were connected to scumbag Third World leaders. Concern's base of operations was thought to be in South America, but Center had not pinpointed the exact location as of yet.

Bastards. Fury tightened Adam's throat. He intended to be on the team that brought down every single member of that ruthless group. But that undertaking had not been sanctioned by the Collective yet. For the time being, Adam would have to placate himself with his current mission—terminating the Judas who had betrayed Archer.

Daniel Archer had been more than his mentor, he had been Adam's friend. Archer was the scientist who'd taken the Eugenic's Project from the brink of failure to unparalleled success. A great man who cared deeply for his work, whose compassion went beyond friend and family to mankind in general. How ironic that his betrayal had come at the hands of the one person whom Archer trusted the most...loved the most, his own daughter.

368

Undeniable proof that relying on one's emotions was a mistake. A mistake Adam had no intention of ever making himself. It wasn't likely that he or any of the other Enforcers would ever find himself in that kind of up close and personal relationship. Still, they were only human. He laughed, the sound strangely loud after the hours of silence. Despite their superior genetic coding, he supposed it wasn't impossible to fall into an emotional trap of some sort.

He never allowed his emotions to show, not even remotely. It wasn't that he lacked the capability of a full range, to some degree, it was simply that he maintained a strict control over himself. Discipline was the key.

That was just one of the reasons he was so good at his work.

He smiled, thinking of what his friend Cain would say about who was the best Enforcer at Center. Adam knew there were those who would like to argue, but the proof was a matter of Center record. Number of failed missions: zero. His skills were unmatched, his instincts always on the money. He was the man for this job. O'Riley wasn't taking chances with this mission. He wanted it done right the first time, and Adam would see to it that it was done with the cold, exacting precision of a surgeon's scalpel.

He forced away the memories of how Daniel Archer had doted on his supposedly loving daughter. Those heartfelt stories had worked their way under Adam's skin. Made him feel as if he knew the woman himself. And he did, on the outside. He would know her anywhere if he saw her. He knew the music she loved, the movies she watched, even her favorite foods. But he hadn't known the evil that had lurked inside her. Her father hadn't even known that.

As tension radiated inside him, making him restless, Adam glanced at his watch once more. It would be over soon, he reminded himself. He took a deep breath and forced himself to relax. He would put this chapter of his life and all its memories behind him after today…but he would never forget. He would keep the coming moment tightly compartmentalized, only to be opened when he needed a reminder of what love and trust could do to a man. Of how emotions could betray even the strongest or most innocent of the species.

A car parked on the side of the road a mile or so in the distance dragged his attention from his less than pleasant thoughts. The hood was raised. Engine trouble. Adam slowed only slightly and surveyed the situation as he approached the vehicle. There were no houses on this section of the two-lane road. Traffic was sparse. In fact, since leaving the interstate he hadn't met the first vehicle. Another one might not come along for several hours.

A woman, twenty, twenty-five maybe, stepped slightly away from the front of the car as he slowly passed it. She held a small child in her arms.

A scowl tugged at Adam's brow as he pulled over to the side of the road in front of the woman's car. He scanned the area once more in his usual cautious manner as he emerged from his rental car and adjusted the Glock at the small of his back. He closed the door, taking another quick look at his watch. He didn't like delays, but he wouldn't leave the woman and child stranded on the side of the road. He doubted even Cain would be that heartless. Adam smiled to himself. Well maybe Cain would have driven on without stopping.

But not Adam. The least he could do was allow her to call a friend or family member for help on his cellular telephone. Five minutes, tops, and he'd be back on his way.

The woman shaded her eyes from the sun with her free hand and peered up at him as he approached. The child studied him curiously, a half-empty bottle clutched in his hand. Or maybe it was a girl. Adam hadn't spent any time around kids. Babies all looked alike to him.

"I don't know what happened," the woman explained. "It just died on me," she added, gesturing to the engine. "I barely got it off the road. I'm sure glad you came along. I was afraid I'd be waiting half the day."

Adam sensed her uneasiness. He was a tall, broad-shouldered man. This was a deserted stretch of road. She had a right to be uneasy. But at the moment, in her eyes, he supposed he was the lesser of the two evils even if he did make her a little nervous.

He didn't look directly at her as he stepped between her and the car. No point in making her any more jumpy than she already was. He took a look at the exposed engine as he reached into his jacket pocket and fished out his cell phone.

"Why don't you call a friend?" he suggested. He offered the phone in an effort to set her at ease as he surveyed the engine. Something wasn't right.

"Thank you." Her voice still sounded a little uncertain, but she took the telephone from him.

His gaze narrowed as his senses assimilated a number of inconsistencies. No heat rising, no ticking sound of the engine cooling.

The engine was cold.

"Have you been waiting long?" He cut a look in her direction as he waited for a response.

She shook her head, her eyes carefully averted from his. "Five minutes, maybe less."

SNEAK PEEK BONUS FEATURE

She was lying.

"I'm just glad you came along," she repeated, her voice too cheery as she pressed a series of numbers on the keypad, then lifted the phone to her ear.

Not enough digits. Any local call in this part of the state would be a long distance one on his phone requiring one and the area code. When she made no move to redial his suspicion was confirmed.

The sound of frosted grass crushing beneath a heavy footstep came from his left.

Adam started to reach for his weapon.

"Don't move, man!" a male voice commanded.

Young, nervous.

Adam felt the unmistakable cold, hard barrel of a pistol press between his shoulder blades.

"You don't want to do this," Adam told him quietly. There was no way to disguise the element of danger in his tone. It was instinctive. The shaky exhaled breath behind him told him the guy had noticed it as well.

"What're you doing?" the woman asked, her voice rising with hysteria as she flung the cell phone to the ground. "You didn't say nothing about guns, Jimmy!" The child in her arms whimpered as if he sensed her anxiety.

"Shut up," the guy, Jimmy, growled. "You said my name, you stupid bitch!"

"Put the gun away, Jimmy, and we'll forget this ever happened," Adam suggested. He didn't have time for this crap. He thought highwaymen had gone out of style about a hundred years ago. The last thing he needed was a nervous one. If he could distract the guy, he might have the opportunity to go for his own weapon. Leaving a trail of dead bodies wasn't exactly on his agenda.

The scrape of a boot heel in the gravel on the side of the road sounded a few feet away.

Adam stilled, listening. Jimmy hadn't moved. Neither had the woman. Someone else had joined their little party.

The distinct scent of cheap aftershave hit Adam's nostrils.

Another man. Jimmy wasn't wearing any deodorant, much less any aftershave. Adam could smell his sweat. Jimmy was scared…the other guy presented an unknown variable with his silence. Adam knew instinctively that the unknown enemy was a far more serious threat. His tension escalated to a new level.

"What's he doing here?" the woman protested. Her child's perpetual fretting underscored her mounting fear.

"Say good-night, big guy."

Not Jimmy's voice. The other man's.

Adam reached for his weapon. His fingers curled around the pistol grip at the same instant that he prepared to pivot toward the threat.

Something crashed into his skull before he could turn. White flashes speared through his brain. His knees buckled. Another blow. He jerked with the impact of it. Brilliant points of light stabbed behind his clenched lids. He had to…

…but it was already too late.

Center
Ghost Mountain in Colorado

RICHARD O'RILEY scanned the latest report on the Judas mission. One target had been eliminated, but not the second. He looked up at the man seated on the other side of his cluttered desk. "Still no word on our man?"

Dupree, Center's top analyst, shook his head. "Nothing. Either his TD has malfunctioned or he's dead."

O'Riley's jaw clenched. Adam was the best Enforcer they had, and O'Riley wasn't ready to give up on him yet. Electronic devices malfunctioned from time to time. It wasn't an impossibility, just not probable. With the tracking devices neurologically implanted, they stopped functioning only when the host stopped breathing. Unless, of course, there was a malfunction, which had to be the case now. O'Riley refused to believe anything else at this point.

"He's only been out of the loop for twenty-four hours," O'Riley pointed out. "No matter how it looks we're going to keep an open mind. I know Adam. Whatever has gone down on this mission, I can assure you he's been in tighter spots. He'll figure a way out."

At least Dupree had the good sense to keep his mouth shut instead of arguing. O'Riley was well aware of how he felt. Dupree had weighed the known data, ran simulations and assessed all the variables but O'Riley didn't give a damn. This was his operation. He would say when it was time to give up on Adam, and that wouldn't be anytime soon. A team had already been dispatched to retrace Adam's steps.

374

Dupree stood, clearly frustrated but lacking the necessary nerve to push the issue. "We'll keep monitoring local law enforcement activities. We know Adam left Alexandria. Considering the time that his TD went down, I'd say he was about halfway to the primary target, maybe closer. If he's been in an accident of some sort, we'll hear about it soon enough. There can't be that much going on along that sleepy stretch of country road. The recon team will be reporting in any time now. They hit ground zero about twenty minutes ago."

When Dupree had left his office, O'Riley tossed the status report aside. Dupree was an uptight ass, but the best intel analyst on staff at Center. O'Riley released a heavy breath. This whole situation stunk. First Daniel Archer is murdered, then Donald Thurlo's betrayal is discovered and Joseph Marsh is suddenly missing, now this. He didn't like it. He didn't like it at all. He couldn't shake the feeling that something vital was missing from the scenario. Something he and all these highly trained, overpaid intel analysts were missing.

The Eugenic's Project was far too valuable to risk for any reason. Anyone involved in this mess would be eliminated. Too tired to think as clearly as he should, O'Riley rubbed his eyes with his thumb and forefinger. Too valuable to risk even for an old friend like Joseph Marsh.

He stood and turned to stare out the window of his office. The scene beyond the specially designed outer shell that encased the entire building was slightly distorted, but welcome nonetheless. Sometimes he hated the copper-lined walls and soundproof glass of this place. Hated it, but it was, undeniably, necessary.

Though Center was located on a remote mountain in Colorado, it was still vulnerable. Ghost Mountain was owned by the U.S. government, operated by the Collective and heavily guarded with state-of-the-art security systems. No one outside this building knew the identities of those who worked inside. But even with those extreme measures in place, secrets could still escape.

They'd just learned that the hard way.

A technology war had long since replaced the Cold War. They weren't fighting the KGB moles and double agents anymore. Now it was the *code* war and some computer geek sitting in a dark room listening to their every uttered word and computer keystroke. The weapons of today were every kind of imaginable electronic and laser device for stealing bytes of communication via the Net, FAX or any one of numerous other analog or digital means of transmission. Nothing was sacred anymore.

Of course, all secrets weren't necessarily stolen. Some violations of security were merely mistakes.

Fatal mistakes.

Archer had known better. The risk he'd taken by keeping a copy of his files, encrypted or not, at home was a very dumb move for such an intelligent man. In the end, he'd had to pay the ultimate price for that error in judgment.

If Adam failed, which was a highly unlikely sce-

376

nario assuming he was still alive, they would send another man to finish the job.

Adam had never failed before. O'Riley wasn't going to admit until necessary that he had this time.

He turned back to his desk and looked at the open dossier lying there. Adam. Thirty years old. Six foot two, one hundred eighty pounds. The cream of the crop. IQ: Unmeasurable. Physical condition: Perfect. Skill level: Unmatched. No one in the program was quite as good.

Well, O'Riley confessed, there was one who could hold his own with Adam. *Cain.* But there was one key element that marred Cain's track record. He was every bit as skilled as Adam but lacked any capacity for compassion or any other essential emotion. That missing component limited his usefulness in many situations. Thankfully Archer had observed that deficit and all who'd come after the original were better for it.

Archer. It was still hard for O'Riley to believe he was dead. They'd worked together for more than twenty years. How could something as simple as a thoughtless mistake lead to this? He shook his head, weary of trying to make sense of it all. It was done. There was no way to change it. O'Riley could only see that the traitors were eliminated. The identity of the primary Judas was just one more reality that added to the unbelievability of the whole situation.

He refused to analyze it any further. It had to be done regardless of his reservations or his personal feelings. No one regretted the decision any more than he did. Joseph Marsh would be next, if they could find him. Fury twisted in O'Riley's chest. He would like to kill that son of a bitch with his own hands. He had to be guilty…otherwise he wouldn't have vanished into thin air. Well, Marsh could run, but he couldn't hide forever. They would find him and when they did, he would die.

For the moment, O'Riley would be happy if Adam would just report in and let him know what was going on.

There had to be a reasonable explanation for why his tracking device had failed. O'Riley was not ready to accept that he was dead.

Not yet anyway.

…NOT THE END…

No Enforcer has ever deviated from his course for any reason…will Adam be the first to fail? Look for the continuation of this story in John Doe on Her Doorstep *by Debra Webb, available in April 2005 from Harlequin Intrigue.*

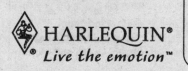

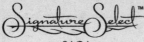

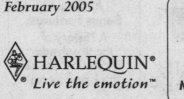

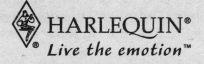

If you enjoyed what you just read,
then we've got an offer you can't resist!

Take 2 bestselling love stories FREE!

Plus get a FREE surprise gift!

Clip this page and mail it to Silhouette Reader Service®

IN U.S.A.
3010 Walden Ave.
P.O. Box 1867
Buffalo, N.Y. 14240-1867

IN CANADA
P.O. Box 609
Fort Erie, Ontario
L2A 5X3

YES! Please send me 2 free Silhouette Bombshell™ novels and my free surprise gift. After receiving them, if I don't wish to receive any more, I can return the shipping statement marked cancel. If I don't cancel, I will receive 4 brand-new novels every month, before they're available in stores! In the U.S.A., bill me at the bargain price of $4.69 plus 25¢ shipping & handling per book and applicable sales tax, if any*. In Canada, bill me at the bargain price of $5.24 plus 25¢ shipping & handling per book and applicable taxes**. That's the complete price and a savings of 10% off the cover prices—what a great deal! I understand that accepting the 2 free books and gift places me under no obligation ever to buy any books. I can always return a shipment and cancel at any time. Even if I never buy another book from Silhouettte, the 2 free books and gift are mine to keep forever.

200 HDN D34H
300 HDN D34J

Name	(PLEASE PRINT)	
Address	Apt.#	
City	State/Prov.	Zip/Postal Code

Not valid to current Silhouette Bombshell™ subscribers.

Want to try another series?
Call 1-800-873-8635 or visit www.morefreebooks.com.

* Terms and prices subject to change without notice. Sales tax applicable in N.Y.
** Canadian residents will be charged applicable provincial taxes and GST.
All orders subject to approval. Offer limited to one per household.
® and ™ are registered trademarks owned and used by the trademark owner and or its licensee.

BOMB04

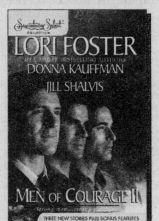
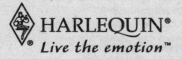